REMBRANDT'S PROMISE

REMBRANDT'S PROMISE

BARBARA LEAHY

eriu

First published in the UK by Eriu
An imprint of Bonnier Books UK

5th Floor, HYLO
103–105 Bunhill Row
London, EC1Y 8LZ

Owned by Bonnier Books
Sveavägen 56, Stockholm, Sweden

Twitter – @eriu_books
Instagram – @eriubooks

Hardback – 978-1-80418-638-1
Trade Paperback – 978-1-80418-639-8
Ebook – 978-1-80418-640-4
Audio – 978-1-80418-884-2

A CIP catalogue of this book is available from the British Library.

Typeset by IDSUK (Data Connection) Ltd
Printed and bound by Clays Ltd, Elcograf S.p.A.

1 3 5 7 9 10 8 6 4 2

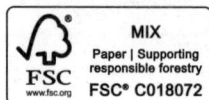

FSC
MIX
Paper | Supporting
responsible forestry
www.fsc.org FSC® C018072

Every reasonable effort has been made to trace copyright holders of material reproduced
in this book, but if any have been inadvertently overlooked the publishers would be
glad to hear from them.

www.bonnierbooks.co.uk

For my mother, and in memory of my father, with all my love

Chapter 1

Amsterdam

March, 1642

A hand on my shoulder wakes me before dawn. I start from the stiff-backed chair.

Pieter looms, candle in hand, surveying me with grudging approval.

'You are ready, Sister. Good. It is time.'

I release a slow breath.

At the door, Pieter stoops to pull on his boots. For a moment I sink into the safety of the chair but he is watching me, and I can endure no rebukes today. I stand and stretch. My fingers brush the feathers of the wood pigeons hanging from the rafters.

I pull my hand away.

Last night, the straw ticking scratched my skin and worked so thin beneath my back I might have been lying on bare boards. From outside came the slow drip of melted snow falling from the eaves. I lay awake, wondering what kind of house I would soon find myself in, and who I would meet there. A weary hour passed, then another, before I gave up on sleep, folded my bedding, dressed, and sat by the fire to wait.

The rug covering the window is tinged with bluish light. I button my jacket, step into shoes swollen with damp. All I own is tied up in a shawl by the hearth. I swing the bundle onto my back. Yesterday's peat has crumbled to ash in the grate. I reach for the scuttle, then remember that I am leaving, and Marit must light her own fires from now on.

Pieter puts on his woollen cloak, feels along the shelf for his pipe and tobacco. From behind the curtain at the far side of the room come his wife's contented snores. He raises a finger to his lips. There will be no leave-taking of Marit.

A good omen, I decide. There must be only good omens today.

Outside, the bitter March air makes me gasp. Grey slush covers the ground and soaks my feet. Pieter's boots slap through the mud. I hurry after him, follow his lantern to the square.

The fire lighting in the bakery glows amid a row of shuttered windows. As we pass, the scent of fresh bread drifts out to meet us. Inside the door, twists of golden pastry hang from wooden pegs. I can almost taste the sugar-sprinkled crust, crunch it between my teeth. Perhaps Pieter will stop to buy me something. But my brother is striding ahead and I dare not delay him. The friendly, red face of the baker appears in the window as he sets a steaming pan on the ledge to cool. I wave, but he does not see me. I have been but three weeks in Rarep. Who here will remember me when I am gone?

Up ahead, Pieter pauses, swings the lamp in my direction. I run a few steps to catch up. His cloak is too good to wear in a carpenter's workshop. This evening Marit will brush curls of wood from his shoulders, complain when they spill onto her swept floor. Lately he has earned good money working on merchant ships, and if his luck continues, he and Marit will move to better rooms before the baby comes.

'I must remind you, Geertje, that you are going to a respectable house.'

'I have never lived in any other kind,' I say tartly, and am immediately sorry.

Without him, I would be destitute. Tears prick my eyes.

Pieter grunts.

'Your husband made no provision,' he says. 'The burden has fallen on me and I am not a rich man.'

I want to lash out at this injustice, to say that Abe was a good man, that it was not his fault he died when he did. But when trouble came, it was Pieter who found me a position with the Beets family in Hoorn. And it was Pieter who took me in, when after seven years the lumber merchant's wife told me I was no longer needed. I had made no plan beyond caring for those boys and girls. How could I have forgotten that children grow up?

'You have been a good brother, and I am grateful.'

'In the city you will find opportunities to improve your prospects. But mind you look outside your master's household. He will not tolerate any careless behaviour with his pupils.'

'I have never been careless,' I say.

A silvery dawn is creeping over the fields as we approach the farmyard. Two men load crates of vegetables onto a wagon. Pieter greets them, hands over the price of my journey.

The horses jangle their harnesses. Breath smokes from their nostrils. Under the eaves of the farmhouse, a cloaked woman and a labourer stand around a barrel, warming their hands at a pan of embers.

I shiver.

Pieter takes out his pipe.

'You have one month to prove yourself. Do not make a fool of me. They are important people.' He screws tobacco into the bowl with his thumb.

The men have almost finished loading. Soon, the farmhand will beckon, Pieter will walk away, and it will be too late to change my mind.

'What if the mistress does not like me?'

Pieter laughs. 'She will like your plain face which will not tempt her husband, and your strong back which will not tire after many hours' work.'

I slide the knotted shawl from my shoulder, draw my arms tightly around it.

'This will be a good life for you, Sister,' he says in a kinder tone. 'The master is wealthy. He collects curiosities from all over the world.'

'I will be his latest curiosity,' I say. He smiles, and looks like the old Pieter who taught me to build dams of mud in the stream behind the cottage where we grew up. But in an instant the smile is gone, replaced with a new sternness as though he regrets his moment of levity.

'Say nothing about the one you lost. I told him the boy is thriving with our mother in Edam.'

I cannot think about that tiny face now, the eyes closed within the caul, the arms curled against the narrow chest.

The farmhand calls out; the other passengers are already climbing up.

Pieter hands me, then my bundle, up into the wagon. I take a seat on a crate next to the woman, who is old and stern-faced and cradles a basket of eggs on her lap. Our backs are to the horses. I will see the last glimpse of Rarep, but miss the first of Amsterdam.

'Marit and I will pray for you,' Pieter says, and the thought of his exacting wife on her knees in prayer for my betterment almost makes me laugh.

There is a jolt, a creak of wheels, and already Pieter is left behind. I half stand to wave but he has turned away, and is attempting to light his pipe from the embers.

The labourer sits on the floor, elbows resting on knees, and begins his breakfast of bread, spiced cheese and beer. His lips smack the mouth of the bottle as he drinks. After a few swigs, he offers it to the old woman. Her body stiffens and she stares out over the fields. The man grins at me, presents the bottle, and I feel a pang of regret for Hoorn and the cheerful, weathered faces of the men working at the port. I smile, shake my head, and look away. I must not arrive in the city smelling of beer, of men.

The village retreats. The road winds through marshland. I close my eyes, listen to the ring of hooves on stone, the lowing of cattle in the fields, and taste the dewy mist lingering in the air. When I open my eyes, the sky is lighter. The scattering of farmhouses, barns, windmills has given way to vegetable gardens, church spires, lumber yards. How will I find my way around a strange city? In my mind, I chant Pieter's directions to the painter's house. The words calm me like a prayer.

Chapter 2

The mist begins to lift as we reach the outskirts of the city. Fingers of pale sun filter through the cloud but offer little warmth. Beside me, the old woman draws her cloak to her chin. Sitting cross-legged on the boards, the labourer has taken out a knife and is intent on paring his fingernails. He catches me watching and winks. Quickly, I turn my head away.

We follow the canal, where horses drag *trekschuiten* filled with passengers along the still water. Through cabin windows I glimpse groups of cheery travellers playing cards, singing songs, drinking mugs of ale. If I earn good money in the painter's house, perhaps I will glide in comfort on my visits back to Edam.

Our wooden wheels turn faster as the road improves. Over roofs of warehouses, ships' masts cut diagonals through the sky. The sea air is tainted with the smell of burning tar. We pass lumber yards teeming with hirelings who rasp logs, shoulder timbers. Overseers shout orders above the groans of cartwheels.

The wagon strains on the incline of a bridge. As we ascend, I twist in my seat. A cluster of red-bricked turrets appears above chimneys and rooftops, drops out of sight when we return to street level. I remember the tales my mother used to tell, of a castle long-submerged in floodwater, its ghostly bells ringing in vain.

'What is that place?'

The labourer looks amused. 'That is the weigh house. Have you never been to Amsterdam before?'

I resolve to ask no more questions.

We pass a clearing where workmen on scaffolds pound enormous wooden piles into the ground. The pulsations shake the wagon, shake us.

The streets narrow. Closely-built houses, two and three storeys high, tilt forward as though craning to catch sight of us. How could anyone live peacefully in a room pitched over a busy street? Painted signs hang from the shopfronts of glove-makers, tobacconists, wine merchants. I must remember all, so that I can describe the city to Trijn, back in Edam, whenever I may see my cousin again.

A couple spills from a tavern: a sailor and a pretty girl, unsteady on her feet. They sway on the canal bank, laughing at a young man who bends and spews into the water.

Had I not married Abe, I might be working at the tavern in Hoorn still, amid the pipe smoke and malt ale, the merry music and lively sailors. But I must not think about those times. Pieter said the painter and his wife would not believe that a woman who served in a tavern could be respectable.

Church bells ring out across the city. Their simple chimes fill me with hope.

We cannot be far from the Nieuwmarkt. The cheerful labourer is tossing nuts into the air, catching and cracking them between his teeth. The stern old woman runs a finger across the pages of a small book, muttering prayers. The printed words are crowded together. I recognise none of the letters I stitched onto samplers as a child and pestered Pieter to read for me.

The wagon turns away from the canal, swings around a bend, and now the weigh house stands like a fortress in our path, its towers stretching to the sky. I grip the sides of the crate that forms my seat.

The labourer smiles.

'Have no fear, your husband will be waiting for you.'

I want to tell the stranger that I no longer have a husband, that my home is far from here and I am friendless in this city, but he is leaning over the side of the wagon, scattering husks onto the road.

Beyond the weigh house lies what must be the Nieuwmarkt. The square is thronged with carts and barrows leaving little room for us to pass. Children duck between stalls, dart in front of horses. Our driver curses, raises his whip. I want him to slow down, to let me admire painted chinaware, copper pans, carved ivory, bolts of red and gold silk. Only yesterday I was trudging through the Rarep market, among sacks of turnips and coops of bad-tempered poultry.

The wagon rocks over the cobblestones, comes to a halt on the south-west corner of the square, and our driver jumps down. Already, the labourer is gallantly taking the old lady's basket, helping her to her feet. He grasps my hand, helps me down too. Do I dare to ask him to escort me to the painter's house?

A young girl, her hair loose about her shoulders, steps in front of me; the labourer slips an arm about her waist, presses a kiss to her lips, they push through the crowd and are gone.

I stand by the wagon, my bundle in my arms. Two men speaking in strange accents unload the crates of carrots and beets onto a sled. Maids bustle past, their faces framed with clean linen caps, their aprons crisp and white. Swinging from their arms are baskets of bread, pails of fish. The elbows of my jacket are worn and my linen, though clean, is no longer white. Pieter did not think to tell me how women dress in Amsterdam. Even if he had, I have no better clothes than these.

Standing beside a stack of cages, a man cups a yellow chick in his hands, thrusts it before my face, saying something I cannot understand. I shake my head, hurry away.

I find myself in an avenue of spice merchants, stalls decked with baskets of bright yellows, muted reds and cinnamon browns. A boy slits open a sack and a cloud of pepper rises, stinging my eyes and nose. He laughs at my wincing. I want to take my bundle and run from this city, run all the way back to Rarep, to tell Pieter and Marit that I will stay to mind the coming baby for no wages at all.

An aroma of fried herring draws juices to my mouth, reminding me I have eaten nothing yet today. Hawkers clamour around me, pulling at my sleeves, and I almost stumble over an old woman tending a stove. A fragrant smell of pancakes rises. From my pocket, I pull the few stuivers Pieter gave me.

The pancake is soft and golden, and drips melted butter over my fingers. I buy another, and find some steps clear of moss where I can sit to eat. I think of Pieter's directions. Beyond the square, I espy the glinting cockerel atop what must be the Zuiderkerk.

I am about to move on when a shadow falls over me. A ragged man, one eye cloudy and streaming with pus, blocks my way. He leans on his stick, says something in an imploring tone. I jump up, shrug his hand from my sleeve, hurry in the direction of the church. At the edge of the square I stop, ashamed. Pieter told me there had been no pestilence in Amsterdam for years, and that lepers who enter the city must sound their clappers in warning. The old man posed no threat to me. By the time I slide a coin into my palm and retrace my steps, he is gone.

Perhaps I imagined him. The agitation of my heart in my chest alarms me. I run from the square, away from the hustling crowds, away from the beggar. Men and women pass by with unseeing eyes, and I fear that I am slowly disappearing, dissolving into the cold morning air. At the bridge, I stop for breath, gripping the iron railings. When I let go, rust stains my hands like dried blood. I look up, and across the bridge, just as Pieter described it, stands the painter's house.

Chapter 3

I walk down what must be the Breestraat, admiring the house with its bright red shutters and windows glittering with dozens of tiny panes. It stands broad and tall; double-fronted, with a lower level half-hidden below the street. In its magnificence, it seems about to push its drab neighbours aside.

Four steps lead from the street to a green front door hung with an iron ring. I imagine the crash the knocker would make, how my unclean hands would dull its sheen. But I will not touch it; Pieter told me I must go around the back.

Returning to the canal, I walk along the bank and find the mouth of the alley leading to the rear of the houses. Boys jostle at the edge of the water, one raising a rod bearing a clump of rags. He waves it at the others and, screeching with laughter, they back away so that I have to jump aside to avoid them. The sodden thing slips from the stick, hits the cobbles with a slap, and I see that it is not a ball of rags after all but a dead bird in early stages of decay.

At the end of the alley I find a stout door which must belong to the painter's house.

Just when I am certain my knock cannot have been heard within, a fair-haired girl of about seventeen opens the door.

'Are you Geertje?' Her eyes are frank with curiosity. She rests a hand on her hip, scans me from head to foot. The patched hem of my skirt, the mismatched buttons of my jacket are barbs which catch her eyes. 'I did not expect you to be so old.'

Can I be exposed so soon? I am in my thirty-third year and Abe has been buried more than seven years, but Pieter told the painter that I am twenty-five and newly widowed.

'Come in.' She smiles, and dimples appear in her pretty, heart-shaped face.

I relax. To this girl, twenty-five would seem old.

'You are to wait here with us,' she says, as I follow her inside.

'I need to see the mistress.'

'Later. Her chest troubles her at night so she often rests by day.'

It is a large kitchen, with a slate floor and a long oak table where a woman works, her back turned. A water pump stands against the far wall, its spout feeding a stone basin. Beside it, a row of waist-high cupboards are lit by a series of windows overlooking an inner courtyard. Along the opposite wall is a stove and griddle, and a wide hearth where a hearty fire burns. The woman at the table turns her haggard face towards mine, nods, looks back to her work. She takes a cleaver, hacks legs from a plucked fowl.

'Maartje, the cook,' the girl says.

She takes my arm, leads me to the fireside where an infant of six months or more lies sleeping in a basket.

'I am very glad you are here. I have been terrified of him dying on my watch. All the others died, you know.'

She lifts a jug of water from the hearth, fills an earthenware bowl on the table. From a cupboard she takes a clean cloth and a scrap of olive soap. 'Is that the only cap you have? We will have to find something better. And you had better put that on.' She points to an apron hanging from a peg.

I take off my jacket and hang it with the worn elbows turned to the wall. The apron is fresh and clean. Someone has pressed the point of a flat-iron into every gather in the linen. At the table, I push my sleeves above my elbows, sink my forearms into the warm water, and wash my hands and face. Beside me, Maartje joints a second fowl, the strike of her cleaver making me jump.

When I am clean, I go to the basket, touch the baby's forehead. He is still sleeping, his cheeks ruddy with heat.

'What is his name?'

'Titus. Their fourth-born.'

The bedding around him is clammy. I try to prise the coverlet from his curled fingers but even in sleep he will not give it up.

'Does his mother nurse him?'

'Not any more. The wet nurse still calls, but he is greedy and prefers his pap.'

'He is too hot.' I drag the basket away from the hearth.

'The mistress said he must be kept warm,' the girl says, but she helps me anyway, peering all the time at the baby's face, as though expecting him to protest.

Titus gurgles, wriggles, settles again. In his embroidered satin smock and coverlet of fringed silk shawl he puts me in mind of a grand old lady. When I say this, the girl laughs.

'Wait,' she says. 'I will bring the apples and then Maartje cannot complain.'

I sit in a low chair at one side of the fire, and wait for Titus to awaken. The girl pours ale from a pitcher on the table, hands a mug to me. 'If you want drinking water you must get it from the barrel in the cellar, never from the pump.'

She stands at the table, deftly peeling apples as she talks.

'Where are you from?' Before I can answer, her voice drops to a whisper. 'The mistress pretends to be stern around us, but she is light-hearted as a girl when the master is in humour. Her people are the Uylenburghs from Friesland. Better blood than his.'

'Has she been unwell since the birth?'

The girl looks wary. 'Longer than that. We thought this one would kill her before it could be born. Her coughing wakes him, so he is to sleep upstairs with you.'

Beyond the hearth is a box bed, and beside it, a panelled door to the rest of the house. Perhaps Maartje sleeps in the kitchen. She is grinding something with a pestle, her flexed arm driving back and forth. The result is a fine black powder, which she tips onto the dismembered fowl and rubs into the skin. Her thick fingers massage the flesh, and I feel a baseless stab of fear. It is the heat of the fire, and this girl with her talk of death.

As the girl chatters on, she tips against the basket and Titus stirs. He smacks his lips, rolls his head and cries. When I lift him into my arms, he is hot and damp. He twists and turns against me. A sour smell rises.

'I will need a fresh basin. And some rags,' I say.

'Ilse,' Maartje says, without looking up from the table.

Ilse wrinkles her nose, but brings all I need. I change the baby's linen, and he cries louder still.

Ilse looks towards the panelled door.

'The mistress will hear.'

But soon Titus is curled against me, sleepy and content.

'He likes you,' Ilse says.

His head lolls. I rub his back and sing to him, a lullaby I used to sing to little Katrijn Beets in Hoorn, and I feel an ache for my old life and the children I loved as though they were my own. I hold the boy fast in one arm, smoothing his blond curls. Loneliness has been snapping at my heels like a fox after a chicken, but here, in the painter's warm kitchen, I feel my strength returning. This child is stirring some old forgotten feeling in my heart.

'I hope we will be friends,' I say to Ilse, when Titus is asleep again.

She squeezes my arm.

'I am very happy you are here, Geertje.'

Maartje approaches, wiping dirty hands on an apron which covers her dress. She is not much older than I am, but her shoulders are hunched, her expression, grim. She opens her mouth, hawks, and spits a mass of phlegm into the fire.

Ilse drops her knife and it clangs against the slate floor. Titus shudders, throws back his head, and bawls.

A flash of fear comes over Ilse's face. I smile, as much to soothe her as the child. But she is not looking at me. I follow her gaze to the panelled door, which has opened, and the lady who stands there, watching us.

Chapter 4

The mistress of the house stares at me. She is all pale prettiness, with mild brown eyes and softly curving brows. A white lace cap covers her hair, its scalloped edges reaching to her neck. Her figure is slight as a girl's. I stand up, conscious of my damp sleeves, my faded linen.

'Geertje Dircx. I am glad to meet you.' Her accent is refined.

Titus turns his head away from his mother, sobs into my shoulder. I perform an off-balance curtsey.

'Bring her to the hall.'

She is looking at me, but the command is for Ilse. Her rich blue skirts rustle as she turns and steps daintily back through the door.

The crying fades to subdued snuffles. I lower the baby into his basket but Ilse stays my arm. 'Bring him. Better she sees you with him.'

Ilse leads me through the panelled door and up a twisting, narrow staircase.

'Wait.' This time, when her eyes fall on my homespun bodice, my wrinkled linen, I sense goodwill in her scrutiny. She straightens my cap and untucks my apron so that it fully covers my skirt. 'It looks better so.'

Titus is quiet now, his cheek warm against mine. Do not cry, I want to whisper in one tiny ear. Stay sweet and serene as you are, until I can persuade your mama to like me.

On the last step, echoes of a faint cough reach us.

'Say nothing about her illness,' Ilse whispers.

We pass through an archway into a hall of double height. Light pours from elegant windows onto a black and white checkered floor. I picture Ilse scrubbing these tiles every morning and wonder if that task will now fall to me.

A tall cabinet dominates the room, and I imagine straining to dust its surface. Every wall is crowded with paintings. To my right, a bearded man in a woven turban fixes me with a stern eye. Above his head, a mischievous Cupid bearing a quiver full of arrows gazes across the room to where a pretty lady is prinking at a mirror. I want to look at all more closely but, seated at a small table on a dais, the mistress is waiting.

'You may sit.' She points her quill towards a leather-covered chair.

A spaniel jumps from her lap to the floor and, wagging his plumed tail, runs playful circles around my feet.

'Luca!' The little dog shrinks to his mistress's side and nuzzles a red leather ball between his paws.

A glance back at the archway tells me Ilse has slipped away.

I sit, gently shifting the baby to my lap. He amuses himself by grabbing at the laces of my bodice.

His mother rests her quill on a marble inkwell. Her hands are very white; her fingernails, delicate pink ovals. A page half-filled with graceful slopes and flourishes lies in front of her. She pushes it aside, unfolds an older sheet of paper, reads a little, and sighs.

'The Beets speak well of you. They say their children loved you like a second mother.'

Unexpected tears water my eyes. 'I loved them too.' I take a long breath, attend to Titus who is cramming my laces between his pink gums.

'I have but one child. Caring for him should be an easy task for you.'

She sits back in her chair, turns weary eyes towards the window. Flurries of snow whirl downwards onto the street, melting before they land. For a few moments, there is no sound but the contented gurgling of her son.

My new mistress is younger than I am, though not by much. I recognise the line of her jaw from one of the portraits hanging nearby, but I dare not turn to compare the image. A fine silk ker-chief is draped over her bodice, fastened with a gold pin set with a pink stone. Around her slender neck hangs a string of pearls. Tiny diamonds flash and bob at her ears. She reminds me of a little girl who has dressed up in her mother's clothes.

When her eyes meet mine, worry cleaves her brow. Her fingers twist her wedding band so that two red stones glow like a bite mark on her skin. The death of my son haunts me; perhaps she can sense it.

Before she can speak, Titus starts to cry. I bounce him on my knee, murmur in his ear, but he quakes and will not be comforted. I stand, put him over my shoulder, rub his back.

'What is wrong with him?' she demands.

I am put in mind of an indulged child, displeased with one of her bejewelled playthings.

'He is too hot, Madam,' I say, though in truth the hall is pleasantly cool after the stifling kitchen. 'He needs fresh air.'

The novelty of rising quells his cries. After one more whimper, he calms, and I ease back into the chair.

'You would take him outside, on a day such as today?' Her chin is high, her mouth, a tight line. She has not yet decided.

I look directly into her grave eyes. 'Yes, Madam. I would wrap him against the cold and take him outside.'

There is a pause, and then, to my relief, she laughs. She reaches out, caresses the baby's rosy cheeks. 'Have I been smothering you with heat?' Her hands look soft and smooth as his skin.

Titus waves his short arms in pleasure at his mother's touch. I hold him out to her but she makes no move to take him.

I feel the balance tipping in my favour.

'See how he loves his mama,' I say.

'He is my fourth child. The others all lie yonder.' She gestures to the window and I realise she is pointing in the direction of the Zuiderkerk, with its spinning golden cockerel. She has had her share of tiny burials, endured what I have endured, three times over. I remember Pieter's falsehoods, how he told this woman and her husband that my dead son thrives in the countryside. For a moment, I am terrified she will inquire after my boy. How can I pretend that he is alive, he who was born a ghost?

But she has no interest in my life.

'Your brother told you the terms?' She seems impatient now, eager for me to be gone.

All Pieter told me was that my main duty would be to tend to the baby and that I was fortunate beyond measure to gain the position.

'Yes, Madam.'

She slides a page across the table, hands me her quill. I hesitate.

'Here.' She taps the space beneath the words.

The dry quill scrapes the paper. I squeeze, and try again. A drop of ink appears. I scratch the mark Abe taught me, the sign that brings luck, onto the page.

'Geertje, I hope you will be happy here,' the mistress says, returning the quill to the inkwell. 'Ilse will show you where you are to sleep.' She bows her head.

I rise and curtsey, prop the baby against my hip, and under pretence of settling him, steal a last look at her before I leave. She has lowered herself deeper into her chair; she sits with eyes half-closed, one white hand held to her chest, the other stretching to stroke the spaniel who stays by her side.

You have trouble, Madam, I think as I descend the stairs. And not just buried in the grounds of the Zuiderkerk, but here, in this grand house.

Chapter 5

I am to sleep in what Ilse calls 'the hanging room', an artful timber construction suspended between ground and first floors. A narrow staircase takes me to a half-landing, where an interior window to the front looks down on the airy hall, and another to the back overlooks a sunny room where a dinner table has been set for two.

An oak-panelled door with a brass handle leads to my room, and the annexe beyond it, where the baby is to sleep.

After the spacious hall, the hanging room feels cluttered. A small bedstead, a cabinet on which an empty basin stands, and a wicker chest crowd the space. A chipped enamel pot on the floor almost trips me. In the annexe are a wooden crib, a chair, and a foot stove. Both rooms are lit by windows onto the inner courtyard and warmed by the southern sun. My cap brushes the low ceiling. It is as though I have been confined to a coop intended for a smaller creature.

I sit on the bed. Seagrass. The mattress will clump under my weight and prickle my skin. In the chest, I find woollen blankets with which to dress it.

I open my bundle, shake out my linen. Wrapped in my spare shift are the tokens that always travel with me. The medal of Sint Nicolaas, which belonged to Abe. My mother's comb; the paint mostly flaked off, and now only visible in specks. The prayer my cousin Trijn gave me, on a page torn about the edges. Everything else I own, my earthenware jug, my mirror, even the ring Abe gave me, are in the pawnshop at Hoorn. It is safest to love things of no value, things that cannot be sold. I set my treasures on a shelf near the window; the comb and medal anchoring Trijn's prayer.

Out in the courtyard, a door slams. The limp crown of Maartje's cap crosses the cobbles as she takes a pail of what look like vegetable peelings to the privy. When she goes back to the kitchen, pail empty, back hunched, I feel a twinge of pity for her.

Men's voices sound on the stairs. The master's pupils. Boots clomp past my door. An explosion of laughter at some jest startles me and echoes around the landing after they are gone.

More footsteps, lighter this time. A tap on the door. When I open it, Ilse is there.

'Geertje, how long you have been!'

I had almost forgotten my duties. But the mistress has a paper with my mark upon it and my time belongs to her.

'Is Titus awake?'

'Sleeping soundly. I left him with Maartje.'

She steps past me without being invited in. Her eyes fly about the room, landing here and there on my few possessions. I almost laugh at the open disappointment in her face. On top of the chest, my shift lies folded. She fingers the inferior cloth.

'We will have to see about your clothes. Sometimes the mistress gifts us her old things.'

Before I can think of an answer, she moves on.

'Are you married?'

The abrupt question discomfits me.

'My husband died not six months after our wedding day.'

'No children?'

I manage a shake of my head. I can hardly hide my irritation. I want her out of my room. But she has tears in her eyes.

'Such sorrow,' she says, touching a hand to her throat.

I soften. What could she know of widowhood, of loneliness? Something in her carefree nature reminds me of how I used to be, before sorrow made its home in my heart.

Her tears disappear as quickly as they arrived.

'I am to be wed a year from now. My sweetheart is a farmer's son, back home in Leiden. I wanted us to be married six months ago, but his parents will not allow it until he turns one-and-twenty.' She sighs in a reverie of thwarted desire, and I wonder if there really is a love-stricken farmer's son in Leiden, if he even knows of this girl and her dreams. At her age, I was already serving in the tavern at Hoorn, learning to evade grasping hands, to dampen obscene suggestions with innocent confusion.

'Would you like to see upstairs?' Her mind has flitted on.

I hesitate, thinking of the men who passed my door.

'We will make no intrusion; the mistress is in the salon, the master is out, and the pupils keep to the top floor.'

By the time I follow her out of the room, she is halfway up the stairs.

The painting room where the master works spans the front of the house. Ilse hangs back as we approach. I stop at the threshold, afraid to venture further without her.

Four large windows look onto the Breestraat, admitting soft northern light. In the centre of the floor is an easel, draped with a cloth, and a rattan stool. An odour of turpentine hangs in the air. How can the painter bear to breathe it all day? Near the door is a table, covered in pots and bottles, some corked, some plugged with wax, some bearing stained tags about their necks. By the farthest window is an oval-shaped grinding stone, mounted on flattened wooden logs. Cast-iron stoves stand at each end of the room.

'Come.' Ilse leads me to the back room. 'I will show you his cabinet.'

Only in the pawnshop have I seen so many objects in one place. Shelves run from floorboards to rafters, crammed with statues, shells, gorgets, skulls.

'We are forbidden to enter here,' Ilse says. She picks up a globe, spins it on its cradle, enjoying my discomfort.

'Have a care,' I say, when it seems a plaster head will slip from her hands.

'Are you afraid to touch?' She trails a hand over antlers and horns of long-dead animals which decorate one wall.

Reluctantly, I stroke the curling fronds of an unfamiliar plant. They are dry and hard as stone.

'Look.' Ilse points to the ceiling. She laughs at my shriek.

The carcass of an animal, half-dragon, half-snake, with legs instead of wings and long, cruel jaws, hangs from a beam.

The tap of a knuckle on wood jolts me from this horror. I whirl around. A clean-shaven man of about two-and-twenty, dressed in a stained smock and old breeches, is standing on the threshold. Ilse had been amusing herself by fitting a polished helmet on her head. When she turns and sees the pupil, she removes it, blushing in abashment or pleasure.

'What are you doing in here?' he asks. His tone is friendly. He leans one arm against the door frame, smiles at Ilse. I try not to think of what Pieter would say if I lost this position on my first day.

'I could ask the same of you,' Ilse replies. 'Should not you be hard at work upstairs?'

'I am weary of sketching my own face and in need of merry company. I heard voices.' He glances at me.

'We have no time to waste in talk with you.' Ilse replaces the helmet, dusts her hands on her apron.

'I would not dare to detain you.' The young man makes a show of stepping aside to allow our free passage from the room. I leave first, holding my skirts close to avoid brushing against him. He smells of linseed oil and tobacco. I hurry down the stairs.

There is some whispering and a stifled laugh before a breathless Ilse joins me outside my room.

'Silly boy,' she says. 'He is not supposed to talk to us. Do you think him handsome? He is not at all as handsome as my Jan.'

'He seems friendly.' I must be wary. She would draw me into her intrigues without a thought and I cannot afford to make any mistakes.

She smiles her beguiling smile, tucks her arm through mine. 'There can be no harm in friendship.'

Chapter 6

Gentle mewling from the baby wakes me at dawn. Once outside the covers, I shiver. The shutters open onto a grey-blue sky singed with orange.

In the annexe, Titus agitates in his crib, waving his fists, his face contorted in woe. 'Hush, little lamb.' I pat his head. 'I will find fresh linen, and a bowl of warm porridge.'

Last night I did not think to ask for a jug of water. I dress blindly, tuck my hair into my cap. Titus looks up at me, chews on the edge of his blanket. I free the wool from his grip, take him in my arms.

In the kitchen, Maartje is filling pails at the water pump. Ilse carries one in each hand, staggering a little under their weight as she crosses the floor. 'Geertje, you will have to prepare your own. I have much else to do.' She tips the pails into the iron pot hanging over the fire.

I smile to diffuse her temper, but she will not be appeased.

'Make haste with that business,' she says, nodding towards the baby. 'You must help me this morning before the visitor arrives.' She lifts a brimming jug from the hearth and without spilling a drop, presses her shoulder to the door and goes upstairs.

I find the bundle of clean rags from yesterday, and soon Titus is chirping into my face, grabbing at my cap, setting it askew. I dress him in a fresh smock and tuck him into his basket, away from the fire.

There is no breakfast on the table for him or for me.

Maartje rakes the fire in silence. The curve of her backbone is pronounced, and I wonder if it is painful for her to reach and bend as she does.

Today, I am braver.

'Maartje,' I say, approaching her. She lifts a pan of dough, shovels it past me into the oven, and pokes the fire so roughly a shower of sparks threatens my skirts.

I jump back. For a few moments, I am too angry to speak.

In his basket, Titus whimpers.

'Maartje,' I say, louder this time. 'I want a bowl of porridge, and fresh milk for Titus.'

She casts me a look somewhere between hostility and respect, lifts a skillet from the hearth, and ladles porridge into two dishes.

Soon I am spooning milky porridge into the baby's smiling mouth, and, in turn, eating my fill. I forget about Ilse's orders until she comes bustling in.

I am to help her scrub the tiled floor in the hall, then dust every surface of the side room where the visitor is to be entertained.

'The art dealer,' Ilse says. 'A man with money to spend.'

She has come from dressing the mistress, and delivers this news with the same irreverence she displayed the day before when showing me the master's collection of strange objects.

Now that she sees I am willing to help, her mood improves. She shows me the laundry room, where mops and brushes are stored. 'The master will be in a gay mood if he sells paintings,' she says. 'Last time, he brought us bags of sugared almonds, and I had Maartje's as well as mine, to save her poor teeth.' Dimples play in her cheeks as she chatters.

In the hall, the floor seems hardly sullied but we set to scrubbing, Ilse making energetic progress across the tiles. I fall into a rhythm of my own, working the cloth, then raising my eyes to the paintings. Opposite the front door, hanging in full sight of any visitor who enters, a naked woman cowers. She cannot yet have seen the man who spies behind her, but some instinct has compelled her to fold her body, to slide bare feet into her slippers. I want to jump up, to warn her of the man's presence.

The smell of vinegar recalls me.

Soon the floor shines wet and clean.

We take dusters to the side room. A mantel supported by columns of mottled red marble makes me gasp in admiration. But the white-veined columns are warm to touch, and, up close, I see that they are carved of wood and painted to feign expensive stone.

'Do not touch,' Ilse warns from behind. 'You will mar the shine.'

I withdraw my hand.

She kneels at the hearth, adds a handful of candle stubs to the kindling in the grate, and opens the tinderbox.

Over the mantel is a painting of a shrouded man sitting in a grave, his eyes half-open, his face ghastly pale. I could be back in Edam, clinging to the edge of a pew in Sint Nicolaaskerk, listening with the other children to a tale of a man raised from the dead.

I turn away, busy myself dusting the frame around a tranquil riverbank where two men are rowing past a stone bridge.

By the window, a table is dressed in a white cloth. On top, a marble basin holds two stoppered bottles. Along the opposite wall, a box bed runs part way, its panels closed and, beside it, stands a virginal. Ilse wipes her sooty hands on a rag. With a fresh cloth, she dusts the lid of the instrument.

I take a soft-bristled brush to the seats and backs of the green velvet chairs arranged around the table. Canvases stand propped on some of the chairs, ready for viewing. What prices must the painter charge in order to maintain his fine house, to feed his family and servants?

'What do you think of this fellow?' Ilse drapes an arm across the top of a painting showing a man at a window. The man wears a flattened cap and old-fashioned coat, rests one puffed sleeve on the sill. I hear a challenge in her voice and hesitate. Could he be an ancestor of the family?

'He is very handsome,' I say, though in truth his round nose is tinged with red, his eyes are murky, lit with mere pinpricks of white.

Ilse laughs. 'This is your new master, Geertje. It is a fancy of his to dress up in old clothes and paint his own image.'

I look again at the shadowed eyes, the reddened rims.

'I would never marry an artist,' Ilse says. 'I heard he once painted the mistress as a harlot in a tavern, and she thought it a great joke until her family made him take it down. How could any wife bear it?'

'I must get back to Titus,' I say.

In the kitchen, Maartje is shucking oysters into a bowl. The smell of baking mingles with the briny odour of shellfish, and for a moment I am back in the market at Hoorn, bargaining for the best of the morning's catch.

While Titus sleeps, I could help her. Four golden loaves, quartered for cooling, rest on the table. The oysters, plump and succulent, bathe in their own juices. Maartje takes a knife and with more force than necessary, splits four lemons. She crushes each half in her strong fists and juice streams through her fingers into a jug.

'Shall I cut the bread?'

Before she decides whether or not to reply, the panelled door swings open and the man from the painting strides into the room.

'Maartje, you old witch,' he says, sniffing the air. He reaches past me for the bread, tears a chunk, and takes a bite.

To my surprise, Maartje laughs, raises her knife in mock threat.

My master is a lively contrast with the sober subject of the portrait upstairs. Out of the shadows, his eyes are large and warm, his expression jovial. He wears a long coat edged with brown fur, and a broad-brimmed hat. His neatly trimmed beard and whiskers bear a copper tint.

He looks at me, chews, swallows.

'The carpenter's sister,' he says.

'Yes, Sir.' I attempt a curtsey, but the formality seems out of keeping with his ease. His eyes rest on me. More than ever, I am conscious of my broad shoulders, my plain face.

'My wife and son seem to like you, that is my only concern.'

At the basket, he bends to touch the boy's forehead. He is not a tall man, but taller than me by perhaps a thumb's width.

'Maartje, we will need more food,' he says. 'Uylenburgh is bringing Dou. Back in Leiden, the cost of feeding that boy nearly exceeded his fees.'

Maartje grunts in displeasure. She scoops discarded half-shells into a pail, steps out into the courtyard.

With his hand on the door, the master turns back to me.

The intensity of his gaze quickens my senses as though one of his fur-lined cuffs had brushed my skin.

'Tell your brother it will take more than a little housework to clear his debt.'

My cheeks burn.

'Debt?' I repeat, but already he is gone. His laughter mingles with the thump of his boots on the stairs.

Chapter 7

By the time Ilse returns, I have cut thin slices of bread for Maartje to toast and am chopping frills of parsley into green flecks.

'Come upstairs, Geertje.' Ilse unhooks a fresh apron from the peg by the door. 'We will see the visitors arrive.'

After the master's stinging words, I am eager for distraction. I look over to Titus asleep in his basket.

'Maartje will watch him,' Ilse says. 'She only pretends to be dis-agreeable.' Maartje says nothing, but does not object when I set down my knife, follow Ilse to the door.

On the half-landing outside the hanging room, Ilse presses a finger to her lips. She nods towards the interior window which overlooks the hall, flattens herself to one side, motions for me to do the same.

From the dais comes the mistress's voice, breathless, as though she had been running.

'Why show them only portraits? The painting of the bittern is finely done.'

I edge closer to the latticework. In the hall, the mistress abandons her letters on the table, steps down to join her husband and leans on his arm. The blue satin of her gown shines with the lustre of sunlight on water.

He touches the back of her hand to his cheek.

'Dou will buy nothing bigger than a dinner plate. And the bittern is too subtle for your uncle's taste.'

She laughs, slides her hand down his throat, presses her palm to his chest.

'Tease my uncle as you will, but you shall not succeed in teasing me.'

His reply is lost as they pass together into the side room.

A sudden longing for the touch of Abe's work-roughened hands, the tang of salt from his skin, makes me light-headed. A surge of jealous grief rises to my throat.

The thud of the iron ring on the front door breaks the spell. Ilse hurries down to admit the visitors.

A clean-shaven old man, round of waist and dressed in black damask, steps into the hall. With him is a younger man, wearing a flamboyant maroon cloak. Both men's cheeks are rosy with cold. Snow falls from their hats and boots onto the pristine floor. Under their arms, they carry flat parcels wrapped in sacking.

Ilse bobs a curtsey. Before she can show them in, the older man pushes past her, thrusts open the door to the side room. 'How fares my niece?' he calls.

Ilse brushes the fallen snow out the front door, then follows the others into the room.

I drift down to the hall. An inner window draws light into a room tucked under the stairs. Inside is a small table piled with papers. A half-spent candle leans from a shelf. I reason by its untidiness that this is a space servants may not enter.

So many paintings hang in the hall! The lowest are at knee-height and the highest almost touch the corbels supporting the rafters. Can all be the master's work? I try to imagine the man I met in the kitchen painting the modest old lady in front of me. A white cap sits high on her thinning hair, and she stares peaceably to the right. Her skin holds tones of pink, purple, gold, and hangs loosely about her face. She reminds me of my mother. I almost expect the corners of her mouth to lift, for her to chide, *Go girl, no stopping with an old woman. Make haste into the world, seek all it has to offer.*

Ilse comes out of the side room, closing the door carefully behind her. 'Geertje, help me bring the oysters.'

On the kitchen table, two platters stand ready. The oysters are speckled with parsley and drizzled with lemon juice. Diamonds of toasted bread fan around them. I would not have thought Maartje capable of such daintiness.

In his basket, Titus is sucking on a crust, regarding me with his mild brown eyes. 'Soon, I will return,' I promise. He chews his bread, unperturbed.

The master is leaning against one of the painted columns, his hand raised to grip the mantel. A fire, more flame than heat, dances in the grate. The younger of the two visitors is holding up a small painting. The master frowns at it, frowns at us as we enter. He has a trick of making himself seem taller, broader than he truly is. In this stance he could be Samson, about to tear down the columns of the temple. 'Over there.' He waves us to his wife's end of the table. 'And pour more wine.'

The mistress's cheeks are flushed as though she had come in from the cold. Behind her fan, she coughs discreetly into a handkerchief. To her left sits her uncle, who has angled his chair to face the other men. I set my platter before her. At the sight or smell of the oysters, a shudder flits across her shoulders. Luca, the spaniel, who rests curled on her lap, lifts his head and sniffs.

'Three days I toiled over that fingernail to get it right,' the young man says.

'Almost right,' the master says. 'Had you restrained yourself to one morning's work, it would have been perfect.'

The art dealer slaps the table, releases a belch of laughter.

The mistress flinches. When Ilse goes to fill her glass she covers it with her hand. 'Bring water,' she says, her voice dry as paper.

Before I can look at the painting, the young man turns it to the wall. The men's glasses are almost empty. I reach across the table to replenish the art dealer's wine. 'Have a care, girl,' he snaps, raising an arm in defence of a canvas he holds close to his chest.

'I beg your pardon, Sir.' I step back, scalded by the rebuke.

'She is new,' the mistress says, touching his elbow.

I feel a rush of warmth towards her. I lower my head, hope the master has not noticed my mistake. When I dare to look at him, he is still frowning, though not at me.

The art dealer grunts, turns back to the two painters.

'You cannot guess what Dou's clients are willing to pay,' he goads.

'Then I will not attempt to do so.' The master comes to the table, moving so swiftly his arm collides with mine. A scent of cedarwood rises from his person. He spills one of Maartje's oysters onto a piece of toast, eats it noisily.

Ilse returns with a tall ewer, fills four water glasses.

'Come and sit,' the master says, throwing an arm across his former pupil's shoulders. 'Oysters are best eaten cold.' When he turns his back to me, I feel strangely bereft. He waves at Ilse to take the second bottle from the marble basin. I am no longer needed.

Back in the kitchen, my charge is wriggling in his basket, eager for amusement. I take him in my arms, sing one of Abe's old songs, about a girl who could love none but a sailor. When he tires of that, I bring him to the window to see snow wheeling into the courtyard. He shows little interest, contenting himself with pulling at the strings of my cap. Across the courtyard, a wooden shed of double-height stands against the neighbouring wall. The master's gallery, Ilse calls it. Another place we must not enter.

Back at the fireside, I cuddle Titus. 'Soon we will explore the city together.'

A scornful sound comes from Maartje's side of the kitchen. But there is no malice in her dourness. When she pours herself a mug of ale, she fills a second, brings it to me.

Ilse appears at the door, empty ewer in one hand.

'You are wanted, Geertje.'

'Both of us are to serve?'

'I will tend to them,' Ilse says quickly. 'The mistress has taken ill. She is in the salon and asks for you.'

'But I must feed the baby.'

Maartje lifts Titus out of my arms with unexpected gentleness. He gazes up at her and she pulls a face so grotesque I shudder. Titus bucks with laughter at this amusement, his little hand reaching up to pat her chin.

When I leave, she is jogging him in the crook of one arm while mashing a plate of beets for his dinner.

It is my first time in the salon, the room above the kitchen where the master and mistress dine and sleep. All the curtains are closed. The only light comes from a low fire in the grate and two candles burning on the table.

The mistress sits on a chair by an ornate bedstead, looking as though she might slide to the floor at any moment. Luca cowers at her feet. I bring one candle closer and see that her silk kerchief is unpinned and slipping to one side. Her face is dewy and pale.

'Help me to undress.' A fit of coughing muffles her words.

I unlace her stiff bodice and ease her out of the gown, which shimmers like a calm sea. When she is bare of foot and in her chemise, she allows me to help her into bed. Eyes half-closed, she reclines against the bolsters while I settle the coverlet around her shoulders.

Awkwardly, I stand beside the bed. Should I leave? Should I call Ilse? The little dog watches me intently from under the chair.

'Stay with me,' the mistress says, as though I had spoken my thoughts aloud. 'Bring some mending. Bring the baby too.'

When I return, she has fallen into an unquiet sleep, her body racked with spasms of coughing. I set Titus on the floor, watch him kick his legs, catch his toes. He waves his arms in delight at his newfound freedom. I stifle a laugh at his rocking attempts to roll onto his front.

'You are a restful companion,' the mistress says. 'I cannot bear idle talk.'

I shift in my chair. I had thought she was sleeping.

'Will you drink some water, Madam?'

I hold a cup to her lips. She sips, then her head falls back as though the effort exhausted her. When she opens her eyes again, she looks stronger and breathes more easily.

'Give him to me,' she says.

She is far too weak to hold the baby, and he is too lively to lie still. But there is an imperious note in her voice, and so I lift Titus carefully onto my lap, then gently place him onto the bed beside her. She smiles, strokes his hair. He seems entranced by her touch, her warmth.

'Go to the kitchen,' she says. 'Ask Ilse if any paintings have been sold.'

The hallway is quiet, save for the rumble of men's voices from the side room. In the kitchen, Maartje is nodding in a chair by the fire, but there is no sign of Ilse.

'No matter,' the mistress says when I return without tidings. 'By my reckoning he will sell none, and acquire at least two. My uncle is a persuasive man.'

Titus lies curled against her chest, deep in sleep.

'Your uncle must be a very clever man.'

'It is easy to sell to those who want to buy.'

Her mood changes. She recovers her usual poise. 'I believe I may sleep a little. Return in an hour.'

I go to take the baby but she waves me away. 'He is better than any bed-warmer,' she says, closing her eyes.

When I place the candle back on the table, I notice a scrap of fabric at my feet and pick it up.

In the hallway, I consider whether to risk Maartje's mood in the kitchen, or go to my low-ceilinged room where I could sew in peace by the window.

Light footsteps approach. Ilse comes down the stairs, slippers in hand.

'I was looking for you,' I say.

She colours. 'I was checking on the stoves in the painting room.' She slides her feet into her slippers. 'I feared disturbing the mistress.'

'She is sleeping; the baby, too.'

'Maartje will be wanting me to scrub pans.'

She seems loath to stop in talk with me. I wonder if she is affronted by the mistress asking for me instead of her. Already forgetting the sleepers in the salon, she clatters down the steps to the kitchen.

Alone in my room, I realise I am still holding the scrap of cloth from the salon floor. In my hand is one of the mistress's fine lawn handkerchiefs, crumpled and spotted with blood.

Chapter 8

On Easter Saturday morning I leave the painter's kitchen, walk down the alley behind the house towards the canal. At the water-side, out of the shade of the houses, the sun's warmth rises up my back, stroking my shoulders, touching my neck, and I feel as though I have emerged from a cold, dark tunnel. I carry Titus in a sling fashioned from a silken shawl, which must have come from India or China years ago. On the bridge, I stop to test again the strength of the knots at my waist and neck.

In the April sunshine, the canal is lively with trade. A tang of decay hangs over the water and I wonder how it will smell at the height of summer. Hirelings are busy unloading furniture from a barge, easing chairs wrapped in sailcloth up onto the banks, roping a cabinet and winching it over the water. Good-humoured shouts pass among them as they work. I hold Titus up, point out a seagull perched on the leg of an upturned table, still as a carving on the bow of a ship. He blows bubbles from his little round mouth, looks not at the bird or the men but at me, stretching out his arm to mimic mine. I laugh, settle him back onto my hip.

In my basket, wrapped in a square of linen, is a pair of the mistress's best leather shoes.

That morning, she sent for me from her bed, and when I entered the salon she directed me to the tall linen cabinet. On the bottom shelf stood a dozen or more pairs of shoes. Such wonderful shoes! For a moment I forgot my task, gazing at the painted satin, the polished square toes, the curling tongues, while the mistress complained of torn silk and scuffed leather.

'Have you found them yet?' she called.

One ash-grey shoe lay fallen on its side. Calf's leather slid into my palm, smooth as a dove's plumage. The trim was frayed and a hole had formed at the heel where a tiny brass stud had been lost.

'Bring both, how else do you expect the shoemaker to match the tassels?' She closed her eyes, as though she could not bear to look at the source of such foolishness. Presently, she recovered herself, and continued in a less petulant tone. 'Take them to Otto; Ilse will give you directions. Tell him I must have them back this afternoon.'

I check the basket again to make sure the shoes are safely resting inside. How long would I have to work to earn their price?

I pass the poulterer's shop, its window strung with game, then the apothecary, shelved with bulbous bottles of blue and green glass. A pair of long-nosed pliers stands in the window, next to a dish of stained teeth.

In a doorway, an old man dressed in a ragged cloak, the hem crusted with mud, plays an out-of-tune fiddle. Plaintive strains of music follow us up the street. We have almost reached the Nieuwmarkt when I see the sign of the shoemaker's anvil swinging from its chains.

The trill of the bell over the door surprises Titus into a stream of delighted babbling. Inside, the air is musty with leather and glue, though two windows gape open onto the street. The shop is small and orderly, with a counter at one end, and a worktable taking up most of the remaining space. From the rafters, shoes and boots hang in pairs from wooden pegs. A girl sits at the table, her back to me, her hand pulling a threaded needle high over her stitching. An elderly man in a buff-coloured jerkin stands at the counter, his head bent over a ledger, his finger creeping down the page.

'I am looking for Meneer Otto, if you please.'

'Elder or younger?' he asks, without looking up. His grey hair is streaked straw-blond.

Why did Ilse not tell me for whom I should ask? I hesitate, place the shoes on the counter beside a row of wooden lasts.

'My mistress sent me.'

At this, he raises his head, looks over my shoulder, and gives a short whistle.

The person I saw seated at the table comes to stand beside me, and I see it is not a girl after all, but a slender young man. He reaches for the mistress's shoes, turns them over in his calloused hands. 'These I made for the painter's wife who lives by Sint Antoniesluis. I recognise her instep.' He returns the shoes to the counter. 'But I do not recognise you.'

'I am Geertje, the new maid. I came in Ilse's place.'

'That is all to the good. Ilse does not like me.' He follows this with an easy laugh, and crooking a finger, chucks Titus under the chin.

A scarf wrapped about the young man's head holds tight brown curls back from his face, which is clean-shaven, with high cheekbones and a long nose. An awl is tucked behind one ear.

'Can you mend them? She needs them today.' As I say this aloud, it rings false. The mistress has not left her bed for two days and cannot be in urgent need of dress shoes. I have been sent here to fulfil a whim, nothing more. I feel a twinge of guilt for lying to this man.

He clucks his tongue, beckons me to sit at the worktable while he examines the shoes by the window.

'Italian leather,' he says, caressing the lining. 'There is no pair like them in the whole of Amsterdam.'

I pull out a stool, ease Titus onto my lap. 'They hardly seem real. That is to say, they are the most beautiful shoes I have ever seen.' I blush at the clumsiness of my praise, wait for him to laugh at a peasant woman's pronouncements on his skill. But he does not laugh.

'Their true beauty is in the fit.'

He sets the shoes aside, drops to his knees, reaches for my heel.

I am so surprised I let him take my foot, suffer his eyes on my thick woollen stockings, his hands on the worn-down clogs Abe bought for me years ago.

'You will walk with greater ease if you stuff the toes with lambswool.'

Before I can reply, Titus grabs a fistful of the shoemaker's hair. The more I try to untwine the little fingers, the more they cling to their prize, and now my hand, too, is deep in the man's hair, and he is laughing over my torrent of apologies, his head held fast at my knees. Finally, I free us, all three.

The shoemaker slips my shoes from my feet, takes a handful of fleecy white fibres from a basket, and tucks the wool inside.

I think of the old man at the counter, his finger working down the ledger. How will this look on the account my mistress receives?

'No charge,' the shoemaker says.

I stand up, my feet light and airy, as though I might take flight. But when I look down and see my lumpish clogs, my coarse-knit stockings, a little of the lightness departs.

Whistling to himself at his bench, the shoemaker takes a knife and a metal rule, scores a line across a piece of hide. The awl holds fast behind his ear, even as he leans over his work.

'Tonight,' he says.

'Pardon?'

'I will bring the shoes to your mistress tonight.'

I pause. 'I will tell her, Sir.'

As I push the door open to leave, he calls something after me.

'Your pardon, Sir?'

'I said my name is Otto. Not Sir.' He smiles at me, showing a row of even white teeth, then turns his attention to his handiwork.

Outside, I have to shield my eyes from the sun. In the distance, I hear a clock chime midday. *Tell him I must have them back this afternoon.*

I am not yet minded to return to the painter's house. I wander along the busy street, stopping at shop windows, admiring displays of linen and lace, velvet and brocade. A pair of gossiping maids pass by, arm in arm, and I envy their companionship. When a drunken man tips his hat to them they shriek with laughter, cover their mouths, hurry away.

At the market I buy a scoop of raisins and feed them, one by one, to Titus. I wander around the stalls, wishing I had means to buy some small trinket; a copper ring, or even a length of woven ribbon. Perhaps, when the painter pays me, I will return.

Titus clamours for more fruit, his mouth sticky with juice. I dare not delay any longer. I feed him the last of the raisins on our walk home.

The tree-lined Zwanenburgwal is cool and shady. As I turn into the alley behind the painter's house, a somehow familiar figure with a hat pulled low over his forehead steps into my path. I jump back, wrap my arms around the baby. But it is only my brother, Pieter, and I have nothing to fear.

Chapter 9

Pieter holds me at arm's length, taking in my old jacket and skirt as though he had never seen them before. 'The peasant comes to the city,' he says, and laughs.

There are curls of wood in his hair and lines of sawdust in the creases of his forehead. A grimy shirt sags loose at the waist of his breeches.

'You startled me,' I say, and then to hide my irritation, 'I am glad to see you.'

I truly am glad to see him. The sight of his face restores a little of my former life. But as we stand in the sheltered alley behind my current home, I find the ache for the past is not as sharp as it once was, and a newfound courage insulates me from my old fears. The woman who clung to the railings on her first morning in the city seems a stranger to me now.

I wonder what has brought him to Amsterdam. 'Did you travel this morning from Rarep?'

As he sucks on his smouldering pipe, a finger of fear touches my heart: the master has complained, has summoned Pieter to take me away. I realise I do not want to leave. Like a blind woman running her hands over an unknown object, I am sensing the shape of a new life forming for me in Amsterdam.

'I had to spend the morning in the city dockyards, overseeing the apprentices, those lazy dogs. We shall be lucky to sail by Whitsun, so pitted with worm is the hull.'

As he talks, I imagine myself growing stronger, taller. My feet seem rooted to the ground as though no wind could sway me. He complains of the laxity of the men, of how they tax his patience. His reproaches are akin to those I often heard him voice against his overseer in Rarep. He is the same Pieter, and yet there is some difference since I last saw him.

After his invective, he nods at the baby on my hip. 'Is the infant in good health?'

'A strong, hearty boy,' I say, tilting Titus towards him.

He grunts. 'Let us hope it lives to keep you employed into summer and beyond.' One foot taps the cobbles; he is impatient to be gone.

'Have you seen our mother? Or Trijn? Tell them I hope to visit before my six-month term is finished.'

'Our mother lives so well she exceeds the monthly stipend I pay her as a matter of course, and reports are that our cousin is meddlesome as ever. For your part, you should not think of visiting Edam until you have secured another term.'

Another term. So it may be September, or later, before I see my family again.

'When I am home, I long to be away, and when I am away, I long for home.'

'The time will pass. Your home is here now.' Pieter gives me a sharp look. 'I hope you give your master no cause for concern.'

It is the master who has given me cause for concern. Whenever I come close to contentment, his mention of Pieter's debt rises to the surface of my mind, scuttling my peace.

'He says you owe him money. Pieter, is it true?'

The question I had resolved not to ask slips from me like a pitcher slipping through my fingers, and the resulting silence seems louder than any crash of pottery on stone.

Pieter takes the pipe from his lips. The eyes I have always considered so like my own seem cold today. From the canal come the screeches of gulls, and I imagine birds fighting for scraps flung from kitchens after the midday meal. I slide my arms around Titus bundled in the shawl. There is comfort in holding that small, warm body closely, as though a pair of reassuring arms also encircles me.

'You should not interfere in the affairs of men, Geertje.' Pieter remains calm. For now, his anger is contained. 'In fact, it is your master who owes me money.'

It is almost laughable. The master's wealth is apparent in the sumptuous furnishings of his house, in the jewels that hang from his wife's ears and throat, in the meat and butter served daily at his table. That he could owe money to a Rarep carpenter seems hardly credible.

Only when I too am calm, controlled, do I dare to probe further.

'You mean that you did work for him. On the house. That you are awaiting payment?'

He puffs smoke into the air. On my hip, Titus whimpers. I realise I am holding him too tightly and relax my grip.

'Work of a different kind. You cannot hope to comprehend the pecuniary dealings of the Company. But we men of the world understand that the value of cargo can go down as well as up.'

I look again at Pieter's work clothes, the wood shavings in his hair. Nobody could take him for a man of the world. But for the past year or more, his talk has been peppered with envy for the merchants who make their fortunes in spices, sugar, lumber, grain. A new zeal spikes all his endeavours.

'So he suffered losses? And you lost money too?'

Pieter frowns. 'It is of no import to you. He is a wealthy man and can afford to lose a little. Lately, it seems his losses only serve to whet his appetite for more spending.'

There is an edge to his voice, an unease behind the bravado as though he is hiding something. I am reminded of nine-year-old Pieter, dragged out of the local orchard by our mother, his pockets bulging, protesting his innocence in vain.

He takes a step towards me, grips my arm. 'Watch him, Sister. Pay heed to how he spends his money. I want to know every ebb and flow of his income.'

The same Pieter, but with ambition sharpened like a knife against stone. His fingers are pinching my arm but I dare not protest. Until now, I had not noticed the lines of care woven around the corners of his eyes like fissures in dried oak. Stale smoke from his breath fills my nostrils.

'I hardly see the master. These days he keeps to his gallery in the courtyard, where he works on a canvas so large it cannot fit inside the house.'

'Cultivate his wife's goodwill then. People say he will do anything for her.'

Titus is crying now, and struggling against me. I nod, knowing not what I am promising.

As the baby's cries grow louder, Pieter drops my arm. 'I will give Marit your compliments,' he says over his shoulder as he walks away.

How could I have forgotten his wife, the approaching birth?

'Come to see me again when there is news,' I call. He raises a hand to the brim of his hat, turns out of the alley and disappears.

I stop by the kitchen door, trying to marry the master's mention of debt with Pieter's talk of losses. If both men have lost, how can each owe the other money?

Chapter 10

At the kitchen table, Ilse is counting eggs in a straw-lined crate.

'How long you have been. I kept some *hutsepot* for you.' She nods towards the hearth.

Titus chews his fingers. I take a seat by the fire, unwind the shawl, shift him to my lap.

'Once you have eaten, you must help me,' Ilse says.

'What do you want me to do?' The baby clambers to my shoulder. One-handed, I gather plates and spoons from the cupboard.

'The mistress has a fancy to paint eggs for his amusement.' She points at Titus. 'All this trouble so that she may stain her dress and he may crush the shells. You can drain the eggs. I will find a darning needle.' She goes in search of the work bag.

I mash a paste of vegetables and gravy. Titus moulds himself into the crook of my arm and I spoon the mess into his mouth.

Ilse returns, needle in hand. 'Where are the shoes?' she asks, seeing the empty basket at my feet.

'Otto said he will bring them tonight.'

She frowns, turns back to the eggs.

The baby's cheeks are speckled brown and orange. I wipe his face, and rub his back until his head droops. When he is tucked into his basket, I eat a plate of lukewarm *hutsepot*, fat congealing in yellow islets on the surface.

'Have you finished?' Ilse calls, the moment I rest my spoon on the empty plate.

The first egg sits smooth and cold in my palm, and in an instant I am back in the lumber merchant's house in Hoorn, the children tugging at my skirts, clamouring for their turn. How many eggs were wasted that day, and yet their mama did not scold them. In

Maartje's kitchen, nothing is wasted. I chip holes at top and tail, pierce the yolk, blow the glossy insides into a basin.

'How dainty you are,' Ilse says. 'I always break the shells.'

'Where is Maartje?'

'Gone to the meat hall. She says Willem Jans cheats me when I go.'

'And the master?' I falter. How can Pieter expect me to spy on my master's affairs?

'Some business took him across town. Likely the mistress will not rise from her bed until he returns.'

I take the next egg, strip a clinging brown feather from the shell.

'Does he sell a great many paintings?'

'He buys more than he sells. But the ones he sells are enough to make him a fortune.'

'Is he really very rich?'

I am asking too many questions. But Ilse likes to talk, and her face registers no suspicion.

'The mistress says he will never be rich, for he casts money about without a care.' She crosses the kitchen to the pump, sluices water into a pail.

'He must know many important people.'

'Yes, and every beggar this side of the Amstel.' She stands the pail on the three-legged stool by the fire. 'After Maartje, the mistress forbade him to bring vagrants home.'

Already I have hollowed half a dozen eggs. Ilse rinses the first two, sets them on a cloth at the hearth to dry.

'Maartje was a vagrant?' I remember the master's familiar manner with her, how she playfully raised a knife against him.

'He found her begging outside the Oude Kerk,' Ilse says in a whisper, though apart from the sleeping baby, we are alone. 'Somehow he discovered she could cook. The mistress can hardly endure her.' She holds a finger to her lips. 'Say nothing of what I have told you.'

The eggs are finished; nothing broken, nothing wasted.

Muffled coughing comes from the salon overhead.

'You had better sit with her awhile.' Ilse gathers the rest of the hollowed eggshells into her apron. 'I will watch the baby.'

I check my apron for stains, tug my cap straight. 'Call if you need me.' I touch a finger to Titus's forehead in farewell.

Afternoon sun streams through the salon windows from the court-yard. The mistress is slumped in a chair beside her bed, Luca resting on her lap.

For a moment, I am reminded of the marionettes at the Edam *kermis*. The other children had clapped their hands, laughed at the puppets' antics. But the painted maidens and soldiers had saddened me, for I could not forget that they were mere rags and wooden pegs; that without their master, they could never dance or sing.

As I approach, she lifts her head.

'Can I get you anything, Madam?' What will I say if she asks for her shoes?

She straightens up a little, spills Luca from her lap, and her shawl slips to the floor. I try to wrap it around her shoulders but she waves me away.

'Geertje, do you feel it very hot?'

'Very hot, Madam,' I say, though the breeze entering the open windows is strong enough to send ripples through the bed curtains.

Two feverish points of colour burn high on her cheeks. A film of moisture coats her skin. For now, she has forgotten the shoes.

'Help me to bed.'

If she meant to play at painting eggs today, she has forgotten that too.

Once propped against her pillows, she seems at greater ease. 'How is my son?' she asks with a faint smile. 'Did he eat well today?'

I take my sewing and sit beside her, tell her Titus is so strong he tries to grab the spoon for himself, that he pulls at my sleeve if I am too slow in serving him. The wet nurse is no longer needed, and his gums are swelling with new teeth. Her eyelids lower and close. I talk until the smile fades from her face and I am certain she is asleep.

A little of her light goes out when the master is away from home.

I dare not leave her side to examine the room's many paintings so I content myself with looking at the one nearest her bed. In a cramped cottage, a young mother holds her breast to an infant's mouth. An older woman looks on, fussing with the baby's coverlet. I wonder if the same painting hung there through all the mistress's births and losses.

It is evening when the master returns. In the dusk, it is becoming difficult to see my stitches but I refrain from lighting candles for fear of waking her. Luca sits, alert, at my feet, as though suspicious of my proximity to his mistress.

The salon door opens. Before I look up, I sense my master in the room. About him hangs a faint smell of turpentine. His shoulders sag, as though he has been hard at labour all day. Raising a finger to his lips, he motions for me to be still. He leans over his sleeping wife, kisses her mouth.

How must it feel to lie on a bed of bevelled oak, to rest a cheek on downy pillows, and awaken to a loving husband's kiss? Ilse told me they will soon be married eight years. As I would be, had Abe lived.

More kissing and murmuring from the bed. I rise and, without taking leave of them, slip out the door.

I meet Ilse on the stairs, bringing a supper of bread and herring to the salon.

'The shoemaker is asking for you,' she says, a note of incredulity in her voice. 'Make haste to the kitchen. The sooner he sees you the sooner he will be gone.'

Downstairs, Otto is sitting by the fire. Maartje tips ale into his mug.

'How are your feet?' His eyes are bright from the flames.

'At far greater ease, thanks to you.'

Maartje returns to the table to beat eggs with a long-stemmed spoon.

I pour myself a mug of ale, take a seat beside Otto.

'I have been hearing about you,' he says.

I look at him in alarm. What can Ilse have said? My discomfit provokes a gentle laugh.

'Maartje told me you come from the country; that you know nobody here.'

He takes a draught of ale, looks into the flames as they lick the grate, dart up the brickwork. 'I know what it is like to be friendless and alone.'

'But you have family here.'

'I have my father. My mother died when I was born.'

'So you never knew her.' I think of my son, whose eyes never opened to my face, then remember that Pieter has forbidden me from speaking of my loss.

'You must have many friends,' I say.

'No friends. I work in the shop all day. Those I knew in school spend their nights in drunkenness and whoring.'

In Hoorn, young men did not sit by firesides speaking to widows of pursuits we should know nothing about. I could feign shock, but this quietly-spoken boy with his brown-black eyes does not mean to shock me. In those eyes, trust is offered, trust is invited.

The fire crackles. Specks of soot land on the tiles and on Ilse's eggs, which lie on the hearth, wrapped in a round of cloth. I push the nest further from the fire.

'Tell me about your home,' he says.

At first I cannot think what to say. I tell him about the cottage in Edam where I was born, about the melodies from the bell tower that quartered every hour we spent at play in the fields. I pause, awaiting the familiar sting of loss that always follows my memories. It does not come.

'Go on,' he says.

I talk more than I have talked in years, telling him about moving to Hoorn and working in the tavern at night, the air spiced with sausage and clouded with smoke, the lively music, the beery kisses of sailors and their sweethearts. I am ready to tell him about Abe when Ilse returns, clattering her tray onto the table.

'You will be happy here.' Otto smiles.

I find myself smiling back at him. He has lost a mother; I have lost a son. We are akin.

Behind us, Ilse rattles pewter plates.

Otto drinks the last of his ale and stands.

I take the lamp from over the fire, walk him down the alley. On cool evenings, the stench of the canal subsides. I breathe fresh sea air.

'How can Ilse dislike you?' I ask on impulse.

He turns to me, his face half in shadow.

'One night, when I sat with her by the fire, as I sat with you tonight, she leaned over, kissed me on the mouth, and I did not kiss her back.'

I cannot think how to reply.

The same gentle laugh as before.

'Come to see me soon,' he calls as he walks away.

I watch the sway of his shoulders until my light no longer reaches him. I lower the lamp, turn back down the alley.

In the kitchen, I remember the shoes.

I find them on the bench by the box bed. At first, when I unfold the cloth, I think he has made a mistake and brought a new pair. Then I recognise the soft grey leather, the tiny brass studs. I turn them over in my hands but cannot discover the repairs.

Chapter 11

I am buttering strips of bread at the kitchen table when Ilse comes in, tapping the empty breakfast tray against one leg.

'The mistress is quite well today.' She leans over my shoulder, snatches a sliver of bread. 'She asked for her blue silk,' she adds, her mouth full.

'Does she mean to go outdoors?'

'She has already gone. Taking flowers to the Zuiderkerk.'

The Zuiderkerk, where her three infants lie buried.

'Perhaps the sunshine coaxed her out,' I say.

Titus crawls across the floor, clattering his wooden horse against the tiles, delighted by the noise. I lure him to my side with a morsel of soft white bread.

Sunlight beams into the courtyard. It is early May, and though it cannot be long after nine, the kitchen is already too hot. Maartje opens the windows.

'You can press the linen in the salon while the mistress is gone,' Ilse says. 'Mind you take him with you.' Titus sits at my feet, squashing bread into his mouth.

It is Ilse's job to press the linen, but I have no objection to spending the morning in the cool salon.

Without the master or mistress, the salon seems bigger, brighter. I set Titus down on the floorboards to explore, then begin my own exploration, free from scrutiny.

How would it be, to eat every meal surrounded by dozens of paintings and carvings? But perhaps the artworks are as ordinary to the master and mistress as the pots and pans of the kitchen are to me.

Opposite the windows, a broad mantel spans the hearth. Wooden tendrils bearing leaves and flowers intertwine in intricate relief. I cannot find where one vine ends and another begins. The weight of the beam is supported on either side by statues of a nearly-naked man and woman, their doleful eyes cast downwards to the slate. Over the mantel hangs an immense painting of the mistress looking younger and stronger than the woman I know. A crown of flowers is woven into her hair. She holds her satin skirts bunched in one hand as though she is about to tread on uneven ground.

Most magnificent of all is the bedstead of carved oak. A faint honeyed perfume lingers over the polished surfaces of the wood. I part the hangings of rich blue velvet, stroke the smooth coverlet, the tasselled bolsters. As if in a dream, I step out of my slippers and climb into the cushioned space. I roll onto my back, the bedding moulding around my body as though I am melting into feather and down. In that moment, I never want to rise again.

A cry startles me. I open my eyes to a dark canopy, and for an instant I feel as though I have been buried alive. Titus wails louder. I scramble down from the bed. He has tumbled over by the grate and holds aloft a blackened hand, no longer recognising it as his own. I examine fingers and palm. The cause of his distress is nothing more than the shock of the fall and the sight of the sooty hand. I kiss and comfort him, chide myself for my neglect. When he is calm, I drizzle water from the pitcher on the table onto a cloth and wipe the tiny hand clean.

'All better. Mama need never know.' Settling him close by, I take an armful of linen to the cedar press in the corner. I catch sight of the mistress, or rather the reflection of her portrait, in the mirror that hangs between the windows. For a moment we stand side by side: she, dressed in a gown trimmed with pearls and wearing a garland of flowers about her face; I, in my plain white cap, my sleeves rolled high above my coarse forearms.

I turn back to my work.

At my feet Titus sits, chewing the head of his toy horse. The creaking of the press draws his curiosity and he clings to my legs, pulling himself upright. I lift him, show him the pressing plates, the turning handle, the finials of carved lions which top the frame. Solemnly, he pats each lion's head in turn. He stretches to grab the handle. 'Not for baby hands.' I set him down.

Aggrieved, he wails and plucks at my skirts. I pull my handkerchief from the fresh linen, show him the sparrow I embroidered long ago in Edam with the sprig of berries in its beak. 'You can fold this one for me.' He dances the handkerchief before his face in triumph.

The crash of the front door resounds through the house. The mistress comes in, Luca scampering at her feet.

'Finish that later, Geertje.' She slips the fur-trimmed mantle from her shoulders. 'I must rest.'

Her face is tired and wan. Stooping, she ruffles her son's downy hair. Too late I notice the parted bed curtains, the impression of my body on the bedding within.

'Put this away.' The mistress drops the mantle onto a chair, goes to the table, pours a glass of water.

Behind her back, I smooth the bedding, close the curtains. I lift Titus from the floor, bounce him in my arms to hide the shaking of my hands.

She looks over one shoulder. 'Have Ilse send my husband to me at noon.'

'I will be in the kitchen if you need me, Madam.'

She makes no reply. Eyes half-closed, she sinks into her usual chair, rests her forehead on one hand.

The kitchen is empty. Maartje has taken her pipe to the courtyard where she squats in the sun. Ilse must have gone to the market.

'Time for your nap.' I tuck Titus into his basket.

The iron knocker falls on the front door. I hurry up the stairs to answer it before the noise disturbs the mistress.

A man in a tight jerkin stands on the steps, his thumbs hooked into the strap of a leather pouch hanging from his waist. Behind him, two boys steady a wooden crate between them. 'Your master, if you please. Tell him Meneer de Groot is here.' He beckons the boys and they shoulder the crate into the hall.

Upstairs, the door to the painting room is open as before, but this time the master is seated at the easel, his back to me. His brush moves swiftly across the canvas.

I raise my hand to knock.

'Geertje Dircx, the carpenter's sister.'

I release a tiny gasp.

He laughs.

'I work with mirrors. I saw you before you saw me.'

I hesitate, unsure if he is mocking me.

He half-turns. 'Come. I will show you.'

To the side of his canvas, a mirror has been propped on a second easel.

'Stand behind me. Now look into the glass. Do you see your reflection?'

'Yes, Sir.' From this angle, his face fills the mirror, blocking mine, but I do not want to disappoint him.

He is adding smudges of brownish-yellow paint to an indistinct form. It is not quite a face, though I can see lighter patches where the eyes and nose should be, and a bare triangle between what might become cheek, jaw, chin.

'I did not know paintings were made like that.'

'And how did you think they were made?' He sounds curious.

'I had supposed there would be an outline, then colours filled in, but it seems your colours come first and have no bounds.'

'Nature sets the bounds.'

The brush stops. He shifts on the stool. Under his gaze, I feel as though a bright light has been turned upon me. I should have untucked my apron and straightened my sleeves before coming upstairs.

'Meneer de Groot is in the hall and asking for you, Sir.'

'Tell him I will be down directly. And wait for me there; I shall need you.'

His smile warms me like an open fire.

Downstairs, the two boys ease an oblong box through the front door. 'Against the far wall,' the master calls in a low voice. 'Make no disturbance; my wife is resting.' Soon, a dozen or more deliveries of all sizes line the wall, and the master is waving Meneer de Groot out the door, the leather pouch at the man's waist bulked with coins.

'Help me unpack these and put everything away before she awakens.' A mischievous smile plays around the master's lips. I cannot help smiling back at him. He looks like a little boy hiding some misdeed.

'You would have me conspire against my mistress, Sir?'

He laughs aloud, checks himself, peers through the passage to the salon. The door remains closed; no sound comes from within.

'Be careful, these are valuable.' He hands me one of the containers. 'I could not trust de Groot's boy with them.'

So he trusts me. It is indirect praise, but I feel a swell of pride as though he had handed me the keys to the household coffers. I take a knife from my pocket, slide the blade till the twine around the box springs free. Inside, lying in a nest of straw, is a porcelain figure of a fantastical animal. I lift it out. It is something like a bird, with a long neck, small head and cockscomb. The legs that end in three-toed feet carry a body too heavy for flight.

'What do you think of it?' The master takes the bird-creature from me.

'I have never seen anything like it.'

'It is a flightless bird. From Java.'

'You have seen such birds?'

He smiles. 'No, but other men have, and they have sketched them, and made models like this one.'

'But they could have conjured the creature from fancy.'

'Would it matter if they had?'

His answer confuses me. I turn my attention back to the boxes. Soon the floor is strewn with sawdust. Paintings, busts and other strange objects surround us.

'Take those books and some of the shells to the back attic. I will follow.' Flexing his knees, he tests the weight of a large frame wrapped in sackcloth.

I pass the salon door, balancing a spiky shell on three heavy books. Pressing the purchases close to my chest, I mount the stairs.

Muted curses drift upwards as the master struggles with the unwieldy frame. I pass the small room where his curios are displayed, take the stairway to the next floor.

Outside the attic room, I await the master's orders. Across the landing, the murmur of a man's voice comes from the small painting room where the pupils work. I rest my armload against the stair rail. Before the master resumes his teaching, I must remember to tell him the mistress wants to see him at midday.

A familiar female laugh comes from the pupils' room.

Ilse.

For an instant, the books sway and almost fall from my arms. I tighten my hold. The shell digs into my chest.

The master rounds the final bend of the stairs, breathing heavily. He rests his burden against the wall, enters the attic.

If he keeps to the back of the house, I might snatch a moment to tap a warning on the pupils' door.

The thought has hardly formed in my mind when he is back, easing the books and shell from my arms, and relaying them to a dust-covered cabinet.

'Thank you, Sir,' I say, as loud as I dare.

As I speak, a woman's muffled cry sounds from the pupils' room.

The master's back stiffens. He turns around, his eyes on the door behind me. I am blocking his path. He grasps my wrist, pulls me to one side as though I am a discarded packing case, and throws the door open.

In the first partition, Ilse sits on the lap of a young man, her skirts pushed to her hips, his hand thrust between her thighs. For a terrible moment, they do not see us. There is hole in her stocking, just below the knee, and the foolish thought comes into my head that I should mend it for her.

The master steps forward. The young man jumps up. Ilse screams, stumbling to the floor. The master grabs her by the forearm, drags her to her feet.

'Get out of my house!' A vein flares in his cheek as he shouts. He flings her from the room. 'Take your trappings and go.'

She staggers towards me, one hand clutching her loosened bodice. I catch her before she falls, wrap my arm around her waist, and half-carry her down the stairs to the hanging room.

Before I can close the door behind us, I hear the mistress in the hallway, calling her husband's name.

Chapter 12

Ilse throws herself face down onto my bed, her body shaking with sobs.

'Do not distress yourself.' I touch her arm, and she sobs even louder.

Footsteps pass the door, descend the stairs. The master's outrage echoes around the hall. I ease the door open. It is impossible to know if the mistress is agreeing or remonstrating with him. Whatever she says seems to calm him. The salon door opens and closes, the footsteps return.

I close the door quickly, sit on the edge of the bed.

'The mistress has soothed him,' I whisper. 'All will be well.'

Ilse moans. Her cap has slid to one side and the knot of hair at the back of her head has come loose. I raise her gently, tidy her dress. Her pretty face is puffed and wet with tears. She sniffs, gulps air.

Boots sound on the stairs. Men's voices approach. I open the door a crack, glimpse the fresh faces of the pupils. At first, I think the master is expelling them from the house. Then the sight of his face confounds me. He is smiling broadly. As they pass, one of the young men says something in a low tone, and a laugh breaks out among the group.

Ilse springs from the bed. I catch her at the doorway.

'You cannot mean to follow them!'

'I must speak to him.' She shrugs me off, darts from the room.

I run down the stairs after her.

The pupils are filing out the front door, following their master onto the street.

'Barent!' Ilse calls.

The last of the young men slows, almost stops, at the threshold.

From outside, a command is issued. As though pulled by an invisible string, the man continues out the door, never looking back.

Ilse's face is white. Silently, she allows me to lead her back to my room.

'Lie down and rest,' I tell her. 'I will help Maartje with dinner. Likely the pupils will eat at the tavern today.'

She huddles on a corner of the mattress, her knees drawn up to her chest.

The hall is littered with packing straw and empty boxes. Footprints cross the tiles where someone trod in the sawdust. I tidy as best as I can, not daring to touch the master's purchases without his supervision.

When I go down to the kitchen, the mistress already stands in the doorway, instructing Maartje. Before I can slip away unseen, she turns around, fixes me with her gaze. I brace myself for an inquisition.

'Send her to me.' Her face is impassive.

I should make an appeal on Ilse's behalf. *She is a silly girl but not a bad one. A hard-working maid deserves a second chance.* Defences form in my mind but find no expression. The blank eyes of the mistress forbid it.

Slowly, she climbs the stairs, her breath rasping in her throat.

Maartje leans on the kitchen table.

'I warned that girl.' She sounds hoarse.

'What is going to happen?'

She shakes her head. 'He is not a forgiving man.'

In his basket, Titus utters a syllable of contentment but does not awaken.

'Sleep on, little lamb.' I smooth his blanket. I should rouse him for dinner, but I cannot bear to breach his peace. As long as he sleeps, there is some harmony left in this house.

Ilse crouches on my bed, in the same position as when I left her.

'I have brought you some bread and cheese.' I set the plate down. 'Try to eat.'

She makes no move to take it.

'He wanted me to run away with him,' she says, as though I had not spoken. 'First, we would be married, then, he would take me north to meet his father.' Her eyes are fixed on the bare wall.

I cannot form a reply. How could she have thought a gentleman's son would wed a servant girl?

'I know what you are thinking.' She raises on one elbow, turns to look at me. 'But his father is only a schoolteacher. That is not so very grand.'

Ilse is calm now; only her eyes betray her distress. A motherly tenderness besets me. I slide an arm around her shoulders, rock her against me.

'The master should throw him out of the house.'

She gives a short laugh. 'And lose a fee of a hundred guilders a year? Far cheaper to rid himself of a wayward maid.'

I remember the drum of feet on the stairs, multiply hundreds in my head.

'You think Barent behaved badly,' Ilse says. 'But he truly loves me. His only failing is his lack of courage.'

I cannot bear to hear more.

'The mistress wants to see you.'

'You will come with me?' Her eyes are threaded with red veins.

I nod.

'Wash your face. I will fix your hair.'

She jumps up from the bed pulls off her cap, drags her fingers through her hair. My mind misgives, but I cannot abandon her.

Outside the salon door, Ilse ducks behind me, skittish with nerves. I raise my hand to knock. On my wrist is the mark of the master's fingers.

The mistress sits, looking down the length of the table at us. Luca watches from her lap, the leather ball clenched in his jaws.

'My husband has complained of your conduct. He insists you quit this house without delay.' Her eyes are focused on some spot on the door behind us. Whatever hope I had of her compassion fades. In this matter, she will be her husband's instrument; a brush in his deft hand.

'I have persuaded him that you should stop one more night, until you secure lodgings elsewhere.' Her tone is gentler now, but resolute. Any struggle that may have existed within her has been quelled.

'If you please, Madam, I would rather leave right away.' Ilse lifts her chin, looks the mistress in the eye.

I had expected tears, entreaties, not quiet determination. I sense a little of Ilse's spirit returning. Her wounds are the quick-healing wounds of the young.

The mistress stirs at this rebuke.

'As you will.' She slides open a drawer in the table, removes a pouch. 'You have friends with whom you may stop awhile?'

'All my friends are in service, Madam, and not at liberty to shelter visitors.'

The mistress pushes the pouch across the table. 'Perhaps it would be best for you to return to your family. There is a little extra in this to cover your passage. If you can find no respectable conveyance at the markets then you must go to the Dam and take a seat in a *trekschuit*.'

On her lap, the spaniel whimpers for attention. 'Down, Luca.'

The dog jumps to the floor.

'Geertje, walk Ilse to the square, see her safely on her way.' She bows her head as though the matter is concluded.

'The permission, Madam,' I prompt.

Her face flushes. 'My husband has refused the permission.'

I gape at her. Can he really mean to banish Ilse with no prospect of finding any employment?

Beside me, Ilse sways and I fear she may faint.

'You have been a good servant.' The mistress rises. 'Were it to me . . .' She stops, swallows.

'Goodbye, Madam,' Ilse says flatly.

The mistress goes to the linen cabinet, searches inside.

She returns with a woollen shawl, ties it around Ilse's shoulders.

'I wish you well,' the mistress says. For the first time in the interview she looks directly at her former maid. I catch the shine of a tear in her eye; she blinks, and it is gone.

All Ilse owns is what she wears, and a small cloth-wrapped bundle tucked into a corner of a kitchen cupboard.

'You could go to the courts.' I cannot put weight behind my words.

'And gratify old grey councillors with my tale? The story would reach Leiden within days.'

From the bundle she pulls a shrivelled rosebud, casts it into the fire. Maartje, who sits at the hearth, Titus on her knee, sends a stream of spittle flying after it.

The pouch the mistress gave Ilse is slung carelessly at her waist. I persuade her to open it, to count half the money into a pocket under her petticoat.

'Two weeks' wages, and a few spare stuivers. No doubt from the mistress's coffers, not his.' She tosses her head. Her lip trembles.

I take Titus from Maartje, wipe his mouth with a cloth. 'I will wait in the alley.'

With a sob, Ilse bounds into Maartje's arms. I slip out the door, the baby settled on my hip. A few moments later, Ilse joins me. Her eyes are wet, but her shoulders are braced as though ready for a day's hard work.

Without thought, I head for the Nieuwmarkt, the only place I know where farm carts arrive and depart all day. The afternoon is stale and sticky. Ilse lags behind. I slow to match her pace. On the bridge, a welcome breeze flutters through our caps and skirts. A laden barge floats under our feet, emerges into sunlight on the other side.

'It may all be for the best. Soon you will be home with your family and your betrothed, and will be mistress of your own household in time.' I mean this to cheer her, but her eyes fill with tears.

'I will miss you.' Her words are almost lost in the tumult of hawkers.

'And I will miss you.' Too late, I realise I had underestimated her. Her dignified leave-taking of the mistress points to a courage I never knew she possessed. 'You were my only friend in that house.'

'Maartje is your friend, though she does not trouble to show it.'

We cross through a maze of stalls to the weigh house at the far side of the square, where Ilse espies a Leiden farmhand loading empty chicken coops onto a cart. While she bargains for her passage, I swap Titus to my other hip, take him to admire a shaggy carthorse tethered outside an inn. The friendly ostler allows him to pat the horse's mane, jingles the harness to amuse him.

Ilse returns. 'It is all settled. I will be in Leiden before dark.'

'You must eat something.'

I buy bread and slices of smoked sausage and we sit on a kerb to eat. Titus jigs in my arms, delighted with his tidbit.

When it is time to leave, I settle Ilse into a corner of the cart, then stand alongside it, uncertain when to commence my farewells. The farmhand puffs on a clay pipe, showing no urgency to depart. I am impatient for her to go, yet I do not want her to be gone.

'How good it will be, never to scrub those steps again.' She manages a weak smile.

I wish I had something to give her. Then I remember my handkerchief, freshly pressed and folded, and draw it from my pocket. She examines the little sparrow, the sprig of strawberries, the jagged leaf.

The driver says something. Ilse throws her arms around my shoulders.

'What if Jan has forgotten me?' Her sudden alarm unsettles me.

'Of course he will not have forgotten you. It will be a wonderful surprise for him to see you.'

She pulls back a little, grasps my hand.

'The farm is not really his father's. But he will always have work there. It could be a good life, could it not?'

I feel a lurch of fear. To what uncertainties is she returning? 'If ever you find yourself in need, seek me out and I will help you.'

The cart rocks on the cobbles. I step aside, uncertain how else to reassure her.

'Godspeed,' I say, raising Titus's hand in farewell.

'I will come back to see you,' Ilse calls as the cart rolls forward. Then, with a burst of her old cheer, 'Though I may be too busy after I am married.' A wave of her arm, a flash of her smile, and I see her no more.

When she is gone, I am lonelier than on my first day in the city. I cuddle Titus, but he is contrary, pounding his little fists against my chest.

In late afternoon, the market stalls are dreary with picked-over goods. A powerful stench rises from the canals.

I remember Otto and his invitation to call upon him. But when I reach the shoemaker's window, no one is within but the old man, and a young boy sweeping the floor.

Titus begins to cry. I think of Abe, of the cramped room we shared above the draper's shop in Hoorn, and how it felt to have loving arms enfold me at the end of each day. In this city, there is nobody to whom I can turn. Ilse's chores and my own are all that await me in the master's house.

I join the stream of peddlers and servants coursing onto the bridge, duck between sleds rocking over cobbles, and turn down the alley towards home.

Chapter 13

The days after Ilse's departure are filled with toil. Every morning I leave Titus with a grumbling Maartje while I light stoves, heat water, dress the mistress and serve breakfast. I scrub floors, my back aching, my hands raw, the checkered tiles of the hall seeming to extend to infinity so that I have to close my eyes, sit back on my haunches to stave off dizziness.

Before noon, the mistress comes to the kitchen to help with dinner. After a little play among the pots and pans, she loses interest and retires to the salon, leaving a chaos of dirty ware for me to wash.

By the end of the first week, the novelty of this new routine has waned, and Lotte is hired, an unmarried woman of twenty who curls up like a cat and sleeps at will if left unchecked. But she is young and strong, and empties pots and lugs water with ease. Maartje ceases grumbling, and I resume care of my charge who has grown peevish at my neglect.

When the mistress is well enough, she bids me to leave Titus in her company while she practises her music. For an hour, the notes of the stately arrangements she plays stab at the heart of the house. All skill and no melody, Abe would have said. The tavern musicians had but to pluck a string or breathe a note into a reed, and a chorus of voices would joyfully carry the tune. The mistress does not sing.

One day, when I go to the side room to collect Titus for his nap, he is sitting on his mother's lap at the virginal. She plays a trill of notes, and his baby hands wave and slap at the keys. She looks up at me and laughs. 'See what a prodigy he is.' She kisses his head.

I go to the window, look onto the street while they play. The bells of the Zuiderkerk ring eleven o'clock. Schoolchildren scatter about the streets, whooping and making mischief on their way home for dinner.

A messenger boy in cut-down breeches runs up our front steps and raps on the door. When I open it, he hands me a bundle of letters and dashes off, pocketing the coin I give him.

In the side room, I stack the letters on the table by the window. Luca sits coiled on one of the green velvet chairs. I reach to stroke his molasses-coloured head. Grudgingly he submits, his eyes on his mistress.

A clang of baby fists on keys makes me jump. The mistress laughs again.

'Geertje, you try it,' she calls, setting Titus on the floor.

She is in one of her playful moods today, her pale face quick with mirth so that her illness is almost hidden. But when I take a seat beside her at the virginal, I hear the familiar catch in her breath, and her face seems to float, ghost-like, over the watery silk of her gown. I remember how she stood by the instrument on one of my first days in this house, how she stretched out an arm as though to shield it. 'Never touch it unless I am with you,' she had warned. 'An unfamiliar hand could put it out of tune and it might never come right.'

Until then, I had not thought of touching it at all.

Today, she is all indulgence. 'Do you understand how it works?'

'No, Madam.'

'A quill plucks a string every time I press a key. Is it not wonderful?' She plays a rapid trio of notes.

I try to picture the inner workings of the virginal, but all I can think of is Maartje plucking fowl in the kitchen, a pile of bloodied feathers growing beside her. While Maartje grunts and wipes her hands across her apron, my mistress sits in velvet and silk, an array of delicate quills primed for her touch.

'Try it.' She takes my hand and places her own on top so that the pads of her small fingers rest on my stubby nails. Then she presses firmly, and from within the virginal comes the sound of a plucked string. My fingers are clumsy, too large for hers to guide, mashing the keys, pounding discordant sounds into the bright fresh room, but I am making music and it thrills me. She breaks off for a moment, amused at my delight, then slips her hand over mine again, and with my forefinger picks out a simple tune, note by note. I wonder if I could learn to play like her. When she stops and pulls her hand away, I look up to see the master at the door.

'Such noise,' he says. 'I buy you the finest instrument in the city and you use it as a plaything.' His eyes are warm and teasing. It is as though the frenzied man who tore Ilse from her lover was some chimera of my imagination.

The mistress stands, her skirts rippling. 'I was teaching them.'

I go to pick up Titus, and excuse myself, but they are not listening.

'I am trying to work.' His voice is gentle. Standing in the doorway, he wipes ink-blackened hands on a handkerchief, and watches his wife. He is never really angry with her.

Her skirts brush the floor as she goes to him, takes his arm. I wince at the closeness of stained fingers to green silk, but he is careful not to touch her with his sullied hands. Hanging beside the door is a painting of a wedding feast. The light is centred on the bride; the guests are banished to the shade. That is how it is when he looks at her: all others fade away.

'Dine with me today,' she says, collecting the bundle of letters as they pass into the hall. Luca jumps from his chair, darts past me to follow them. 'Your pupils can spare you for an hour.' Over her shoulder, she calls to me. 'You may bring dinner.'

Without them, the room seems duller, darker. The instrument, the noise, their son, all are forgotten for now. I wonder how much longer the lesson would have amused her. Titus starts to cry and I raise him to my shoulder, whisper comforts into his neck. I drop the lid of the virginal and the slam echoes around the room.

In the salon, the master and mistress are seated at the dining table. Outside, gathering clouds obscure the sky. The unclothed figures supporting the mantel seem even more dejected in the grey light.

The mistress examines a fold of rich cream paper, sealed with vermilion.

'From my sister.' She breaks the seal, and reads.

I unload my tray, pour ale. The mistress takes hers with a little jug of water and a spoon of honey. The master reaches for a platter of pork stuffed with dates and fills his plate.

'Hiskia is in Amsterdam and means to call on us.' The mistress folds the letter. 'Geertje, tell Maartje my sister will visit this afternoon and we must have refreshments.'

'I have no time for entertaining.' The master takes a rind of pork from his plate, feeds it to Luca under the table. 'She is your kin, you may do with her as you please.'

His rudeness startles me, but the mistress laughs.

'I will make your apologies,' she says.

I am about to go back to the kitchen when she calls me. 'This one is for you.' She holds out the smallest of the letters.

With a beat of excitement, I reach for the slip of paper. At once, I recognise the orderly hand of the Edam schoolteacher.

'It could be from my cousin.' I picture Trijn striding across the pasture to the old schoolhouse, a cleft of concentration between her brows as she plans all she wants to tell me.

In her present good humour, the mistress might read it for me.

'We must have dishes of almonds and raisins. And perhaps a little of the pork served cold,' she says, as though I had not spoken.

'Yes, Madam.'

I tuck the letter into my pocket. It will not be read today.

Chapter 14

The mistress is gazing into the mirror in the salon, her fingertips exploring her face. She pulls the skin of her cheeks taut, stretches her lower lids downwards as though searching for something amiss.

'How do I look, Geertje? Do I look quite well?'

'Very well, Madam,' I lie. Her kerchief only partly disguises the sharpness of her collarbones, and there are dark shadows under her eyes. Titus struggles in my arms, vying for her attention.

'You must change his smock.' She goes to the linen cabinet, takes out a snow-white garment edged with brocade.

I ease his arms into the little shirt, foreseeing an evening of scrubbing stains from linen.

The fall of the knocker on the front door makes the mistress jump.

'I will go,' she says. 'No, you go. We will wait here.' She sits in her chair by the hearth, holds out her arms for Titus.

On the steps, Hiskia van Uylenburgh stands tall and broad, dressed in black. Under her starched cap, her dark hair is streaked with grey. At once she is like the mistress, and not at all like her. She has a long nose and arched brows: all strength where the mistress's face has delicacy. Her brown eyes could be her sister's but for their alert, commanding expression.

'You are new,' she says, as I curtsey my greeting, take her cloak to the cabinet in the hall. 'Where is Ilse?'

'Ilse is gone.' The words drop like a weight to the floor.

Her eyes fix on mine. She misses nothing.

'And how do you get along here?'

'Very well, Madam,' I say, relieved at the warmth of her tone.

'How is my sister?'

I hesitate. Already, I am convinced of the impossibility of lying to this woman.

'She says that she feels quite well.' The sharp eyes survey my face again but she asks no further questions.

In the salon, the sisters cry out in mutual affection, and embrace. I go to take Titus from the mistress's arms but she stops me.

'I want to show him off.' She starts to cough, sinks back into her chair. I bring her a glass of water. She sips, hands it back to me with a little gasping laugh. 'It is the excitement of seeing you,' she tells her sister as I leave them.

Later, after they have eaten, the mistress sends for me. I worry I have left Titus too long and expect a reprimand. But in the salon the two women are at ease by the fire, while the baby sleeps in his basket, his arms raised to either side of his head.

'My sister's dress is torn,' the mistress announces.

Hiskia is stroking Luca who gazes up at her with adoring eyes. When I kneel to examine the damage I find not a tear but a dropped hem, which has trailed in the muddy streets. I bring the work bag from the kitchen, thread my needle and push it through the border of rich damask.

'Geertje is a neat seamstress,' the mistress says.

'I trust her skills more than yours,' Hiskia says with a laugh. She bunches her skirts so that I can reach the soiled silk with ease. 'That vase in the hall is new, is it not?'

The mistress's heels scrape the floorboards as she draws her feet under her chair.

'A gift from my husband.'

'A very handsome gift. It must be Chinese.'

'We are fortunate, Sister. Demand for his work is such that he could paint day and night and still not satisfy all requests.' There is pride in her voice; defiance, too.

'And yet, many of the paintings displayed in the hall are not his. Whereas here, in your private chamber, I see his hand all around me.' Some minute movement of Hiskia's causes the damask to tense between my fingertips.

'Sales are conducted in the side room, where most of his paintings hang. You need have no concerns. God be thanked, we want for nothing.' The mistress turns her face to the fire.

I reach the end of my thread, tie it off, unspool a new length. Hiskia sits so still I fear the motion of my needle may disturb her.

'While you were in my charge, I protected you as best I could. Now you are in the charge of another.'

I feel Hiskia's eyes on the top of my head. She wants me to leave. But how can I leave, when my mistress has engaged me in this task?

Before I can think of a reason to slip away, she continues.

'Have you thought over the matter we discussed last time?'

'I have thought on it, and will follow your counsel,' the mistress says. 'But first I must discuss it with my husband.'

'Sister, do not waver from this course. Your son's future may depend upon it.'

Hiskia rises, tugging black silk through my fingers. I risk looking at the mistress. Silent tears are running down her face.

'It is a safeguard, nothing more.' Hiskia takes the younger woman's hands. 'Now tell me, may I send the notary to you?'

The mistress nods, pressing her sister's hand to her cheek.

I shift a little, my knees aching on the hard floor.

'Why, I have abandoned you.' Hiskia resumes her seat, bends to appraise my handiwork. 'Such tiny stitches.'

She looks over to the mistress. 'Hold on to this maid.'

So they discussed Ilse's departure while I was in the kitchen. How much did the mistress disclose of her husband's conduct on that terrible day? I bow my head, stitch on.

When it is time for leave-taking, I go to collect Hiskia's cloak. On my return, I meet her at the salon door.

'Walk with me,' she says, and so I follow her through the hall and out onto the front steps.

'I find my sister sadly altered.' Her eyes are grave. 'Does the physician call?'

'Yes, Madam. He has been twice this past month.'

'And what remedy does he suggest?'

'A tincture of honey to ease the throat, and aniseed for the chills.'

Her lips tremble, then tighten. She presses a heavy coin into my hand.

'Oh no, Madam.'

She raises a gloved finger to her lips.

'Geertje, look after my sister.'

'May I conduct you to the *trekschuit*?'

Hiskia shakes her head. 'Tonight I stop with my late husband's friends, on the Dam. And I have some business to settle on the way.'

So she intends to call upon the notary today. She looks right then left, steps into the street and leaves behind the sister she may never see again.

Chapter 15

The mistress's ragged coughs wake me during the night. In my room, tucked between ground and first floors, her gasps for breath seem to echo around the walls. Gradually, the coughing subsides.

I drift in and out of sleep. I am back in Hoorn again, in my old bed with Abe, his broad back rising and falling with gentle snores beside me. I stretch against him, savour his warmth.

A door slams and I awaken.

Abe is dead, and I am alone in a stranger's house.

Not alone. Gentle whimpers rise from next door. I feel my way to Titus's room, lean over to stroke his hair. He is not quite awake. I resist the urge to pick him up. He sighs, rubs one fist against his cheek, settles back to sleep.

The coughs start again, louder this time. Somewhere, a door opens and closes. Footsteps are coming up the stairs. I slide back into bed, pull up the coverlet. A fist thumps on my door.

'Wake up!' the master says.

'Is something amiss?' My voice startles me, as though a stranger had spoken in the darkness.

'My wife is ill. She asks for you.'

'I am not dressed,' I say, foolishly.

'Then dress yourself, and go to her.' Footsteps fade down the stairs.

I open the shutters, dress by the light of a pale moon. Before leaving, I touch the warmth of Titus's cheek.

The master is waiting for me at the salon door.

'She complains of pain in her chest. Why did you not give her the doctor's physic?' He spits out the words.

A rush of dread chills me. This is how it feels to displease him.

'I believe she took it before bed.'

I want to tell him the truth: that I brought the medicine to the mistress and stood by as she faithfully swallowed the preparation. But something in him moves me; the proud painter standing in his nightshirt and gown, his eyes full of fear and rage, and I cannot press the point. For now, I have lost his favour. Later, I will find a way to win it back.

At the other side of the door, the coughing resumes.

'I will go to her now, Sir.'

With an oath, he surges past me into the hallway, his candle guttering, trailing a rope of smoke behind him. One-handed, he grabs a tall-backed chair, drags it to the salon door. 'I will wait here while you tend to her.'

The salon is warm and close, every window fastened against the night air. In her bed, the mistress lies rolled onto her side, coughing in helpless spasms. She looks at me with dazed eyes, tries to speak, coughs again. On my approach, the jealous spaniel springs from his basket.

'Madam, you need to sit upright.'

She is too weak or too bewildered to heed me. I slide one arm under her shoulders, take her helpless weight in my arms. She is light as a child. I slip a bolster behind her back. By candlelight, her face bears a waxy sheen.

'You will be easier now.' She nods without looking at me.

On the dining table stands a basin of water, a dripping cloth overhanging the rim. I wring out the cloth, press it to her forehead. Her eyes are closed, her face is white and still, like those of the plaster heads her husband treasures.

Soon, she will die. The thought drops into my mind with the stealth of a raven. Perhaps she, too, has had this thought tonight and the idea has sent her into a nervous panic.

I sit beside the bed. Wisps of hair lie slicked against her damp forehead. Her chest hardly rises, her lips do not move, but the sound of her breathing reassures me.

When they took Abe from the sea, he looked perfect but for the graze on his cheek. In death, my husband looked more alive than the woman before me now.

'Water,' she whispers.

I fill a glass and bring it to her. She makes no attempt to take it, so I gently lift her chin, tilt the glass to her lips. She seems to drink, then turns her face away. Droplets scatter across her cheek.

After that, she is silent for a long time. When I think she must be asleep, I rise to summon the master. Though I am careful to make no sound, she senses my movement.

'Stay with me.' There is a hint of her usual authority.

I sit back down. The heat of the room, the comfort of the chair induces a heady torpor. What will become of me, of her son, when she dies? I think of Titus waking upstairs, calling for me the way he does. At dawn, I will bring him to the kitchen where Maartje may tend to him, and later I will take him to the harbour to see the tall cranes swinging their heavy loads, the waiting ships emblazoned with flags, the warehouse where we will meet Abe, who will tickle his cheeks, say what a fine son we have, how there cannot be lives luckier than ours.

Someone grips my shoulder, shakes me from my dreams.

'You may go now.' The master's candle casts one half of his face in shadow. For a moment, I think I am looking at one of his portraits. I stare at him, my head dull and confused. Then I remember the coughing, the dressing in the dark, his anger. I stand up, smooth my skirts, bow my head, but already he has forgotten me and is half-sitting, half-lying across the bed, stroking his wife's face.

'Saskia, my love.' His voice is so tender it compels me to look. I see her gaze up at him, her eyes wide, their light almost restored.

In the morning, the mistress does not leave her bed. She takes no breakfast, refusing even the honey-sweetened porridge I bring her. The heat of the coverlet oppresses her; she shrugs it off, and moments later, shakes with cold. She calls on me to arrange her pillows, then twists about so that I must arrange them again. When this fretfulness passes, she lies in a stupor, her linen clinging to her clammy skin.

I touch her sleeve. 'Let me change this for you, Madam.'

She submits, and I ease the damp chemise over her head. Crouching forward, she crosses her arms over her chest. Hollow chambers form above her collarbones. I thread her gaunt arms through fresh sleeves, draw the lengths down over the wasted muscles of her legs. When I pull the coverlet to her shoulders, she is already asleep.

I bring Titus, and my mending, to her bedside.

'Hush while Mama sleeps.'

To lure him from the bed, I march his wooden soldiers across the floor. In no time he is back at my chair, pulling at the bedsheet, querulous when his mama makes no move to pet him. His contrivances fail to wake his mother; nor does she awaken when the master enters the room, a drawing board and papers under his arm.

He stands over her for a moment, then turns to me.

'Her colour returns,' he whispers.

His wife's face is grey against the white of her chemise.

'I am glad you see an improvement, Sir.'

He has forgotten his anger of the night before. I almost sway with relief.

At my side, their son cries for attention, burying his face in my skirts. The master tries to lift him but he clings to my legs, cries even louder.

'Take him away.' The master snaps with impatience. 'Go to the market and buy oranges. And for God's sake keep him outdoors till noon.'

When I rise, the master takes my seat, settles his board on his knees. His pen scores dark lines across the page.

Titus, satisfied now that he is in my arms, busies himself with tugging at the laces of my cap. 'We are going for a walk,' I tell him, patting the letter in my pocket.

Otto waves from the shoemaker's shop.

We stop at the open window and watch him work. He pierces a row of holes in a strip of leather and hammers tiny rivets in place.

Titus observes with interest, stretches out his plump arm to grab the hammer.

'I already have an apprentice,' Otto tells him, and I laugh.

At the worktable, Otto's father spreads out rich brown hides. He pinches the thickness of the leather, smooths his hands over surfaces, his fingers searching for flaws.

'I will return in an hour, Father,' Otto says, wiping his hands on a towel. The elder man raises a hand to me in greeting.

'Are you on your way to the market?' Otto asks, when he joins me outside.

'Yes, but that is not really why I have come. I have much to tell you.'

He raises one dark eyebrow and tickles Titus's chin.

'Would you like to see the barges, young master?'

Otto guides me along the fringes of the bustling Nieuwmarkt. We cross onto the quiet Kloveniersburgwal, where a gentle breeze rustles the canopies of the trees.

I tell him about Ilse's disgrace, how she has returned to Leiden, and may be married by now. I tell him about the mistress's illness, how I may soon be seeking a new position. Finally, I tell him about Trijn's letter.

Otto listens without comment until I mention the letter, then directs me to a scattering of wooden crates abandoned at a mooring post. Titus weighs heavily on my hip, and I gladly take a makeshift seat.

Otto unfolds the letter I hand him, and reads.

My dear Cousin,

May God grant this finds you well.

Your brother's wife was this week delivered of a healthy baby girl, God be thanked. I had the news from the sister of the midwife with whom I shared the poultice for my poor knee that keeps me awake nights, and it brings great ease, though the stink of the concoction forbids sleep, and were I not a widow, I would be good as widowed now, for this physic would have driven Albert from the bed, and though she took an hour of stitching all is well and you should not worry.

Your mother is in good health, though she laments your absence, and gives me cause to reprove her. Would she have you settle in Edam, daily scraping dung from some dullard's boots? Nay, said I, my cousin is destined for a better life than that.

Cousin, I will visit you on the second Saturday of June. Though it is a weary journey and my poor shoulder pains me grievously, I come to steer you on the course I have long advised, for I fear without my gentle guidance you may never take another husband, and without one, you cannot remain in a strange place, far-removed from those who hold you dear.

In devoted friendship,

Trijn.

'Wait, there is more.' Otto turns over the page.

I will wait for you by the weigh house at one o'clock. Tell your mistress your first quarter's work has more than earned you a half day's leisure.

I imagine the inquisitive eyes of the schoolmistress growing rounder as Trijn dictated her missive, and how the contents will be relayed throughout the village. But I am too happy to care much about the gossips of Edam.

'Good news.' Otto hands the letter back.

'I was married once. My husband died, and Trijn will not rest until I find another.'

'And do you intend to marry again?'

'Yes.' My certainty surprises me.

'And whom will you marry?'

'I have yet to meet that fortunate man.' We laugh together.

'You must make haste to find him, you have not quite one week before your cousin's gentle guidance bears down upon you.'

'There was a farmhand in Edam, a widower with two children, who asked for me.' I had almost forgotten the man's honest face, the disappointment in the eyes that could never compare to Abe's.

'That life would suit you, would it not?' Otto is serious now.

'For a while, I thought it might. But I found that though I could love his children, I could never love him.'

'You loved your husband?'

'Very much.'

A warm silence falls between us. I marvel at the ease with which I can sit, side by side, with this young man, talking of love and marriage. Had my son lived, this is the kind of man I would have wanted him to become.

'And what of you? Are you happy in love?' As soon as I ask, I sense a withdrawal. Otto looks out across the canal.

'My father wants me to marry. But I think marriage is not for me.'

'You are young. You have plenty of time to find a sweetheart.'

A glossy red barge approaches. The deck is laden with oak barrels stamped with legends in black ink.

Titus arches his back, tries to slide through the loop of my arms.

'How strong he is growing.' Otto stands, takes one of the small hands. 'Come, we will bring you for a closer look.'

I grip the other hand, and we raise the little boy to a tottering stance. Smiling, he sways between us. Otto counts to three, upon which we swing him forward and he crows in pleasure. The barge glides past, dragging a churning fork of water behind it. The lighterman lifts his cap, waves it gaily above his head, and I find myself waving back at him, as though greeting an old friend.

Anyone would take us for a family. As we cross the next bridge, I peer down to where our reflections shudder on the water, and remember how Abe returned to me the night before, the cruel trick of that moment in which this child became our child.

'You are cold,' Otto says in surprise. He lifts Titus onto his shoulders. 'I will walk you back to the Breestraat.'

The bells of the Zuiderkerk chime noon as we reach Sint Antoniesluis.

High on Otto's shoulders, Titus plucks at the young man's dark brown curls, intrigued at how they spring from his grasp. He captures one, crams it into his mouth. Otto lifts him over his head, hands him into my arms.

'Come to see me after your cousin's visit so that I may congratulate you on your forthcoming nuptials.'

'Knowing Trijn's devices, you may hear of them before I do.'

He walks a few steps backwards, waving at us.

'I hope your father will not be angry at my delaying you,' I call.

'He will not be angry. He thinks you are my sweetheart.' One last wave, and he is gone.

For a moment I stand, looking after him in confusion.

When I turn to face the master's house, I remember the travails of the morning, and how I promised to buy oranges for his dying wife.

Chapter 16

At the end of the alley, the new maid is sitting on the kitchen step. She dangles a length of string over a cat's head. The cat leaps to catch it, pawing the air in futile effort.

'Lotte,' I say. Without looking up, she shuffles a fraction to one side to let me pass and continues her play.

A smell of boiling bones hangs in the steamy air. Marrow vapours spill from the pot over the fire. Maartje strains a batch of beef stock through muslin. She wrings the mouth of the cloth with both hands, squeezing a stream of amber liquid into a basin.

On seeing me, she ladles the stock into bowls.

'Eat.' She pushes a bowl across the table to me. 'Then take some up to her.'

A lace-like froth of bubbles clouds the surface. I take a few spoonfuls, taste only bones.

I leave Maartje to feed Titus, and take a tray upstairs.

The salon windows are half-shrouded against the sun. Where the curtains are slightly parted, narrow rectangles of light enter the room. A low fire burns in the grate.

The master is helping the mistress out of bed. She touches the hand that grips her waist as though she might draw from his strength. He drapes her left arm over his shoulder. Together, they move towards the hearth where he lowers her so gently she seems to sink weightlessly into the chair. A pang of jealousy vibrates within me. When he sees me watching I am ashamed, as though I have intruded upon their lovemaking.

'Give my wife some broth,' he says. 'Barcman will soon be here.'

The mistress tries to say something but her words are lost in a cough.

I open my mouth to tell the master that she is too unwell to receive visitors, but he has turned back to her. 'Spare your voice for now. We will laugh about this when you are well again.'

She allows me to feed her a few spoonfuls of broth while her husband paces behind us. When she closes her eyes and shakes her head, I return the bowl to the table.

I wrap a woollen shawl around her shoulders and she smiles faintly at me. One slipper slides from a blue-veined foot and when I bend to fix it in place, the coldness of her flesh shocks my fingers.

I take a fire iron, shovel a cake of smouldering peat into the foot-warmer.

'Sir, you should eat too.'

Maartje has sent a plate of cold meats and bread for him. He nods, sits at the table and picks apart a rye loaf.

Illness paints the grand salon dull as any sick room I have known. Ornaments and paintings shrink into shadows. Even the bed linen has turned grey. A dejected Luca lies by the hearth, ignoring his ball. The dining table is strewn with empty drinking glasses, burnt-out candle stubs and discarded cloths. I stack the tray and prepare to return to the kitchen when the fall of the knocker sounds from the hall.

'I will go.' The master rises, wipes his mouth with a napkin. 'Clear this mess away and bring refreshments for the clerks.'

When I return, two young men in oversleeves are seated at the table. One leafs through a cloth-bound book, while the other scratches in a folio with a goose quill. A white-haired man sits with the mistress by the fire. The master stands behind her, his hands resting on the back of her chair. I set out plates and glasses, careful not to disturb documents.

The man by the fire reads from a yellowed page. His voice hums like that of the Edam pastor, one word running into the next.

'All of that stands.' The master leans forward, bristling with impatience. 'The purpose is to include our son. Can you not add a codicil and be done with it?'

Their guest leans back in his chair, resting the paper on his knees. A pair of wired spectacles balances on his nose. He tucks a finger inside his old-fashioned ruff and tugs at the linen. The room is uncomfortably hot.

'The birth of your son brings a fundamental change,' he says. 'I must caution you against haste in this matter.' He looks at the mistress. Her head is bowed. On her lap, her fingers pluck at a lace handkerchief. I remember how her sister urged her to this meeting: *Your son's future may depend upon it.*

The notary clears his throat. He is looking at me.

The master stirs. 'You may go,' he tells me. 'All here will serve themselves.'

The clerk with the goose quill has already drunk one glass of wine, and is pouring himself another.

I curtsey and leave, closing the door behind me. Within the room, the notary's voice summons one of the clerks. A chair scrapes on boards, and I imagine the young man in attendance, quill poised to note the mistress's directions.

Outside the door, I hesitate. Pieter will want to hear of this. If the master owes him money, then should not my brother be privy to these matters? I pass an uneasy few moments straining to hear the undertakings. The mistress's hollow whisper is lost inside the room. I lean closer, and hear *remarriage* and *family money* pronounced in the notary's leaden tone. Perhaps the mistress means to safeguard her inheritance for her son. But surely the master's success would be enough to secure the boy's fortune, even if she left nothing behind.

The master's response is obscured by a cry from the kitchen.

I have left Titus too long with Maartje. I hurry down the stairs.

Titus has fallen on the hard floor. He lies on his front, propped up on his forearms, eyes screwed closed with the effort of bawling. Maartje looks on helplessly, burdened with the weight of the iron stockpot.

I take Titus in my arms, examine the rising bump on his fore-head. What will the mistress say? I rub his back and sing to him until the cries die down. He gulps for air, his little body shudders, then he settles his head against my shoulder and sucks comfort from his fingers.

Lotte is reclining in the courtyard, her face turned like a flower towards the sun, an abandoned basket of peas set on the cobbles beside her.

I lean out the door. 'I need you to go to the apothecary.'

She yawns and stretches as I direct her to the shop where the mistress's physic is prepared.

When she leaves, I sit at the table with Titus and shell the peas. Maartje shovels a tray of fresh bones into the oven for roasting. The spent muslin from earlier lies collapsed on the table. Titus grabs a blackened bone from the jellied mass. I prise it from his fingers before he can cram it into his mouth.

'Not for you. This is for your mama, to make her well again.'

He looks up at me, eyes wide with trust.

Chapter 17

On the day of Trijn's visit I awaken before dawn, and realise the master has not called for me during the night. I sit up, hold my breath, strain to hear. When a faint cough sounds from downstairs, I relax.

I get out of bed and open the shutters. Stars are scattered across the sky as though flicked from the bristles of a brush. On nights when Abe was at sea, it used to comfort me to look up at the moon and know that the same light was shining down on him, wherever he was. I lean my cheek against the cold glass and think of Trijn in Edam, kneeling stiffly at her morning prayers, or already about her chores, washing the kitchen floor, water pooling in the depression worn over a lifetime by her feet and her mother's feet before her.

A murmur from next door draws me from the window. In his crib, Titus lies sleeping, his face serene. He has been chewing on the blanket to ease his sore gums and his fingers are fastened around the damp hem. I smooth his hair. Yesterday's bump has subsided.

Too early to wake him.

In my room, I fill the basin from the ewer. How must it be, to strive for air, for no breath to come? I lower my face into the cold water so that it covers my nose, mouth, cheeks, forehead. How was it for Abe, to draw salt water with his last breath? I pull my head up, shake the water from my skin.

I dress quickly. In near darkness, I tie on my cap, test the crispness of its folds against my fingertips. Trijn will approve.

Downstairs, the salon door is closed. No sound rises from the kitchen where Maartje and Lotte must still be sleeping.

I follow the light that falters through the upper windows in the hall. Faces gaze at me from every wall. How will I describe this room to Trijn? I stare at the old woman who reminds me of my mother, try to memorise the lines of her face, the drape of her collar. A laughing soldier displays a row of crumbling, yellow teeth. There is an image of the master, his face cast half in darkness, and I remember the mirror beside his easel, how he wanted me to find my reflection in it. I move swiftly past a tortured Christ, and on to the preening young lady admiring herself in her mirror. She cups a hand about one ear, well satisfied with the effect of her pearl ear-bobs. How did I not realise before now that she must be a courtesan?

At the dais where the mistress writes her letters, I sit in her leather-backed chair, imagining lives for the painted figures around me.

When I hear a voice I start, as though one of the portraits had spoken.

The master stands half-hidden in the archway. 'You are needed.'

'I will come directly.' I jump up from his wife's chair, a blaze of heat on my cheeks.

At the salon door, he is waiting for me with the candle. He is already dressed, though his shirt hangs loose from his breeches. His eyes are shot through with red.

'You have not slept, Sir,' I say, without thinking.

'She coughs less.' He presses a hand to his forehead. 'It is a good sign, is it not?'

Before I can think of some way to reassure him, he swings the door open, and I find the mistress awake in bed, struggling to breathe, fluid rattling in her throat.

I raise her gently to a sitting position, tilt her forward and rub her back the way I rub her son's. 'You must cough, Madam, then you will find relief.'

A stale odour of sickness hangs about her person, overpowering her coconut-scented soap, her lavender-pressed linen. The master turns away as his wife expels a bloodied scum from her lungs. He no longer sketches when he sits by her sickbed, no longer questions the doctor and nurse who alternate visits. He is afraid, and I am afraid for him.

For now, the mistress seems to find some comfort in my ministrations. Soon there will be no more I can do to ease her distress. I look around for a cloth to cleanse her face.

'I will fetch fresh water,' I tell the master.

He shows no sign of having heard, but when I step towards the door, he stops me.

'I will have Lotte bring it,' he says, and leaves.

I push aside the heavy curtains and open a window, wide as I dare. From the canal come the shouts of bargemen, the thud of cargo deposited on banks. The mistress sleeps, untroubled by the sounds.

I quench candles, tidy the table. The master's nightgown is thrown over the back of a chair and I bundle it up with the rest of yesterday's linen.

Lotte enters with a basin, sets it on the table.

'Bring porridge, a jug of milk, and whatever the master will have,' I tell her.

'The master has eaten already and is away.' Lotte tucks a wayward strand of hair into her cap and it tumbles loose again.

'But he has pupils this morning.'

'Nay, for he sent them all home.'

I stare at her. Every Saturday the master takes pupils in the mornings and sits with his wife from noon.

'When will he be back?'

'He did not say.' She yawns, twirls the stray lock of hair about one finger, and turns towards the door.

'Empty the pots, then come back for the linen,' I say, more sharply than I intended.

She seems about to protest, but when the mistress shifts in bed she shrugs, and takes the pots away.

I soak a clean cloth in water, take it to the bedside, wipe the mistress's face.

She opens her eyes.

'Stay with me.' Her lips are blue.

'I will bring the baby, Madam.' I try to stay calm. 'Then you must eat.'

She nods, closes her eyes.

When I have dressed and fed Titus, I help the mistress to bathe. I change her bed linen, and when I ease her back into her fresh sheets she seems a little stronger. I sit her son on my lap at her bedside. She smooths his swollen cheeks with the backs of her fingers.

'How he has taken to you, Geertje.'

'Show your mama your new tooth,' I tell him. 'You kept me up nights this past week with the trouble it caused you.' Immediately, he clamps his mouth shut, and I laugh.

'And how well you care for him.' Her smile fades.

I lift Titus to her, and she kisses his forehead. For a moment, he holds her face in both hands, and mother and son gaze upon one another. Then he wriggles in my arms, and I set him down on the floor to play with his wooden blocks.

I persuade her to take a few spoonfuls of milky porridge. A tinge of colour returns to her cheeks.

'Bring me my rings.'

On the mantel, in a Chinese dish, she keeps the gold band with the two red stones and the tiny ring with the cluster of dia-monds which does not fit over the tip of my forefinger. She slips them on.

'This was my wedding band,' she says, holding out her hand. The ring hangs loosely, the weight of the two stones dragging it askew. 'And this was my mother's.'

The smaller of the rings sits on her little finger. 'She died when I was seven.'

In the distance, church bells chime eleven o'clock. Where is the master?

'You must rest, Madam. Save your strength for when the master comes home.'

She studies the rings, working her thumb over the stones. Then she slides them into her palm, returns them to me.

'My chemise,' she says.

'Would you have me change it again?'

She shakes her head in frustration. 'Bring me the chemise with the jasmine flowers.'

It is one I have never known her to wear, a filmy silk so finely woven I fear my hands will snag the lengths as I take it from the cabinet.

'As soon as we were betrothed, I began the embroidery. How I toiled over those petals.' She sighs, running her hands over the delicate work.

I fold it for her, but when I move to put it away, she takes my wrist.

'Did you bury your husband in his wedding shirt?'

Never before has she asked me about my past life.

'He had but one, Madam. There was no choice to be made.'

Abe taken from the water, bare-chested, his shirt half-dragged over his head as though the sea would have stolen that too. I knew my husband at once, before I saw the ink on his shoulder, before the men pulled his linen back down and turned his dead face towards mine.

Eyes closed, her head slumps on the pillow. I return the garment that will be her shroud to the linen cabinet. Her breath comes heavy and slow. I try to sit her up so that she might force fluid from her lungs. When she opens her eyes, she seems not to recognise me.

I hardly know how I reach the kitchen but in an instant I am downstairs, calling for Lotte.

'Go find the master. Bring him home directly.'

Maartje sets down her knife.

'And where am I to find him?' Lotte asks, looking about for her outdoor shoes.

'Ask for him at the art dealer's. Or at the Kloveniers' hall.'

'And where is that?'

I give her the best directions I can, while Maartje goes upstairs.

'I remember now,' Lotte replies calmly, when I finish. 'He said he was meeting Meneer Decker about a sale.'

I want to slap her. I push her towards the door. 'Go to the Decker house and ask for him. If he is not there, try the auction houses at the Dam. And be quick.'

Upstairs, Titus is crying in Maartje's arms. The mistress draws laboured breaths, her face contorted in effort. I raise her in the bed and she coughs up foaming blood. Her head falls against my shoulder.

'The master is on his way,' I tell her. 'He will want to see you well when he arrives.'

She inclines her face towards mine. 'He cannot bear it,' she whispers.

She will not wait for him.

'Check if Lotte is back,' I tell Maartje. She sets Titus down by my feet, moves swiftly to the door. The little boy raises his fists and howls.

I should have sent Maartje to find the master. Lotte with her ambling walk and idle mind will seek every distraction along the way.

The mistress is no longer conscious. I start to pray. Too late to send for the doctor; too late even for the pastor.

The front door crashes. My heart leaps, but it not the master, or even Lotte, just Maartje back to say the girl is nowhere to be seen.

The mistress is choking, drowning inside her own body. Her breath rattles in her throat. I hold her in my arms, reciting my childhood prayers, until her body convulses one last time. When she is quite still, I rest her back against the pillows.

Maartje comes to my side, Titus calm now and in her arms. She guides me to a chair. I am shaking so much I cannot speak.

Maartje closes the mistress's eyes, lays her son beside her on the bed.

'Go outside,' she says. 'Get some air. I will stay with her.'

I stumble to the hall and out the front door. Lotte is sitting on the steps. She looks up at me, untroubled. 'I could not find him.' She shrugs.

Down in the street, I whirl around, realising I have no idea where else to seek the master. A brewer's sled nearly rolls over my foot, and the drayman shouts an insult, making a group of children laugh. Wind whips my apron over my face. For a moment, I am blinded. Panic takes hold of me, the like of which I have not known since my first day in this city.

Then the cloth falls from my face and I see the master coming over the bridge.

It is him, and yet it is not him. There is a sway to his walk which I have often seen in other men. The master, who takes little beer and less wine, is in his cups.

When he notices me standing in the street, he jolts into action, like a horse touched by a whip, and runs to the house.

Chapter 18

I take the steps up to the house, my legs heavy as though I have walked a great distance since morning. Once inside, I close the door, press my back against the oak.

Silence.

If I could hear the master's grief before seeing it, divide it into morsels of sound, then sight, would it be easier to consume the whole?

My footsteps echo around the hall. On my toes, I continue to the salon. From within comes Titus's contented humming.

Everything is normal, until I enter the room.

The curtains are closed, the mirror draped with a heavy shawl. A single spot of light falls on the floor, cast from the interior window above the door. Maartje stands at the table, her crooked back stooped as she lights a row of candles. At first I think the master is not there, then my eyes adjust to the dimness. He has thrown himself upon the bed in which his dead wife lies, his face buried in her hair, his arms wrapped around her body.

Titus still sits by his mother's side where Maartje placed him. Sensing something amiss, he pats his mother's forehead. Then his attention is caught by some movement of his father's hair. He plucks gently at the curls as though wary of interrupting his parents' last embrace.

'I will send Lotte for the pastor,' I whisper to Maartje.

'She has already gone.'

The neighbours will soon be at the door. I dare not disturb the master. His mouth is pressed close to his wife's cheek and he murmurs something I cannot hear.

Did I fall upon Abe's body in the same way? Did I beg my husband's spirit not to leave me?

The thud of the iron knocker jolts me back to the painter's house.

I hurry from the salon to the front door. On the steps a woman leans over the railing, peering down to the quarters half-hidden below the street. Her thin shawl is neatly darned at the shoulder.

Though I cannot read my name in letters, I recognise my hand in those stitches.

'Trijn!'

Trijn's good-natured face, with its weave of red veins about the cheeks and bright eyes, quick with purpose, draws my tears.

'I have found you!' she cries.

In the hall, she captures me in an embrace of baskets, pockets and parcels. She is dressed in her city clothes, as she calls them, though the skirt and bodice are those she wears every day. All that differs is that her jacket is buttoned to the neck, a concession to her notion of urban fashion, and she wears her best cap, the one that belonged to her mother, and must have been very fine when that good woman stitched it a score of years ago or more.

I hug what I can of Trijn while provisions tumble to the floor.

'Finding you was no easy task, for I stood by the weigh house close on an hour until my poor legs grew weary, then I waylaid a young man and bade him direct me to the house of the finest painter in Amsterdam, whereupon the ruffian laughed and called me Oma, and presumed to ask what business I could have with the finest of anyone anywhere, and when I finally reached your kitchen, I smote upon the door and found nobody within.'

Here she breaks off. 'But you are crying! Take me where I may rest my feet and then you must tell me what is troubling you, and I will take a cup of ale to wet my throat if your mistress has no objection.'

At the mention of the mistress, I cry harder.

Lotte mounts the steps from the street and, with a simper, ushers in the pastor, a grey-haired old man with a pointed beard. For once, she is a little out of breath. She looks from me to Trijn.

'The infant has died?' Trijn cries.

'Nay, not the infant, the mistress.' Lotte's curious eyes travel over Trijn's laden form. 'What wares do you peddle?'

The pastor clears his throat, shifts a book from under one arm.

Trijn sets down the rest of her trappings, sweeps her shawl from her back and presents it to a confounded Lotte. 'Take my things to the kitchen. We shall call if we need you.' Lotte looks at me, opens her mouth, but does not speak.

Trijn taps my arm. 'Lead the way. We shall escort the pastor to his unhappy station.'

In the salon, the master is sitting at the bedside, his hands covering his face. Luca crouches at his feet, emitting low growls as strangers enter the room.

Trijn approaches the master with a sweeping curtsey and makes her condolences. He looks uncomprehendingly at her. His eyes are haggard, his face sober with shock. I want to take his hands in mine, share the weight of his loss.

The pastor steps forward to greet him, places a hand on his shoulder, speaks in a low voice.

On seeing Titus, Trijn leans over the mistress's body and lifts him from the bed.

'We must take him away, lest his mother's spirit coaxes him to follow,' she says in a loud whisper.

Titus's mouth drops open, his lips quiver. Trijn frowns, passes him to me.

Maartje looks up from the table where she is pouring the master a glass of brandy wine.

'He has had enough of that,' Trijn says, forgetting to whisper this time. 'Warm ale with honey is the thing; I shall prepare it.'

Before Maartje can react, I bustle Trijn out the door and down the stairs to the kitchen.

Trijn rises on her toes to sniff the cured hams hanging from the rafters, looks into various pots on the hearth, then takes a copper bucket to the pump.

'Geertje, you must send for your mistress's kinswomen without delay,' she calls over her shoulder.

'Her mother is dead, and her sister lives a day's journey away.'

'Then the task must fall to the neighbours.' Trijn hangs the bucket of water over the fire. 'Where is that servant girl?'

Titus agitates in my arms. I sit him in his basket, and he yelps with displeasure.

'Hush,' Trijn tells him. Astonished, he stares back at her.

From overhead comes the drum of feet on boards.

The panelled door swings open and Lotte sails in, her cheeks pink with excitement. 'The art dealer is here and moaning at the mistress's bedside. And the pastor's wife is come, and I think her far too pretty for one so dull as he. She asks for you,' she says, nodding at me.

'Go,' Trijn says. 'I shall manage very well here. Now, girl, lay out your best meats for never yet have I met a pastor loath to eat and drink his fill in a house of the dead.'

Upstairs, the art dealer and the pastor are leading the master to the side room. The men support his crumpled weight between them, effect each of his staggering steps. How often Maartje and I took Titus's hands, raised him onto his untested feet and walked him between us while the mistress coaxed him forward. I want to touch the master's arm, tell him I know the size and shape of the burden he bears, for I have borne it alone for seven years.

The art dealer glares at me. 'Why stand you idle there? You are needed within.'

In the salon, the bed curtains are closed. The ornate bedstead has become a mausoleum. I remember climbing into the space that now entombs the mistress. From the linen cabinet I take the chemise that formed part of her trousseau. It is so white, so delicate, I dare not set it down.

The pastor's wife stands at the hearth, dispatching Maartje with a litany of instructions. She cannot be more than five-and-twenty. Her pretty face is solemn as she takes the chemise, nods her approval, and drapes it over the back of a chair. Deftly, she moves candles to a corner of the mantel where they cast light onto the bedstead. She has the air of a woman who has seen much of other people's grief but known little of her own.

'Should I send for the neighbouring women, Madam?'

'He will have only you and me.'

At first, I cannot grasp her meaning.

'Your master has sent the Breestraat women away,' she says, speaking slowly as though she thinks I am not in my wits. She draws open the bed curtains, the velvet bunching softly at the sides.

The mistress lies, smaller, somehow, than in life, and younger too, her long hair loose about her cheeks.

As the pastor's wife reaches to draw back the coverlet, I turn my face away. The door opens and Maartje enters, carrying a basin of water.

Chapter 19

'Not bad,' Trijn says. 'A little thin about the face. Wads of linen in the cheeks would have helped. Why did you not call for me?'

Fortunately, Trijn's arrival at the salon comes at the end of our task.

The pastor's wife tightens her pretty mouth into a thin line. She opens the door to the passage, stands beside it, arms folded.

Undaunted, Trijn settles into one of her favourite stories. 'There was no better-looking corpse in all of Edam than my Albert, God rest him. In his case, there was no need of added bulk, rather I feared I would not find a casket to accommodate him, and the carpenter who contrived it, rogue that he was, demanded payment for the extra lumber, though I am certain the mason's wife was later buried in the excess.'

'Trijn, we have stayed over-long.' I press her arm, steer her towards the door.

Trijn stops short of the threshold to make amends to the pastor's wife. 'You, my dear, will be an asset to your good husband when his time comes, for you will have had a little more practice by then.'

As we descend to the kitchen, the pastor's wife traces a few steps behind us, as though to make certain of our departure.

The Zuiderkerk chimes two o'clock. The farmer's cart in which Trijn intends to travel leaves at four. On the kitchen table lies an array of unwashed dishes, Titus's bowl and spoon among them. His basket has been moved away from the table, and set against the back wall. Curled up inside, he sleeps soundly.

'I ate dinner without you,' Trijn says. 'Journeys make me ravenous.'

Lotte nods wisely at this remark. Maartje has tasked her with raking ashes from the fire but she has not progressed beyond the table, on which she leans, shovel in hand, enthralled by Trijn.

'Bring my cousin a dish of stew,' Trijn tells her, and, in moments, Lotte sets a steaming bowl before me.

While I eat, Trijn talks of life in Edam, of my mother and the old cottage where I grew up, of the wheelwright's wife who lately died, and of the baker's youngest daughter who ran off with a deckhand and has not been heard of since.

I want to ask about Pieter, to tell Trijn of his interest in the master's affairs, but Lotte sits, chin on hand, following every volley of our conversation. Finally, Maartje sends the girl upstairs with a tray of bread and meats. Lotte returns briefly to tell us the mourners are come, that the women are dressed in silk, the men in damask, and that the pastor's wife has instructed her to remain in attendance at the front door.

'Back you go, then,' Trijn says, and Lotte looks at her in surprise, as though it had not occurred to her to obey the instruction. When she is gone, Maartje takes a jug of wine and pitcher of ale upstairs.

'Do they treat you well here?' Trijn asks. 'A fine house your master keeps. The larder is filled with meat and butter. He must be rich, though I cannot conceive how any person in their wits would purchase one of those gloomy paintings that cover the walls and must need dusting every day, and why, pray, if he takes the trouble of painting his own face, does he leave it half in darkness?'

'I am treated very well. Had the mistress lived longer, I could have grown fond of her.'

'Your master cannot be more than five-and-thirty. Likely he will marry again, and soon. Being young and strong, his new wife will care for his child and her own to come, and you will lose your place and have to return to Edam, and it is as well you pack your things and come away with me now, until your brother can find you a new position in the city.'

I stare at Trijn. How can she ask me to abandon the master? Who this day, needed the help of two men to walk. Who would have only me to assist in the laying-out of his wife.

'I cannot leave him.'

'Speak you of the child or the master?'

My cheeks grow hot. I go to the basket, adjust Titus's coverlet.

'I love him as though he were my own.'

Trijn does not miss the catch in my voice.

'But he is not your own.' The gentleness of her tone is unbearable. 'Tell me, have you found a sweetheart here?'

'I have not looked for one.'

Trijn becomes stern. 'The city throngs with men. Why, I had half a dozen or more selected for you in the market and on my way here. Delay your choosing too long and you will grow old and thin and be forced to take a mate from among the boors of Edam.'

A light knock interrupts Trijn's advice. I escape to the back door and find Otto outside, his face serious.

'Then you have heard,' I say, bringing him in.

'Heard what?'

'Young man, this is a house of mourning.' Trijn gets to her feet. 'The mistress of the house expired this very day.'

'I am sorry to hear it,' Otto says, looking at me.

'And who might you be?' Trijn asks.

'I am the shoemaker, and you, I believe, are Cousin Trijn.'

From his basket, Titus emits a shrill cry.

'Healthy lungs, unlike his poor mother.' Trijn is now occupied in packing her bags and pockets.

I pour Otto a mug of ale. 'It has been a terrible day. The master is distraught.'

Titus's cries grow louder. Trijn wraps her shawl about her shoulders, clucks her tongue. 'My nerves cannot abide that clamour. Geertje, you must wait here and see to the child. Young man, may I prevail upon you to escort me to the weigh house?'

Otto makes a half-bow and Trijn promptly unloads several of her purchases into his arms. She hugs me closely. 'I will tell your mother I found you fat and well. Think on what I have said, and tarry no more. A happy life awaits you, Cousin, if you will only grasp it with both hands.'

Trijn's stout form has the solid reliability of a mooring post. I cannot speak through my tears. I nod, follow my friends outside.

Otto looks back over his shoulder. 'I must speak with you. Another time will do.'

'Is something wrong?'

He hesitates. 'Not yet.'

Before I can question him further, Trijn tucks her arm through his. 'We must make haste, for the wretch who drove me here threatened to leave without me should I delay him a fraction after four.'

I wave them off. Trijn's voice carries back down the alley. 'What is your name, young man? Are you married? And why not?'

In the kitchen, Titus's cries have turned to high shrieks.

'My lamb, I have neglected you.' In my arms he lies limp, his head falling against my shoulder as though he cannot bear its weight. His linen is damp, his forehead hot.

Not this. Not now.

I run to the foot of the stairs. Maartje is descending with heavy tread, grumbling to herself. When she sees me holding Titus, she stops.

'Go for the doctor. Make haste!'

She says nothing, asks nothing, departs in an instant.

Titus cries in such a frenzy I fear he will take a fit. I strip his sodden linen, pull a fresh smock over his head. I return him to his basket, wring a cloth in cold water for his forehead. The coolness seems to comfort him.

I have nursed babies through fevers before. The Beets family survived every ailment that passed through the household. The only child I ever lost was my own.

Titus lies, listless, before me.

'You must not die,' I beg him. 'Please, please, you must not die.'

Chapter 20

That night I keep Titus in the kitchen, where Maartje and Lotte sleep. I set a chair by the back door, the coolest part of the room, and pull his basket close to my side.

I have Lotte bring me one of the mistress's pressed handkerchiefs so that I may fan the little boy's blazing face, but the motion of air agitates rather than calms him.

Lotte shrinks from the basket. The doctor told us the fever is not infectious, but she eyes Titus suspiciously, and soon rolls up her bedding and departs to the laundry room for the night.

The doctor's instructions run through my mind like an incantation, though there is no magic in cold compresses and spoonfuls of broth. When I attempt to give the child a little milk, he cries so piteously I abandon the task.

Maartje unties her apron, hangs it on a peg. Barefoot, she crosses the floor to peer into the basket.

I hold my breath. Does she see an omen in his face that I cannot?

Her expression is stoic. For a moment I hope she will draw up a chair and join me, but she only grunts and walks away. At the fireside she steps out of her petticoats, loosens her bodice and turns the hearth lamp low. Before clambering into the box bed she snuffs out her candle with a pinch. Soon her snores mingle with the baby's cries.

At the pump, I fill a bucket with cold water. The crank whines, a sound I never noticed by day. From overhead comes the scrape of a chair on floorboards. Who watches in the salon with the master? Perhaps one of the party will persuade him to take a few hours' rest.

One cloth soaks in the bucket, while the other cools Titus's forehead. His smock is wet through. I free his struggling arms, pull the sopping linen over his head. His chest swells with vexed cries.

I wring out a fresh cloth and press its coldness along the length of his body. The chill startles him into momentary silence. Eyes wide, he gulps for air. His cries grow softer now, though whether through improvement or exhaustion, I cannot tell. With the back of one cold hand, I stroke his cheek.

'Sleep,' I whisper. 'Sleep, and save your strength.'

Throughout the night, my arms seem to move of their own accord as I soak and wring cloths, press anxious fingers to his forehead. Eventually he falls into an uneasy slumber. What if he should worsen before dawn? Trijn would prepare a poultice of lavender and lemon balm, brew elderflower tea by the fire. But Trijn and her herbs are in Edam, and I cannot replicate her cures. Across the kitchen, Maartje reclines with her back to me, her bulk rising and falling with her breath. I will rouse her, and Lotte too, if I must.

Overhead, men's voices thrum over the tread of outdoor shoes on boards. My mistress lies cold in her bed and beside me, her child burns. What did Trijn say about the mother's spirit calling the son? I should not have left him so long with the corpse.

I shake myself. Old women's talk from Edam. I am in the city now, far from foolish country notions. 'You will be well,' I tell Titus, making circles on his cheek. 'You will be well.'

When I awaken, my candle has burned out. A figure looms in the dim light of the hearth lamp. I leap from my chair. Maartje bends over the basket, her hand on the boy's forehead.

'The fever has broken,' she says. 'Go to bed. I will watch over him.'

Before I can stop myself, I throw my arms around her unwieldy form and sob onto her shoulder. Maartje's hands, more accustomed to wringing necks of fowl and hoisting sacks of oats, land awkwardly on my back.

When Titus is sleeping peacefully, I climb the steps to the hallway. It is still dark, but the joy of the baby's deliverance glows like sunrise in my heart. The door to the oak-press room, wherein I have never been, stands ajar. Against the low ceiling, the halo of a single candle's shadow quivers.

The master is seated in a far corner of the room, his back turned to me, his head bent low over a book. In the centre of the floor, almost reaching the rafters, stands the great oak press. The frame is as wide as it is tall, and attached to one side is a cross-shaped lever, pinioned at its centre-point like the sails of a windmill.

The only movement is the rise of smoke from his candle.

'Sir?'

Too late, I remember Maartje warned me to tell him nothing of his son's illness, to keep even the doctor's visit from him. He has not endured the worry from which I have come to deliver him.

The head of untidy curls lifts. His shirt hangs open at the neck, the wide sleeves crushed from the weight of the doublet he wore earlier.

'It is you.' His shoulders relax.

'Forgive me for disturbing you.'

I can give him no good reason for my intrusion, but he seems unsurprised to see me at this hour, in his printing room, which no servant is permitted to enter.

'Come here.'

I hesitate, unsure if I have heard correctly. An inclination of his head decides me.

My candle flickers past the ink-stained press. One wooden arm stretches above my head, casting a long shadow before me like an additional threshold to be crossed. A table lines the back wall, and here the master sits, a sketchbook open in front of him.

I stand by his side. On a loose leaf is a drawing of a young woman in a straw hat, her hair dressed low over her forehead, her cheek resting lightly on one hand.

The mistress, smiling shyly, returning her lover's gaze.

'It was my first drawing of her. We were three days betrothed before she would agree to sit for me, and even then she hid beneath that great hat.' His fingers hover above the paper as though it is too precious to touch.

'She looks happy.'

Untroubled eyes look out from the page. This morning, Maartje's thumbs were on the lids, pressing them closed.

The master takes a long breath. 'The burgomaster's daughter and the miller's son. How her eyes shone when her uncle gave his consent. I promised her she would want for nothing.'

How can I comfort him, when in seven long years I have found no comfort for myself?

'Sir, you should try to sleep. There are long days ahead.'

'Sleep,' he repeats, as though it is the name of some slight acquaintance he had forgotten.

How many hours has he been awake? I want to work my thumb over the crease of weariness in his forehead, smooth the pain from his face. He throws himself forward onto his elbows, drives his fingers through his hair. For a moment I think he is weeping. Sweet saltiness rises from his skin. On the nape of his neck shines a tiny crimson bead. I imagine the careless drag of his painting smock over his head, a fleck of paint landing unseen on his skin. I withdraw my finger before I realise I had extended it.

'I could keep vigil in the salon while you rest.'

He sighs, rubs his eyes. 'There are people and prayers enough in that room. Go to bed. I will wait here for dawn. Perhaps then, I may sleep.'

I go to the window. It must look onto the courtyard, but all I see is my own reflection: a servant holding a candle; an image ill-deserving a frame.

I am at the door when he speaks again.

'Geertje.'

I pause, mid-step.

'Thank you.'

He blows out his candle, and I leave him alone in the dark.

Chapter 21

The mistress is to be buried on Thursday.

All morning, throughout the prayers in the salon, Titus sleeps in my arms. In the days following his fever, he has fallen into a lethargy from which none of my efforts can rouse him. I have to wake him for meals, and before the last spoonful, his eyes are already closing, his head drooping to his chest. He only becomes alert at night, when I am in need of sleep. It is then his gums most trouble him, and he crams fingers into his mouth, emitting piteous cries until I fetch an ice-cold cloth for him to chew on.

The pastor reads from the Bible, casting his eyes aloft at the end of each verse. A belt of moisture shines across his forehead, under the brim of his conical hat. From over his shoulder, his wife surveys the room with solemn rigour. Lotte has been charged with diverting preparations for the prohibited funeral feast from their notice. Several of the Breestraat householders have brought their servants to help, and from the kitchen below come bursts of giddy greetings and stifled laughter as Lotte directs the maids.

The master grips the side of his wife's coffin, his fingers sinking into the silk lining. His lips are parted, his tumid eyes half-closed. In fastening his black doublet, he missed one button and I chide myself for not having noticed before the room filled with mourners. Beside him stands the mistress's sister, her face puckered with grief, her iron-grey hair pulled sharply under her stiff cap. As the prayers come to a close, her eyes fall upon me.

The pastor calls the family forward. A trio of men I take to be the mistress's brothers cluster about the coffin. The men's wives bow their heads. The rest of the mourners shuffle out to the hall, murmurs breaking out among them before the salon door is fully closed.

The mistress's sister beckons me. 'Wake him,' she says. 'It is time.'

I rock Titus gently, shift him to my shoulder, but there is no waking him. The pastor's wife steps forward, lips pursed, and I fear she will pluck the child from my arms. I dandle him to the floor and the shock of his feet touching the boards jolts him into fretful alertness. The mistress's sister lifts him to kiss his mother's face. He wails, slaps at the coffin, kicks his aunt with vigour.

'Take him away.' Hiskia thrusts him into my arms.

I avoid the crowd in the hall, take Titus halfway up the stairs to the interior window. Back in the comfort of my arms, he calms himself by chewing his fingers.

A hush falls. Through the lattice, I watch as seated ladies abruptly stand and gentlemen bow their heads. The coffin is borne on a bier to the front door. The master follows it, walking beside his sister-in-law. In her hands she holds an open prayer book. His arms hang empty at his sides.

A bell tolls as the mistress leaves the house for the last time. The train of mourners follows in her wake.

Titus struggles in my arms. 'You are getting your strength back,' I tell him, and he chirps in agreement.

When I reach the bottom of the stairs, a whimpering comes from the hall. On the dais, Luca stands on his hind legs, paws pressed onto the window ledge. Nothing I can say will coax the little dog away.

The kitchen is hot and steamy, smelling of baked white loaves. At the back door, Maartje is taking delivery of a cask of ale and a side of Friesland pork. One of the Breestraat maids soaks dried fruit in a generous quantity of brandy wine, while another rolls pastry as they chatter. Lotte leans on her elbows, having appointed herself supervisor of their work. 'Not too thin,' she admonishes.

'We are going out for a while,' I tell her, and she frowns and nods, as though I am interrupting important matters.

Over the Breestraat, clouds roll slowly past the sun. The bridge is cast in welcome shade. I stop with Titus to look over the side, but the canal is quiet today, with little traffic to amuse him.

'Look at the clouds swimming beneath the bridge. And see the upside-down trees and houses.'

Our reflections loom below us, though the canal is too muddy for our features to be discerned. It is not yet midday, but already a fetid smell rises from the water.

A crisp breeze ruffles my cap. Titus grows heavy on my hip as I move on. 'Soon I will ask your papa to buy you a *loopwagen* so you can learn to walk for yourself. How will you like that?' His reply is a babbling song he repeats all the way to Otto's shop.

Inside, Otto is replacing a pair of silk slippers on a shelf.

'Never do business with the rich,' he says. 'How they hate to pay.'

'My only business today is with the fruit-sellers at the market. Can you come with us?'

At the worktable, Otto's father is cutting out a pattern in leather. The young apprentice, who looked up with hopeful interest upon my arrival, resumes sweeping.

I want to ask Otto what it was he came to tell me on the day of Trijn's visit, the day the mistress died.

The elder man nods a greeting to me, waves his curved knife in assent.

Otto hangs up his apron. Out in the street, he lifts Titus to his shoulders, and the boy's small hands grip his head.

'You survived Trijn's onslaught?' Relieved of the baby's weight, I feel light-footed and a little unsteady.

'Only because I was forewarned,' he says.

'She has a good heart.'

'And great regard for you.'

He falls silent after this, and so I talk on about Trijn, and Edam, and how I have not seen my brother since his baby girl was safely delivered.

'Let us sit,' Otto says, at the first bench we reach at the Nieuwmarkt, a seat where hawkers too old or weary to stand often gather to trade.

I buy a scoop of cherries from a stall and sit the baby on my lap while I squeeze the pits into my handkerchief. Titus chews on a cherry, removes it for further inspection before popping it back into his mouth.

'You must tell nobody what I am about to tell you,' Otto says.

'I have none to tell anything to but you.'

He nods, looks straight ahead. A ragged old woman thrusts an arm sleeved in beaded bracelets at us.

'Not today, Oma,' Otto says, before she can begin her patter. When she moves away, he clears his throat.

'The night before I last saw you, I had been to the Rapenburgh, to visit a friend.'

He pauses. It is the first time he has spoken to me of a friend.

'I arrived a little earlier than I had intended, and the evening being hot, I betook me to the Blue Anchor for a mug of ale.'

Impossible to picture Otto with his slender frame, his scarf full of curls, seated in a sailors' tavern. But what do I really know of him, this young man I have come to like so well?

'The house was empty but for one table, around which sat a dozen or more men, braying their way through a drinking song and spilling waves of froth over their sleeves. I took a quiet seat in the back, meeting nobody but the crone who frequents the place and knows well enough to leave me alone.

'After half an hour it was time for me to go, and yet I delayed. Presently a girl's voice carried from the door to where I was sitting, and though I could not hear her properly above the din, it was clear she was in dispute with the old woman. I drank the last of my ale, threw coins on the table, and got up to leave before their fray attracted more players. But the crone was already at the open door, shaking her fist, and the girl was laughing and crossing the street. She cast one backwards look, and though her face has taken the sun since I last saw her, I recognised Ilse.'

'Ilse? But she is in Leiden.'

'I called her name without thinking,' Otto says. 'Until then she had not seen me.'

'You spoke to her?'

'She turned down an alley, nearly colliding with a beggar in her haste to get away.'

'Did you follow her?'

'Ilse does not like me, remember? I would not embarrass her by seeking her out.'

'Then I will go to look for her.'

'You cannot go there.' Otto stands. 'Your master would not like it.'

'Likely she has come back to the city to earn money for her marriage by serving in one of the taverns. It is honest work; I have done it myself.'

He frowns, as though I have missed his import.

'You are her friend, I have told you what I saw, and now I must go.'

He makes a sharp bow, turns, and disappears into the crowd, leaving me with the sinking feeling that follows an unexpected quarrel.

I tuck Titus into the shawl at my hip. 'Otto imagines catastrophe where there is none,' I tell him. 'I will find Ilse, and prove him wrong.'

Chapter 22

One of the Breestraat maids kneels inside the back door, unpacking pears from a crate. As I approach from the alley, she smiles and flattens herself against the wall to let me pass. At the table, her companion sings to herself while scraping gnawed bones and scraps into a bucket. A pungent smell of boiled cabbage rises from the waste. When she sees Titus, she crooks a finger, runs a red knuckle down his cheek.

Maartje takes a tray of fruit breads from the oven, slams it onto the table. Both maids and loaves jump. The girls titter, exchange looks. I press a finger to my lips, ease Titus into his basket.

Lotte enters from the stairwell, swinging an empty jug. 'The master wants more wine,' she announces, teasing a currant from the crust of one of Maartje's breads. On seeing me, she makes great work of decanting a bottle into the jug, slopping wine over the spout.

'Let me do it.' I take the bottle from her, and she slinks over to the hearth to inspect the contents of the oven.

When two jugs are full, I bring them upstairs. In the hall, an overflow of guests sits at cloth-draped trestle tables. Here are the pupils, the local traders, and a group of guild members, their embroidered pennant hanging from the back of a chair. Hands reach for the jug as soon as I set it down. A beardless young man is on his feet, attempting a speech, but without age or authority he cannot command the room. Knives clatter on plates, mugs rise and fall. Conversation continues unabated.

I stop at the door to the side room. A dozen or more mourners dine therein, the mistress's sister and relatives among them. The master sits hunched over the head of the table, swirling a half-empty goblet. He tugs at his collar, pulling the linen askew. The weight of the day is carved into his forehead. At his elbow, the art dealer holds forth, stabbing the air with a speared morsel of meat.

'The delay is understandable given these sad circumstances.' Here the man pauses to chew and swallow. 'But you cannot allow yourself to be outdone by Pickenoy.' He points his greasy knife down the table to the elderly painter who lives next door and is presently occupied in sucking on a bone.

To the master's right sits Meneer Decker, his poet friend, a kindly man with heavy-lidded eyes who nods at me from across the room. I go to the hearth to wait for a break in the conversation, careful not to look up at the painting of the shrouded man rising from his grave.

The art dealer drops his knife onto his plate, leans forward as though preparing for a long invective. 'You have spent too much time upon that canvas to the detriment of your trade.'

The master's plate lies untouched. He studies the raised pattern of his glass, rubbing his thumb up and down the stem.

'More wine, Sir?'

He starts, sits upright. 'Geertje, where have you been? I sent that girl back to the kitchen where she is less likely to injure one of my guests. Jeremias had to relieve her of the carving knife.'

'I will stay as long as you need me, Sir.' My wrist shakes under the weight of the jug. I wrap my hand around the belly as I pour.

'I must show you something,' the master says.

I look up, but the words were spoken to the poet.

'The commission of which Uylenburgh inquires has been finished for some weeks, and yet, I struggle to let it go.'

He lifts his glass, tilts his head back and his throat bobs once, twice. When the glass is drained, he stands, throws his napkin to the table.

'With God's grace this crowd will remove to the tavern before we return.'

His voice is thick with wine. I take his plate as he leaves. Later, I will persuade him to eat.

As I gather more plates, the maid who unpacked the fruit arrives, lugging a pitcher of ale and a basket filled with crisp green pears, walnuts and wheels of cheese. The diners, sluggish from their feast, revive at the sight of fresh provisions. In the hall, ale flows, and tributes are paid to the master and his dead wife.

The mistress's sister summons me with a curl of her finger.

'Where is your master?'

'Engaged on business, Madam.'

'A sale?'

I struggle to let it go.

My arms are filled with soiled dishes. I shift the load as though in discomfort at the weight. Under her scrutiny, my cheeks grow hot.

She nods towards the crowded hall. 'Let the pitchers run dry. And tell your master I wish to speak with him.' She adds her plate to the stack in my arms. 'I will detain you no longer from your work.'

I nod, drop an awkward curtsey.

Though it is early evening, the courtyard is soaked in sun. The bells of the Zuiderkerk chime as I cross the yard. Under the cloudless sky, their music seems closer than before.

The gallery door opens. The poet is speaking, earnest and low. The master pays him no heed, throws his head back with a mirthless laugh. He stops when he sees me, propping one arm high against the door frame.

'The Uylenburghs have sent you in search of me. Tell them I have repaired to a gamblers' den to squander the family money.'

'Perhaps you should tell them yourself, Sir, before you depart.'

He smiles, though the smile does not reach his eyes.

'The sight of their stiff faces will sober me. Jeremias, help me clear the hall of ruffians before their pipes set my house alight.'

By the time I put Titus to bed and come back downstairs, the guests are gone, leaving behind a pall of smoke and a scattering of empty glasses. Tables and chairs fill the room, yet the emptiness is palpable. My throat tightens. I go to open the windows and find Lotte sobbing on the dais. Luca lies stretched out beside her, his water bowl hardly touched.

'You must not cry. The mistress is at peace.' I pat her shoulder. She looks up at me, wide-eyed.

'They are gone, and have taken their maids with them. How am I to clear this room alone?'

I want to shake her.

'Where is the master?'

She sniffs. 'In the salon with the mistress's people. The lady said they are not to be disturbed, but she may fear no disturbance from me, for everything seems to vex her and I have suffered enough of her *stand straight, girl* and *be quick about it, girl* all day.'

'Tonight we will clear the tables and air the room,' I tell her. 'All the borrowed furniture may be returned tomorrow.'

After an hour, I send a yawning Lotte to bed. By candlelight, I brush the chairs, sweep the side room, then sweep the hall too. The salon door remains closed.

I am resolved to wait up for the master, to see that he takes at least a little bread and cheese before he sleeps. On a turn of the stairs I sit, out of sight, waiting for the mistress's family to leave.

The closing of the front door rouses me. On stiff legs, I make my way downstairs. In the sconces, the candles burn low. From the salon comes a flicker of light.

The master has sunk into a chair by the hearth. I tap on the inside of the open door.

'Sir, may I get you something to eat?'

He stirs. 'Geertje. You are up late.'

'I was waiting to see if you needed anything.'

He rubs his forehead. 'Maartje fed me; she seems intent on keeping me alive.'

So I cannot perform this small office for him. I swallow my disappointment.

'Then I wish you goodnight, Sir.'

'Wait.' He straightens up. 'Sit with me. I cannot endure to drink alone. Bring two glasses.'

An open bottle stands on the table, a cluster of clean and unclean glasses beside it. How can I tell him that I have never drunk anything stronger than ale? I pour a full glass of wine for him, and a half for me.

'You must be in need of sleep, Sir.' I take a seat opposite him.

'I have not slept alone since I was married. These past nights, it seems I have not slept at all.'

'I could bring you some lavender oil.'

He shakes his head.

'It was her favourite scent. Once, I had a merchant bring oil of roses from Persia for her birthday gift, and still that night I smelled French lavender on her skin.' He drinks deeply, holds out his glass for more.

The wine is purple-red as I pour, and settles in the glass with an oily sheen.

It is sweet, and smooth as velvet on my tongue, but stings the back of my throat and I have to hide a cough. The master does not notice. He leans back into his chair, closes his eyes. The hand holding his glass is flung out to one side, the wine tipping towards the rim.

'My sister-in-law thinks me a charlatan, that I preyed on my wife's wealth. But I would have married her had she been selling posies at the flower market.'

It is true. He is incapable of pretension and would as soon converse with a beggar as with a burgomaster.

'I know it, Sir, for often have I witnessed the tender attentions you paid your lady, and likewise her devotion to you.'

I have said too much. I set my glass down, clasp my hands. Have I affronted him?

His eyes are closed, his breathing steady.

As he sleeps, I ease the glass from his hand.

The bed has been made with fresh linen. All I have to do is open the bed curtains, take his nightshirt from the cabinet and lay it on the coverlet. Before I leave, I fold a blanket of soft wool over his knees, and quench all but one of the candles.

A restless energy seizes me. I should go to bed, but I will not sleep until I have seen the painting in the gallery.

I creep down the stairs, enter the courtyard from the laundry room. Cool air fans my face. Overhead, the sky is punctured with white stars. All is quiet.

The city has taken a deep breath, waits and watches.

I shake this fancy from my mind.

The door of the gallery is closed but unlocked. On days when the master leaves it open and unrolls the tarpaulin to admit more light, I have caught sight of the dark and crowded canvas within. So close am I now to the painting, it is as though I have climbed into the scene.

I move my candle along its width, casting light on small parts of the whole. Military men loom above me, charging muskets, waving standards, thrusting bayonets. Among them, a girl in yellow glows like a beacon. It is the mistress, or how I imagine she once was, long before she had met her husband, borne four children and suffered the loss of three. Her face and gown shine with a light that seems to burn from within. Does it pain or comfort him to imagine her thus, her life still waiting to be lived? My eyes fill with tears.

I swing my candle high across the rest of the canvas. At the forefront of the company, the captain stands, his arm outstretched as though inviting me into the fray. His assured eyes gaze into the darkness behind me. I reach out, and can almost feel the warmth of his hand closing around mine.

Chapter 23

On an overcast morning, two weeks after the mistress is buried, her sister returns, accompanied by her maid and two large travelling chests.

When I enter the salon, Hiskia is holding Luca under one arm, and inspecting the cuff of a fur-lined mantle.

'Sable,' she tells the maid. 'Take care not to crush the nap.'

The doors of the linen cabinet gape open. Petticoats, gowns, and chemises lie heaped upon the bed. Some garments have already been folded and stacked on chairs.

'You sent for me, Madam.'

She hands the little dog to the maid. 'Go to the kitchen and find a basket for him to travel in. And some scraps, before he starves.'

I dare not say that Luca, who only ever dined on tidbits from his mistress's hand, has refused to eat since her death.

When the door closes, Hiskia takes a seat, and motions for me to join her. A thick Turkey rug, rarely used, now covers the dining table.

'Geertje, I have spoken to your master regarding your position in this household.'

I press my palms against the rich pile of the rug.

'It is my view, and his also, that you should stay, at least until the child starts his schooling.'

I am too relieved to speak.

'There will be more duties. Now that my sister is no longer with us, you will be taxed with running the house. The maid can look after the infant until you find a more capable replacement.'

How can I hand Titus over to Lotte? Lotte, who boasts of sleeping through the crowing of cockerels and has been known to deem a pocket knife a suitable plaything for a child.

'Naturally, you will be compensated for your extra work.'

She has read my silence as reluctance.

'I am happy to stay, Madam.'

'You were good to my sister, more so than the gorgon in the kitchen or that girl downstairs. I have chosen some things for you.'

From the back of a chair, she takes a finely woven woollen petticoat, old, but little worn, and two chemises of white linen. I imagine her thumbing through the mistress's cabinet, discounting silks and taffetas, searching for garments befitting a servant.

'Thank you, Madam.'

Leaving the clothes on the table, she rises and goes to face the portrait of her sister over the mantel. Am I dismissed? I stand to leave.

'Tarry awhile.'

She returns, coming so close her face is barely a palm's width from mine.

'Your master, as you know, trades in an uncertain market.'

How can her eyes be so like her sister's, yet so full of steel?

'His patrons grow impatient. His future prosperity, and that of my nephew, may hang upon the success of this current commission. I want you to see that he finishes it promptly.'

'I have no influence over such matters, Madam.'

'All I require is that you relieve him of household distractions, smooth his path towards painting again. I hear he has not lifted a brush in over a month.'

I want to tell her that he has never been idle, that he passed long afternoons in this room sketching his ailing wife. Sketches none of his patrons will buy.

'Domestic matters need never trouble him, Madam.'

She nods.

'I will return to see that all progresses as it should.'

What would she say if she knew the commission was already finished, that he cannot bear to part with a canvas that includes his last painting of his wife?

'I have one more gift before I go.' From a half-filled chest, she takes a filmy length of silk.

The mistress's white kerchief, the one she often wore pinned about her neck, pours into my hands. So fine is the silk, it seems about to spill like water through my fingers.

The other garments feel coarse and heavy when I gather them into my arms.

'Geertje.'

I halt on the threshold.

'Mind you give me no cause for regret.'

'No, Madam.'

I climb the stairs, unsure whether I have been encouraged or threatened.

In my room, I drape the kerchief over my bodice, peer into the scratched piece of tin that serves as my mirror. How rich it feels, to own something I do not need. I can almost feel Trijn's hand on my shoulder, warning me to say nothing to Maartje and Lotte about this extravagant gift. What if Lotte pokes through my things and comes upon it? She will think I stole it. I will have to tell the master. But I cannot tell him, or he will want to know the reason such a fine garment was given to me.

How did the master say he wanted me to stay? Did he raise the matter, or merely assent to Hiskia's proposal? Perhaps later, he will tell me.

In the evenings, the salon becomes warm and stuffy. Though it is still summer, spots of mould have lately formed on the bed curtains and so I have Lotte light a small fire in here every day.

The master sits by the hearth in one of his melancholic moods, staring into the embers.

At the table I try to lift the pitcher, but my hand is slippery with sweat. Ale splashes onto the rug. I wipe my hands on my apron. This time, I raise the pitcher with no mishaps, replenish the master's pewter mug, and top up my smaller brown one with half water, half ale.

I take the chair opposite his. Ale foams in the mugs like miniature seas.

'Next time, bring the pitcher.'

'Yes, Sir.'

Just last night he chided me for resting it on the warm hearth.

'It will spare you a journey.' A faint smile forms, vanishes. He leans forward, takes a draught. 'Go on.'

Where was I in my story? The details of my unremarkable life must make poor listening for a man who counts princes and poets among his patrons.

'Hoorn,' he prompts. 'The tavern.'

I remember then how I promised Pieter not to speak of the time I spent at the Moor's Head, lest serving men with beer offend the sensibilities of a moral household. But every night since his wife's funeral, I have served the master wine or beer, and my nights in the tavern were no less respectable than those spent in his house. In any case, the tale is too advanced for me to stop telling it now.

'At seventeen, I went to Hoorn to take a position my mother's brother had found for me. Till then, I had never left Edam and knew no work other than the dairy.'

In an instant, I am standing again under the Westerpoort at Hoorn, an ignorant country girl in worn-down clogs, my belongings bundled into a threadbare shawl. Afraid of going forward, determined not to go back.

'Go on.'

'On the first night at the tavern, smoke stung my eyes and my arms ached from hauling pitchers. I filled drinks too full, slopped beer onto tables.'

My hands are damp again. I press them against my apron.

'Men shouted orders through the music of the fiddle-players and I had to cup my ears, beg them to call again. At dusk, the shipyards closed. Labourers came from the docks, and masons from their workshops, eyebrows dusted with powdered stone. The room heaved with men, shirts slicked to their backs, runnels of sweat streaking their necks. When I stepped out into the alley for a breath of air, the smell of piss drove me back inside.'

I pause. Surely he has heard enough. But his eyes are intent upon me.

'That night in the attic room, I cried in my narrow bed while the other serving girls slept. In the morning, they gathered round, petted me like a child. "It gets better," they said. And it did.'

The master could spend his evenings sipping wine with friends on the Prinsengracht, the lady of the house directing servants with gestures of her creamy white hands. Instead, he leans forward. 'Tell me more about the tavern.'

I tell him about the merry sailors who bawled songs of faithless women and treacherous seas, and clinked tankards till dawn. I tell him about the landlord's doughty wife who kept order with a broom handle and steered many a drunken labourer to the door.

The master's cloth cap casts a shadow over his face. When he reaches for his mug, his eyes are far away. I wonder if he is sketching in his mind.

When next we sit together at night, I take no water with my ale. I want to talk, and it seems the master is content to listen.

I tell him about the night a fair-haired young man came into the tavern with a group of weathered deckhands. 'The old sailors circled a table, calling for beer and herring. I poured drinks, avoided straying hands. When I served the young man, he smiled at me, asked my name, and if I liked music. His eyes were grey-green, the colour of the sea after a storm. Later, we sat together and talked. Every night after that when he saw me, he changed the girl in his song to the maid of Edam.'

The master smiles, and his warmth pours into me, fills chambers that have lain empty for years. I take a long drink.

'How soon after were you married?' he asks.

'Three months later, on his next leave. The wedding feast was held in the tavern and we roomed there for the first weeks, until Abe found us a place.'

I lick my lips to moisten them. In an instant they are dry again. I could tell him no more, light my candle, go to bed. For a moment,

I close my eyes. The ale wraps around me like a thick cloth protecting a hand thrust into an oven.

'We were barely six months wed when he drowned in the harbour, not far from shore.'

I get up too quickly, and for a moment it seems my body moves faster than my head. The room sways. I reach for the mantel.

The master rises. 'You were not with him when he died?'

'No.' Sorrow bites, but with fewer teeth than before. In the hearth, a log flakes and crumbles, exposing the fire's glowing orange heart.

He comes closer. 'You were with my wife in her last moments. You comforted her through her pain. I could not bear to be apart from her, yet I ran away.'

The candle on the mantel flickers as he speaks. If I look up, I will see her portrait hanging above us, how she stands resplendent in her cloak of green and gold, her white hand holding the bunched satin to her breast. I know every fold of her voluminous sleeve, can almost weigh the brocade in my hands.

Now the master's breath is soft on my cheek. But when I face him, he is looking at her.

'She understood,' I say. 'Do not reproach yourself.'

'She understood all and still loved me, I know not why.' He gazes up at his wife, his eyes glassy with tears.

I can no longer bear the quiet triumph of her pose. I back away, take a stub of candle from my pocket and light it at the table. Across the room, he stands before the portrait, reduced to a silhouette of slumped shoulders, his crumpled shirt pulling loose from his neck.

With every tread of my feet on the boards, I hope to break the thrall. When I reach the door, the house beyond the salon is so silent it is hard to believe that any living being breathes within it.

'Goodnight, Sir.'

He does not turn around.

Chapter 24

Though the windows of the side room are open onto the street, no breeze stirs, and the small fire lit for hospitality's sake gives forth intense heat. Dusk is falling, but I cannot bear to closet the room against the evening air. At the fireside sits the merchant, his satin-cased knees thrust wide apart, his broad belly resting between his thighs. One hand toys with the silver head of his cane. 'I imparted good intelligence, did I not, Sir?' The triumphant inflection is marred by a rattle of phlegm in his throat.

'You did,' the master replies.

The merchant hawks into a handkerchief, screws the scrap of cloth into his fist and resumes. 'Not six months ago I told you demand would increase, and increase it did; threefold since my first cargo arrived. There is not a shipyard in this city without a stock of green timber bearing my stamp.'

In her seat by the window, the merchant's wife coughs delicately. She nods towards the virginal. 'What a beautiful instrument. Amalia plays delightfully. Her tutor says she astounds him with her prowess.'

Their daughter winces. She is a young woman of perhaps twenty with mild, discerning eyes, her hair fashionably loose beneath her cap. Over her glossy black gown she wears a fallen collar of layered lace. A black stone set in gold hangs about her neck, the weight of the jewel dragging the chain into a sharp point above her bosom. When I pour her wine, she thanks me in a whisper.

'My wife played,' the master says.

The virginal is already closed, but his words fall like the slamming of a lid.

The merchant's wife is undeterred. 'I encourage Amalia to perform at every opportunity. It sets off her wrists. She has most elegantly turned wrists, would you not agree, Sir?'

'Most elegant,' the master says.

The merchant's daughter casts him a look of rueful amusement, draws her hands a little deeper into her wide sleeves. He glances at her, the corners of his lips approaching a smile.

The merchant's chin sinks onto his chest. The pouches of his cheeks slacken, his eyelids droop.

'Naturally the eye of an artist is drawn to such detail,' his wife continues. 'Her elder sisters, all married now, have many accomplishments among them, but none share the freshness of Amalia's complexion.'

The young woman lowers her eyes. Her forehead is tinged with pink. The master seems about to speak to her, changes his mind, and addresses her mother instead.

'I would be happy, Madam, to advise you of my terms, but alas, my workshop is oversubscribed, and likely to remain so for many months.'

The merchant's cane slides from his fingers and clatters to the floor, rousing him from his doze. I abandon a dish of almonds on the table and restore the cane to his hand.

His wife bridles. 'You mistake me, Sir. The only time my daughter will sit for her portrait will be on the occasion of her marriage, whenever that happy event may transpire. Let us intrude no longer upon your valuable time. Come, Lucas.'

I hurry to open the door, and follow the guests into the hall. When Amalia takes leave of the master, her eyes hint at amusement. *My parents are vulgar, forgive them*, she seems to say. The master smiles broadly, kisses her hand. *You are even lovelier than your mama boasts.*

When they are gone, I press my weight against the door behind them.

This is how it will be. An onslaught of simpering mothers parading their daughters before the rich and famous painter. How long before he chooses a new wife?

The master retreats through the hallway. 'Sir,' I call. He pauses under the archway, half-turns.

Is he in love with her? His countenance displays good temper; more than that I cannot divine.

'I would speak with you, if you please.' My broad vowels echo under the high ceiling.

'Come to the salon.' He strides ahead, and when I follow him into the room, he is already at the table filling two mugs. Lotte has laid out bread, cold meats and cheese for two. She no longer questions where I plan to take my evening meals.

The master spears an olive, crunches it against his teeth as he stacks his plate. Lately, his appetite has improved.

'Thank heaven they left when they did,' he says. 'I feared I should have to endure their company through supper.'

'The daughter is a fine young lady, is she not?' I cannot look at him.

'In future, you may spare me the company of fine young ladies and their chaperones by telling them I am not at home. I could find better conversation among the beggars at the almshouse.'

He works his jaw on a crust of bread.

I have not lost him yet.

With one knuckle he pushes the plate towards me. 'Why do you not eat?' he asks through a mouthful.

After the meal, we take our mugs and sit by the fire. A candle stands on the mantel as usual, but tonight I set it to one side so that the portrait of the mistress is obliquely lit.

'You wanted to speak to me,' he says. 'What troubles you?'

How can I speak of the fear of losing him to a new wife who will beguile him as the mistress did? The fear of spending long evenings alone in the hanging room while they exchange caresses by the fireside and lie together in the curtained bed.

'Is my son well?'

'Quite well.' I force a smile. 'Soon he will be walking. Already he pulls himself up by the leg of the table. He should have a *loopwagen*, and a hat to protect from falls.'

The master laughs. 'I cannot have my boy falling on his head. Send for whatever he needs.'

In a rush to embrace this good mood, I talk of the baker's wife who gives Titus a wafer when we pass, and the fishmonger who flexes the claws of freshly caught crabs for his amusement. I am lost in tales of our rambles around the city when the master interrupts.

'Why do you never speak of your own son?'

For a moment, I am bewildered. Then I remember Pieter's lie. I meet his gaze.

'My son died before he was born. Pieter thought you would not want me if you knew. I was widowed at twenty-five and that was more than seven years ago.'

I see no shock, no outrage on his face. He looks at me with new recognition, as though he had always sensed affinity between us and now finds proof.

He leans forward, wraps his hands around his mug. 'Tell me.'

And so I take him back with me to the room I shared with Abe in Hoorn. Abe is not there, for he was buried weeks before the pains rose in my womb. Somewhere in the house a loose shutter bangs relentlessly against a wall. Old women circle my bed. Their chatter swells, subsides, gains rhythm, turns to prayer. The reek of mutton-fat candles makes me retch, and someone thrusts a basin under my chin.

'By morning your pains will be over,' the midwife says.

Slowly, night leaches from the sky. When daylight comes it seems a ragged thing, a length of linen rinsed not quite clear of dye. At the end of the bed, my son lies pale and still, his arms crossed as though he had long prepared for death. The midwife wipes her bloodied hands. 'You have birthed your first and last,' she says.

I am grateful for the silence that follows. Peat smoulders in the hearth. The master rises, takes the fire iron, stirs up flames.

'What did you do?'

'After they took him away, I lay in that room for days. At first, I wanted to die. I felt trapped at the bottom of a well, with no will to climb the sides. But like an intruder, my strength came creeping back. On the day the landlord was to put me out, Pieter came.'

He smiles. 'The loyal brother. The ship's carpenter who aspires to be a merchant, and were he a merchant he would aspire to be burgomaster. Of all things, he is best at being a rogue.'

'Pieter saved me. When I lost Abe I became a widow, but when I lost my son I knew not what I became.'

The master sets the fire iron down, crosses the room. He stops at the table, as though examining the pattern of the rug that covers it. 'I did not mean to offend you. I would sooner spend an evening in a tavern with your brother and his fellows than dine at the richest table in the Herengracht. Yes, I court personages who strut about this city in satin and furs but that is how I make my living.'

While his back is turned, I am brave.

'The merchant who visited today intends you to marry his daughter, does he not?'

A beat, then another. I have gone too far.

'I have nothing to offer such a woman.'

I have little time to puzzle over his answer.

'Come, Geertje.'

He has moved to the window and pushed aside one of the curtains. Outside, daubs of cloud obscure the moon and the courtyard lies in near darkness. The narrow gallery that houses his work is cast in shadow. Faint light falls from the kitchen windows beneath us. I sense his warmth beside me as he holds the curtain clear.

'The painting in the gallery is finished. Today it was taken from the stretchers and rolled up. Tomorrow it will be carried across the city to the hall where it is to hang.'

A shy resolve has crept into his voice, as though he hopes for my approval. We are so close I could trap my little finger in one of the curls that spring from his cap. When he looks at me, I am drunk on his presence. He is letting her go.

He talks of how men march out of the canvas, how the paint blazes and roars with action. His face comes closer, his eyes shining like his son's. 'Soon, I will show it to you.'

I flinch.

He steps back in confusion.

A new lie unfolds between us. How can I tell him I have already seen the painting? It is as though the whole company he depicted is bearing down upon me, pikes clashing, gunpowder exploding and I cannot move, cannot make myself heard above the tumult.

After he bids me goodnight, I stand alone at the window. The courtyard is in darkness; the gallery has blended into the night. All I see in the glass is the reflection of my candle, and the glow of my face behind it.

Chapter 25

After breakfast, the pupils gather in the courtyard to await the master. A respectful air hangs about the young men, as though they have been charged with conveying a casket rather than a canvas.

When the master enters, he answers our greetings with a curt 'Clear the room.'

Maartje thrusts a handful of sage into the fowl sprawled on the table and heads for the stairs, patting her pockets for her pipe. I follow with Titus in my arms, pulling a gaping Lotte along with me.

I want to watch the proceedings from my room, but Lotte is in a companionable mood and will not be shaken off. I go to the salon and she follows, entertaining herself with her chatter.

Down in the courtyard the pupils file out of the gallery, the rolled-up painting hoisted onto their shoulders. Lotte opens a window, smudging the glass. 'It could be an old rug,' she says, leaning out over the ledge for a better view.

'Have a care, they will hear.'

The procession crosses the courtyard and is swallowed by the kitchen door.

Footsteps sound beneath us. I hear the master's sharp 'Ach!' and imagine one of the young men nudging the canvas against a hanging pan, or taking too sharp a turn at the door to the alley. I picture the loading of the sled on the Zwanenburgwal, the master settling the painting for its short journey as though it were a beloved child.

'I forgot to tell you about the man.' Lotte has lost interest in the activity and now stands before the mirror, tweaking her cap. 'I think I should wear it further back.'

'What man?'

'It shows my face better so, do you not agree?' She pivots towards me.

'Much better. Was it Otto?'

'Nay, not he.' She pats her hair, simpers at her reflection. 'I think you are right, it sits well so.'

I wait for her to tire of this game.

'Some country fellow, I forget his name. I told him I knew not where you were and that he had better return after breakfast. He said you should seek him at the Old Barge instead.'

Pieter. And it must be an hour or more since he was here.

'You should have told me sooner.' I am halfway to the door.

'Worry not, I am sure your new beau will wait for you,' Lotte calls after me. 'Let us hope he will not make the master jealous.'

Every day her gibes grow more daring.

In the shade of the linden trees, I wait, Titus humming in my arms, while a boy fetches Pieter from the tavern. Pieter emerges, shading his eyes, scanning the canal bank. He is clad not in his work clothes but in his best shirt and breeches.

'Over here.' I beckon him forward.

For all his care in dressing, he has neglected to clip his beard. Unruly grey hairs spring from his chin. 'What are you doing in the city?'

He grabs my arm, pulls me close. I stagger under Titus's weight.

'I am more interested, Sister, to hear what you are doing.'

'What do you mean?'

He lifts his pipe to his lips, studies my face.

'Why did you not send me word of your mistress's passing?'

'I knew Trijn would tell you. No matter, tell me how does your daughter fare? And Marit?'

He sucks on the pipe, blows a ring of smoke into the air.

'Marit has grown fat, and the baby never ceases her plaints. Enough of that. Such a tale I heard from your neighbours when I inquired about the grieving painter, can you guess at it?'

Too late I remember that Lotte's cousin serves in the Old Barge, a girl as idle and eager for gossip as herself. Did Lotte direct Pieter there purposefully? My stomach tightens.

'It seems the painter has found a new favourite among his household, a homely woman to comfort him by night.'

I keep my voice calm, but cannot control the flaming of my cheeks.

'It is not true. Yes, he invites me to sit with him after dinner, but we talk; that is all.'

'Then you are a bigger fool than I thought. He is a powerful man and he is showing you favour. Encourage him.'

'No man could compare to Abe. All others are lost in his shadow.' I blink back tears, switch Titus to my other hip.

'Abe was a drunk.'

The words strike like a cudgel. All breath is sucked from my body.

'The night your sainted husband died, he had been brawling with a Russian crew. They had their sport, then rid themselves of him, as one does of a troublesome cur.' Pieter spits a plug of tar short of the canal.

My hand feels for something solid. I find a tree trunk, lean against it. 'Abe's death was an accident. He fell from the wharf. His foot became tangled in the moorings.'

'So it did, but not before he had drunk more than his fill and earned a thrashing.'

My arms are weak. Titus slides to my feet. I sink to my haunches, cling to the little boy.

Pieter stands over me. 'Grieve no more. That matter is long past. Now is your chance. Who knows what rich presents you might receive?'

'Go,' I say. 'Please go.'

'Geertje, you will make your eyes red with crying.' All at once he becomes kinder, offers me his handkerchief. I pull out my own, mop my face. Titus is crying now too, and flapping his hands against my arm.

Pieter tips ash from his pipe, grinds it with his heel. 'I will return to see your master another day. It is thanks to me that you are in his house at all; do not forget it.'

I cover my face, resolve to say no more. Titus cries louder, prises my fingers from my eyes.

When I look up, Pieter is gone.

Grieve no more. Pieter's words seem to echo around the kitchen. Maartje's spoon beats the refrain. The water pump cranks the tune.

I take Titus onto my lap, busy myself with stirring his dinner, but it is as though sluice gates have opened in my mind and memories come rushing through. Abe, hoisted home on the shoulders of drunken deckhands, bellowing 'The Maid of Amsterdam' all down the street. Abe dancing me round the room to the rhythm of our neighbour's fist on the adjoining wall. Abe collapsing, limbs thrown across our bed. Waking hours later, eyes bloodshot, calling for ale.

'Grieve no more,' I whisper. Abe is gone and no amount of sorrow will bring him back. My future is here in Amsterdam, with the master and his son.

Titus rocks forward, swatting air with chubby hands, reaching for the spoonful of poached fish I have been holding. I feed it to him, he smacks his lips and smiles. A white paste gluts the corners of his mouth. I kiss the top of his head. 'You are my one true love,' I tell him.

I send Lotte to sweep the hall that I might escape her talk, and trail Maartje about the kitchen, asking the names of the tradesmen, what they are owed, when they should be paid. She takes a tattered book from her pocket and teaches me its ciphers: a cask for the brewer, a cow for the dairy, and more. The pages are closely filled with rows of ticks for deliveries, scored through for every bill settled. A crudely sketched boot marks Otto's account and I am glad to see he has lately been paid. I stop at the outline of a bull's head. 'Is this the butcher who used to cheat Ilse?'

'Willem Jans,' Maartje spits into the fire.

'He will not cheat me.'

She nods in approval. Since the terrible day the mistress died, I have come to rely on her solid presence, and she, in turn, has softened towards me. Every morning while I eat breakfast she takes Titus to the courtyard and distracts him by blowing smoke rings from her pipe.

I study the rest of the entries, take stock of sacks of flour and sugar, count cured meats and casks of ale. By evening, I am certain I can run the house better than the mistress ever did.

When I carry Titus upstairs, I feel lighter, as though casting off burdens with every step. The hall looks smaller than it did before, and the painted faces hanging on the walls seem familiar as old friends.

'I am in charge,' I tell them. My voice echoes and fades.

Though the windows have been open since morning, the hanging room is hot and still. Titus's smock is already damp, his mother's embroidery sticking to his chest. I strip it away, let him lie in his tailclout under a sheet.

An orange sun burns low in the sky. I fold my arms on the sill, cup my elbows. Pink clouds streak across a horizon of rooftops, spires, sails of distant windmills. Soon the master will be home. Last night, I made him doubt me. This time, I will make him certain.

It is the end of the day, but feels like a beginning. I lift the ewer, fill the basin, and undress slowly, dropping cap, bodice, skirts to the floor. My old shift peels away like a shed skin. I take a precious scrap of coconut soap, lather my neck and arms. The cold water tingles. My body hums with memories of Abe. I wring a cloth, smooth it over my face.

The sun sinks ever lower. In the scratched mirror, my wet skin glows with a pearly sheen.

Down in the courtyard, a door opens. A man's boots ring on stone.

Coconut scent rises, fresh and sweet as I move to the window. Silvery streams of water run down my breasts, my thighs.

He is alone and crossing the courtyard, his shirt billowing loose at the waist of his breeches. He has almost reached the gallery.

The hinges sing out, as they always do, when I force the window to its fullest opening.

He looks up, and sees me. The flattened cap he wears casts a shadow over his eyes. I want to tear it from his head, see what I saw in him last night. The set of his shoulders, the angle of his jaw give me no sign. Slowly, he turns away, enters the gallery, and is gone.

I push the window closed, rattling the glass in the frame. How long before he sends for Maartje, or worse, Lotte, to throw me out? My body convulses but I cannot cry. I drag my shift on over my head, struggle into the sleeves. Linen clings to my wet skin. The hair at the nape of my neck drips onto my bodice and dampness seeps through my cap. My trembling hands stab the pins in place. When I am dressed, I go to Titus's crib and sit on the floor, threading a wisp of his hair around my little finger.

At supper, a smirking Lotte will bring the usual jug of ale and two mugs to the salon. Will the master look up from the table, frown at the second mug, bid her remove it?

In the distance, the bells of the Zuiderkerk chime the half and then the full hour's passing. Soon, it is time for the evening meal to be cleared away, and the master to sit with his books and letters.

I have no candle, and for an hour or more the moon stays in hiding. Then clouds part, and a ghostly light crosses the floor, passes over the sleeping baby, slides up the walls.

The house is still. By now, doors must be locked, candles snuffed out, and all gone to bed. I rest my head against the crib. Every catch and release of Titus's breath seems a tremulous thing. Though my legs are cramped and my arm has long grown stiff, I cannot bear to move away.

Downstairs, a drawer slams shut, jerking me back to wakefulness. Someone is in the oak-press room. Has he gone there to gaze upon the sketch of his young bride-to-be, her cheek resting on one hand, her amused eyes so sure of herself, of him? How could I have expected him to forget his peerless wife, I, who have been so stubborn in devotion to my flawed husband?

Footsteps enter the hallway, weigh on each step of the stairs.

The strand of Titus's hair slips through my fingers. I am on my feet and moving into my room where the door is opening.

The candle shines so close to his face I see his pulse beat in his throat.

'I was waiting for you,' he says.

I reach out in near darkness. The door swings closed behind him. The candle clatters to the floor, smokes, and dies. His mouth lands crookedly on mine. For an instant, I taste Abe in the malt on his tongue, then comes a sweet vinegar all his own. His fingers are in my hair, forcing my cap from my head, and his breath is hot on my face, my neck. I try for his mouth again but his beard scrubs my lips. One hand grips my waist, the other pulls at the tangled strings of my bodice. He drags my shift from my shoulder, flattens one breast under his hand with a pressure that makes me gasp.

We land awkwardly on the bed, his elbow digging into my belly so that I cannot breathe. He eases onto one side, pushes my skirts to my thighs, and twists to loosen his breeches. I want to rise to meet him, but now his knee is on the length of my shift, pinning me down. The coverlet twines about my ankles, trapping my legs. He tears at the bedding, forces the shift high above my waist. As he thrusts, I stifle a cry. I am back in the tavern at Hoorn, wincing at boasts of coarse couplings.

When he finishes, I pull the linen down to cover my bare skin. In moments, his breathing is steady.

I remember how Abe honed my desire, how we used to lie entwined till dawn, exhausted by love. Tears sting my eyes. I turn away, feign sleep, tensing my body lest it graze that of the man lying next to me. The room is so dark I hardly know whether my eyes are open or closed.

Beside me, his weight shifts.

'Forgive me. It will not always be like that, I promise you.'

Something stirs inside me, like the plucking of a quill deep within the instrument downstairs.

I lie still as he raises himself to kiss my shoulder, my hair, my cheek. Caresses land soft as brushstrokes on my skin. When I turn around, his lips meet mine.

By morning, I have almost forgotten how he hurt me.

Chapter 26

The gentle touch of sunlight on my face wakes me. Beneath my eyelids, an orange glow blends into rose-pink, earth-brown. If I could show these colours to him, would he paint them for me?

I open my eyes.

Alone.

When I close my eyes again, the colours have gone.

Last night, I forgot to fasten the shutters. I should rise to open the windows, admit the morning air, but I want to preserve whatever of the master still lingers in the room. I touch a finger to my damp skin, taste him on the tip of my tongue. How can I have lived seven years without love?

In his annexe, Titus starts to cry. I pull on my shift and go to him.

Downstairs with Maartje and Lotte, I take care to hide my smiles. My fumbling hands upset the porringer, spill the milk. It is as though a marionette parodies my tasks while I still lie upstairs in the master's arms. Before I fell asleep, he made me promise to come to him tonight. I lower my face to the baby's, and kiss his nose. My accomplice capers with delight, and I allow myself to laugh aloud.

Lotte eyes me from the hearth.

'Do not forget to collect the *loopwagen* this morning,' I tell her. 'And take Titus with you that he might try it for size.'

She scowls. 'Can you not take him? There is laundry to be done.'

'I have other matters to see to.'

Before she objects further, I hand the child over.

Weeks have passed since Otto told me he saw Ilse at the tavern. Today, I am resolved to find her and satisfy myself that all is well.

After Lotte leaves, I seize my chance. 'Maartje, how do I get to the Rapenburgh?'

She looks up from her pastry, licks a fingertip and commences drawing on the flour-dusted table.

From over her shoulder I make out a street; no, a bridge; an island. 'This way?' I point north-east.

Maartje nods. She throws the lump of white pastry onto her map and rolls it into oblivion.

'Geertje!'

I turn back from the door.

'Take a knife.'

On the Breestraat, I turn away from the canal and take an unfamiliar route past the tobacco traders' shops. Patrons spill onto the street, puffing on pipes. A young man in slashed sleeves blows a ring of smoke into my face. I hurry past, his friends' laughter following me to the corner.

After I cross an arched bridge, a tang of brine sharpens the air. Soon another odour penetrates: somewhere, fish guts are rotting. The wind carries and drops the stench on a whim. Every time I think I have walked clear, a drag of putrid air returns.

The buildings are of dark red brick, crammed close together. At street level, some are washed in gleaming lime. Older houses make crutches of their neighbours, as though the wooden piles that once supported them have surrendered to the suck of mud and water. Under eaves and in alleyways, sailors link arms with bare-necked girls in brightly coloured shawls. Their laughter trickles onto the street. A lean mongrel circles my feet, threatening to trip me. I bend to scratch the dog's ear, swiftly withdraw my hand. Diseased skin flakes from his coat.

I cross soiled cobbles, turn a corner, and shield my eyes. High above the gables, ships' masts criss-cross the sky. I remember Maartje's map; how lines seemed to radiate from rooftops. This is the Rapenburgh, and all I need now is to find the sign of the Blue Anchor.

A twinge of worry pinches my stomach. All will be well, I tell myself. I will find Ilse and we will laugh together about our days in the painter's house.

Another twinge. I wanted to forget how the master treated her, and so I made myself forget her. But the man capable of explosive anger is capable of tender love too. Likely he regretted casting her out and would have relented, had she not hastened away.

I am about to stop a respectable maid and appeal for directions when I happen upon a tavern with an anchor slung above the lintel, not fully blue, but fading to rust-bitten white. An old woman leans in the doorway, a pipe held to her slack lips.

'Is this the Blue Anchor?'

She removes the pipe, smiles a gummy smile.

'What is your business?'

'I am looking for a friend.'

She laughs, spits into the straw at her feet. 'Come in, and I will soon find you a friend.'

From within, I hear women talking. I push my way inside.

Beyond the door, a woman and a girl are seated at a table fashioned from a barrel, a scattering of playing cards before them. What little light there is enters through two half-shuttered windows, which stretch to almost the full height of the room. Half a dozen men sit at a long table. Their pipe smoke cannot mask the smell of unwashed bodies.

The woman is leaning on her elbows, rolling a pitcher back and forth on its belly. 'S'empty.' She looks up at me. Her face is pitted with scars.

From my pocket I take the price of filling the pitcher afresh. Her companion, who cannot be more than sixteen, snatches the coins with glee. 'More ale, Joris!'

Sweat stains the underarms of the girl's bodice. In her red hair she wears a greasy ribbon.

'I am looking for my friend, Ilse. She may once have served here.'

The girl's eyes flick from the coins to my face, and back again. 'Nobody of that name works here.'

'She is of an age with you, pretty with flaxen hair, and comes from Leiden.'

The girl shrugs her shoulders, counts the money into the hand of a sour-looking man who delivers a new pitcher.

The woman at the table lifts her head. 'There was a country girl. She lasted but a day.'

'Her name was not Ilse,' the red-haired girl says, righting two upturned mugs. 'And she came from Friesland.' She pours the ale with care, measuring one cup against the other.

Friesland. Ilse once told me the mistress came from there.

A shout comes from the street. Arm in arm, three sailors stumble through the door. The old woman follows close behind.

'Quiet, you dogs,' the first fellow calls. 'There are ladies present, one apiece.' He doffs his hat, performs an elaborate bow.

My new acquaintances titter.

The old woman leads the sailors to a table, beckons the young girl to follow.

Her friend levers herself to her feet, leans on the barrel, takes a long draught of ale. 'The country girl,' I say. 'Where will I find her?'

'Try the Three Crowns.' She wipes her mouth with the back of her hand.

Under the old woman's gaze, I dare not question her further.

I am on the front step, unsure which way to go, when a hand grasps my arm and the woman's scarred face is once more before mine. In daylight, her eyelids are thin as paper and branched with purple veins.

'I remember now,' she says. 'Her name was Saskia.'

I leave the tavern, plunge headlong into the street and run as though I might outrun all memory of the mistress. Even here, far from genteel society, her ghost follows me. A washerwoman forced into a sidestep sends curses in my wake. At a stone bench I throw myself down, try to calm my racing heart.

Gulls screech overhead. From the shipyards comes the clang of hammers on steel. I shiver, though the sun is hot. The red door of a nearby house opens, and a maid flings the contents of a bucket down the steps. By the time I decide to ask her where I might find the Three Crowns, the door has been closed and a tide of soapy water laps my feet.

Throngs of darting children are returning to school. Across the street, a girl emerges from a doorway. Sunlight catches on her hair.

'Ilse!'

Eyes wide with fright, she ducks back into the shade. I smile and wave though I can no longer make her out. A drayman drags a sled over the cobbles, blocking my path. On the gable of the building are three crowns, painted in gilt.

As I approach, two men stagger out the door. One is bearded and grey, and clamps a hat bearing a flaccid plume to his head. The second is fleshy and red of face. He slaps his thigh. 'Where is my darling?' He locks one hand about Ilse's wrist, pulls her from the shadows.

'*Godverdomme*, I saw her first,' the older man replies, then laughs at his own folly. He grabs her other arm, jerks her towards him.

Ilse has grown thin. The skirt and bodice are the same she wore in the master's service, but now she seems lost inside them. Her face and bosom have been burned by the sun and she wears no cap. The bearded man slides an arm about her waist, the other forces a kiss onto her cheek. They drag her to the corner.

'Ilse!' I call again.

For a moment she breaks free, raises a hand and smiles. It is her old smile, tempered with a new wariness. I step closer, and she shakes her head in warning.

'Come to see me,' I call, but already the men have renewed their hold, and now they lead her down an alley, out of sight.

Chapter 27

Maartje leans out the door to the courtyard, holds up a palm to the morning rain. She curses, pulls the door closed.

'I can go to the meat hall, and anywhere else you want,' I call from the table. It will give me a chance to visit Otto and tell him that I have seen Ilse.

Maartje hands me the pail. 'Bring the mutton home with you. No deliveries. That villain would cheat his own mother.'

I kiss the sleeping Titus, cover my head with my shawl, and head out into the alley.

The rain lightens to little more than a mist and the day becomes sultry. I lift the neck of the mistress's old chemise, waft warm air onto my skin. By the time I reach the Nes, the shawl is shrugged to my elbows and I long to rid myself of its weight.

I enter the coolness of the converted church where the butchers keep their stalls. A sled laden with freshly slaughtered oxen is dragged inwards. The metallic tang of blood fills my nostrils.

Flayed carcasses swing from a wooden scaffold running the length of the hall. Maids linger to examine the offerings, pinching pale fat and ruddy flesh between their knuckles. The purple-pink hues remind me of the old woman whose painting hangs in the master's house. How does he see what lies beneath the skin?

Two dogs snarl over a tangle of entrails. I step carefully over dark puddles which threaten to spatter my skirts. Soon I lose count of the stalls but it matters not because when I reach the one where the master's account is held, I recognise Willem Jans. He was among the tradesmen who came to sympathise with the master, and drink his fill at the funeral feast. A man who freely partook of my master's hospitality, yet would cheat him in every dealing.

The butcher's cap slants over his yellow hair and his shirt is loosely laced, showing much of his pale chest. He hacks at a rack of ribs on a table livid with fresh stains. Behind him, a woman sharpens knives at a whetstone.

'Well, my pretty,' he says, looking up from his knife. 'What takes your fancy?'

'Maartje sent me. From the Breestraat.'

He smiles, showing gapped teeth. 'A nice piece of rump?' He slaps a fatty loin and laughs. 'Or I could show you a fine plump sausage.'

'A leg of mutton,' I say. 'I will have that one.'

He glances to where I point.

'Too heavy for pretty maids' hands. I will send my boy with it later.'

'I will take it now if you please. Last time it lost a quarter of its weight on the journey.'

His grin disappears. He hawks, spits onto the ground.

'Cornelia, you confounded the orders again.'

The woman at the whetstone glances over her shoulder. For an instant I am confronted by a pair of dark eyes glittering with spite. I take a sharp breath. She turns back to her work, her blade scraping the stone with renewed force.

'I know your master. We were schoolfellows in Leiden.' The coldness of Willem Jans' tone unnerves me.

A boy wraps the mutton in a scrap of waxed linen and I force it into the pail. A shining knob of bone thrusts out from under my arm as I hurry away, past swaying sides of beef, with the uneasy sense of Willem Jans and his wife watching me.

In my haste to leave the hall, I all but run to the shoemaker's shop. Inside, the bulwark of the counter seems to rush to meet me. I steady myself against its weight. The apprentice leans on his broom and stares. Strands of hair cling to my face. I force them into my cap.

Otto emerges from the back room, humming a tune. When he sees me, he stops.

'I found Ilse, and did nothing to help her.' My shoulders shake.

Otto takes the pail from my arm, bids me sit at the worktable.

'Marten, have your dinner at the Whaler today.' He hands a coin to the apprentice and the boy skips out onto the street. Otto latches the door, goes to the back room, and returns with two mugs.

'Drink,' he says, handing one over.

'Is your father here?' The brown ale smells of glue.

'At home. He has the dropsy again and must lie abed three days.'

I take a long drink, set the mug down amid snaking strips of leather, and tell him what I saw on the Rapenburgh.

He rubs his bare chin. 'Nothing could be done. The deal was already struck; intervening could have placed you in danger. The women thereabouts look out for one another.'

'So I should abandon her?' My pitch rises.

Otto sighs. 'You have no money, no shelter to offer. You have but few acquaintances in the city. Ilse had best call upon her friends in service, find a position with one of their mistresses.'

'Without a recommendation from the master, she will find no position in Amsterdam.'

I cannot meet Otto's eyes. I have betrayed Ilse, and now I betray the master too.

Otto rolls a spool of twine towards the table edge, stops it, rolls it back again.

'Your master is a man not to be crossed.' Now it is he who avoids my face. He winds a loop of twine about one fingertip.

'What have you heard?'

He frees the finger, binds it again. At last, his calm brown eyes meet mine. 'That he has grown close to a servant of his household.'

'It is true.' The words come in a whisper. A tremor of relief runs through my body.

'Are you in love with him?' His voice is gentle.

'I cannot help myself.'

I talk, and Otto listens. When I finish, he smiles.

'I am happy for you.'

'I thought you would caution me, urge me to give him up.'

'I am no one to preach caution.' He reaches for my hand, squeezes it. 'Did not you wonder what business I had on the Rapenburgh that evening?'

I try to picture Otto stepping past the old woman into the gloom of the Blue Anchor, being greeted by the girl with the dirty ribbon in her hair.

'You told me you were meeting a friend.'

'So I was. One who is more than a friend.'

'I saw a girl there.' I stop, uncertain. I cannot imagine Otto calling for ale, making merry with the girl and the jaded older woman.

'There is something I have long wanted to tell you.' He falters. 'You have trusted me with your secret; now I am trusting you with mine.'

This new trepidation alarms me. 'You may tell me anything in confidence.'

'It may shock you.'

'Little you say could shock me. I was routing drunken sailors from the Moor's Head when you were still a boy, trundling a hoop over cobbles.'

Some of the tension in his shoulders eases. 'That night, after I left the tavern and saw Ilse darting across the street, I continued to my appointment. The arrangement was a tenuous one, wrought from hints and gestures.'

He pauses, looks at me, and I smile to reassure him. How his fine features, his fresh complexion, must have marked him out from the seasoned sailors and work-weary labourers of the Rapenburgh.

'To my relief I found the bait-shop as described, with the old man scooping dried worms at the counter, and an outdoor stairs leading to a room overhead. I had been wary of being late and scuttling my hopes. Now, ascending the steps, I was wary of seeming too eager, or of being lured into a trap.' He stops, lifts his mug, but replaces it without drinking. This is a new Otto; this timid youth who must be coaxed at every turn. I nod, and he continues.

'I closed my eyes, tried to recall the face of the man I had met at the harbour that morning. His hand had glanced against mine as he pointed out the wharf where all day he would load bales of linen onto a ship bound for Muscovy.'

A memory floats into my mind: Abe telling tales of sailors who grew lonely on long voyages, and took to comforting one another when far from home. After weary months at sea, when the ships returned to port, the men returned to the embraces of their wives and sweethearts waiting on the docks.

Otto searches my face.

'Go on.'

'Before I could knock upon the door, the man opened it, and beckoned me inside. One window cast little light on a drab but orderly room. There were no chairs, just a bedstead in the corner, with a cedar chest and small table nearby. I stood while he reached for a bottle, poured me a drink I could not taste. He wore his tunic loose at the neck, the sleeves rolled above the muscles of his forearms. When he saw how my hand shook, he eased the mug from my grip, and I smelled the sea on his skin.'

Otto's eyes are bright. For a few moments, I lose him to the dimly-lit room on the Rapenburgh.

'I stayed with him all night, in that low-ceilinged room, and slipped back to my father's house at dawn.'

I can hardly recognise the man who once sat with me in the master's kitchen and told me he knew how it felt to be friendless and alone. But it is the same Otto, with an awl behind one ear, and a scarf wrapped about his curls.

'You are not shocked?' A nervous smile.

'Not shocked. But I cannot help being a little afraid for you. Do you mean to see him again?'

'I already have. I would spend every night with him if I could.' His face glows. Speaking of his lover gives him courage.

'You must be careful.'

'Now who urges caution?'

'You are young and have no fear. I am glad to see you happy, but you must not be discovered.'

'That is the price of friendship. I worry for you, and you worry for me, yet in our own affairs we are as two lovesick maidens, incapable of prudence.'

When I have finished laughing, I attempt a serious tone. 'Otto, who else knows of this?'

'None but you. Though my cousin in Haarlem, Aefje, has long known my nature.'

'You have never spoken of a cousin.'

'A distant cousin. From childhood we have been intended for one another, though Aefje is even less inclined for marriage than I. She takes lovers, and on her every visit brings me tales of their ridiculousness.'

It is well past midday. The rain has stopped. Outside the shop, Marten has returned and occupies himself in kicking over stones.

'Do not worry, Geertje,' Otto says. 'I am not so foolhardy as you think. I have no plan to wear a rope around my neck.'

I shudder, and he laughs.

'I cannot forget poor Ilse.' I stand up, smooth my apron. 'I told her to come to see me. She should have been married by now.'

'Tell her to go back to Leiden,' Otto says. 'I will give you the price of her fare and you may pretend that you have paid it.'

At the door, a thought seizes me. 'The mistress's sister will soon pay a visit. What will she say when she finds me out?'

'You owe her no explanation.'

'I have broken her trust, and she will discover it. I have failed her, as I did Ilse.'

'You have failed nobody. And we will find some way to help Ilse. In the meantime, let us enjoy what happiness we have found.'

Already, I long for night to come, for the master's arms to surround me.

Otto unlatches the door, and the bell trills as I step outside. Marten slips past, casting me a curious look.

I hesitate, turn back to the shop. 'I hardly know to whom I should be loyal anymore.'

'That is simple,' Otto says. 'To yourself.'

Chapter 28

The leading straps Lotte stitched onto Titus's gown come loose on first trial, sending him sprawling towards the floor. When I catch him, his forehead is a thumb's width from the slate.

'I told you to sew them yourself,' Lotte says.

'Remind me to follow your counsel in future.' This remark is ignored by Lotte, who is already holding out the work bag and the mistress's shears.

Leaving her in charge of Titus, who is now clad only in his undershirt, I make for the salon.

The room is cool and quiet. I have hope of an hour's peaceful needlework before I must return to the kitchen. Today, the master's great commission is to be unveiled, and he must depart for the ceremony soon after the midday meal.

The salon is his favourite part of the house, other than his painting room. Lotte is careful to concentrate her efforts in here, where he is most likely to observe any deficiencies. The hearth shines like black glass, and the honeyed scent in the air tells me the mantel has lately been polished. Behind me is the window where we stood, the night he told me the painting was finished.

Soon, I will show it to you.

Later, after we have eaten, I will kiss the place where his cap meets his forehead, and remind him of this promise.

Under the gaze of the mistress's portrait, I spread her son's dress across my knees, and reattach the straps with double thread. What would she think, to know that I spend my evenings in this room sitting on her husband's lap, drinking in his kisses, feeding him mine? That by night, he comes to my room, returns here alone before dawn? In the corner, her bedstead stands, inviolate. The bed curtains remain closed in daytime, a thing she could not endure, for she hated stale air to surround her sheets.

I shiver. I should not have lain on her bed, the morning she left the house to put flowers on her children's graves. What if some unlucky seed was planted for me on that day?

My elbow catches the work bag, spilling spools and bodkins to the floor. I cram them back inside.

A cry of laughter makes me jump. I follow the sound to the hall, where Lotte is sitting on the checkered tiles, arms wrapped about her shaking sides. In the middle of the floor, Titus struggles within his *loopwagen*. The padded hat, which is yet a little big for him, has slipped over one eye. Grunting with effort, he pushes forward on the wooden frame. When the rollers move, his feet slide, his hands lose purchase, and he lands on his behind.

Perplexed, he grips the struts, stares out at us like a tiny prisoner.

Lotte drums her feet, laughs louder.

'Help him,' I say, but I am laughing too.

'Heertee!' he calls, waving his arms. I raise him to his feet within the frame, guide his hands to the rail and coax him forward. One tottering step, then another.

'Look, Lotte, he can do it.'

Lotte jumps up. 'Good-day, Sir.'

The master is standing in the archway, observing us with a smile. Already, he is dressed for the afternoon's ceremony. His slashed doublet is threaded with gold, and a velvet cap crosses his forehead at an angle. On his feet are boots of calfskin leather. What would it be like, to enter the hall on his arm, to greet artists, burghers, patricians as the consort of such a man?

Lotte casts me a sly look, slips past him to the stairs.

The master crosses the floor, bends to rub Titus's padded head.

'So this is what happens when I leave women in charge. They put you in a cage.'

Footsteps descend to the kitchen. I picture Lotte creeping back up again, her slippers in one hand. When she or Maartje are nearby, I become shy around the man who shares my bed.

'Soon your son will walk unaided. And I am teaching him to say your name.'

'The painting is to be unveiled at three o'clock. Will you bring him?'

The hall will be crowded. All the artists of the Breestraat will be there, all his pupils and friends, many of whom already know me.

'But what will I wear?'

'What you always wear.' His face is puzzled. He turns to Titus, lifts him high into the air and the little boy squeals with delight. 'I must have you there to witness my triumph.'

Whether this last remark is addressed to me or to his son, I cannot tell. He sets the boy down on the floor.

'Maartje will tell you how to get there. It is not far.'

'I know where it is.'

'Then I will see you there.'

He steps close to me, touches my face. I want to press his palm to my lips, breathe his olive-soap scent.

Too soon, he withdraws his hand. 'I must be gone. I cannot trust those military men to shade the windows as I directed.'

While Titus naps, I examine the contents of the wicker chest in my room. The few garments I possess fail to improve upon close inspection. The best among them is the woollen petticoat which was once the mistress's. Though the day is hot and humid, I slip off my apron and skirt, step into its folds. Hidden at the bottom of the chest is the silk kerchief I resolved never to wear. But that was before the master spent his nights pressed against me, whispering words of love.

The silk caresses my neck. It pains me to knot the delicate corners but I have no pin to fasten it. My reflection in the tin mirror satisfies me. Something of the girl I was looks back at me. A softness in my eyes counteracts the firmness of my chin. 'Not a beautiful face,' my cousin Trijn once conceded, 'but a strong one. A face with the power to imprint itself on the mind of a man.'

I will wear the kerchief, and later, I will tell my lover how I came by it, and we will laugh together at his sister-in-law's connivances. As for Lotte and Maartje, I care not what they think.

A faint cry from Titus recalls me.

'Come my lamb, you must wear your new gown and make your papa proud.'

On the last step of the stairs, with the baby in my arms, a nervous agitation rises within me. I will keep to the back of the hall, come forward only when the speeches are over and spectators dwindle to groups of twos and threes. Then might I approach the master, commend him on his success. Titus reaches out, pats my shoulder as though he approves this plan.

'I have nothing to fear when you are with me.' I kiss the top of his head, and the master's intention becomes clear. Bringing his son to the ceremony explains my presence there. With this request, the master seeks only to protect my reputation. My care now must be to praise the painting as though I had never seen it before. By tonight, all will be understood between us.

Today, I will leave through the front door. I want to skip through the streets with Titus in my arms, to throw open the doors of the great hall where the master awaits me.

The thud of the knocker echoes under the ceiling. I set Titus down on the tiles.

When I open the door, the mistress's sister is standing outside.

Chapter 29

Hiskia's greeting is cordial, her expression friendly, as she steps into the hall. Her cap sits tightly on her head as though moulded to her iron-streaked hair. A shawl of intricate lace wraps about her shoulders like a black web. She waves away my attempt to relieve her of this garment.

'I cannot stay. I have only come to congratulate your master. But perhaps he has already departed?'

Titus clings to my leg, pulls himself to his feet. I lift him into my arms so that his face shields mine.

'Yes, Madam. He was needed early at the hall and left before midday.'

'No matter. I will find him there. I have a curiosity to see this vaunted painting.'

I try to hide my dismay.

Her eyes linger on my face an instant longer than is necessary. She reaches for the hem of the baby's gown, folds it over and back between her fingers as though searching for a flaw in the brocade.

'I did not expect to find my nephew bedecked in satin.'

'I am taking him to the ceremony.' I aim to sound casual, indifferent.

The brocade drops from her hand. 'There can be little purpose in bringing an infant to such an event.'

'Nevertheless, the master desires it.' My impertinence astounds me but I do not waver.

She stares coolly back at me. 'Your duties are here, within this house. The child may come with me.'

Muffled footsteps sound from the hallway. I imagine Lotte skulking behind the arch, eager for intrigue.

'He may be restless in unfamiliar company, Madam.' Steeped in defeat, the words ring hollow.

'Have no fear on that account; I shall take the servant girl with me.' She inclines her head, looks over my shoulder. 'Tarry, girl!'

I turn to see Lotte arrested in mid-flight. She delays a teasing moment at the top of the stairs, but even Lotte does not dare oppose this woman. Sullen-faced, she drags her feet to join us at the door.

'Then it is settled.' Hiskia smiles, but her eyes maintain their chill.

Lotte gapes at the kerchief knotted about my neck. Why did I wear it? Rage blazes within me. I want to tear it from my neck, fling it back at the giver who wields such power over me. But the mistress's sister is already passing through the front door and descending the steps to the street.

Titus whimpers, sensing the impending handover. These nights he sleeps on the truckle bed in the kitchen where Lotte is supposed to watch over him. More often she takes her bedding to the laundry room, leaving him to Maartje's care.

'There are turnips to be scraped,' Lotte says, taking him from my arms. 'Better change your clothes.'

The bells of the Zuiderkerk chime three o'clock as I knead and stretch dough on the kitchen table. Now the master mounts the dais. Now the city official takes a golden cord, tugs the velvet curtains open.

I slap the bread onto the shovel, thrust it deep into the oven. Does the master look for me in the crowd?

I want to see his painting, not by candlelight in a cramped gallery, but in a great hall with my lover standing, triumphant, before it.

I wipe my hands on a cloth.

'Maartje, I am going out.'

In my haste, I cannot determine the fastest route, and it seems a long time before I turn a corner and the spire of the Regulierstoren pierces the sky.

There is still time. The speeches may be over, but the guardsmen will surely linger, admiring their likenesses on the canvas.

Instead of the mistress's silk I am wearing a linen kerchief knotted under my chin. A feeble disguise. I will slip in at the back of the hall, pray Hiskia and Lotte do not see me, and that none of the master's fine friends remember the maid who served them at his wife's funeral feast.

The civic guardsmen's hall is fronted by a great turret. At the top of the steps, a guard in a buff coat is in attendance, a musket resting against one shoulder. He interrupts the picking of his teeth to point to the basement. 'Servants go through the kitchen.'

Down at the kitchen door, I hesitate. At a table, a maid is scooping pastries onto platters, ignoring a dog begging at her feet. The meaty odour of game thickens the air. A serving girl takes dishes of candied fruit and sugared almonds, climbs the stairs.

Another maid decants wine from a cask into large pewter-lidded jugs. She looks up and sees me. 'You are late. We sent for help an hour ago.'

She bends her knees, lifts two of the jugs. 'Take these.'

The weight of the wine drags on my arms as I follow the serving girl upstairs. When I reach the banqueting hall, I want to pull my kerchief lower about my face. The room is filled with people. Most have their backs to me, their attention focused on the other end of the hall where a man is speaking. Somewhere, the master is hidden among this crowd.

The hall is the grandest I have ever seen. An immense chandelier, its arms arced like serpents' necks, is chained to the stuccoed ceiling. Four tall windows have been thrust open onto the glittering Amstel. On the opposite wall hangs the master's painting.

In the gallery, I had observed the painting piecemeal and stitched the fragments together in my mind. Now its true magnificence is revealed. To the right, the captain thrusts one hand forward, commanding his men. Beside him, the lieutenant tightens his grip on his spear. The ensign raises the flag. The entire company seems about to march into the hall. I stretch onto my toes, strain to see the girl who reminded me of the mistress, but the crowd obscures my view.

A trestle table has been set up against the back wall where a maid is setting out glasses. She takes one of my jugs, commences pouring. My hand shakes as I lift the first glass, fill it with crimson wine.

The speaker finishes. A drumbeat ripples and a horn blows. There is a pounding of boots as military men assemble on the dais. A flag is hoisted, then the master ascends like a newly crowned king.

Cascades of applause fill the room. The master speaks, but I hear none of what he says. His smile is exultant. The goldwork on his doublet gleams. He seems to grow in stature, as though nourished by the adulation. Last night, I held his face in my hands, feasting on his noble imperfections. Today, his visage rivals that of any emperor cast in bronze. How easily he outshines the military men in their ill-fitting gorgets, their plumes and tassels. I want to reach across the hall, draw him into my arms.

The captain of the company steps forward to address the crowd. The scarlet sash and flounced collar, which in the painting denote authority, now give him the air of a hastily costumed *kermis* player. It is the master who bestowed greatness upon this man; the master who elevated a company of retired soldiers to a noble army.

Somewhere in the hall, Hiskia is looking on, seeing his future, our future, assured.

The captain finishes his speech with a flourish. I wonder how the floor can withstand the stamping of so many boots. I push past a cluster of guardsmen pointing stems of pipes at their own images. Silk-gowned wives murmur in admiration.

At last, I will see the master's greatest work as he wanted to show it to me.

Too late. Ahead of me, Hiskia's cap floats like a black buoy on a surge of velvet and lace. I imagine her steely eyes counting heads on canvas, multiplying fees, calculating the increase to her nephew's bounty.

While her back is turned, there is a chance to see the master. I am desperate to share his joy. I take a glass of wine from one of the serving girls and push towards him. I will meet his eyes, if only for a moment, and let him know that I have witnessed his glory. But among the men circling him I recognise the art dealer, the poet, and I dare not mount the dais. Instead, I reach up, brush his elbow with the glass.

'Wine, Sir?'

He half-turns, takes the glass without seeing me, carries on talking.

Out in the glaring sunshine, I pull off the kerchief, crumple the linen in my hand.

Perhaps Hiskia has saved me. Had I worn my second-hand finery as I intended and joined the gathering on the dais, I would have succeeded only in delighting the gossips of Amsterdam.

I must get home before she returns and notices my absence.

I am nearing the mouth of the alley behind the master's house when I hear a call.

'Geertje!'

I turn wearily, expecting Lotte.

Coming down the Zwanenburgwal, keeping close to the eaves with her head held low, is Ilse. She hurries to meet me and I hug her thin shoulders.

'You will squeeze all breath out of me,' she says with a little laugh. Her lower lip is swollen.

'Come inside where we can talk.'

She hesitates.

'The master is not at home, and we do not expect him until evening.'

Once in the kitchen, I latch the door behind us. Maartje cries out in surprise and Ilse rushes into her arms.

'You are both unchanged,' Ilse says, looking from Maartje back to me.

'It has been but three months.'

'It seems far longer. I have seen none of my old friends since I returned.'

Her weariness disquiets me. The changes I saw on the Rapenburgh are more pronounced now that she is back in her former home. Her hair has grown dull, her complexion florid. She has been carrying a cloth bundle on her back and when she sets this down on the table, her shoulder blades poke hillocks through her bodice.

Maartje ladles stew into a dish.

'Eat.'

'I am not hungry,' Ilse says, looking at the food.

When she has eaten two dishes full and drunk a mug of ale, she sighs, half-closes her eyes, and pushes the empty ware away.

'What of the mistress?'

'She died in June.'

Ilse nods. 'And how does the master do without her?'

Before I can think how to answer, she holds up a hand. 'Nay, I care not.'

'Perhaps I could talk to him, persuade him to take you back.'

She stares at me, incredulous. 'And have him turn you out, as swiftly as he did me?'

Maartje is inscrutable. She takes her empty pipe out of her pocket, chews on the stem.

A stale smell hangs about Ilse's person. What did it cost her pride, to come here in this state? I open the door to the courtyard. 'The breeze will cool our faces.'

'Can it really be only three months since I was here? It seems an age ago.'

'What happened when you got to Leiden?'

She emits a bitter laugh.

'At first they were glad to see me, for my mother had been ill and my sister and her children now share our cottage. The two boys were in my care all day and I was happy to bide my time with them till Jan returned from his uncle's farm. But within a week, a letter came from the master.'

Ilse tests her swollen lip between her teeth. Dread pours into the chambers of my heart.

'My father had the neighbour's boy read it for us. In front of my mother and sister he read on and on, my father making no attempt to stop him.'

I cannot move. My skin is cold and damp. Beneath my bodice, the mistress's chemise sticks to my back.

Ilse wipes tears away. For a moment I glimpse the tiny sparrow I once sewed before she crushes the handkerchief into her fist.

Maartje pours more ale, and they drink.

Ilse composes herself, fixes her eyes on the table. 'That evening, the same boy brought a message to say that Jan is to be married before Christmas to the butcher's daughter. So you see, I cannot stay in Leiden. Nor can I stop here, for I owe money to the hag who keeps my room. From her girdle hangs a long knife, and she would cut my throat without a thought.'

'Where will you go?' Maartje tucks strands of hair behind Ilse's ears.

A little of the old Ilse returns. She straightens her shoulders, raises her chin. 'I am going to Rotterdam, where my cousin Neeltje went a year ago. She will help me, when I find her.'

'You will need money.' I empty my pocket onto the table. A few coppers rattle free.

Ilse laughs. 'Infants do not pay well, Geertje.'

Maartje goes to the hearth, picks at a loose tile, and comes back to the table with a leather pouch.

'I cannot take your runaway money,' Ilse cries.

Maartje's coins are already spilling onto the table. She divides them into two squat columns, slides one over to Ilse.

'I will pay you back one day,' Ilse says. 'Geertje, keep your coins; they would not take me as far as the city gates. There is something else I need from you.'

'Anything,' I say.

'Let me stay in your room tonight, for I have nowhere to go. I will be gone by dawn. I dare not sleep in the kitchen for fear the master might discover me, but in your room I will be out of sight, and can slip away before he rises.'

There must be some excuse I can make, some reason I can give to dissuade her. I grip the edge of the table, open my mouth but cannot speak.

Ilse's forehead puckers. She looks from me to Maartje, then back to me again. When she finally speaks, it is in a slow and careful voice, unlike her own.

'When you said that you would talk to the master on my behalf, I did not understand you. Now I see I must thank you for that offer.' She scoops Maartje's coins into her pocket, takes up her bundle.

'Ilse, do not go.' How can I fail her again?

But already she is embracing Maartje at the door. Before she leaves, she throws me a look of pity. 'Do not cry, Geertje. There are far worse things to cry about.'

Maartje lifts the latch, the door swings open, and Ilse is gone.

Chapter 30

After Ilse leaves, Maartje stops at the back door, pressing a corner of her dirty apron to her eyes. Dragging her feet, she returns to the table, scoops the remaining coins back into the leather pouch. The only sound is the scuff of her worn-down soles across the floor. At the left side of the hearth, she crouches to replace her hoard. The loose tile scrapes back into place.

Why does she not fear my stealing her money? Any night while she lies snoring I could go to her hiding place, take the coins, leave behind the pouch fattened with stones. By first light, I could escape through the city gates.

But I will not run away, and Maartje knows it.

With a grunt of discomfort, she stands, rubs her back. Ignoring me, she goes to the pump and sluices water into an iron pot. Any utterance, any rebuke would be better than this.

'Maartje, forgive me. I should have told you I had seen Ilse on Rapenburgh.'

The cranking ceases. Maartje seems heavier, older, as she bends to lift the pot. I jump up from the table, grab one of the iron rings, and we carry the water to the fire.

'It matters little now,' she says.

'Perhaps her cousin will find her a position.'

Maartje's breath comes whistling through her teeth.

There are no flames, but when I reach for the chain, fasten it to the ring, the fire seems to scorch my face. The pot lurches as Maartje hooks up her side.

She takes the poker, stirs up a storm of grey ash.

'I love him, Maartje.'

Her arm stills. She leans on the poker as though it is a crutch. When she withdraws it from the fire, the tip glows red.

'Then you are a fool.'

I back away from her, stumble against the table.

From the hall comes the thump of the front door. He is home.

I pull off my apron, and run up the narrow stairs to meet him. But before I reach the top, Titus's cries and Lotte's irritated 'hush' come echoing from the hall.

'You take him,' Lotte says, when I meet her in the hallway. She thrusts the sobbing child into my arms. 'All the way back he howled in my ear. He weighs heavier than a sack of beets.'

'Did the mistress's sister accompany you here?'

Lotte scowls. 'Nay, not she. Once all the fussing and speeches were done, she bade me walk ahead. It is no short journey with such a burden as he.'

'So she does not mean to call on us?'

'She stayed on to speak to the master, though I am full sure he did not want to speak to her.' Lotte giggles. 'Likely they are talking of you.'

I grab her arm. 'What did you tell her?'

'Nothing.' She shrugs me off. 'Why would I speak with one who never fails to reproach me?' Her eyes narrow with sly intent. 'But there was much talk among our neighbours gathered in the hall.'

Titus wriggles, rakes my face with his fingers. A pungent smell rises from his linen. Taking advantage of this distraction, Lotte skips past me and, tittering to herself, descends the stairs to the kitchen.

The bells of the Zuiderkerk chime eight times and still the master is not home. In the salon, Lotte has set out cold mutton, bread and pickled herring. There can be no feasting in a house of mourning. Only the jugs of red and white wine the master ordered that morning hint at celebration.

Outside the window, ripples of gauzy cloud spread purple and pink across the sky. I could defy the curiosity of the neighbours, go onto the street and wait for him in the last of the evening sun. But when I look into his eyes, will I find my lover there or the man who ruined Ilse's hopes?

In the painting over the mantel, the mistress's gaze is serene. Was she always so untroubled in her husband's mercurial company? When he cast Ilse out, she deferred to his wishes. Must I, too, learn to curb my feelings, bend my will to his?

I draw the bed curtains open. The coverlet is smooth as though the bed has not been slept in since the mistress was taken from it. What does the master think about, after he descends the stairs from my room and comes here to lie alone at night? Perhaps he does not think at all, but sated, sleeps at once.

My hands are shaking. At the table, I lift the jug of white wine and fill a glass. I drink it down, and a shudder runs through me. But within moments, a comforting warmth spreads through my limbs, and I fill it again. When I hold the glass up to the window, the fading light imbues the wine with a silvery glow. 'I am drinking enchantment.'

I did not mean to speak aloud. I wheel around. The room is empty. I slip into the mistress's old chair by the hearth, gaze up at her gentle face framed with flowers. I fancy she regards me with benevolence; that she understands my plight and would console me if she could.

When I awaken, the room is almost dark and the master is kneeling before me, shaking my arm.

'It was a success; a great success.' He trips over the words and laughs. An odour of brandy wine hangs on his breath.

For a moment I do not want to speak, I only want to look at his boyish smile, his eager eyes, the curls springing from his velvet cap. I hold his face, raise it to meet mine.

'I have something for you,' he whispers. 'I had it from the silversmith tonight.'

He opens my hand, slides what feels like a coin into my palm. Moving his candle closer, he shows what he has given me. It is a marriage medal, embossed with the figures of a man and woman, standing either side of a twisting vine. On the reverse are letters. I look at him in wonder.

'Geertje, I would marry you.'

I could think it a dream, were it not for the cold hard metal in my hand.

'I love you,' I tell him.

He hesitates.

I squeeze the medal inside my fist as though to brand the tiny figures onto my skin. Then his mouth meets mine and I twine my arms about his neck. He carries me past the open bed curtains, out into the hallway and up the stairs to the hanging room.

Chapter 31

'It could be silver.' Pieter weighs the marriage medal in one hand. 'I need more light.'

Before I can object, he is halfway down the alley. I hurry after him. Every step on the cobbles sends an ache through my head. Since morning, my throat has been dry, my tongue uncomfortably large in my mouth. All I want to do is drink mug after mug of cold rainwater from the barrel in the cellar. Instead, I follow my brother into the glare of the sun.

Pieter crosses to the canal bank and squints at the medal.

A noxious odour rises from the fermenting water. Barges glide below us, trailing films of foaming scum. Across the canal, the Zuiderkerk chimes eleven o'clock.

'A simple design, but well-crafted,' Pieter says. 'I will take it to a dealer and have it appraised.'

'But I would not be parted from it.' What foolish impulse made me show it to him?

'You have attached yourself to such a trinket?'

'When giving it, he said that he would marry me.' The confession makes me proud, yet shy.

Pieter snorts. 'A painter's promise. What can that be worth?'

The promise of a man who adds figures to scenes on a whim, paints over any which displease him. A knot of pain gathers between my eyes. In Pieter's hand, the medal becomes a grubby coin. But there are words chased in the silver which cannot be erased.

'What does it say?'

'It is Latin. Nothing of consequence. He has not troubled to have your name upon it.' He flicks the medal over and back between his fingers. 'Likely it is made of tin.'

I reach out, but his hand closes. The knot tightens. Later, when my head is clear, when I am lying in the master's arms, I will enjoy my happiness again. First, I must have my medal back.

'What would the master think if I gave up his gift so soon?'

Pieter pinches a wisp of his beard.

'Perhaps he will expect you to carry it about with you.' He frowns. 'If you cannot produce it, he will certainly suspect you of selling it, or giving it to another.'

Patience, I tell myself.

'I have more pressing concerns than this trifle of yours.' Pieter takes one last look at the medal before giving it up.

Once more, I feel the reassuring pressure of the betrothed figures inside my hand.

'Mind you look after it, Sister.'

'I shall, though as you say it may hold no worth.'

Pieter grunts, takes out his pipe. 'Let us hope the painter does not tire of you and ask for it back.'

We walk over the bridge, talking of Marit and the baby.

'Does Trijn mean to visit soon? I have much to talk over with her.'

'Unlikely. Last time she claimed the journey made her ill for a week.'

'How so?'

He shrugs. 'Alas, it was not a malady of the tongue.'

'Then I will go to Edam to visit her.'

Pieter wrenches my arm.

'You must not leave your master, not even for a day.'

'Why not?'

'I have important business to conduct with him. Until it is concluded, you cannot allow his attention to wander.'

'What business?'

'I am dealing with powerful men, Geertje. Men who demand great returns. Your master should oblige me in these matters, much as you are obliging him.'

Who are these men? Fear scuttles across my heart. 'You would have the master pay your debts?'

'Do as you are told and there will be no trouble.'

He drops my arm, threads through the crowd, and is gone.

The medal lies damp in my palm. I close my fist around it, as though Pieter's talk of trouble could cause it to slip through my fingers. Once it is safe in my pocket, I relax. I have the master's love, and no debt can threaten that.

Perhaps there will be time to lie a quarter hour in my room before the midday meal. I turn back towards the Breestraat, quickening my step. A woman dressed in black is mounting the steps to the painter's house.

Hiskia raises a hand to the knocker, glances down the street and sees me.

Too late to make for the canal bank and the safety of the alley. I stop on the bridge, bob a greeting. The disdain in her expression strikes me like an arrow. Then the door opens and she disappears inside.

I am going to be sick. Hanging on to the railings, I lean over the canal and retch. Nothing comes. Shaking, I straighten up, press my handkerchief to my mouth. My back is slick with sweat.

'They are shut up together in the side room,' Lotte crows by way of greeting when I enter the kitchen. 'I was dusting in the hall and could have overheard all but for her sending me to find you.'

I am too weary to pretend I know not of whom she speaks. Titus clatters across the floor in his *loopwagen*, babbling happily up at me. Ignoring Lotte, I tickle him under the chin and he laughs. In silence, Maartje stirs a pot over the fire.

'You are to wait in the salon,' Lotte persists.

There will be no escaping to the cool, dark cellar, no hiding away in my room. On the kitchen table stands a jug of ale. I fill a mug and drink it down. Though its sour warmth makes me shudder, it gives me strength.

'I will see her when I am ready,' I say. Lotte gapes. 'Take Titus out to the courtyard that I may watch him from the salon windows.'

When she is safely outside, I climb the stairs. I would not have her creeping up behind me to press her ear to the door.

Hiskia stands at the hearth in front of her sister's portrait so that it seems I am facing not one adversary, but two. At the table, I grip the back of the master's chair.

'It seems I have been much deceived in you.' Her coldness grieves me. 'You need not dissemble; I have seen your master and know all.'

'It was not my intention to deceive, Madam.'

'Then you do not deny your disgrace?'

'No, Madam.' My legs are weak.

This answer appears to surprise her. She folds her arms, clutches her elbows. 'I am rarely wrong in my judgement of character . . .' Here she breaks off, strangely unsure of herself. Her strength has buckled under the weight of her youngest sister's death.

She recovers, crosses the room and leans on the table, bringing her face close to mine. I step back, abandoning the support of the chair. Does she smell the ale on my breath, notice the tangle of red veins in my eyes?

'Answer me this, and answer truthfully or it will be worse for you.'

Fear courses through me. Down in the courtyard, Titus starts to cry.

'When did you first lie with my sister's husband?'

'It was after her passing. After his great painting was sent to the militia men's hall.'

There is nothing worse to be told. Giddy relief swims in my head. It is as though I have been released, limping, from the bite of a trap. I meet her gaze throughout the pause that follows.

'I believe you,' she says. 'On the day of the funeral feast I saw him look at you without seeing you. He was in need of comfort but had not yet recognised it within your form.' She draws herself up to her full height. 'It should come as no surprise that he chooses the most proximate of women with whom to console himself.'

'He cares for me. We care for each other.'

'He is grieving. He knows not what he does.'

'He has given me a token.' My fingers slide across my pocket, touch the medal through my skirt.

'All that he has belongs to my nephew and is not his to give.'

'I have had his pledge and want nothing more.'

Her eyes widen. 'You cannot imagine he means to marry you? He will never marry you, nor any of your kind. My sister saw to that. Half of her money returns to my family upon his re-marrying. And the greater portion has been traded for the bricks and mortar that surround you.'

'He has no need of her money. His paintings command great sums.' My courage is wilting.

'My brother-in-law is a fool with money. Likely the bread you eat has not been paid for. And he has stopped painting.' Hiskia draws the web of her shawl tightly around her shoulders. 'I will return to this house before long. Do not think that I will neglect my nephew's interests.'

'His interests I place above my own.' But already she is leaving the room, her stiff back and shoulders betraying no sign that she has heard.

Chapter 32

Alone in the hanging room, I stretch out across my bed. Though I have fastened the shutters against the sun, sleep will not come.

The bells of the Zuiderkerk chime four o'clock. In an hour or less, Lotte will surely seek me out. I finally find comfort when I unlace my bodice, kick off my skirts and turn over the pillow so my cheek rests on cool linen.

Upstairs, an easel is dragged across floorboards. By now, the pupils will be draping damp cloths over palettes, hanging besmirched smocks on pegs. I imagine the master moving from canvas to canvas. Is he generous with praise, or does he frown, seize a brush and repair tentative under-drawings with impatient strokes? From the kitchen comes the muffled clang of a dropped pot. I curl up on my bed, suspended between two worlds. Hiskia's spite echoes in my head. *He will never marry you, nor any of your kind.*

Boots tramp along the landing outside my door, the noise jolting me from confused dreams. Jocular voices echo down the stairs and out into the hall. When the front door slams, I get out of bed, open the shutters and unlatch the window. I lean out over the ledge, take a deep breath. The wafting scent of Maartje's mutton stew masks the unwholesome vapours of the canal.

At the sheet of tin that serves as my mirror, I tidy my cap, dress myself. My head no longer aches. Only the sting of Hiskia's words remains.

When I open the door, a faint creaking of boards overhead tells me the master is still at work. I remember the day I stood on the threshold with Ilse. How fearful I was of him then, how wary of disturbing his work.

I tread gently on the winding stairs, stop at the open door of the painting room. Here, at the front of the house, the light is softer and bathes the floorboards in a buttery glow. The four windows stand open, dispelling the odour of turpentine. The master sits in a chair of studded leather, his back to me. His shoulders are sloped, his head tilted, as though he might be sleeping. On the easel facing him is a newly-stretched canvas, tinted with ochre, but otherwise unmarked.

'Sir?'

Only the slightest turn of his head tells me he has heard. Though clad in his painting garb, he carries neither brush nor palette. The rattan stool is pushed to one side.

'Is supper served already?'

'I must speak to you and it cannot wait till then.' I cross the room, stand at his elbow. I wait for him to slide an arm about my waist, pull me onto his lap.

His eyelids are heavy. He sighs, fixes his eyes on the empty canvas.

'No doubt my sister-in-law has spoken to you. Have you come to renounce all sin?' His attempt at a wry smile is soon abandoned.

'She told me things.' I hesitate. Why did I not plan what I wanted to say?

'What things?' He speaks with concentrated calm. There is danger in his tone but I cannot stop now. I will make him look at me.

'Why did you give me this?' I hold out the marriage medal.

He is out of his chair. A vein reddens on his cheek.

'I gave it to you as a token of my affection. You liked it well enough last night.'

His menace chills me.

'I liked the promise that came with it.'

He presses fingertips to his temples, closes his eyes.

'Were circumstances different ...' For a moment he seems to struggle with some unexpressed emotion, then checks himself. He hauls his smock over head and shoulders and lashes it to the floor. With one foot, he kicks it aside and makes for the door.

'Then it is true?' I call after him. 'You are bound by the terms of your wife's will?'

He pauses in the doorway.

'You are my wife.' The muttered words are half lost to the staircase.

If only he would look at me, tell me again, with tenderness. But already he is descending the steps.

'Tell Maartje not to keep supper,' he calls.

I wait for him in the salon but he does not come. Across the court-yard, his candle burns in the oak-press room. What work can he be doing in this light? I close the curtains, return to the table. I long to go to him, but I crossed one threshold to find him today and I will not cross another.

Though I had told Maartje he wanted nothing, a platter stands on the table. Under the cloth is a loaf of wheaten bread, a round of spiced cheese and a dish of almonds. I tear chunks of bread, eat them with the cumin-scented cheese. A mug of cool ale slakes my throat.

When I can eat no more, I rise from the table. My place is here with the master and always will be. We may not be wed, but he is my husband as surely as Abe ever was. I will wait no longer. Let him follow me to bed if he will.

When I reach the foot of the stairs, the door of the oak-press room opens. The master stands in the half-light.

'Geertje. I want to show you something.'

I follow him across the lines of shadow cast by the wooden press to his chair in the corner. On the table lies the sketchbook, with loose leaves protruding from its pages. Has he been brooding over his first drawing of the mistress again, pining for her tranquil eyes?

'Some work I keep for my own amusement.' He opens the book and slides a sheet over to me. In the centre of the page is a picture of the master, an image scratched in black ink and hatched with wayward lines. His mouth is open, his forehead contorted in rage. I suppress a shudder. It is the man who faced me today in the painting room.

Before I can respond, he slides a second sheet over the first. His face again, but this time the eyebrows are raised in surprise, the rounded lips seem about to whistle a tune. In an instant, I see how his son will look as a young man.

'I like this one better,' I tell him, but he is busy turning pages.

Next, he shows me a pitiful array of beggars. They lean on sticks, stretch out hands, stagger on feet bound in rags. An old man warms his hands by a stove. 'I know him,' I say. 'Or someone just like him. A poor soul who roamed the eastern harbour at Hoorn, sweeping dung from shop fronts for the price of his dinner.'

Abruptly, he gathers the sketches, sets them to one side.

'This is the one I want to show you.'

A sheet of thick, yellowish paper lies face down inside the leather cover of the book. When he turns it over, I see a crouched beggar wrapped in a blanket, his shoulders hunched, his miserable eyes fixed imploringly on some point beyond the page. It is the master, the master whom I have only ever known to paint himself in splendour befitting a courtier or a prince. One hand is folded in the meagre warmth of his cloak, the other he holds cupped for alms.

'She hated it,' he says. 'I told her I had burned it.'

I stare at the image which frightened the mistress as it frightens me.

'All that saves me from such a life is layer after layer of paint brushed onto canvas.'

And the mistress's money. The disloyalty of this thought shames me.

Beside me, the master opens a drawer, takes something from the darkness within.

'I want you to have this.' A gold ring shines in the palm of his hand. He slides the band onto my little finger. 'I promise you, I will marry nobody else.'

His arms draw me close, his lips touch my neck. As I lean into his caresses, I hold my hand to the candle's light. Two familiar red stones glint on my finger like the puncture marks of some tiny creature's teeth.

Chapter 33

On a September morning the master stands at the window, tucking his shirt into his breeches. 'The first frost of the year has fallen,' he says.

Until he spoke, I had not felt the cold. I climb out of bed, wrap myself in a shawl, rest my head against his shoulder. Roof tiles of nearby houses shine like fish scales. Down in the courtyard, rimed cobbles catch the first rays of light.

'Must you go so early?' I smooth a hand over the stubble of his chin, draw his face towards mine. Gently, he breaks my hold.

'I have work to do. And the model will be here by nine, unless she finds better business on her way.'

'So you are to spend the day gazing upon a pretty girl while I toil in your kitchen.'

'Precisely.' He flees to the door, pretending to duck the pillow I pretend to throw. I have not seen him so light-hearted since before the mistress died.

He pauses in the doorway. 'Mind you feed the woman before you bring her up. And have Lotte light the stoves.'

The shawl has slipped to my waist. He smiles at me, and a sensation deeper than desire wells within me. I am brimful of love for him.

When he is gone, I go back to bed, twine my body in the sheets that bear his scent.

'Not even your shift?'

Lotte's voice, full of thrilled revulsion, carries from the kitchen up the stairs to meet me.

'Nothing but my pelt, and all my working parts laid out for the young gentlemen to see.' A throaty chuckle follows this remark, succeeded by Lotte's shriek of laughter.

When I walk in, Lotte looks up, flicks the hearth with her broom. By the fire sits a woman dressed in a tattered skirt and shawl.

'Anke is teaching me about art,' Lotte says.

The master's model would not look out of place in his catalogue of beggars. Her cheeks sag, and her bloated form shows no deline-ation of bosom, waist, or hip. Crimped yellow hair protrudes from her greasy cap. On her lap is a plate of pearly-grey bones sucked clean of meat.

The woman's eyes pick over my dress, land on the gold ring on my little finger.

'You must be the mistress.'

Lotte titters.

'When you have finished eating, I will bring you upstairs,' I say.

Anke licks her fingers, wipes them on her skirt.

'You need not trouble, Mistress, for I know the way.'

From the far side of the table comes a crash of wood. Titus has escaped his *loopwagen* and made of it a battering ram, gleefully driving his new toy against the courtyard door.

'What a strong son you have, God be thanked.' Anke lifts her hem and there is a flash of red wool as she thrusts one stockinged foot, then the other, into a pair of worn mules. 'He looks of an age with my youngest but one.'

The master must pity her indeed. His benevolence casts no judge-ment, perceives only a cold and hungry mother forced to leave her children to seek work. When she stands, I take her arm. A reek of vinegar almost masks the stale odour of her body.

'Come, I will take you to him.'

The master is alone in the painting room. He has set his easel to one side and is dragging stools across the floor to form a half-circle. The lower panes of the windows are shuttered and the air is close and dry. Smouldering peat stings my nostrils.

'Well, Master,' Anke says. 'It is a long time since we have had this pleasure. Where will you have me?'

The master lifts his leather chair, lands it close to the stove. 'I would not suffer you to gripe about the cold.'

Anke unties her shawl, throws it onto the chair.

I move to the door. 'If you do not need me, Sir . . .'

He is watching Anke. 'There is more of you to draw than when you last sat for me. I hope your price has not risen in proportion.'

Her hearty laugh turns into a cough.

'Get her some ale,' the master says, still looking at her.

I go to the jug on the table. When I deliver the ale, the model is already out of her skirts and pulling her shift over her head. With her clothes lying in a ragged heap, she takes the mug and drinks. Distended breasts patched with large nipples overhang the belly, which overhangs her hips. Garters have gouged tracks below her knees. I fold each unclean garment, tuck the red stockings beneath the bundle.

'I will leave your things on the table.'

'Thank you, Mistress.'

I brace myself, but the master does not correct her.

'Sir, I will come back in two hours,' I say.

He nods, arranging Anke's arms and shoulders to his liking as she settles her bare flesh into his chair.

Men's voices sound on the stairs. I leave quickly before the pupils descend.

'How do you know that woman?'

'What woman?'

We are lying on our backs in my bed. The ceiling is dark as a starless sky. I slide a hand to his chest, circle fingertips around his heart. 'The woman with whom you spent your morning.'

'Anke?' The inquiry seems to surprise him. 'One or other of the pupils always seems to be acquainted with Anke or her sisters. If I send a request on a Monday, I am certain of a sitter by Wednesday.'

I would sit for him. Can he only find favour with my body in a darkened room? I remember Anke's puckered belly, her low-slung breasts. A mean impulse garners within me. 'I felt sorry for her.'

The master snorts. 'Feel sorry rather for me. On her last visit she helped herself to two wax candles from the hall.'

'It was a kindness to have her brought into your kitchen and served a meal.'

He grunts. 'Unless sated with food and heat she is wont to fits of trembling liable to challenge the steadiest of eyes.'

'Is it true that you once discovered Maartje on the streets? That you persuaded the mistress to take her into the household?'

'I have no idea from whence Maartje came. One morning I found her in the kitchen, frying herrings in butter so delicious that on my knees I begged her never to leave me.'

I squeeze his arm. 'I want to know.'

'All right then.' His tone is serious. 'I will tell you, but you must swear not to tell a soul. I rescued her from the harem of a Sultan. Her teeth were pulled to prevent her from telling his secrets.'

The thin sheet covering us quakes as he laughs. 'Some day soon Maartje will disappear and we will never hear of her again,' he says. 'Already I have lost favour with her; she no longer crimps the pastry crust to my liking.'

For him, a wavering line separates what is true from what is false. How easily he skips over it and back again. His work is filled with figures posing in borrowed clothing, their faces bearing emotions they do not own. For a dizzying moment I feel trapped in an artifice of his making. I strain my eyes for some pinpoint of light in the room, some marker to guide me back to what is real.

The master shifts beside me, slides his body over mine. For a moment his weight stops my breath. He captures me with every long stroke of his fingers, every teasing dab of his tongue. I lie beneath him, allow him to arrange me as he will.

Chapter 34

On an October afternoon Pieter strides into the hall, tracking mud across the polished tiles. I push the door closed against the driving rain, and take the cape he swings from his shoulders. 'Why did you not come to the back door?'

'You would have your brother call to the kitchen like a common tradesman?'

I refrain from reminding Pieter that he is a tradesman, common or otherwise. His over-large hat lists to one side and a dripping plume hangs from the brim like a broken wing.

'I am here to see your master.'

I hesitate, folding the woollen cape in my arms. Pieter espies the ring on my finger and grabs my wrist. 'Very fine,' he says, examining the stones. He glances upwards to the interior window that opens from the landing, lowers his voice. 'You have done well, Geertje.'

'Have you news from Edam? How fares our mother?'

'Asking for money as usual. I must collect a portion from you today.'

I cannot meet his eyes. 'I have no money to give you.'

'You have spent it all?' Pieter's voice ascends to its customary volume.

'This quarter I have been given none to spend.'

From upstairs comes a crash of wood, followed by a hearty oath. I picture the master glowering, a pupil scrabbling to retrieve a painting board.

'The master did not tell me you were calling,' I say quickly.

'I did not alert him in advance. Must he have notice of every visitor?'

'He is loath to be disturbed during working hours.'

'Would you have him miss an opportunity to increase his fortune?'

How alike the two men are. Neither will be thwarted. A shiver crosses my shoulders. It is well for me that both are on my side.

'Wait here, and I will ask him to see you.'

'Here, in the hall, like a messenger boy? Where does your master receive his guests?'

I take Pieter into the side room where he turns a full circle, appraising all around him. He goes to the hearth, runs a hand over the false marble columns.

'The master may be occupied for some time.'

'I will wait.' Surrounded by fine furnishings, Pieter is suddenly rendered poor and unkempt, his ill-fitting breeches and limp plume more revealing than any carpenter's smock and cap.

I find Lotte in the hallway, swinging a duster from one hand, and send her to fetch the master.

When I return, Pieter is at the virginal, lifting the lid.

'You must not touch that.'

He scowls, but closes it.

'What of your master's melancholy moods? Does he paint?'

'He takes walks in the countryside and returns with drawings to work upon.'

Pieter snorts. 'Who buys drawings of windmills and bridges? City merchants are willing to pay fistfuls of guilders for counterfeits of their wives.'

'The days grow shorter. There is less time in which to work.'

'Then you must encourage him to paint by candlelight. Your livelihood and mine depend upon it.'

A familiar footfall sounds on the stairs, crosses the hall. Pieter adjusts his hat.

When the master comes in, the room fills with bristling energy. He responds to Pieter's greeting with a curt nod.

'I told you not to call when I am working.' The master is clad not in his painting smock but in an outdoor shirt and breeches.

'It grieves me to interrupt your work; however, a pressing matter demands your attention. Sister, you may go.'

'You forget yourself, my friend.'

Pieter colours. 'Forgive me. My affection for my sister means I regard her as part of my household.'

The master turns to me and nods. I leave the room, not daring to linger outside the door.

Later, in the salon, I pour a mug of light ale for the master, and one of double for me. After he has eaten, he pushes aside his plate of bones and takes his mug to his chair by the fire. He sits, brow contracted, shuffling through letters.

Since Pieter's visit we have hardly spoken, and now I struggle to break the silence. The room smells of drying wool. His coat hangs on the back of my chair, wet through after one of his long walks. Earlier, when the front door banged closed behind Pieter, I discovered the master had left too.

I turn the coat, check the sleeves for dampness. I should remove it to the laundry room.

'What did Pieter want today?'

'What he always wants. Money.'

'You mean he seeks an investment from you?'

He laughs without mirth. 'That is how he termed it, yes. Your brother draws enemies as a dog draws fleas. And with every passing day, they bite more keenly.'

I fill his mug too quickly. Ale froths over the brim, soaks his cuff.

'Ach!' Anger leaps into his face.

I pull out my handkerchief but he waves me away, wipes his wrist against his breeches. He clenches his teeth as though enduring some great trial.

Then, as suddenly as it arose, the anger passes. His face relaxes.

'That is two drenchings I have had today.'

'I am glad mine was the lesser of the two.'

A half-smile twitches on his lips.

'Is Pieter in trouble?'

'Not for now. Though he should know my generosity has limits.'

I kneel on the floor by his feet, rest my head on his lap. He lifts a hand and for a moment it floats uncertainly above my cheek. Then it lands on my head and his fingers work under the linen of my cap, stroking the nape of my neck. I wait for him to draw out the pins, tumble out my hair.

The motion stops. He sighs, pats my head: a signal for me to rise.

I take the poker to the fire, turn over grey logs, expose the glowing undersides.

'I would like to be of service in your work. Are there tasks within the painting room I could undertake?'

'I have apprentices enough to mix paint and stretch canvas. In truth they do little more than clutter my space.'

'Perhaps I could sit for you. You may have need of a servant in one of your compositions.' The offer tastes of bitter smoke. I set down the poker, fix my eyes on the embers. Is he looking at me, or at the portrait over the mantel? I should have made this request late at night, when promises are readily exchanged between us, not here, under the steadfast brown eyes of his wife.

'What brings about this sudden vanity?'

'Not vanity. I want to see what you make of me, that is all.'

'It is no use,' he says. 'I can paint nothing, nobody.'

I close my eyes against my tears. When I look at him, there is a distant expression on his face. He has moved on in his thoughts, unconscious of the wound so casually inflicted.

From the table, I take a candle. 'I will go to bed.'

'Geertje.'

A beat of hope. I turn back to face him.

'I will sit and read awhile. Do not wait up for me.'

Chapter 35

Rain pounds the Breestraat, bouncing up from the saturated cobbles so that the street seems to boil. There will be no walk through the countryside for the master and pupils today. I stand on the dais, peering out of windows streaked with rain. A maid ducks past, her empty pail clamped to her head like the helmet of an impoverished mercenary. As I look on, the girl stumbles, raises an arm in hopeless defence against sleds which drive waves into her path.

'I feel nothing.' My voice echoes around the hall, startling me. I turn away from the window and discover Lotte leaning in the archway, her eyes full of mischief.

'I was taking water to the master when I heard you say something.' Her arm is curled around a pitcher resting against her hip.

'I will take it to him.' I cross the floor quickly.

Lotte sways deeper into the archway, clutching the vessel to her chest.

'I should not go up there if I were you.' Her face takes on an expression of concern so unnatural to her I take a step back.

'What do you mean?' My head is light on my shoulders, as though I had drunk a cup of wine too fast.

Lotte leans forward, lowers her voice. 'Have a care, Geertje, in case the master tries to paint you without your shift.'

I grab the pitcher, sending a spray of water onto her apron. She skips away from me, shaking droplets from the linen. Her laughter runs down the stairs, fades beyond the kitchen door.

In the painting room, the master is at the table, selecting a palette of colours with one of his pupils. When he hears me deposit the pitcher, he looks up.

'Here is my wife, just when I am in need of a model!'

How easily the monotony of the rain, the numbness of the morning, Lotte's provocations can be dismissed. Like a weathercock, I swing with his moods. Were it not for the boy by his side, I would take his face in my hands, press a kiss to his lips.

He drags his old chair into the centre of the room. 'Come.' He pats the worn leather. 'Sam needs a subject.'

I cannot move. I look from him to the boy, who wears a shy smile.

Impatience flickers across the master's face. He seems on the point of chastisement when he releases a sudden laugh. 'Do not be alarmed, Geertje, you do not need to remove any clothing. In fact, I have a better plan.'

He goes to the back room where his treasures are kept, and returns with a dun-coloured jacket and a string of carnelian beads. The jacket is too small and smells of tobacco but he feeds my arms into the sleeves before I can object. The beads rattle as he twines them round my neck. He places me behind the chair with my hands resting on its back. I shift, and he frowns, corrects my position.

The work is to be on a canvas already coated with a brownish ground. The master holds the stretchers up to the light, invites the pupil to smooth a hand over the surface. A ghostly image manifests as though conjured by the boy's fingers: the long-rejected work of some predecessor, almost hidden beneath a layer of ochre.

The master tightens the screws on the easel. After some terse instruction, he repairs to the upper floor where the rest of the pupils are at work, and I am left alone with the boy.

I am a prisoner until the painting is finished.

The boy peers at me, measures my distance from him with the stem of his brush, and dabs at the board. I want to straighten my back, loosen the laces of the stifling jacket, but I dare not move. Perhaps the master will come back to complete the portrait when the under-painting has been prepared. This pupil cannot be more than fifteen years old, a smooth-skinned child with a habit of shrugging his shoulder-length hair back from his forehead.

'Madam, are you comfortable? May I fetch water for you?'

I shake my head, then apologise for the movement, and he smiles.

'It is my first day. I have much to learn and humbly beg your patience.'

His voice bears both the confidence of wealth and the polish of education. The strong forehead and nose, the full lips, foreshadow a handsome maturity. I ask where he is from, and soon he is telling me about his father's workshop in Dordrecht where he learned to chase arabesques on silver goblets and emboss scrolls on handles of knives.

After an hour or so, the master returns and makes some rapid corrections to the work. When he looks at me, his gaze is impersonal as though I am a vase of flowers or a porcelain figure. In those moments, my emotions seem strangely suspended, as though I have been transformed into the object he sees. But when his eyes are on the canvas, I find myself tracking every flourish of his hand, consigning the movements to memory that I might identify his strokes in the finished work.

In a few moments he is gone and I am alone with the pupil again.

When I leave my post at noon to tend the stove and fetch our dinner, I am astounded by the boy's progress. The woman's pale forehead and red cheeks are undoubtedly mine but there is a harmony to her visage I never knew I owned.

'You flatter me,' I say, then fear I have offended him.

'It is faithfully done,' he says politely.

We eat bowls of mutton stew which I bring on a tray from the kitchen. I tell him about Rarep and Edam and the farmland where I grew up, and he listens attentively, his head tilted, his hair falling over one shoulder. The rain continues unabated and the room darkens.

We resume, I, with my aching neck and shoulders fixed into the morning's pose, and the boy seated on the rattan stool pulled close to the easel. His brushstrokes are so delicate his arm hardly seems to move at all.

It is nearing time to light the candles in the sconces when the master returns. Without waiting for permission, I join him at the easel.

The harmony I earlier observed in the painting has ripened in the balance of the brow, the symmetry of the cheeks. I touch my own chin, search for evidence to support the image the boy has claimed for me. I remember my first day in the city, the strange fear of dissolving into the streets and waterways. The woman in the painting is vital and assured. She will not disappear.

'It is not finished, Sir,' the boy says timidly. 'Another morning's work should complete it.'

'It is not worth pursuing,' the master says. 'I cannot sell it in its present state and you would be better served to start afresh. Set it aside for over-painting.'

The boy betrays no disappointment. He nods, wipes his hands on a rag, and sets about removing the canvas from the easel.

'May I have it?' I ask, above the squeak of the wooden screws.

'It is not mine to give, Madam,' the boy says with a little bow.

I turn to the master who is lighting a candle at the stove. 'May I?'

He looks at me, amused. 'Whatever for? I tell you, it has no value.'

'I want it. Is that not reason enough?'

The painting is the only proof of my existence, proof that I am seen, as well as seeing.

He laughs. 'Take it by all means, for no client of mine could be persuaded to purchase it.'

When I am alone in my room with the painting, the oils smell stronger, the painted shadows loom darker. I search the image by candlelight but the master's hand is lost in the composition.

He will never paint me. Had I not intervened, he would have had an apprentice scrape my partly dried image from the board, then hide any remaining trace of me beneath another layer of ground.

'I have saved you,' I tell the woman, who is, and is not, me. For a moment it is as though the painting has spoken. A feeling of strength rises within me, as if I have been joined by a new ally. I stand the canvas on its stretchers against the wall in the annexe where Titus used to sleep. The painting will outlast me, the master, and all within his house.

Chapter 36

January, 1648

When I open the front door, cold air hits my cheeks and forehead as though I have pressed my face to a slab of stone. It is not yet dawn. Across the canal, the spire of the Zuiderkerk points like a black finger towards the sky. A floating fragment of moon shimmers above the belfry. Since Twelfth Day, the gables of the Breestraat have glittered with frost. Now they are crowned with snow. In the low morning light the landscape is so changed, lines of houses softened, corners turned to curves, that it seems I have woken in a different city from the one in which I went to sleep.

A sudden pain clenches my abdomen. I lean against the door frame, breathe deeply. Titus ducks under my arm and out the door. 'Hold the railing,' I call in vain, as his feet crunch down the gritted steps.

As I walk, the discomfort eases. We tramp through grey slush that will stain my skirts and soak his boots. A breeze ruffles the linden trees on the canal bank and their laden branches drop cascades of snow into the icy water. Boats moored along the Zwanenburgwal have collected miniature drifts on their sagging tarpaulins. We cross the bridge, the yellow smudge of my lantern's reflection moving silently along the water below. Soon, the canals will freeze.

'Geertje, I will be late.' Titus tugs my arm.

I had not realised I had stopped. 'My legs have frozen,' I say, but he is already running ahead. Though my limbs are cold, my head is uncomfortably hot. I fan my face with a corner of my shawl and hasten after him. Since his sixth birthday, he no longer permits me to accompany him all the way to the schoolhouse, or even to hold his hand on the bridge. For an instant, he loses his footing and skids off-balance, turns back to me, smiling his father's smile. A pang of love drops like a grain of silt to the bottom of my heart.

By the gates of the Zuiderkerk, I straighten his coat and collar, pull him into a reluctant embrace. His russet cap bobs as he runs down the narrow street. For a moment I lose him, then he reappears under the lantern outside the schoolmaster's house. I wave, but he does not look back. How these daily partings grieve me. I will walk to the Nieuwmarkt and buy him a sugarplum for later. First, I must speak to Otto.

Most windows are still shuttered. I trudge through unswept snow, my feet growing heavier with every step. A trickle of sweat runs down my back. I loosen my shawl at the neck and shiver. The shoemaker's shop is so close I can hear the painted sign swinging on its chains. Before I reach the door, a cramp squeezes my womb. I double over, brace myself against the wall until the spasm passes.

Otto is behind the counter where his father used to stand. At the trill of the bell he looks up. The gentle inquiry in his kind brown eyes is quickly replaced by concern.

'I was mistaken.' I start to cry.

In an instant his arm is around me and he is guiding me to the back room, a space hardly big enough to contain its two stools. He delivers instructions to Marten, then returns and pours mugs of ale.

As I sit, the laces of my bodice pull against my swollen midriff. When my tears are spent, I take a long draught of the bitter ale.

'I knew it could not be so, and yet I wanted to believe it.'

Otto studies me. 'How tired you look.'

'The pains wake me at night. I cannot sleep until they subside.'

'You must see a doctor.'

'No doctor can change what the midwife told me years ago.'

From the shop comes the sound of Marten's knife scoring leather in long, decisive strikes.

'You are ill, Geertje. There may be a simple cure.'

I think of the master, how he fled from his wife in her final hours.

'I did not tell him of my hope.'

Otto's eyes narrow. 'Surely he sees that you are unwell?'

'Some days he hardly looks at me. This past week he has been away from home. He is painting the baker's daughter, a girl of fourteen whose father will not permit her to enter a painter's house.' I try to laugh, gulp air instead.

'It is good that he is painting again,' Otto says cautiously.

'He says that she inspires him.'

The ale Otto favours leaves a brackish taste in my throat. When he moves to fill my mug again, I cover it with one hand. My forehead is hot, my mouth filling with thick juices. Sweat gathers on my skin. I hold my apron to my face until the nausea passes.

'I used to hope that if he could paint again he would have no need of his wife's money and we would be married.' Tremors run up and down my body. Otto takes the mug from my hand.

'You must go home and see a doctor.' He is on his feet, taking his cloak from a peg.

I stand, lean on the seat of the stool, try to smile at him.

'Did I tell you the daughter of the lumber merchant came to visit me? I cared for her in Hoorn when she was an infant.' I stop for breath, swallow, begin again. 'Her father brought her to Amsterdam to seek me out.'

Otto says something, hooks an arm through mine.

'She said that losing me grieved her more than losing her own mother. For years, she prayed every night that she might never forget my face.'

I want to tell him everything about the Beets family, how I loved those children and they loved me, but I cannot keep up with my thoughts and my head aches with the effort of trying to make myself understood.

'You have a fever,' Otto says.

A violent cramp sends water to my eyes. I clutch his arm. His face fills with apprehension.

'You must stop here. I will close the shop and call Doctor Sanders.'

'I must go back.' Panic courses through me. I am filled with dread that the door of the house on the Breestraat will be locked against me if I do not return immediately. I try to tell Otto that I can walk if he will help me, if he will only bring me back to the master's house.

Men's voices interrupt my sleep. The coverlet is too tight. I shrug it from my shoulders. Firm hands press it back into place.

'Sleep,' a man commands.

Something cold and wet is held to my forehead. I want to call for the master but a great weariness overcomes me.

When I awaken, I am back in the hanging room and the mistress stands by my bed, her back to me. The sheet of tin is propped against a basin on the cabinet and she is studying her reflection, her hands adjusting the silk kerchief about her neck. I gasp in fright but cannot move.

She turns and speaks in Lotte's voice. 'You are awake! How ill you look. The doctor said it is nothing infectious but I think Maartje should sit with you instead of me for she is already an old woman and has no mother to grieve for her if she dies.'

Lotte whips the mistress's kerchief from her neck and bundles the silk back into the wicker chest.

'How long have I been ill?' My mouth tastes foul. She fills a mug with water and holds it to my lips, spilling much onto my chest.

'Two days and two nights. Your shoemaker half-carried you into the kitchen. I thought you were drunk.' She giggles. 'He was shouting at us to call a doctor and carry you to bed, but you were struggling and saying that you had to go to Hoorn, that you had left your baby behind in Hoorn. When the master heard the commotion he sent your young man for the doctor.' She claps a hand over her mouth. 'The master warned me to call him the instant you awoke.'

'I cannot see him now, like this.' A dried paste clings to the corner of my mouth. My head burns.

Lotte soaks a cloth in the basin and wipes my face with cold water. She takes my comb from the window ledge, drags it through my hair.

'Let me sleep first,' I beg her.

A look of fear crosses her face. 'I promised to call him directly.' She opens the door and is gone.

The bolster under my back is damp. I try to turn it but the effort makes me dizzy. I must seem well when the master arrives. I draw back my elbows, haul myself upright. I should have had Lotte open a window to freshen the room.

There are voices on the stairs but I cannot tell who speaks. Steps approach. I close my eyes, and wait.

'Geertje, please wake.' The master is whispering so close to my ear his lips brush my skin. His tenderness makes me weep. I turn my head and our foreheads meet. On his breath is the scent of the red wine served to visitors.

A cough comes from the doorway.

'This is Laurens.' The master straightens up.

A thin man in a tightly buttoned jerkin stands at the open door. Wire spectacles pinch his long nose. Under his arm he clutches a leather folio.

I have never seen this man before and yet there is something familiar about him. 'You are not the doctor.' I sound hoarse.

'I cannot work in here,' the man says.

'Take some particulars. You can write more fully at the table downstairs.' The master goes to the annexe and returns, carrying a chair. He sets it at my bedside and motions for the man to sit.

I watch the visitor draw on a pair of oversleeves. Though I do not recognise him, I now recognise his profession. He is a notary, just like the men who came to the mistress's sickbed to record her final testament in the last days of her illness.

Chapter 37

The notary extracts a quill from a leather case and sets his ink pot on the shelf by the window, pushing aside my comb, my medal of Sint Nicolaas.

'You labour in vain. I have no intention of dying on this day or any soon to come.' I aim for levity but there is a quaver in my voice I cannot control.

The notary is unamused.

I look to the master for reassurance. He turns an abashed face to the window and gazes out at the falling snow.

My hands creep down the coverlet towards my thickened waist, then shrink back to my sides. Did I dream the strange hands probing my belly? While I lay in fever, did the doctor discover a knot of diseased flesh? I imagine an elderly physician shaking his head, washing his hands and going downstairs to join the master. In the salon, a good supper of salt pork and wine would not be spoiled with talk of cankers and black blood.

'You are not dying.' The master turns abruptly to face me. 'There is no immediate danger. Doctor Brehmer will return before dark.'

He comes to take my hand. I am filled with an uneasy sense that the two men flanking my bedside know more of my fate than I do.

'Geertje, you will soon regain your strength. In the meantime, it seems prudent to record your wishes.'

'My wishes?'

A crease darts between his brows. 'Titus must inherit his mother's jewels.'

My hand falls limp within his.

'That has long been understood between us, has it not?'

'The law has ways of confounding such matters.' He drops my hand, pulls the cloth cap from his head, rummages through his hair. 'With no direct line, it is best to make intentions explicit.'

A realisation forms within me, as clearly as though the master had snatched the notary's quill and sketched its outline on the coverlet of my bed. He is afraid, but his fear is not for me. This time I allow myself to touch my swollen belly through the sheets. He thinks that I am with child. Or mortally ill. It matters not, as long as he secures all he has given me.

'Laurens has commenced the testament for you, and I will have Lotte and Maartje witness it.'

I imagine the two men sitting at the table in the salon, the notary's quill scratching on paper, the master detailing the three gold rings he gave me, the purse of foreign coins, the marriage medal without an inscription.

'No.' I am so loud the notary stays his quill and stares at me from behind his spectacles.

The master halts close to the door. The eyes that meet mine are cold as iron. Otto's voice floats into my mind. *Your master is a man not to be crossed.*

'As soon as I am well enough, I will go to the notary's rooms with witnesses of my own choosing.'

'All can be resolved here and now, within the hour.' Impatience sparks within him. A breath from me could fan his rage.

'If I am in no immediate danger there can be no need for haste.' I smile at him, at the notary. 'Today, I fear the fever still clouds my mind. When I am recovered, all will be done as it should be.'

The notary lays down his quill, looks at the master. There is a long pause. Even the clamour of bargemen on the canal seems to quieten.

'Come, Laurens,' the master says. 'We will draft the document together. In three days' time Geertje will go to your rooms and sign it.' He does not wait while the man scrabbles his papers together. The door swings closed behind him.

Dusk is falling when Doctor Brehmer enters my room, clad in his outdoor cloak. A draught of icy air accompanies him, and his nose and cheeks are tipped with pink.

'I am glad to see the fever has broken, but that is not all that troubles you.' He motions for me to lift the coverlet.

The pan of peat on the floor now holds only ash. When his cold fingers meet my skin, I shiver, close my eyes. He presses circular patterns into my belly as though attempting to rub away stains.

'Married?'

'Widowed.'

I try to recall when the master last called me his wife. Did he identify me to the physician as a mere servant of the house?

'It is as I thought,' Doctor Brehmer says. 'A growth has formed in your womb. You are healthy and strong and there is no cause for alarm. There will be discomfort from time to time but it cannot be much.'

His face is kind. 'I will tell your master that you must rest.'

When he leaves, I sit upright. The torpor of fever is gone and I am flooded with heady relief. I will find the master, tell him all will be well. I push back the covers, slide my feet to the floor. Once out of bed, a wave of weakness causes me to stagger. I steady myself against the cabinet. Someone is coming up the stairs. In the scrap of mirror, my face is wan, my hair lank. I pinch my cheeks, drag on a cap.

The door opens and Lotte comes in, carrying a bowl of broth on a tray.

'How glad I am to see you on your feet. Since you have been ill, I have had no rest. Every trifle vexes Maartje, and that child wearies me with his demands.' She settles herself at the end of the bed with the tray. 'Are you hungry?'

The floorboards list as though the house is setting sail. I grope my way to the window. Outside, trapped snow is piled up in the courtyard.

Lotte watches my progress back to bed. 'What a time old people take to get well. When I had the smallpox I was abed but a day.' She breaks a crust of bread, dips it into the bowl.

I lift a corner of the coverlet and when she does not move aside, I give it a gentle tug to oust her.

'You cannot go back to bed, Geertje. And it is a sin to waste good food.' She blows on a brimming spoon of barley and shredded meat. 'I added extra pepper while Maartje was in the privy.'

My legs seem fit to fold beneath me. 'I need to sleep.'

'You are to sleep downstairs,' she says through a mouthful.

I stare at her. For years I have wanted to lie with the master in the salon's oaken bed, to watch its carvings glow in candlelight like facets of a dark jewel.

Lotte eats hungrily. I wait until the spoon clanks against the empty bowl. She sops up the remaining juices with a morsel of bread.

'The master said we are to watch over you in case you sicken in the night. "Master," said I. "Maartje has the box bed, Titus the truckle, and there is room for but one roll of bedding on the floor. Would you have me sleep in the courtyard?" Then he said Titus is to sleep in the side room, and you are to have the truckle. It is well he arranged it so, for I could not sleep close to Maartje without a pomander pressed to my nose.'

She finishes her bread, sighs with contentment.

I slide onto the bolster, press my face against its softness to hide my tears.

'Do not cry, Geertje,' Lotte says, alarmed. Her weight shifts from the mattress, then her strong arms are around me, easing me onto the chair the notary lately occupied. 'Sit here while I remove the linen.'

The unexpected kindness in her voice undoes me. I sob helplessly as she strips the sheets from my bed, casts them to the floor.

Chapter 38

The cold kitchen floor shocks my feet as though I had stepped onto a frozen canal. I walk to the table in near darkness, testing my balance with each step. From the hearth, the lamp's glow swells like a rising sun as Maartje adjusts the wick. Lotte's bedding has already been rolled up against the wall. Out in the courtyard, a spade clangs against stone.

Maartje fills a mug of buttermilk, pushes it towards me. She turns away from my thanks, bends to stir a pot of broth bubbling over the fire.

The discomfort of which the doctor warned has not returned. On my first night in the kitchen, I slept little. The orange eye of the hearth lamp coupled with Maartje's snores conjured delirious dreams of dragon-like beasts. But last night I slept so deeply I did not awaken even when Maartje clambered past me to dress herself and crank the day's first pail of water.

After breakfast, I sit by the fire sewing while Maartje scrapes turnips into a bucket. Lotte, whose shovelling progressed from the courtyard to the alley, now returns. 'How my back aches.' She throws herself onto a stool. Melting snow drips from her shoes.

A pounding on the back door disturbs my peace. 'It is too early for Otto,' I say.

Lotte shrugs, pulls off her shoes and stretches her feet towards the fire. I set aside my mending, get up to answer the door.

A smaller, older version of Lotte stands outside. The fury in the woman's expression alarms me. I take a step back and she bustles past me into the kitchen, a pair of shears dangling from a girdle about her waist.

Lotte shrieks, leaps like a cat from the stool, and shields herself behind Maartje.

The woman stabs a finger at her. 'Fetch your master.'

Lotte cowers. Maartje stands like a bulwark between her and the visitor, a curl of turnip rind still hanging from the blade of her knife.

I clear my throat. 'I am mistress here, Madam.'

The woman rounds on me. It is as though Lotte's plump youthfulness had been stretched taut over brow and chin. An apron washed of all colour is tucked over the woman's skirt and her hair is scraped beneath a grey cap. She rests her hands on her hips, tilts her head as though measuring me from head to foot.

'You must be the harlot upon whom he spends my daughter's wages. I will have no more of it. He pays me now, else I take her home.'

Lotte pops her head up over Maartje's shoulder. 'Geertje is no harlot!'

I feel a rush of gratitude for her indignation.

'Why, she has not been paid for even longer than I.'

'Do not provoke me, girl,' her mother says. Lotte ducks back down.

'The master is with his pupils and cannot be disturbed,' I say, though in truth I know not where he is. I have not seen him since the day of the notary's visit.

Lotte's mother folds her arms. 'Pack your things.'

For a moment I think the order is for me. Lotte starts to cry but obeys, going to the cupboard where her linen and few trinkets are stored. I move to help her but her mother blocks my path. She leans forward, rising onto her toes to match my height.

'You may tell your master I will have the bailiffs after him if my money does not arrive this very day.'

'You are too hasty, Madam,' I say, but already the woman has seized her daughter's arm and is dragging her to the back door. Lotte breaks free, rushes to embrace me.

'I cannot leave you, Geertje. Not with all the trouble in this house.'

Feckless Lotte, whose only care has ever been for her own comfort. I hug her back. In spite of all, I will miss her.

She presses a crumpled handkerchief to her eyes. 'In my last household the young master got the neighbour's maid with child, yet it was not so interesting as here.'

Her mother jerks her arm, they stagger out the door and are gone.

Maartje steps into the courtyard. Flakes swirl into the kitchen.

Maartje is your friend, though she does not trouble to show it. Ilse's words on the day she left.

I watch through the window as the older woman coughs over her pipe, sends a stream of black spittle flying into the snow.

When the master returns at noon, I am waiting for him in the hall. Dressed in a black coat and breeches, he could be taken for a member of the church council. The wind has ruffled his beard, a sign that it has grown over-long. When last did I trim those copper wires, his jaw cupped in my hand?

'I am glad to see you well.' He pulls at the fingertips of one glove, then the other, slaps them onto the seat of the chair beneath the window.

I make no move to take them. When he sits, and tugs at his leather boots, he looks up at me expectantly but I come no closer. I draw my feet together, within the perimeter of a white floor tile. Before his schooling began, Titus used to play a game in which the black squares were the sea, the white, dry land. He would hop a precarious course from one wall to the other, shrieking in mock-terror if his foot slid onto blackness.

The master's first boot lands on its heel, flops to one side.

I start to shake.

'This house grows colder by the hour.' He grapples with the second boot. 'Today I must suffer a visit from the guild. Have Lotte lay a fire in the side room.'

'Lotte is gone.' My throat tightens.

'Gone?' He looks up. 'Why so distressed? Has she taken the silver with her?'

'She is owed wages. Her mother took her away.' Words are hard to form and I am wasting them upon Lotte.

'I have met her mother and would readily pay any sum to avoid meeting her again.' He gets up, takes a pair of slippers from the cabinet by the dais.

'But what of me?'

'Maartje will have to help you until I find someone else.'

I am desperate to make him understand but already he is walking away. He enters the office under the stairs. I watch through the interior window as he unlocks a wooden chest, removes a leather pouch. Like a jailer, he beckons me to the grating. My fingers hook around the metal.

'The doctor said you are in need of rest. Tomorrow, go to Edam to visit your mother.' He thrusts the pouch through the lattice, shakes it, and coins rattle within. 'A gift. Take it.'

The leather is cool and damp to touch, like the mice the cat deposits outside the back door. I drop it into my pocket and its weight drags upon the linen.

My eyes cloud with tears.

He comes to meet me in the archway, slides his hands over my shoulders. 'In a few short weeks the country air will restore your health. In the meantime, Maartje will see to Titus, I will see to myself, and all will be well.'

The thought of Edam makes me long for my mother and Trijn, and the salve of their love. But how can I bear to leave him? I fall against his chest and he strokes my back. He murmurs something I cannot hear.

The Zuiderkerk chimes the third hour. Gently, he eases me back onto my feet. 'I will say goodbye now, for guild officials are irredeemably punctual.' He touches my cheek, and steps away.

I lean against the archway. All will be well. He has promised me that all will be well.

On the threshold of the salon, he turns.

'Geertje.'

Framed in the doorway, he stands like a nobleman in one of his full-length canvases.

'Do not forget to visit the notary's rooms before you leave.'

The salon door closes, and the portrait is gone.

Chapter 39

The farmer's wagon is rigged with canvas, which protects against sleet but channels icy wind into our faces. I draw my hands under my shawl, clutch my bundle to my chest.

On hearing of my trip to Edam, Titus had clung to my neck and had to be appeased with the promise of a swift return. By way of farewell, Maartje surprised me with a present of a cake stuck with almonds, and surprised me further still by clasping me in a brief embrace.

As the wagon pulls into the deserted square, misgivings grow like evening shadows. *Go back*, the horses' hooves seem to say. *Go back, go back.*

In the rain, even the canals are empty, the ducks sheltering among tall reeds along the banks. I pass the bell tower and turn on to Molensteeg.

Trijn's door swings open at the first push of my hand. My cousin is busy chopping cabbage into a copper pot. When she sees me, her knife clatters to the table.

'Geertje! I took you for a ghost!'

I laugh, then start to shake with cold. Trijn wipes her hands on her apron and comes to hug me. She holds me at arm's length for a moment, clucks her tongue, and leads me to the fire.

'You are grown so pale. Why did you not send word that you were coming? But no matter, sit down, I will pour you a mug of ale and we will talk.'

The cottage has not changed in the six years since I joined the master's household. The familiar smell of boiled vegetables and peat smoke is still undercut with a faint tang of lye. Overhead, the wooden beams are cluttered as always with phials and flasks and hung with bunches of dried roots.

I reach out to the flames. The tiles around the hearth have been chipped and crazed for as long as I can remember. A leaping stag bears a crack down the centre and a gambolling dog has a bloom of chalky whiteness where his tail should be.

Trijn rattles plates on the table and fills two mugs.

Once I have eaten a dish of stew and Trijn has relayed all the town's news, she draws her chair close to mine. 'I have much to tell you; I am in despair over my poor knee and though the new doctor promised he would cure the ache in my shoulder, I fear his physic has made it worse, and now my back aches too, but first you must tell me how it has been with your master this past year, for I read trouble in your face.'

I am resolved to tell Trijn everything. How the master spends his evenings on the Prinsengracht, among the society he once told me he abhors. How I burn candles to the wick as I wait for him, hoping he will not send me to bed alone. How he avoids my eyes when I ask about those gatherings. *It would not have interested you. The men talked of poetry and politics; the wives, of servants and children.*

I tell her about my illness, about the doctor who pronounced me well. Here she interrupts to make me promise to see a doctor of her choosing. When I tell her the master has sent me home to recover, and that Otto accompanied me to the notary's house, she stops me with a lift of her hand. 'Why does your master ask you to perform this office now, while your brother is at sea?'

I have no good answer. I dare not think what Pieter will say when he hears the master's terms.

'Otto can read and write as well as Pieter.'

'And was all written down as your master directed?'

'All was done as we agreed. Anything I acquired while in his house is for Titus.'

Trijn folds her arms. 'No doubt the child's aunt will trouble about his prospects. Who will trouble about yours?'

I drain the last of my ale.

Trijn gestures to the back window. 'I am suspicious as the old hen who guards my coop. While the chicks tip their beaks to the dirt, she holds her head alert. I have seen foxes creep forward, tails slung low, only to be vanquished by the beating of her wings.'

'Thankfully I am in no such mortal danger.'

Trijn does not laugh.

I take my shawl from the mantel where she hung it to dry. In the distance, the bell tower marks the quarter hour. The melody that rings so sweetly by day jangles in the dusk.

'It is growing late. You had better stop for the night.' Trijn lights a candle from the fire, sets it in a sconce by the door.

'I could find my way to my mother's house blindfolded, with nothing but the chimes to orient me.'

'If you will not stay then you must take a lantern.'

Trijn wraps the remainder of the bread in muslin and adds it to my bundle. She lights the old lantern with its cracked pane and rusted latch, and touches my hand. 'All will be well now that you are home, Geertje. Once you are fully recovered, Pieter must find you a position with the Company in Rarep, or better still, he may know of a respectable merchant, a widower, perhaps, older than you but in good health, his brood reared . . .'

She talks on. I stare at her in astonishment.

'You cannot think I mean to stay?'

Trijn breaks off mid-sentence. 'Stay? Of course you must not stay in Edam. There is nothing for you here. Perhaps you should go back to Hoorn, they say the burghers there dine from platters of gold.'

'Trijn, I am going back to Amsterdam, back to the master's house. I will stop with my mother no later than Shrove Tuesday.'

'You mean to return to a man who has all but cast you from his home?'

A residue of ale rises to my mouth. I swallow down the bitterness. How old my cousin looks in candlelight. The skin about her eyes is crimped, the white of her hair ill-concealed beneath the folds of her cap.

'You cannot understand love, you who buried an invalid husband a dozen years ago.' The poisonous words burn my throat.

Trijn's gaze holds firm. 'No, Geertje. I understand very well. And that is why I am afraid for you.'

The lantern slips from my hand and oil splashes onto my foot. I wrench the door open and run down the steps into the darkening street.

Rain pelts my face as I make the half hour's journey through mud and slush to my old home.

At dusk, the fields blend into one desolate plain. Candles glimmer in distant cottages: specks of light guiding me along the dirt road like seeds scattered in a furrow. The intermittent melody from the bell tower grows fainter. I imagine Trijn in her warm kitchen hearing the chimes and knowing I must be nearing home.

If she had not spoken as she did, I would not have responded in kind. My words cannot have stung her as much as hers stung me.

The light from my mother's window is weakest of all. I find her asleep in a chair by the fire, her arms crossed in front of her chest. The points of her shoulders seem about to pierce her shawl. In the half-light, her face has a greyish hue. Pieter told me she lived well but I see no sign of plenty in her face.

I light candles, set them along the mantel. On the chimney breast there is a shadow where the shepherdess painting used to hang. A lone nail still protrudes from the render.

I take off my wet shawl and stockings. The cottage is tidy, though it needs sweeping, and a fuzz of dust coats the higher shelves. Smoke mingles with a scent of dried lavender. When I add a cake of peat to the fire, a rising ember catches my hand. I stifle a gasp but make enough noise to wake my mother.

'Trijntje, is that you?' She sits upright, her face alert. Her clouded eyes look past me to the door.

I kneel at her feet, take her thin hands in mine. 'Now can you guess who it is?'

The larder is empty save for some wizened carrots and parsnips, a sack of ground oats and a pot half-full of broth. I sniff the broth, hang the pot over the fire. From my bundle I take Trijn's bread and cut it into chunks. 'When did you last have meat?'

'These days I have little appetite.'

I set a steaming bowl of broth in front of her.

Her fingers flutter over the surface of the table. 'Where is my spoon? You must not move things.'

I give her the spoon, guide her hand to the bowl. She dips a morsel of bread into the broth and chews.

A draught blows around our shoulders. 'Is it always so cold?'

'A pane is missing. I have to stuff the hole with a rag.'

A twist of sodden linen lies on the floor. I force it into the diamond-shaped opening, then find another gap in the leading, and another. The window is checkered with lost panes. The empty lead chills my fingertips, and for a moment I am back in the master's house, his hand brushing mine as he passes a pouch of money through a grating.

'Tomorrow I will buy firewood. When was Pieter last here?'

'Your brother visits whenever he can. I expect him very soon for the rent is due and Jan Ecker has already come scratching at my door like a hungry dog.'

'Pieter must see him and have the window repaired.'

'I worry for your brother's health. He works too hard.'

'And what of your health? You cannot live on cabbage water.' Already she has refused Maartje's cake and bade me take it to the Ecker children.

She clucks her tongue. 'Never mind about that. Tell me again about your fine house in Amsterdam. Does your master eat meat every day?'

Up in the garret, the musty air makes me cough. Swathes of dusty cobwebs carry dried insects in their nets. The window that looks out, one-eyed, from the gable will not open. On rainy days when we could not play outside, that window became a porthole, the cottage, a ship lost at sea. Pieter always played the captain, and I was always a lowly deckhand.

'Come down, Geertje, the ladder is half-rotten,' my mother calls.

When I climb into my mother's old bed, she is already asleep, her mouth slightly open, a braid of hair cutting across her neck.

For a long time, I lie awake. When I think of the master, his face is blurred and I cannot summon his likeness. Then Trijn's face comes unbidden to my mind, wearing the severe look she wore when I left her. Never before have we argued. How could I have spoken as I did?

I push the thought away. Tomorrow she will visit with a conciliatory loaf of bread, or a round of cheese, and I will have my stalwart to guide me again.

The next day it rains, and Trijn does not come.

The master's money pays for firewood and butter and cheese, and enough smoked pork to last a month. When I return from the market, clay clings to my shoes and stains the broken flags that line the floor. The barren fields, the leaching damp, even the raven's hoarse call, seem to mock me. Amsterdam is like a painting I once glimpsed through a rich man's window. Edam is the mud that sucks at my feet.

A week passes, then another. The days grow brighter. My mother stops asking when I mean to visit my cousin. I want to tell Trijn that I am ashamed of what I said and beg her forgiveness. But to admit shame would be to admit there could be truth in her words.

When the new moon rises, my pains return. After my mother falls asleep, I pace the room, walking to Amsterdam. Back in bed, half-dreaming, I smell the sea, the tar from the shipyards, and hear the strike of picks on stone. I watch barges pass through Sint Antoniesluis, slide under the arch of the bridge. When I turn to face the master's house, I awaken.

I get out of bed, heat a brick among the embers, wrap it in cloth, and clutch it to my belly.

'You are sick,' my mother says in the morning. 'That is why you have come home.'

'I am much improved. Soon, I will go back.'

Tears form in her weak eyes. She blinks them away. 'You cannot spend your days here with an old woman and bare fields for company.'

After breakfast, I sweep the floor and take the broom outside to shake it clean. It is a cold spring morning but the pale sun gives an illusion of warmth.

The Ecker children are at play in the clearing, a pup yelping at their feet. One of the older boys calls a greeting to someone approaching from the fields.

I strain my eyes.

The man stops, thrusts his stick into the ground. 'What are you doing here?' my brother Pieter shouts.

Chapter 40

My mother sits by the fire, her hands clasped on her lap. 'Tell your brother to come back inside and warm himself.'

Pieter paces in the clearing. He kicks at a lump of snow, sends a clod of earth knocking against the door.

'There is no time. He will not wait.'

'Ach, young people. Always in a hurry.'

I kiss the top of her cap and she strokes my sleeve.

Sitting on the arm of her chair, I lift the hem of my petticoat. Through the folds, I count the gold rings, the coins, the marriage medal slipped from its ribbon, all sewn inside for safekeeping. I want to prise open the stitches, hold the master's gifts before my eyes once more. Instead, I drop the cloth, feel its gentle pull as it settles around my ankles.

'You must take the rest of the bread with you or it will grow stale.'

'Toast it on the fire later. I will worry if you do not eat.'

The purse the master gave me is half-empty. I leave it on the table for my mother. Then I remember that I have no money and take back some coins.

The door opens and Pieter stands on the threshold.

'How lucky you are to have a brother who takes such interest in your affairs,' my mother says. 'God willing, he will stay with me a few days.'

I go to hug my mother. It is like embracing a sack of kindling. She pulls me close and I breathe in her lavender pomade.

'Mend your quarrel with your cousin before you go,' she whispers, sliding a papery hand into mine.

'There was no quarrel.' I can hardly keep from crying.

We walk to the town centre in silence, Pieter always ahead.

Without the clutter of stalls on market day, the square seems bigger, barer. We turn onto a narrow street. By the butcher's shop we brush past a cart laden with carcasses. Mingled smells of blood and manure fill my nostrils. Pieter stops at the Silver Goblet. Outside the tavern, two boys tussle on a stone bench. One holds a terrier pup and the other means to have it. 'Wait here,' Pieter says, the first time he has spoken to me since the diatribe delivered at the cottage.

'I want to buy tobacco,' I call after him. 'A gift for the master.'

He turns. The onset of a beard is already darkening his shaven face.

'Be quick about it.' He pushes the door open, releasing a condensed odour of beer and smoke and unwashed bodies into my face.

How long will it take Pieter to secure my passage to Amsterdam? I imagine old acquaintances gathering round him, work-worn hands slapping his back. A tankard will be placed in front of him, his pipe filled again and again. With no clear plan of what to say, I dash through the winding streets to Trijn's house.

As I run, my feet grow lighter and my heart grows giddy with relief. I turn into Molensteeg, climb the steps, push open the door.

But the woman inside is not Trijn.

The neighbour, whose name I have forgotten, clutches her scrubbed red hands to her bosom. 'Geertje, is that you? You startled me.' On the table between us stand three of Trijn's remedies, the bottles uncorked. 'You grow more like your poor mother every day.'

I greet the woman as shortly as politeness will allow.

'Where is my cousin?'

'Did you not hear?' She edges around the table. Her eager eyes put me in dread of what she is going to say.

'She has gone to Volendam; her brother's wife sent word that Gerrit is dying and she would have nobody but Trijn to help her. Had you knocked on my door these past three weeks I could have told you so.'

'I have been busy. My mother . . .'

'She asked me to tend to the hens. I wonder she did not charge you with that task.' A sly smile cuts across her face.

I sidestep her, nod at the phials on the table. 'Are the hens ailing?'

'You are dressed for travel. I will not delay you. Is there any message you want to leave for your cousin?'

In that instant, what I want to say to Trijn becomes clear in my mind. *I am sorry; I was wrong to use you so. In truth, I am afraid of how the master will meet me on my return.*

It could be months before I speak to her again.

'Tell her I had to go back,' I say slowly.

The woman cannot hide her disappointment. 'Is that all?'

I should hurry back to Pieter but my feet drag on the cobbles. I take a meandering route down streets I have not walked in years.

'Geertje!' A woman leans out of the moneylender's shop. Wary, I cross to the door, intending to go no further.

'I thought it was you.' Giertgen Nanningh's smile falters. She looks up and down the street, takes a backwards step inside.

'Come in.'

Pieter could be waiting outside the tavern, or perhaps he is walking the streets in his impatient way and has already seen me enter here. Trijn once told me it was a kindness to fail to recognise the women who hid their faces behind their shawls as they ducked into Mistress Nanningh's shop with their husband's winter coat, or a set of tarnished spoons. Never before had I spoken to the moneylender, nor could I guess how she knew me.

An oblong window, set too high to encourage onlookers, admits little light into the shop. Every wall is covered in pictures and paintings and maps. More frames stand on the ground, propped against the walls. A prickling of my skin tells me the eyes of my mother's shepherdess are upon me.

I turn my attention to the counter and a heap of coats, breeches and gowns. An edge of fur sweeps the floor like a tail. Further up the pile, a lace cuff pokes out as though attempting to escape the weight of its fellows.

'I remember you as a little girl, playing on the canal banks with your brother. You always looked so happy. One day as I watched from the bridge, you called out to me to join you. But by then, I was already working here.' Giertgen rests a hand on a child's smock, fingering the embroidered linen.

'That same brother awaits me now.'

'I will not delay you.' For a moment I think she is about to take my arm; her hand reaches into the air between us, falls to her side.

'Lately your mother sent word that she would visit me when your brother returned. I want you to tell her she must not venture out in this cold weather. In fact, I do not expect her before *kermis* time.'

One of the neighbours would have brought my mother to the square, pretending not to notice the parcel wrapped in cloth. Guided by the bells, my mother would have found the street corner, counted shopfronts with her hands until she reached Giertgen's door.

'I will tell her,' I say, though I know not when I will see my mother again.

By the time I reach the tavern I remember that I was supposed to be buying tobacco for the master, who rarely takes a pipe.

When Pieter emerges, he has forgotten the ruse. He leads me to a corner of the square where a boy is sluicing buckets of canal water over a soiled cart. Once the driver is satisfied with Pieter's offer, the boy covers an empty cage with sacking to make my seat. He hands me up, then slides the bolts home.

Pieter leans over the side, his breath thick with malt.

'Fix this, Geertje, or it will be worse for all of us.'

I remember the enemies the master mentioned. Have Pieter's troubles resurfaced?

The driver touches a switch to the horse's flank.

'I have little money.' The wheels roll forward. 'The master says he pays my wages directly to you.'

'As well he might,' Pieter says. 'You have no small mouths to feed.'

The cart pulls out of the square, crosses the town walls, passes the fields and meadows surrounding my mother's cottage. As I take my last sight of Edam, the bells chime, tinny and discordant, in the distance.

Chapter 41

After the quiet of Edam, Amsterdam thrums with activity. A babble of competing voices rises from the market. Beaks, claws, feathers thrust from cages. Hands pull at my elbows, forcing me to look upon basins of purple crayfish, trays of writhing eels. I shrug them off.

It is a crisp day; already past noon. At this hour, the master will have set his pupils their tasks for the rest of the day. Leaving them in their partitions, he will descend the stairs to his pigments and brushes and the easel that dominates the room like a scaffold. I see him, standing in the northern light, his hand moving swiftly across the canvas, laying one assured stroke upon another, smiling at his own skill. I could tiptoe upstairs, fasten teasing hands about his eyes, whisper in his ear that I am returned.

In the distance, clouds hang over the Zuiderkerk, painting the cockerel dull as pewter. The notion that I should not leave the square until its colour is restored anchors my feet to the ground. I stand, still as the church spire, and wait until the clouds part, the sun performs its alchemy, and once again the cockerel shines like gold.

Too soon I am crossing the bridge by the sluice, climbing the steps to the master's house. The iron knocker gleams like a blue-black bracelet. My reflection stares back at me from the polished front door. When I press the flat of my hand to the smooth surface, a ghost-hand reaches out to push me away. The door is bolted.

The handrails have been polished too, and the steps are freshly scrubbed. I descend to street level, round the corner by the canal, and enter the alley. A smell of lye rises from the shaded cobbles.

In the kitchen Maartje looks up from the table, her face blank, as though she does not know me. I clasp her stiff shoulders in a hug.

'Where is Titus?'

She points her knife to the window.

Titus is in the courtyard, his cheeks flushed with cold, wearing a cap pulled low over his ears. About his neck hangs a drum, which he strikes at intervals with one of Maartje's wooden spoons. While he beats time, a woman's voice rises and falls in song.

The woman stands outside the open door to the courtyard, her back to me. She wears a skirt of russet wool, and an embroidered bodice over ballooning white sleeves. Her song promises victory in battle for brave-hearted men. Titus marches solemnly across the yard.

'Geertje!' He pushes past the woman and I am almost bowled over by the force of his embrace. I lift him up, and his small fierce arms clamp around my neck. I hug him as tightly as his drum will allow.

'You are grown taller! And heavier too.' I set him down, smooth my hands over his cheeks.

'Are you better now?' His little forehead wrinkles in concern.

'Much better.'

The woman in the doorway has turned around and I feel her eyes upon me.

'You will not leave again?' Titus presses.

I laugh. 'I will not leave again.' I kiss the top of his head and look up at the woman.

She is perhaps twenty, plump and pretty, with round cheeks and large dark eyes. A half-smile hangs about her lips as though some amusing thought is playing through her mind.

'I am newly returned from Edam,' I say, and she makes a slight nod with no change of expression.

'See my new drum!' Titus thumps a fist against the skin.

'It is very fine. You must play it for me.'

'Hendrickje says I must not play it in the house when Papa is working.'

The young woman is at the back door, taking Titus's coat from a peg. He lifts the drum from around his neck, catching his curls in the strap.

I reach to take the coat but already Hendrickje is holding it out to him. She slides it onto his shoulders and waves him off from the alley.

When she goes upstairs to retrieve the master's tray, I join Maartje at the table.

'When did the new maid arrive?'

Maartje does not answer. A smell of rotting fish wafts from the parcel of cod she is unwrapping. She tosses the offender into the bucket of waste by her feet, takes a knife to its fellows.

'She may help you down here,' I say. 'I am fully recovered, and will hardly need her at all.'

Maartje's blade whittles at the fish, strips lattices of bone from flesh.

'Why did you come back?' Her usual gruffness, but with a new note of concern. I would rather face her darkest mood than know that she is worried about me.

An oily hand shoots out to grip my wrist. 'Five tiles to the left of the fire, behind the picture of a ship, is the hollow wherein my money is hid.'

The words come thickly through the stumps of her teeth. I am too frightened to break her hold.

'Why are you telling me this?' My voice scratches my throat like sand.

'Have you ever lived on the streets, begged for your bread? Put a little aside this quarter, a little more the next.'

'The master would never put you out, Maartje,' I say carefully.

She casts my hand away as though tossing a fish bone into the cesspit.

My eyes slide to the hearth, seeking the tile she described, and there it is: a ship in stormy waters, its sails full, its bow rearing in the waves.

In the hanging room, the bed has been stripped of its covers and someone has beaten the imprint of my body from the mattress. The lid of the wicker chest sits a fraction higher than it should. When I open it, I find the contents neatly folded, but not as I left them. The mistress's silk scarf sits atop my clothing.

The bareness of the shelf by the window discomfits me until I reinstate my comb, my medal, my half-torn prayer.

With a cry, I remember the painting. I drop to the floor. The portrait lies under the bed, wrapped in muslin, as I left it.

Gently I unroll the canvas, see again how the young apprentice saw me three years ago, and how, with a few strokes of his brush, the master altered me. The painted woman's sidelong glance makes me uneasy, as though she sees some consequence beyond the frayed edges. Did she always avoid my gaze? I roll the painting up in its cloth, push it back beneath the bed.

From the chest I take a bodice the master gave me years ago. In the half-light of my room, it could be earth-brown, or even black. Tonight, by candlelight, it will glow burgundy-red. 'Choose anything,' he had said, that day in the draper's shop. In the end, he chose for me, draping a swathe of red satin across my shoulders.

The bodice slides over my arms, cool and smooth as glass. I lace up the front. Tiny bumps rise on my skin.

I go to the window where I first undressed for him and look across the empty courtyard. The new maid is lighting candles in the salon. Soon she will call the master for his meal. Better to meet him downstairs than disturb him at his work.

When I reach the salon, I almost collide with Hendrickje who is about to leave the room. A hearty fire burns in the grate. On the table she has laid one plate, one mug and one wine glass, which throws a pale green glow across the cloth.

'You may tell the master that I am home and will dine with him tonight.'

Her head bobs, betraying no surprise.

'I will bring another setting.' The door closes softly behind her.

I close my eyes, take every step of the stairs with her. I am there when she leans in the doorway of the painting room, there too, when she calls out to the master.

Soon, he will come to me.

But when the salon door opens, it is Hendrickje again, this time carrying a large tray. I help her to unload the basket of bread, the platter of cured ham, the jug of wine. She waits for me to take the second plate, glass and mug, as though uncertain of where to place them.

I smile at her. 'Where do you come from?'

'Bredevoort. This is my first time away from home.'

Was that the sound of a door closing upstairs? In moments, I will be alone with him. I arrange and rearrange the settings.

Hendrickje polishes the blade of a paring knife against her apron.

When the master comes in, a reeling sensation makes me grasp the back of a chair. It is the old master, the man I fell in love with. A faint smell of linseed oil rises from his person. He is painting again, and in as buoyant a mood as I have ever seen him. Beard and whiskers are neatly trimmed, and his unruly hair has been tamed beneath a flat velvet cap. With hearty force he drags his chair out from the table, throws his bulk onto the seat.

'So it is true, you have come back. How are all in Edam?'

Hendrickje straightens the breadbasket, wipes a drop from the lip of the jug.

'All are well. I hope I find you well too.' The blandness of my answer pains me. Hendrickje turns her attention to the candles, taking the one from the mantel and bringing it to the table. As she sets it down, the flame flares against her cheek.

The master takes a roundel of bread, tears it in two, bites and chews.

At last, Hendrickje asks if that will be all. He waves her away, and we are alone.

'Be kind to her,' he says, as her footsteps fade. 'She has lost her father, her brothers, too.'

'I am always kind.'

He makes no reply, nor does he rise to embrace me, only fills my glass and his. I take my usual seat by his side.

'We must drink to your health, Geertje.'

When did he start to take wine instead of ale in the evenings? My hand shakes as I bring the glass to my lips. The wine is thick and purplish. It prickles my throat. I take another mouthful.

'What have you been painting?'

He talks about his work in the way he did when the mistress was alive, eyes bright, hands shaping air. He tells me of a supper-scene at an inn; draws imaginary lines to illustrate points of perspective, jumps up and pulls out another chair to mark where the third figure will sit.

I pour more wine. Moisture collects on the prunts of my glass, trickles down my wrist as I drink. When he pushes his plate away, I rise and go to him. Before he can speak, I slide onto the warmth of his thighs, touch my lips to his forehead. His breath comes hot and fast against my breasts. One arm clutches my waist, pulling me closer, then his fingers are tugging at the strings of my bodice, his mouth is on my neck. The joy of having him restored to me makes me want to cry aloud.

He stands, gripping my thighs, and presses me against the wall between the windows. My fingers drink the textures of his face: the furrow that cleaves his brow, the wires that spring from his jaw.

The ebony mirror with its frame of twining foliage digs into my back. Ahead of me hangs the mistress's portrait. I close my eyes to all but him.

When it is over he releases me, leans back on the table as though dazed. I try to take his hand but he half-turns, reaches for the last of his wine and drinks it down.

The house is too quiet. For a moment I imagine Maartje and Hendrickje crouching outside the door, listening to all that passes between us. Would he laugh if I shared the fancy with him?

The empty glass thumps the table. 'It is late. I have work to do.' He takes a candle, goes to the door.

'I will wait up for you.' An eyelet at the top of my bodice has been torn out. I fasten the laces as best I can.

He pauses without turning around. 'You must be tired. You should sleep. I bid you goodnight.'

After he leaves, I go to the window, push the curtain aside. Across the courtyard, a candle flickers in the oak-press room.

I let the curtain fall back into place.

The last of the wine has grown warm. It coats my teeth, makes me crave pure water.

When all candles but one are snuffed out, I go to the mistress's portrait.

'I am back.'

Her gentle eyes gaze down upon me.

I drag a chair closer to the fire. Standing on the seat, I lift the candle to her face. Her eyes I know to be brown, yet they are painted with green, pink, yellow, black. Their radiance comes from the slightest touch of white in each iris. How does he capture truth with deceit?

I blow out the flame, climb down, and find my way to the door in the dark.

Chapter 42

June, 1649

'It is nothing.' Otto touches the purple stain around his eye and winces.

Instead of whistling over his work, Otto crouches on a stool in the back room, dabbing his cheek with a wet cloth. The walls exude midday heat as though we are trapped in a firebox. The only window in here overlooks a yard shared with a brewer, and is kept closed against the stifling smell of hops. A drizzle of sweat escapes my cap, runs down the nape of my neck.

Ignoring Otto's protestations, I take his chin in my hand, turn his face to examine the damage. A raw patch shines on his cheekbone where the signet ring tore skin. Clear liquid oozes from the fissure.

Out front, the bell over the door trills. A woman in black silk enters the shop, an ebony fan held in one languid hand. Marten looks up from the worktable, sets his knife down with a sigh.

'The sight of me might startle the fine ladies of Amsterdam,' Otto says.

I close the curtain, hiding us from view.

'How did you get away?'

'His second swing missed, threw him off-balance. I left him rolling in a piss-filled gutter.'

Otto gulps a mouthful of ale, rattles the mug onto the window ledge.

I take the crumpled cloth from his hand, swap it for a fresh one from the basin.

He holds the compress to his eye for a moment, then tosses it back into the water. 'I cannot work with a cloth held to my face.'

'Trijn would know what to do. An unguent of comfrey might help.'

'I have no need of plasters or potions.' He lifts the mug again but instead of drinking, presses the cool metal to his burning cheek.

I sit beside him. 'You must be more careful.'

'How often have I heard you say that?'

'Perhaps now you will pay heed.'

Out in the shop, the woman is protesting: the calfskin is too thick or too thin, too light or too dark.

Otto wipes his brow on his sleeve. The awl tumbles from behind his ear, clatters to the floor.

'Aefje has been ill.'

'Your cousin?'

'She is not really a cousin.' He seems about to say more, stops. The anguish on his face alarms me.

'What ails her?'

'She called here last week, so frail it frightened me. It is more of the same trouble.' Stooping, he retrieves the awl, turns it over in his hands. 'This time she thought she would die on the old woman's table. I begged her never to take such a risk again.'

For a moment I close my eyes, will away the image of a writhing girl, a rag in her mouth, her linen soaked in blood.

'Does her lover know?'

'He is the rogue who sent her to the witch. Now his house is locked up and he is gone with his wife to Milan.'

Otto shields his injured eye from a sudden dart of sunshine. 'Enough of my worries. How is it with your master?'

'He has taken to his walks again. It seems he is more often out of the house than in it.'

'What of the new maid, have you befriended her?'

'She has no need of friends.'

When I address Hendrickje, her polite replies have the finality of rebuffs. If we are alone in the kitchen together, she sings to herself, as though to ward off conversation. She never hurries, not even when Maartje calls sharply, and yet fires are lit, water is heated and floors are scrubbed ahead of time. No fault can be found with her work, except that it is so thorough as to make my role superfluous.

'Then Maartje is your only friend in that house.'

'Maartje thinks I am a fool.'

'At least you have Titus.'

I make a task of wringing water from the compresses, folding them into neat squares.

On returning from school, Titus runs first to Hendrickje's arms. His favourite game is to clamber upon her back and cling to her neck as she capers around the courtyard. Their whoops would disturb the master's work, if he were home.

Until bedtime, she indulges the boy so that he pays my directions no heed. If I try to speak to him alone she is likely to approach sidelong with some stratagem to draw his attention. There are days when I suspect her of inciting him against me, then suspect myself of baseless jealousy.

I hand Otto a wad of damp linen and obediently he presses it to his eye.

'Hendrickje is young and pretty,' I say. 'Titus is charmed by her.'

The bell over the front door sounds again, marking the customer's departure. Otto drops the compress, pulls his scarf low over his injured eye.

'You might be taken for a pirate.'

He manages to laugh. He holds the curtain aside for me and we go out into the shop. On seeing us, Marten's eyes brighten; it is past his dinner time.

Otto stops short of the door to the street. 'Have you had any reply from Trijn?'

'None.'

Since he wrote my letter, carefully coded to disappoint the schoolteacher's curiosity, I have become desperate for a response. Every morning I search the master's correspondence for a fold of paper bearing the shape of my name.

'She may still be at her brother's house,' Otto says. 'Why not visit her there?'

'I dare not leave Amsterdam. Pieter has forbidden it.'

'A device to protect his interests or yours?'

'Our interests are the same.'

Marten clears his throat.

'Go,' Otto says. 'Eat!' He claps the boy on the shoulder, hands him a coin. Marten skips out onto the street.

'I must go home.'

Otto lays a hand on my arm. 'Tarry a while.' He bolts the door. The bruise around his eye is edging onto the bridge of his nose. Today, no one would suppose he is not yet thirty.

'My father grows weaker every day, Geertje. Soon this shop and all in it will belong to Marten.'

'Your father would put his grandson before his son?'

Otto laughs. 'The man I call my father puts blood before water. Have you never noticed how unalike we are?'

It must be a year since I last saw Otto's father, and longer again since the old man stood at the shop counter, his head bent over the ledger.

'My mother confessed her transgression and he loved her enough to forgive her. When I was born, he gave me his name. But the first day of my life proved to be the last of hers. I think he has never recovered from losing her.'

'And what of your true father?'

'Of him, I know nothing. He may have been a sailor. Or a soldier. Perhaps I have Spanish blood.'

'So the man you call your father means to leave you with nothing?'

'Not nothing. He has made a match for me with Aefje. Her father has money. Enough to buy us a house with room for a shop.'

'You cannot marry for money.'

'Aefje and I have long agreed that one should save the other, if trouble comes.' Otto touches his cheek. 'I suspect that I am being followed. And Aefje has lately been in mortal danger. Sooner or later the marriage will take place and I must leave the city for good.'

'So I am to lose my only friend in Amsterdam?' My eyes are hot with tears.

'It may not happen for six months, perhaps a year, and when it does, you can take the *trekschuit* to visit me. You will like Aefje, and she will like you.'

He slides the bolt free. When the door swings open, heat and dust blast my face.

'Was I wrong to tell you this now? We do not have to speak of it again.'

I shake my head, nod my head, cannot answer. I step out onto the street, unsteady as though I have spent a day at sea.

Chapter 43

All the way home, my legs are heavy as though I am wading through soup. Three days of sunshine have made cesspools of the canals. Noxious fumes rise from the water, funnel through the narrow streets. I swallow to quell my rising nausea.

Never had I thought of losing Otto. Without his friendship, Amsterdam is a sieve I could slip through and disappear. I remember when I first arrived in the city, how I clung to the railings of the bridge until they stained my hands with rust.

My fists are clenched. I release them, walk on through the crowd.

A group has formed outside the gates of the Zuiderkerk. On a platform of wooden crates, a quacksalver displays his wares. Though the man's tunic and cap are worn, they are clean, and his beard is neatly slicked against his chin. Some allure in his green eyes and singsong patter entices me into the circle.

An array of coloured bottles is spread out before the man. There are phials of liquid, bags of powder, and what look like fish scales collected in jars. Above his head he holds a flask of silver liquid, tilting and turning it in the sun, all the while chanting a list of ailments it can cure. When he calls for a stuiver, a pock-faced young man steps forward. The stranger floats the stuiver on the shining surface, swills the flask to demonstrate that the coin will not sink. He pours a drop of the liquid into his palm where it rolls about like a bauble before he tips it back into the flask.

I look at the remedies and think of the bruises on Otto's skin. But Trijn often warned me against charlatans who travel from town to town, never lingering long enough to account for the harm done by their potions. In vain, the scarred young man calls for his coin to be returned. The stranger has turned his attention to the women in the crowd, telling of creams to smooth the complexion. I turn away, head for the bridge.

As I pass a flower cart, a girl in a grey apron catches my arm, thrusts a bunch of yarrow under my nose. I mean to free myself and walk away, but the pure, sweet scent refreshes my senses as though the blossoms are the only clean things left in the city.

I dig into the pocket at my waist.

Now that I have smelled the yarrow, I cannot leave it behind.

'It is past its best.' The girl returns one coin to me. Broken teeth shine through her smile.

I take an armful of stems and hold the blossoms close to my face until I reach the house.

Indoors, the scent is stronger. At the kitchen table, I trim the water-logged ends, fill a pitcher at the pump. Out in the courtyard, Maartje squats on the step, sucking peaceably on her pipe. A strain of song floats across the cobbles from the open door of the laundry room.

Upstairs in the salon a breeze enters the open windows, ruffling the curtains as I rest the pitcher on the table.

'Where have you been?'

The unexpected voice makes me jump. The master is sitting in one of the tall-backed chairs at the hearth, his eyes fixed on the empty grate. About his person I see no chalk, no book, no letters.

'You startled me. I am surprised to find you home so early.'

'I ask you again, where have you been this past hour and more?' His coldness frightens me more than his anger ever could.

'I called to Otto's shop, then walked around a little. I did not expect to see you before evening.'

'The shoemaker gives you flowers?'

'I bought them to mask the smell of the canals.' I hold out a spray and he waves it away.

'They cause my eyes to water.'

His mood is unsteady as a ship pitched on a swell. I set the yarrow down on the table, go to place a hand on his shoulder. 'I am sorry I was not here when you came home.'

He stands, shrugging off my hand. 'I intend to be home more often. I have had enough of outdoor sketching.'

'I am glad to hear it.'

'I will need a model.'

How I used to long for him to paint me. Now I have learned not to hope.

'Will you have Anke back again?'

'Anke grows less reliable and more expensive every day.'

My legs are trembling. I sink into the opposing chair.

He raises a hand to the mantel. His fine lawn shirt and twilled breeches are those he normally wears to evening gatherings at the homes of burghers and diplomats on the Prinsengracht. Perhaps he has secured a new commission.

'I want Hendrickje to sit for me.' He frowns. 'I expect you will object.'

Does he mean to seek my approval? But these are statements, not requests. I lift my chin, straighten my back. 'Your work comes first, that has always been understood.'

His forehead relaxes. 'The extra duties might prove taxing for you.'

'Do not think of it.'

He nods. 'We start tomorrow, as soon as the pupils leave.'

On his way out, he calls over his shoulder. 'Tell Maartje I will dine late.'

The door closes behind him.

In the hall, I stand on a chair to take the Chinese vase with its swooping blue birds and robed figures down from the oak cabinet.

What kind of painting does he mean to make?

Back in the salon, I pour water into the vase and fill it with the yarrow. Loose blossoms scatter onto the tablecloth like tiny white stars.

I remember Anke's bloated body, her coarse laugh, how she leaned towards the stove to soak up its paltry heat.

Some flower heads have browned around the edges. I set those stems aside. When the rest are arranged to my satisfaction, I centre the vase on the table. Something else is lying on the cloth. I pick up the small, fuzzed body of a dead bee, turn it over in my palm. Its back is arched, its body curled as though it had been trying to roll onto its feet.

I take the bee to one of the open windows. When I blow it from my hand, a gust of wind catches and lifts it in a mockery of flight.

Chapter 44

Next morning I rise later than usual and find Maartje alone in the kitchen. A cloudy spoon abandoned in a scraped dish tells me Titus has already eaten breakfast and gone to school. When I clear the ware, a telltale ring of brown sugar is left behind on the table.

'Maartje, you are spoiling him.'

She is tipping a jug of sour milk into a bowl. Without looking up, she inclines her head towards the courtyard.

White linen glares in the sun. Hendrickje is hanging washing out to dry. Fragments of her song drift inwards as she nears the window. I should rap on the glass, tell her to take the washing back down, to wait until Maartje has had her morning pipe lest she puff smoke onto the master's sheets. But the thought of Hendrickje displeasing the master pleases some new meanness in me.

Maartje slaps a floury ball onto the table, sending a cloud of white dust over her notebook and my breakfast. She stretches and folds the dough. I blow flour from the book's worn cover. The pages serve me as a fan while I eat a plate of yesterday's bread and herring. Maartje mops her forehead with her sleeve and I fan her too. She laughs, waves me away.

Hendrickje pushes in through the door, sets down the linen basket. She acknowledges me with a demure nod. At the table, she pours a mug of ale, drinks too quickly, and catches a drizzle from her chin with a fingertip. Her face is dewy and the channel between her breasts glistens. Is this how she will pose for him: eyes lowered, neck bare? A fancy grips me that if I sank my fingers into her pliant cheeks, twisted and kneaded her face, her flesh would recover itself and bear no mark of my hands.

'I will work in the kitchen with Maartje this morning,' I tell her.

She nods again.

Do I imagine a curling of the corners of her lips? She fills a pail, takes a scrubbing brush, and goes upstairs to the hall.

I open the delivery book, study the last page of signs and ticks. None but the butcher's account has been paid.

'Maartje, why did you not ask the master to settle this week's accounts?'

For a moment Maartje stops her pummelling, glances at me, her face inscrutable.

I turn back one page, then another. The bills have not been paid these past three weeks.

I close the book and smile. 'Likely he is waiting on settlement from a customer.'

A tear drops from my eye, clears a spot on the flour-coated table.

Maartje dumps the dough into a pan, covers it with a cloth. She fills two mugs with ale, brings one to me.

'He is going to paint her, Maartje, did you know that?'

My tears are falling freely now. She stands by my chair, exhaling wheezy breaths. Her familiar stale odour comforts me. I want to rest my head on her shoulder, weep like a child.

'Take yourself away from this house.'

'I have nothing. I have nowhere to go. My brother will not let me leave.'

Maartje makes a noise at the back of her throat, screws her mouth into a knot, spits into the fire.

Next morning, I enter the salon early. Already, the master's pitcher and basin have been removed, the floor has been swept, the bed curtains closed. Did he even sleep at home last night? I touch the neatly folded sheets. His scent is lost beneath the fragrant beeswax Hendrickje rubs into the oak bedstead.

A warm breeze ruffles the yarrow, reviving its perfume. The stems are fewer in number than yesterday. I imagine Hendrickje stopping by the vase, seeking out tattered blossoms, reaching for her knife.

I throw the door open, go to the hall and walk across the wet tiles Hendrickje is scrubbing. She lifts her head, gapes as I pass.

The front door crashes closed behind me. Outside on the steps, I breathe deeply.

Across the street, a woman is standing in the shade. For a moment I take her for the maid of the tobacco merchant's house, and am minded to ask her to walk with me. But the woman I see is not the friendly maid. As I pass, she ducks her head, and I continue alone.

I head for the Nieuwmarkt in search of distraction, casting not a glance towards Otto's shop. If I am soon to lose him, then best to spread the pain thin over time.

Among the bustling stalls, I play a game from childhood: I am a rich lady who lives in a fine house and I may buy anything I desire. I fill an imaginary basket with the best of fruit and nuts, pastries and cheeses. But the game fails, as it always does, because I have no money. My eyes slide from fat lemons and cloudy green grapes back to bruised apples rolling in the bottom of a crate.

I have almost reached the weigh house when I notice the quack-salver from yesterday, addressing a gathering on the fringes of the market. Gone is the wooden platform; today, a smaller sample of remedies is ranged on top of a case and his call has quietened almost to a murmur. A dozen eager women circle the makeshift stall.

'Three drops on the tongue before and after the act.' He passes a phial of dark liquid around the group. Some refuse to take it; others hold it up to the light and tilt the bottle as though they can determine efficacy by sight alone.

'On which tongue must it drop,' a woman in a yellowing cap shouts, and a burst of coarse laughter follows.

The peddler shows no sign of irritation. He pauses, his eyes calculating the appropriate interval.

'While no gentlemen are present, I have something special to show you.' He beckons the women closer.

'They all think they have something special to show us,' the woman in the faded cap calls.

This time, the laughter is muted. There is a gentle jogging of elbows; the women move forward. I find an opening and draw nearer. He holds up a fist, flicks his hand open to reveal a muslin sachet, snaps his fingers closed as though he fears someone will snatch the prize.

'This powder will stir desire in the most indifferent of men. It is tasteless, odourless; ground so fine it may be mixed with the plainest of food and drink and escape detection. Within weeks, lovesick maids become happy brides, and married women enjoy their husband's renewed vigour.'

His fingers uncurl, his outstretched hand brushes my shoulder. The sachet, tied with golden thread, sits on his palm. Without thinking, I reach out and take it. I press my thumb to the muslin. Warmth radiates from within. The peddler's green eyes meet mine, and in that moment I am certain he can help me.

A shoulder jostles me from behind. The sachet is plucked from my hand. Women ply the man with questions. Trijn's scornful voice floats into my mind. *These fools believe the sand they feed their lovers is made of dried lizard's pizzles and henbane gathered at moonlight. Let us hope they conduct their lovemaking near a privy.*

I turn abruptly, almost colliding with a figure dressed in a plain grey bodice and skirt. She looks away, but I recognise her as the woman I saw earlier on the Breestraat, and I have seen her elsewhere too, though I cannot recollect where. Before I can study her face, she lowers her head, pushes past a hawker whose outstretched arms are draped with strings of amber beads, and slips into the crowd.

Chapter 45

Too soon, I reach the bridge, and the master's house looms. I slow my step.

A barge laden with sacks of coal is waiting to pass through Sint Antoniesluis. On the bank, the lock-keeper bites down on his pipe, turns the windlass with both hands. His shoulders strain against the spokes. Water gushes into the chamber. Across the channel, his counterpart shouts; they leave their posts, push the barriers open. The skipper waves and the barge glides forward, its green-fringed bow clearing the gates by a palm's width.

How often I held a wriggling Titus up to see this spectacle. If he were here now, he would scowl, pull at my sleeve. *Geertje, you are too slow!*

For a moment I imagine running along the bank beside the departing barge, jumping the narrow passage of water, landing on the deck. I could crouch among the sacks, the glittering coal dust stinging my palms, and let the canals take me far from here.

Sun beats down on my forehead. Behind me, the bells of the Zuiderkerk chime six o'clock. Today, the master is unlikely to have noticed my absence.

Titus sits at the kitchen table, kicking his feet against the chair legs, a primer open in front of him.

'Geertje, will you hear my verse? The schoolmaster said I did not know it, but I did, only I forgot it when he asked, and the other boys laughed.'

On hearing his aggrieved tone, I almost laugh too, but take the book and assume a serious expression. He recites a string of Latin and when he finishes, I praise him, land a kiss on his head of curls.

'You smell of leaves,' I tell him, but he has turned his attention to the contents of his pockets. A handful of polished knuckle bones spills onto the table, colliding with a cloth-covered tray.

I lift the cloth to discover a cold meal ready to be served. Among the dishes, a ham hock shines, pink and fatty, on a platter. Beside it, a jug brims with burgundy wine.

'Where is Hendrickje?'

'My father is painting her picture. He has been a long time and Maartje says he will take his dinner while he works.'

The tray is heavy; the earthenware jug throws the load off-balance.

'Geertje, I know a secret!'

I land the tray awkwardly, upsetting a dish of olives.

'What secret?'

He holds his finger to his lips, shakes his head, and goes back to swapping bones in and out of line.

I take a long breath. His grubby hands range the bones by size.

'Is it about Hendrickje?'

He looks up, his face triumphant. 'I knew you would not guess it!'

I press my palms flat against the grain of the table, study restless whorls and knots in the oak.

Titus glances over his shoulder to the courtyard, leans back towards me. 'It is about a ship,' he whispers.

Maartje comes in through the open door, sees the scattering of bones. 'I warned you.'

He crams his treasures into his pocket. 'Tonight I am going to beat Joost, and then I will be champion.' He heads for the backdoor.

'Come home when the bells ring seven o'clock,' I call as his feet clatter down the alley.

I scoop stray olives back into the dish, lift the tray again.

Maartje stands by my shoulder. 'He asked me to bring it.'

I force a smile. 'Then I will surprise him.'

Every tread of the stairs seems narrower than before, every foot-hold, uncertain. The gloom on the bends alternates with shafts of light channelled through the interior windows.

Hendrickje's voice drifts downwards from the painting room. Has she not yet learned that the master prefers to work in silence? At the top of the stairs, a peal of laughter rings out. The master's timbre soon joins it.

Wine slops from the lip of the jug, splashes my arm.

I push the door open with my foot.

He sits in the centre of the room, the easel hiding his face.

To the right, Hendrickje reclines on a settle, leaning on one elbow as though about to rise. She wears the same skirt and bodice from this morning, but draped across one shoulder and tucked beneath her breasts is a length of antique cambric.

The master lifts his head, sees me at the door. 'Stay as you are,' he says to Hendrickje.

On the table by the window, I set down the platter, the jug.

'You block the light.' The master stows his brush and rises from his stool. Joining me at the table, he takes out his knife.

'Have you been bathing in my wine, Geertje?'

A purple stain seeps through my sleeve. I blot it with my handkerchief, staining that too.

He cuts a sliver of meat, flicks it from the blade into his mouth.

Without the tray, my hands seem weightless. I clasp them together.

Hendrickje's head is thrust forward, her back curved. The pose must hurt her neck.

'How does the painting come along?'

'As yet, I cannot tell.'

'May I see it?'

He chews on a seeded crust of bread.

'Not now.'

In the salon, I count seven chimes from the Zuiderkerk. What if the master brings Hendrickje in here to discuss the painting? Must I endure his proclamations, her coy returns? I pour a glass of sweet white wine. At a quarter past the hour, Titus's excited voice rises from the kitchen. He has won the evening's contest. I imagine him pulling on his nightgown while Maartje stoops to gather a trail of discarded garments. I pour more wine, rest my chin on my hand.

Nine chimes. Hendrickje's footsteps pass the salon door.

Maartje must be asleep by now, her bed shutters closed against the last of the light. In a corner of the dim kitchen, Hendrickje will unroll her ticking and sleep there as she always does.

The slam of the front door wakes me. The master's boots rattle down the stone steps and fade into the street.

The flocked curtain had been cushioning my cheek. I raise my head, rub my neck. How often have I waited here alone, while he dines with artists and burghers in the mansions of the Herengracht?

A smell of decay hangs about the yarrow. Stems droop under wilting blooms. Let Hendrickje dispose of them in the morning.

I will wait no more for him. I swallow the last of the wine.

In the hallway I take a candle from the sconce, climb the stairs, and climb again, steadying myself against the wall. The dull pounding in my head grows heavier with every step.

Moonlight filters into the painting room. He forgot to close the shutters.

The painting is covered with a cloth and rests on its easel, facing the window. I stand behind it, touch the wooden skeleton on which the canvas is stretched. How much force would it take to punch a hole through its taut skin? Or I could daub the surface with crimson, ochre, bone-black, making it mine. A burst of laughter echoes around the room. I clasp a hand over my mouth.

Slowly, I bring the candle round to see what he has made.

When I lift the cloth, Hendrickje undresses.

The skirt and bodice from today are gone. One bare shoulder thrusts forward. The length of cambric is about to slip; she clutches it to her breasts. She is gazing to the right, waiting for someone.

It is not her body, I tell myself. It is only how he imagines it to be.

As I move the candle, a pulse seems to quicken beneath her skin. He has worked a nameless colour through her flesh, revealing some essence she has shown only to him.

Hot wax drips onto my hand. I stifle a cry.

If I dropped the candle, if the flame caught a splash of oil, the painting would blaze. At first Hendrickje's face would glow, then shadows would darken her expectant eyes. A shower of sparks would fall to the floor and the discarded rags at my feet would smoulder. When I close my eyes, darting fingers of flame cross the room, ride the walls, array the rafters. In a fiery dawn, I float above the house, watching it burn.

Chapter 46

Someone bangs at my door. Pain orbits my head, waxes and wanes, waxes again.

I am lying on top of the coverlet, my shift damp with sweat. The banging sounds once more, closer this time. The noise comes not from the door, but from the unlatched shutters pounding against my window.

When I try to stand, my legs will not hold. I lean against the window ledge, drag the shutters home. A bitter sap floods my mouth. I double over, vomit into the pot on the floor.

My body shakes. Tears squeeze from my eyes. I crawl across the bed, press my face into the crook of my elbow. The foul taste in my mouth threatens to sicken my stomach again. I whisper a prayer. If I do not move, do not think, then surely sleep must come.

When I am well enough to come downstairs, Hendrickje is frying pancakes on the griddle. Breakfast is late. Titus has tipped his empty plate onto its side and rolls it from one hand to the other. The smell of burning butter makes me queasy. I pour a beaker of ale, rub Titus's head. 'Where is Maartje?'

He ducks from under my hand. 'Gone.'

'Gone where?'

'I woke up, and she was gone.' He sighs, as though he has told the story many times before.

The panels of the box bed are closed. Inside, the mattress has been stripped. The pegs where Maartje used to hang her comb, her hempen bag, are empty.

'She cannot be gone.'

I check the cupboard where she keeps her clothes. The only garment left behind is the serge petticoat the mistress's sister gave her.

Hendrickje scoops a golden pancake onto Titus's plate. At the griddle, she lifts a jug of batter, pours a fresh roundel onto the hissing fat.

I come so close she cannot ignore me. 'Where is Maartje?'

An islet of batter puckers on the hot iron. She turns it deftly before answering. 'I know not. I woke before dawn and she was not here.'

'Maybe she has gone to the harbour,' Titus says.

The door to the courtyard is open. I stumble out into the fresh air, cross the cobbles to the laundry room.

'Geertje,' Titus calls after me, his mouth full.

Nothing within the room looks amiss. I search a basket of unwashed linen for a crumpled cap or a stained apron; any sign of Maartje's presence.

'Geertje!' Titus cries with greater urgency.

Stale body odours rise from the clothes. I need air.

Outside, the courtyard is too bright, too hot. Blinded by the sun, I turn back to the kitchen, lean in the doorway. I want to climb onto Maartje's bed, pull the panels closed behind me, lie face down in the dark.

Titus pulls at my sleeve.

'You will be late for school,' Hendrickje tells him.

'Geertje, Maartje said I must tell you the secret before I go to school and I have been trying very hard to remember to tell it to you.'

'She told you where she was going?'

'You never listen!' He stamps his foot. 'The secret! Last night she made me promise not to tell until today.'

Hendrickje is calmly clearing breakfast plates, moving slowly between the table and the stone basin where she rinses the ware under the pump. I give Titus's shoulder a sharp squeeze and he stiffens beside me.

'Go to the hall,' I tell Hendrickje. 'Sweep the dais and wash the floor.'

'I already washed it this morning.'

Then wash it again, I want to say.

'The front steps need scrubbing.'

When she finally leaves, I pull up a chair and sit before Titus, taking his hands in mine. He beams with importance.

'Now tell me very carefully. What did Maartje say?'

'She said you must look behind the ship. Do you think she has sailed to China?'

'Is that all?'

'Just that. Look behind the ship. She made me say it over and over again so that I would not forget, and now I have told you and I do not have to remember it anymore. I did well to keep the secret so long, did I not?'

'You did very well.' When I stand, my head is dizzy.

Titus claps a hand to his chest. 'I will be late!'

He hurries to the back door, shouts a farewell from the alley.

By the hearth, I kneel on the slate floor. The tile that bears the image of the ship hangs flush with its fellows, showing no sign of ever having been removed. The rough edges snag my fingertips. When I prise it from the wall, a jagged crust of mortar frames the scene. The sprightly angle of the bow surging on the waves gives the galleon a merry air, despite the gathering storm clouds and the swirling ink sea.

Maartje's leather pouch lies within the hollow; limp, but not empty. I remember the day she made two columns of her coins, slid one across the table to Ilse, kept the other for herself. Now she has halved her store again.

The coins clink into my pocket. I take a handkerchief and knot them inside to stop their noise.

Before the pupils arrive, before Hendrickje takes up her pose on the settle, there is time for me to go to him.

In the painting room he sits at the easel, his shirtsleeves furled above his elbows. The window is open and a breeze stirs the room, teasing the corners of papers stacked on the table. At the sound of my step he glances in my direction, then quickly returns his eyes to the portrait. I cross the room, stand by his side, see the painting as he sees it.

I look, not at Hendrickje's ivory shoulder or her expectant face, but at the surround of oak, the familiar lace of the pillow. He is painting her into his bed.

'Maartje is gone.' The words ring with desolation, as if I had shouted into an empty room.

He stirs, as though rousing from a deep sleep.

'Maartje reads the air better than any flask of mercury.'

The curling ends of his hair are still damp from his wash cloth. A new scent of sandalwood rises from his skin.

'I must speak with you.'

'Then speak.'

He will not look at me. I step between him and the easel.

'You are in love with her.'

The thought must not be spoken, yet it can no longer be contained. My arms reach out, as though his denial is something that may be caught and held fast against me.

'It cannot be helped.' His hands lift to his temples, fall to his sides.

The city stops. The bargemen on the canals, the horses on the streets, all traders from here to the Nieuwmarkt fall silent. Nobody breathes, but in this room.

'What of your promise to me?' Something catches in my throat, threatens to choke me.

'I promised you nothing.' The old impatience flashes in his eyes. He looks away. 'You must see that things have changed between us.'

'I have not changed.'

But it is not entirely true. I am no longer the dreamer I was when I came to this house, my heart vulnerable as a pink-bodied crab. Since then, a shell has grown steadily around me, arming me for treachery such as this.

He stands with a force that rocks his stool. 'In any case, I mean to send Titus away to school. For too long, he has been cosseted by women.'

I am to lose Titus. I struggle for air, find my own hand clenching my neck. The morning's dizziness returns.

'Have a care.' The master reaches out to protect his painting. With one foot he pushes the stool towards me, and I sink onto it.

He goes to the window, studies the view he sees every day.

'There is no need for alarm. You may keep your room here for now. We will agree a reasonable time period.'

Already, he has discussed my departure with Hendrickje. How long have they been plotting against me?

Anger surges within me. Every muscle of my body strains to contain it. I fumble at my neck, pull out the ribbon on which the token he gave me is strung.

'Have you forgotten this?'

The marriage medal is hot in my hand. I remember the night he gave it to me, how I wanted to imprint the betrothed couple onto my flesh.

He leaves the window, stands before me.

'The jewellery is for Titus. You agreed as much.'

The contours of the bride and groom are unchanged. The vine still branches out to circle the couple. But to him, it is no more than a chip of silver to be rated on a jeweller's scale.

'Geertje, let us remain on good terms. I would not have you suffer any adversity on the breaking of our friendship.'

His hand takes mine. His skin feels like leather. It is as though he had pulled on an invisible glove before touching me.

'Should you ever be in need, I will help if I can.'

'And who will determine the need?'

My insolence amazes me. There is power in no longer having to please him.

Abruptly, he drops my hand and it falls like a dead bird onto my lap. He looks at me as though I am one of his overpriced curiosities which has long lost its charm. I hold the gaze until his eyes falter.

'You are upset.' He turns away. 'We will speak later. Now, I must work.'

Chapter 47

The room above the Black Flounder pitches forward over the street, as if straining against its brick-and-mortar moorings. On the floor, by the window, a narrow strip of daylight is in withdrawal. I step across the threshold, feeling as though I am mounting a gangway to a listing ship.

Otto slides the bolt behind us, tests his weight against the door. 'At least you will be safe here.'

A bedstead is dressed in linen, surprisingly clean, and dry to touch. The only other furniture is a cabinet on which stands a pitcher and a basin. One door hangs askew on warped hinges. When I try to force it home, it swings back open.

An odour of mutton stew seeps up through the floorboards. My stomach quails. The hasp whines as I drag the window open.

Out on the Rapenburgh, sailors are drinking at a wooden bench. Lusty voices swell in a cheer. Across the street, above the rooftops, masts cut the sky like clashing pikes. A sea breeze blows, sweet and heavy with the smell of rot. Beneath my window, the tavern sign creaks on its chains.

'It will be noisy by night,' Otto says.

'I care not.'

He swings the bag of my belongings from his shoulder onto the bed.

'You must go back, Geertje.'

The ceiling forces me to stoop as I pull my tangled clothes out onto the coverlet. Wrapped in the mistress's kerchief are my comb, Abe's medal, Trijn's prayer.

'You must go back, and agree a settlement.'

I shake the sacking, though it is already empty. My thumb catches on a corner of the bedstead and my knuckle rings with pain. The raw skin tastes of salt.

'I will go back to say goodbye to Titus and to determine what wages I am owed.'

Every word, every action, feels stiff and unnatural. It is as though a marionette has taken over the folding of my spare shift and shawl, the stowing of my belongings into the broken cabinet.

'How long is it since he last paid you?'

'He pays Pieter, and Pieter is at sea.'

What will my brother say when he hears I have left the painter's house? My body tenses as though a hand pulled sharply on my puppet strings.

'This time, you must be paid. Then I will help you to find better lodgings. You may refuse my money, but you cannot relinquish what you have already earned.'

'I have no need of better lodgings. I lived above a tavern before and can do so again.'

There is a pause in which Otto does not tell me that I am older now, and frailer than the girl who once lived in the garret above the Moor's Head in Hoorn.

The pendulum of Maartje's coins swings beneath my petticoat. How long will her few guilders last?

Otto touches my arm. 'You have not had time to think.'

I press a hand to my eyes to stop tears forming.

'He said he would not see me in need.'

'He will see you today,' Otto says. 'And we will not leave until all is settled. Have you eaten?'

Downstairs, a squat stoneware jug props open the tavern door. Otto leads me through a porch and under an arched lintel to a smoky interior furnished with mismatched tables and stools. A tall window, its panes checkered with crude repairs, casts splintered light across the room. By the fire, two men play at tric-trac while a third dozes beside them, his pipe resting on the floor against a crock of smouldering peat.

A barrel standing against the back wall serves us for a table. When a servant girl comes up from the kitchen, Otto bids her to pour ale and bring a dish of stew for me.

'I cannot eat,' I tell him.

'Take a few spoonfuls while I speak to the innkeeper.'

A sturdy man is coming through the door, carrying a cask under one arm. Otto goes to meet him in the porch.

The girl brings the stew. It tastes of nothing. Puddles of mutton fat cool on the surface while Otto negotiates the price of my room. The innkeeper looks over. I push away gristle with my spoon.

'A month in advance; then payment by the week.' An iron key with a kidney-shaped bow hangs from Otto's finger. 'No visitors.'

On the bridge, with the painter's house in sight, I stop, clutch Otto's arm.

'What if he did not receive your note?'

'Then I will send the maid to fetch him.' He pats my shoulder. 'An hour's work and all will be done, Geertje.'

Instead of turning onto the canal bank and following the alley to the kitchen door, Otto leads me along the Breestraat and up the familiar stone steps.

Otto lifts the iron ring and raps twice. The mouthful of stew I ate sits at the top of my stomach. There is no more time to ask him what I must say, how I must behave, in front of Hendrickje.

When the door opens, it is the master who confronts us. He is dressed as he was this morning, but the sleeves of his shirt now sag about his forearms and the rolled ends bear a bloom of reddish chalk.

'You have come for your things.' He might be speaking to a peddler who had dropped a card of pins in the hall.

'And to speak with you, Sir,' Otto says.

'The shoemaker.'

There is something more than hostility in the pronouncement; a note of derision I cannot fathom.

He steps back to admit us. A tiny creak sounds as the door closes. Never again will I dip a feather in oil to brush those hinges.

Some subtle change has come about the hall, as though Hendrickje's hand has shifted all within. Nothing has been moved, yet all seems displaced. Even the paintings have changed. Figures fade into shadowy backgrounds. Today, the laughing man exults in his mockery. The old woman who once reminded me of my mother stares into the distance, indifferent to my plight.

'This business is best conducted in the kitchen.'

The master disappears through the archway and down the stairs.

Hendrickje sits with her back to the window, her hands on her lap, calm and composed as a cat in the sun. She looks up as we enter, then quickly dips her head. I cannot bear to greet her.

Otto glances towards her. 'This is a private matter.'

'Geertje has her witness and I have mine.' The master pulls out a chair at one end of the table.

I sit beside Otto, the heat of the fire behind us. Never has the kitchen been so quiet. By now, Maartje should be muttering to herself at the cupboards, contriving an evening meal from the midday surplus. Titus should be skipping around her, begging for almonds, rattling pots to inspect the contents.

The master looks past us to the wall where the aprons hang.

'Geertje, you have led a comfortable life in my home. Too often, my generosity has outweighed my prudence. Nevertheless, now that we are to part, I seek no return of my many gifts. You may leave this house unencumbered with that obligation.'

My fingers fly to the marriage medal safe under my chemise. For a moment I cannot recall where I have put the rings, the gold and silver coins. Then I remember; they are here with me now, sewn into the hem of my petticoat.

'Geertje has debts. And she will need an income,' Otto says.

The master directs his gaze to him and frowns.

'I will write the permission so she may seek a new position.'

'There may be no such position to be had. Maids are wanted young and strong.'

'As already promised, I will help Geertje if she finds herself in need.'

Some slight movement by Hendrickje distracts me. I will myself not to look at her.

'It is not a question of help, Sir. There is a matter of unpaid wages. And Geertje has fallen ill in the past; God forbid that she may fall ill again. The sale of the jewellery will not sustain her beyond a year.'

'The jewellery must not be sold.' The master's fist pounds the table. His chair scrapes slate and he is on his feet, the vein livid in his left cheek.

Otto flinches.

'The will remains inviolate, do you hear?' The master is shouting now, pointing at me.

'I would never change the will. All is for Titus, as we agreed,' I say quickly.

His chest rises and falls. For a few moments, the only sound is the rush of his breath.

Otto recovers himself. 'An annual settlement must be agreed.'

The master takes his seat.

'I am a generous man. I wish no hardship to befall Geertje. In consideration of her age, her infirmity, I will allow fifty guilders a year.'

'That will not keep her,' Otto says. 'It must be at least a hundred guilders.'

'I have heard enough.' He holds up a hand. 'Sixty guilders, not a stuiver more. I will have Laurens write it up.'

Otto starts to speak, but the master's hand slaps air once more. 'Hendrickje will fetch Geertje's things.'

Hendrickje raises a bowl of peas from her lap. Her nails are clogged with green. Beneath the table, her fingers have been busy stripping husks.

'I will fetch them myself. And Otto will accompany me.'

How easy it is, after all, to defy him.

Hendrickje's mouth opens. She looks to the master for direction. He sits back in his chair.

'Go then,' he says. 'I care not.'

For now, I have forced a retreat.

In the hanging room, I sense further dislocation. The chest I stirred through that morning is now open and empty. My remaining clothes, folded by a neater hand than mine, sit on the bare mattress. Rolled up beside them is my portrait.

'They must have been looking for the jewellery.' I sit on the bed.

'Is everything here?' Otto asks.

I nod.

In my haste this morning I left behind my jacket, the mistress's old woollen petticoat, the satin bodice. I touch the pucker where the eyelet was torn from the fabric. I will never wear it again. Nor will I leave it here for Hendrickje. I stuff it into Otto's bag.

'Is this the painting the student made?' Otto touches a frayed corner of the canvas.

I unroll the painting on the mattress, flatten the curling edges. The woman I see startles me with her youth, her courage. In her oblique gaze, I read a warning. The master has withdrawn only to attune his weaponry.

'I can carry it,' Otto says.

'Leave it. One day it will belong to Titus. Till then, it may remind him of me.'

Otto studies the canvas. 'It is a pretty picture, if a little dark. How can we trust that his father will not defy the notary, sign and sell it in your absence?'

I shake my head. 'Had he written his name beside me, he would now scratch the letters out.'

Gently, Otto raises me to my feet. 'Come away, Geertje. We can wait for Titus outside.'

The bells of the Zuiderkerk chime as we cross the bridge. The sun hangs low among spires and towers, glittering like a golden coin. Schoolboys stream along the canal bank but none of them are Titus. One runs onto the bridge, folds his body over the railings, and dangles a cap over the reeking water. Almost immediately, he is set upon by a merry group of schoolboy bandits. There is much jeering and pushing until the cap is returned to its owner, who tucks it deep inside the waist of his breeches.

At last Titus appears on the bank, three tousle-headed boys in tow.

'Otto,' he cries when he comes onto the bridge. 'Joost has found a dog. Come and see!'

A boy of eight or nine carries a bundle half-hidden in the folds of his shirt. As we draw closer, he uncovers the head of a lively pup.

'We are going to teach him tricks,' Joost says.

'What a fine fellow he is.' Otto strokes the dog's brown fur. 'What shall you feed him, Joost?'

Titus looks in confusion at the bag of clothes in my arms. 'Where are you going, Geertje?'

What am I to tell him? I look to Otto, who is explaining to the boys the care the dog will need, how he is to be fed, exercised, housed.

'I have to go away,' I say.

'To look for Maartje?'

I touch his forehead, and though he has long forbidden caresses in the street, he does not shrug me away.

'I am going to live in another house but I will visit you often.'

'Will you visit tomorrow?'

'I could meet you here at midday.'

He frowns. 'That is no good. We are taking the dog to the park.' He rubs his thumb against the strap of his satchel. 'Is Hendrickje making you leave?'

Otto glances at me. He is asking Joost where he found the dog, telling him there may be a reward for its return.

For a moment, I cannot speak.

'I do not want you to go,' Titus says.

'Nor do I want to go.' I smile, to prove I am not crying.

Titus's face reddens. But the anger inherited from his father is governed by his mother's restraint. He casts a sideways look at his friend who has relinquished the dog to Otto, and is pointing at houses further down the Zwanenburgwal. He clasps me in a hug.

'I will miss you.'

I hug him back, kiss his head, quickly walk away.

I am almost at the Nieuwmarkt when Otto catches up, takes my arm, tells me I am going the wrong way.

Chapter 48

A gaudy sunset fires the sky above the Rapenburgh. But when I cross the bridge and turn onto the street, the forward-tilting houses collude to obscure the light. I walk in their shade, careful to turn my face away from the Three Crowns where I discovered Ilse, and the mouth of the alley the men dragged her down. Up ahead, a drunken sailor leans against a limewashed wall, muddy tide marks circling the ankles of his slops. Two comrades seize his arms, jerk him forward with cheerful oaths.

Women loiter on corners, clacking beads and flapping paper fans. One hitches her skirts, calls on the others to admire her new garters. As I pass, she thrusts out a white knee, scabbed like a child's. I think of Titus at play in the street this evening, adding to the ever-changing map of scrapes and bruises on his legs. A sob swells in my throat. I quell it, walk on.

Men are drinking and singing at the wooden benches outside my lodgings. A clash of tankards punctuates their song, making me jump. I lower my head, feeling as though I have been strung upon a lute, the tension pulling ever tighter.

The tavern is quieter inside than out. By the archway, I hesitate. The close air is seasoned with malt. I lick my dry lips. Men are playing cards at the largest table, tobacco smoke curling over their heads. In the corner where I sat with Otto, a dog is lapping at a greasy platter.

The innkeeper's wife circles the group, filling tankards from a pitcher, one hand balanced against her hip. She looks up, sees me, and nods. Soon she comes over, wiping the lip of the pitcher on her apron. Her hands are big as a man's. A wedding band is embedded in the flesh of one finger.

'You cannot get to your room from here,' she says.

'I want a jug of ale. To take upstairs.'

I feel men's eyes upon me and concentrate my gaze on the little dog washing the pewter clean with his tongue.

She brings the jug and a beaker, counts my coins into a pocket swinging at her waist.

I would rather pass time in talk with a stranger than go up to that narrow room alone.

'Do you have other guests tonight?'

'My husband lets the rooms, not I.'

She does not want me here. What vices does she suspect in me?

In the porch, she reaches up over the door, feels along a shelf until she finds something. She hands me a stub of candle. This unexpected kindness confuses me.

'Your cousin seems a fine young man.'

She means Otto. My pause is short, but long enough for her eyes to narrow.

'He is like a son to me.'

The door swings open and a man in a dusty smock comes in, a fiddle resting on one shoulder like an axe. He casts me a curious look, calls a greeting to the house, and settles by the fire. The dog abandons the platter to come yapping around his feet.

'Thank you for the candle.'

She scrutinises me, as though I am a column of figures she is attempting to tally. I brace myself for her curiosity.

One of the men calls for a drink for the fiddler.

'Rest well.' She turns away.

Outside, the drunken sailor I saw earlier is gripping the side of a horse trough and spewing into the water. For sport, his friends force his head below the surface, release, then force him down again. A cluster of women in brightly coloured shawls cheers them on. When I think he must be half-drowned, his companions haul him upright. Gasping and swearing, he shakes like a dog hauled out of a canal. The women shriek in mock horror as droplets spatter their bare necks and arms.

I follow the broken cobbles around the side of the tavern, climb the stone steps, breathing through my mouth to avoid the stench rising from the privies.

The door at the top swings open at a push, and I wonder if it is ever bolted against outsiders. A patch of light falls into the passage-way from an oval of glass set high in the back wall. I remember then that I forgot to light my candle.

I cannot bear to go downstairs again.

There are four doors, and mine is the second. I set down the jug and bag of clothes. The base of the door is scuffed and splintered as though someone has been kicking at the wood. At first the key refuses to turn. I stop, take a breath. Out on the alley, boots grind on loose stones. Someone is coming. On the next attempt, I wrench the key with both hands. It yields.

The mellow evening light entering my room is enough to see by. I pour some ale, take it to the window to watch the merry-making outside. The sailor has been shocked into sobriety. He links arms with his friends and they head towards the docks. The women who earlier surrounded them wave corners of their shawls in farewell. When a lively group of labourers approaches, the shawls flutter again, revealing flashes of bosoms.

Daylight ebbs from the Rapenburgh, steeping my room in gloom. I will bolt my door, go early to bed and think of nothing.

Tomorrow, I will contrive a curtain for the window. Tonight, I care not who sees me undress.

The coarse mattress crackles under my weight. I turn onto one side, draw my knees to my chest. In this room, even my body feels unfamiliar. From downstairs comes a maelstrom of men's voices and the thumping of tankards on tables.

About now, Hendrickje will be pouring claret wine for the master, for herself. Will they toast my absence? I imagine him raising his glass, her image multiplying in its facets. When she lifts hers to her lips, will he study the candlelight falling on her face, its reflection in the white underside of her arm? He used to pull me onto his thighs, have me feed him drops of wine from my fingertips. With

Hendrickje, it will be different. He will watch her all evening with his artist's eyes, before taking her hand and leading her to his wife's bed.

I remember the lace pillow in the painting. How many times has he already bedded Hendrickje? How many times has he seen her cheek rest on that linen?

When I stand, the boards warm my feet. I fill the beaker to the brim and sit on the floor to drink. My back rests against a wall, a mere partition of wood separating me from some other soul with no better place to be.

Downstairs, a slow, sliding note plays on a fiddle. Without warning, the pace quickens. Joyous notes gambol throughout the tavern. Soon there is the pound of feet, and whoops and claps as the music plays on. The boards vibrate beneath me. Music enters my body, warms my blood. In places, the gaps between the boards are wide enough to hint at the revelry below. By one foot of the cabinet, I spy a hole, no larger than my thumbnail, and in another instant I lie flat on the ground, my eye pressed to the hollow.

Skirts and smocks swirl beneath me, blending with bared arms and necks. Amid greys and browns and whites, a bodice blazes yellow; a stockinged ankle flares crimson-red. I feel I am dancing among them, swinging my skirts, kicking my feet, hooking elbows with every outstretched arm. I whirl so fast my head is dizzy.

It was Abe who taught me to dance; Abe who smiled at my shyness, bade me hold his shoulders, follow his feet. When he held me, I felt as though I were flying.

An ache sharper than hunger or thirst makes me lift my face from the floor. I crawl back to my seat against the wall. The jug of ale has shifted from atop the cabinet and now sits beside me. When I tip it sideways, not a drop flows out. I wrap my arms around the clay, hug it to my chest like a pot-bellied lover and doze against the wall.

A thump, like the weight of a shoulder against my door, wakes me. The jug rolls from my lap. In the darkness, I stumble across the room, check the bolt holds fast. I flatten my back against the wood, hold my breath.

'*Godverdomme!*' The man's voice is so close his lips seem held to my ear. My chest tightens and burns. I imagine a labourer after an evening's drinking, the great slab of one hand pressed to my door to steady himself. Muttering, he launches himself back into the passageway. I track every uneven footstep until at last a key turns, a door opens, closes.

In bed, I lie awake waiting for dawn to strike my bare window.

Chapter 49

By the docks, the wind blows harder, and today, it blows from the north. I sit on the hull of an upturned rowboat, waiting for Otto.

It is already September; too warm for a woollen shawl yet too cold to go without. I button my jacket to the neck, and take a lump of stale bread from my pocket. As though sensing my intent, gulls swoop lower, perching on the wooden scaffold where slimy green steps descend to the water. I toss chunks to the shyest, ignoring those who come close enough to peck my feet. When the bread is gone, they line the quay in disaffected conference. Wings flap like the cracking of whips as they depart for the wharves where fishermen are gutting their catches, blades flashing in the sun.

I want to take up a knife with those men, slice through scale and skin and bone, relish every merciless cut.

Since I left the master's house, a ball of anger has been fattening within me like a black pearl. Every moment spent on the Rapenburgh lacquers the surface. It grows as I carry my pot to the privy, as I hide at the corner till I am certain no man with half-fastened breeches will cross my path. Each meal I take in the kitchen, where my portion is whatever the household has left behind, adds another layer. By night, its lustre glows as it feeds on memories, mocks past happinesses. It whispers in my ear like a malicious familiar, scrabbles through my mind like the rats on the waste heap behind the tavern. At times it climbs so high in my throat, I fear it will choke me.

'Geertje!'

Otto bears down upon me.

'I did not mean to startle you.'

I shield my eyes, try to smile at him. A ridge of concern divides his brow.

'Well?' he asks.

'Nothing.'

I slide along the wooden ridges to make room for him, avoiding splays the birds left behind.

He throws himself down, rocking our seat.

'No message?'

'None.'

He sighs. He pulls off his cap, shakes out his hair, the awl balancing all the while behind his ear. 'The house is shut up. There is talk they have gone to Bredevoort for some days.'

'That is where she comes from.' I trap a stone underfoot, grind it back and forth on the cobbles. 'He will post no banns for her, if that is what she is planning.'

The stone escapes my shoe, rattles beyond reach.

'Geertje, you have waited long enough. He has a case to answer. We must go to the Chamber.'

I picture an airless room at the back of the church, its walls lined with cabinets, and seated around a table, an assembly of magistrates noting the city's nuptials in leather-bound folios. When it comes to my turn, there will be a pause. Grey heads will confer. For me, the clerk will select a different volume.

'Soon,' I say. 'Soon, I will go, if I have to.'

'We must go today. Now.'

Out in the harbour, the gulls are scavenging on the deck of a trawler. A deckhand disperses them with a shaking of nets. They wheel overhead, screeching their displeasure, swoop in fresh onslaughts.

I stand and brush my skirts. Every day, the pocket at my waist grows lighter. The coins I earned from the sale of the satin bodice are already dwindling.

'I once had a hope of entering the Oude Kerk as a bride. Never as a plaintiff.'

'Had there been a contract between you . . .' Otto hesitates.

I drag at the ribbon around my neck. 'Here is the contract.'

The marriage medal glints between my fingers.

The church tower sprouts improbably from a snare of narrow streets, as though grown from an acorn dropped among brambles. Otto leads me down an alley and across a gutter of sluggish waste flowing to the canal. A young man sluices the channel with a bucket of water and I have to lift my skirts to avoid the surge which threatens our feet. Even if the canal burst its banks, it could not wash this stench away.

Women lean from casements, jostling bare arms and shoulders. They call to passing sailors and gesture crudely, listing prices on their fingers. A boy in a dirty smock tugs at my sleeve, offering a clumsy posey tied with reeds.

At last we come to a clearing. Beggars gather outside the church. A girl sits by the portico, legs huddled beneath her, an infant at her breast. For a moment I think it is Ilse. She stares back at me with listless eyes. But Ilse left Amsterdam long ago. Are these the streets where the master first encountered Maartje? A shiver like the touch of a cold finger runs down my back.

We enter the church from the southern side. Inside, columns stretch so high it seems I can see into the heavens. The sun that curdles the fetid streets now streams through immense windows of clear and coloured glass, casting hallowed light around us. I remember Sint Nicolaaskerk in Edam, the terror I felt as a child lest lightning should strike its tower again. I think of the mistress taking flowers to her children buried in the Zuiderkerk, then remember that she, herself, is buried here.

The floor is laid with tombstones. My feet seem to shrink within my shoes. At any moment, I could be stepping on her grave.

Otto walks ahead. I hang behind, press my back to the cool stone of a pillar. Near the entrance to a side chapel, a group of grey-haired men in black capes has gathered. They may be the commissioners who hear cases. A lean dog darts about their legs. One of their number, a stout man in buckskin boots, taps a cane on the slabs. The sound echoes under the vaulted ceiling.

How am I to tell such men about my life with the master?

I want to call for Otto, tell him I cannot do it. The dog has parted from the group and is running circles around his feet. Otto crouches to stroke her ears, and she rests her head on his knee. A young man shifts a leather satchel onto his shoulder, reaches out to coax her back. She ignores his efforts, and he laughs, lifting his hands in mock despair.

I want to slink into a pew, hide from these men and their judgements.

Otto takes the dog in his arms, carries her over to the group. Soon the stout man lifts his cane, points out a doorway further down the nave. Sun flashes on the silver hilt as though he is a sorcerer conjuring the chamber from dust.

'This way, Geertje.' Otto calls.

When I leave the safety of the pillar, I expect the arched ceiling to crumble and bury me in rubble.

I walk across the graves, follow Otto through the studded door.

Chapter 50

Two weeks later, we are back in the Oude Kerk, waiting for the master.

The Chamber of Marital Affairs is not the dusty vault I expected. Light from two large windows falls across a polished table and spills onto the shining marble floor. A gilded mirror hangs over the mantel. At the head of the table stands a silver clock, shaped like a turret. The room could be one of the grand salons overlooking the Herengracht, were it not for the three commissioners sitting opposite us.

The chamber is stifling. Dark patches have formed on the under-arms of Otto's smock. A faint smell of leather rises from his skin. The nape of my neck is damp with sweat. I slide a finger under the back of my cap to loosen the ties.

'We are busy men.' The eldest of the commissioners smooths the tip of his grey beard between thumb and forefinger. He seems to address the two empty chairs beside us.

'We are grateful for your time, Sirs,' Otto says.

Drunken voices rise in disharmony outside the window. *Three kisses and you may pass.*

'The young have no respect.' The commissioner seated between the other two sets his quill down. 'Jacob. The window.'

The third man rises. At the window, he lifts his hat and wafts incoming air across his face. His flattened hair still bears the impression of the band. When he fastens the hasp, a housefly buzzes, trapped inside the glass.

I want to take out my handkerchief, mop my face, but the men are watching me.

Now that he is standing, Jacob seems reluctant to sit. He goes to the head of the table, taps the clock. A bell chimes the quarter hour.

'They may be held up by crowds going to the *kermis*,' Otto says.

The man seated at the centre of the table takes up his quill, regards us with contempt.

'Do you think yours is the only case to be heard today?'

'A fine of one guilder to be issued to Meneer van Rijn,' the bearded man says. His neighbour scratches down the penalty.

'And a further summons to this chamber for three weeks' time.' He closes his folio with a slap.

'And how is Geertje to live until then?' Otto tenses, as though about to spring from his seat.

I wish Trijn were here, with her strong voice, her way of centring herself in a room, her sharp gaze sweeping around the gathering like the hands of a clock.

The bearded man sits back in his chair. Its curved arms are finished with the grimacing heads of fanciful fish. I realise my wet palms are resting on a pair of the same creatures.

'Go to the painter's house. Form an agreement with him.'

Otto laughs. 'And how are we to make him pay?'

'We will make him pay.' Jacob comes back to his chair but does not sit. 'The law is not unsympathetic to your case.'

The man with the quill grunts.

When I stand, the floor seems to melt beneath my feet. Otto takes my arm, leads me to the door.

Outside, a breeze is blowing from the canal. A lull has fallen over the streets. Otto finds a pump and I splash water onto my face.

'I cannot return to the master's house.'

'It does not have to be today. In any case, I must get back to the shop. Come with me; it is too early for you to go to your room.'

I shake my head. 'I feel better. I will sit for a while, then follow the crowd to the *kermis*.'

'Perhaps you will find the man who wants three kisses,' Otto says, and I laugh.

He squeezes my hand. 'It is good to hear you laugh again.'

As I reach the square, the sound of a bugle cuts cleanly through the air. Rolling drum beats swell to a tumult, and a troop of guardsmen marches in formation, halberds hoisted high on their shoulders. Through the crowd, I catch glimpses of polished helmets and frisking plumes. Cheers resound as the guardsmen ascend the wooden platform before the weigh house.

Beside me, a sailor lifts his sweetheart onto his back and she squeals with delight. Something strikes my knee. One of her mules has flown off and is stumbled over by a labourer holding a brown bottle to his lips. I snatch it like bait from a trap, replace it on the bobbing foot before its owner even registers the loss.

Rows of tents are pitched across the square. As I pass brightly laden stalls I shuffle my last coins, feel the pinch of pleasure denied.

How Titus would enjoy the clowns! In a clearing, they roll and tumble. Lithe performers in silver-threaded costumes climb onto each other's shoulders, forming a pyramid five men high. When a merman with a painted face jangles a bucket before me I mutter an excuse, elbow my way back through the crowd.

At the west side of the square an ox hangs above a firepit, its glossy brown skin crackling and spitting over the logs. The city smells of roast beef. One man hews chunks from the carcass while another slices the meat onto rounds of bread. As customers gather, the men work harder, their stained shirts open to the waist, their faces red with heat. A boy with quick, greasy fingers takes the money, ignoring two dogs begging by his feet.

The spoonful of watery stew I ate in the tavern must feed me for the day.

Families cluster around tables, eating and drinking their fill. At the end of one bench, a husband is embracing his plump wife who dandles a baby on her knee. The infant waves a pin-wheel, her chubby fingers grabbing the sails. When they do not turn as they should, she flings the toy away and it lands at my feet. I pick it up, place it back into her hand. She smiles at me, reaches as far as her small arm will allow, and flings it away again.

Her mother, a fair-haired woman with sunburned cheeks, laughs. 'Now she makes a game of it, and you will have no peace. Lately, her father carved her a doll. And did you play with it?' She addresses the baby with mock sternness. 'No, you did not! You pounded it upon the floor and cried for your brother's horse and wagon.'

At this renewed attention, the little girl convulses with delight.

Her father nuzzles his wife's neck, squeezes her waist. She shrugs him off, hugs the baby closer. 'Joris, make room and let this good woman sit, can you not see how tired she is?'

Joris throws me a bleary-eyed smile and slides along the bench. Soon I am eating strips of tender beef and drinking warm ale with my new friend whose name is Magda. From a pocket she takes out two pears, hands one to me. She wears her bodice loosely laced, and a thin shawl has fallen from her shoulders to the crooks of her elbows.

'How tired I am of men,' she says, waving a hand at her family. Her husband sits beside her; on the opposite side of the table, a man I guess to be her brother is whittling at a scrap of wood. Beside him is a group of small boys who do not sit long enough for me to count them. 'A husband and four living sons, God be thanked, but here is my greatest treasure.' Magda kisses the top of the baby girl's head through a little linen cap.

I take up the discarded pin-wheel, spin the sails. 'Your husband is a toy-maker?'

'A carpenter. The toys are just for *kermis*. Every year we come from Waterland to sell them.' She winks. 'In truth, we come for the fun.'

At the next table, a fiddler lifts his bow, strikes up a jig. Joris pulls Magda to her feet, and I take the baby onto my lap.

Dancers form a circle. The fiddler grins and quickens the pace.

After a few rounds, Magda returns, breathless and sweating, and throws herself down onto the bench. She takes a long drink of ale, then pulls at the laces of her bodice and lifts out one breast.

I hand over the baby who settles against her chest and begins to suckle.

'Is your husband at sea? You must not miss the dancing on his account.' She nods at our empty tankards. I pour more ale.

'Joris has had enough,' she whispers. 'One day the blade will slip and cut off our income along with his fingers.'

Pitchers are emptied and replenished. Joris and Magda dance again, while I clap the baby's hands to the music.

Across the table, their sons are staging battles between the wooden figures their uncle has carved. He is at work on some intricate detail of a fox's tail, his knife hardly grazing the surface.

I pick up a miniature hare. It stands on hind legs, head turned, ears cocked. I can hardly bear the tension in its pose.

'Do you like it?' The uncle's knife has stopped.

'Very much.'

'Then I will make one for you. Anything you want.'

I hear Magda laugh before I realise she has returned.

'My brother wants to dance with you.'

'Then he should ask me.'

Magda's brother's hand is ridged with scars. Under my fingers, his callouses rub hard as barnacles. I want to open his palm, examine the rough and the smooth, but we are pulled into a merry circle, and now a burly farmer grabs my other hand, a pipe gripped between his brown teeth.

When the music stops, Magda's brother laces his fingers through mine, and we stroll away from the dancers towards the weigh house. The platform is now empty save for a trio of little boys baring their buttocks to the crowd. I turn my head away, catch sight of a figure ducking behind the wooden scaffold.

It is the woman who followed me along the Breestraat, the day I stopped to watch the quacksalver. My back stiffens. I remember where I have seen her before. Cornelia Jans, the wife of the butcher who cheats the master's household as a matter of course.

Magda's brother slides an arm about my waist. Back in Edam, I would have thought him handsome. I wonder if a wife and children are waiting for him in Waterland.

He murmurs something, pulls me into a doorway.

'I cannot.' I look over my shoulder. Cornelia Jans has disappeared. Who else may be watching?

His mouth comes close to mine. Cider sweetens his breath.

When I step back, I recognise the gable stone of the painters' guild set into the lintel above his head.

'My master. I must go.'

'You are in service?'

He tries to take my hand. I turn away, and run.

I run all the way back to the Rapenburgh. At the horse trough, I stop, steady myself against the cold stone, avoiding my reflection in the water.

The sign with the painted fish creaks on its salt-bitten chains. I could bring a man to this place, with its stinking privies and infested cesspool, climb the stone steps, take him into my bed. And all the while the master's spies could be watching.

I look up and down the street. All is quiet. The usual revellers have gone to the *kermis* and are probably drinking there still. A grey veil has drawn across the sky. From the harbour comes a cloying whiff of decay.

The sign creaks again. The ugly flat fish, both eyes bulging on one side of its face, swings in the breeze.

I mount the steps slowly. *Anything you want.*

My room is cold and bare. Nothing is missing, yet it seems something has been taken away. I lie in bed, unable to sleep. In the darkness behind my eyelids, a knife whittles wood. In my mind, a fiddle plays a relentless jig.

Tomorrow I will go back to the *kermis* and care not if the whole city sees me. What can the master do to me that he has not already done?

Chapter 51

A knee to the hollow of my back forces me forward. My arms are pin-
ioned; my feet lose purchase with every surge of the jeering crowd.
Bodies smelling of vomit and sweat press against me. I search faces for
the master, but cannot find him. My shins scrape steps as the bearers
drag me to the scaffold. A cloaked figure waits. When he turns around,
the hood falls from his face, and the beggar from the Nieuwmarkt is
standing before me. His left eye, no longer clouded, bulges from the
socket and in its glassy sheen, my stricken face is reflected. Before I can
cry out, his cudgel pounds my belly.

I scream, roll onto my side, fall from the bed to the floor.

A familiar pulse of agony makes me gasp for breath. I press palms
and knees to the boards, brace for the next spasm. When it comes,
I moan aloud.

Someone bangs on my door.

'Mistress Dircx, are you ill?'

The innkeeper's wife.

Mean grey light fills the room. The twisted bedsheet hangs from
the mattress, knots about my ankles. When I try to free myself, a
glossy clot of blood clings to my fingers. A dark stain has spread
across my shift.

'Let me in!' the woman cries, rattling the door.

'Wait.' I manage only a croak. 'Wait,' I call, louder this time.

The rattling stops. A man's voice says something.

Acid burns my throat. I press a fistful of the sheet to my mouth.
I must send them away, outpace the pain, and when it is over, fall
back into the mercy of my bed.

Outside the door, the innkeeper is remonstrating with his wife. Her
response serves to banish him down the passageway. I cling to the

bedpost, try to ease onto my feet. My fingers slide down the turned wood. At last, I am upright and shuffling across the floor. I lift the bolt, open the door a thumb's width.

My landlady's quick eyes set to work, surveying the disorder in me, in the room beyond.

'A bad dream.' The door sways towards me. I push back against its weight. 'I hope I did not alarm you.'

Her shoe drives into the gap.

'Send for the doctor,' she calls over her shoulder.

'No doctor,' I say quickly.

'This is no ward for invalids. The doctor must come, and your cousin must pay.'

'I am recovered.'

But I can stand no longer. My cheek presses against the scarred wall. I want to curl up on the floor, wrap my arms about my knees.

'Go back to bed. I will send fresh linen.' Her foot withdraws, and the door closes.

By the time the doctor arrives, the pain has subsided. I have washed and dressed, and the maid has taken away the basin of bloody water. The innkeeper's wife chaperones the visit, arms tightly folded against her chest.

'A passing ailment of the womb,' the doctor says, though he has heard only her account of events, and scarcely glanced at me. 'I wonder at this trouble.'

'I had to take a cup of wine for the fright.' Having satisfied herself that there is no danger of an imminent birth or death on the premises, the innkeeper's wife is almost jovial.

The doctor's flat white collar is shiny and spotted with wear. He scratches his scalp, examines his fingernails.

'I could purge her, but it will cost you.'

I hold my breath, pray I may be spared his probing fingers. If Trijn were here, she would swiftly rout him. *Geertje, I would not trust that* piskijker *to remove a splinter from your thumb.*

The innkeeper's wife frowns. 'What other cure is there?'

'Give her a cup of bone broth, and send her back to her husband.' He replaces his hat and immediately the ceiling forces him to stoop.

Outside my door, they haggle in low voices. What price will he charge for this remedy?

When the innkeeper's wife returns, her face is grim.

'How much money do you have?'

'I will pay. In two weeks, I will pay all I owe.'

'This is no house of charity. I have kept you too long already. Tomorrow, when you are recovered, you must pay your debt, and a month in advance. And from now on, you must wash your own linen. None in the kitchen will touch it for fear your disease is catching.'

I lower my eyes, will her to leave. Instead, she comes closer. Pickled herring taints her breath.

'Last night, you went to the *kermis*. You got drunk, made yourself ill.'

'Ale did not cause this illness.'

'You have money for ale but none for rent.' She backs away, well satisfied with her thrust. 'This is a respectable house. There must be no trouble here.'

When she is gone, I lie on the bed, listening to the tavern sign swinging on its chains. By now, Magda is likely directing her sons at their stall. On her lap sits the lively baby, and strung from her girdle is a leather pouch, fat with coins. Beside her is her husband, his arm twined about her waist, while her brother's knife whittles enchanted creatures from scraps of wood.

I stand, roll up my skirts. The stitches I thought so secure pick apart in moments. I shake the contents of the hem onto the coverlet. The silver coins have turned to grey but the three gold rings are bright as when the mistress wore them. I slide her wedding ring onto my finger. The two red stones shine like jewelled eyes. The band with the diamond cluster would best fit a child. The third ring is bigger; a plain gold circlet, with someone's name engraved inside.

I am only losing what was never really mine.

For now, perhaps the coins will be enough. Next month, all will be settled, if the master is true to his word.

I wait by the window until shadows span the width of the street outside. Rain clouds drift in from the sea, mingling with smoke from the foundry. Already, candles are appearing in windows. A bad evening to go out.

I must not be seen.

Drizzling rain has subdued the Rapenburgh, dampened its smells, dulled its hues. My feet feel numb on the stone steps. I press against the wall, ease my way down. The prescribed bone broth was substituted for a thin gruel. At this time last night I was eating succulent beef, and wiping pear juice from my chin.

The street is deserted. Where in the city have I seen the pawnbroker's sign? I pull my shawl up around my neck, shun the neighbouring dealers where the landlady's informants might spy on the transaction.

The rain gathers strength, pelting my face and breaching the shawl to drench my shoulders. I meet no bands of sailors, no laughing girls. Those who have not already been lured to the *kermis* are conducting their merry-making indoors. I shelter under the eaves of the money-changer's shop until the grizzled owner comes to the door, sucking on his pipe and silently observing me. I turn down an alley where gutters brim with streaming filth and head for the canal, taking a circular route to confound any watchers.

I cross the Oudeschans, never looking towards the master's house. Rain smacks the tarpaulin-covered boats, pools on the decks of barges moored for the night. By the tower, I stop to lean against the red bricks darkened with damp. I should go further, far from the master's house and friends. A chill shakes my body. Soon it will be night and I have no light to guide me along the treacherous quays.

At the mouth of an alley, three golden spheres hanging above a doorway have turned to base metal in the dimming light. A half hour later, and I would have missed them.

Inside the shop, a young woman rests her elbows on a counter. As I enter, she lifts her cheek from her hand, and I wonder if I have interrupted her sleep.

'Good evening, Mother,' she says with a yawn. 'What have you brought me?'

I blink in the dim interior. The floor is strewn with dark shapes. A wooden crate catches my foot, snags my skirts. The girl laughs as I struggle to free myself. 'Always he must spare the candles.'

Behind her hangs a heavy curtain. A ripple of movement disturbs its folds.

I spill half a dozen coins onto the counter. When the metal rattles on wood, the curtain is thrust aside, and a man in a tunic with rolled-up sleeves emerges. His daughter, or wife, shrinks into the recess.

'How came you by these, Mistress?' The man takes one of the master's coins and bites it between his yellow teeth.

'They were a gift.'

He laughs. 'And more where they came from?'

'These are all I have.' Six more are concealed within my hem and tip against my ankles as I speak.

He names a sum not half what I had hoped for.

'The silver alone is worth more than that.'

He leans across the counter. I try not to recoil from the smell of unwashed skin.

'Tell me again how you came by them.'

Back in my room, I peel off my sodden clothes. I loosen my hair, comb my fingers through the lengths. Outside, the rain has eased and a faint moon has risen. Merry music floats up from the tavern and soon there is the scrape of stools pushed aside, the gallop of feet across boards, the shouts and laughter of the dancers. I lie on the bed, wet hair clinging to my neck. Tomorrow, I will clear my debts at the inn. And as soon as I have my strength back, I will go to the master's house to claim all he owes me.

Chapter 52

When the door on the Breestraat opens, I am ready.

'Good morning, Hendrickje.'

Her head tilts. She looks from me to Otto as though considering whether or not to admit us. A new shawl of maroon wool is draped over her shoulders. Around her neck hangs a silk cord, its unseen ornament caught inside her chemise. She wears no apron.

I step over the threshold, my skirts brushing hers, forcing her to back away.

'How well you keep the house.' I cross the hall, leaving Otto to close the front door behind him. 'You must have been scrubbing tiles at dawn.'

A flush highlights the tip of Hendrickje's nose, her cheeks. I imagine the master dipping a fine-bristled brush in madder, blending one drop of rose-coloured pigment with the creamy white of her skin.

When I pause before the painting of the old lady, the aged eyes seem pensive, the brows slightly raised.

Nothing will daunt me today. 'Fetch your master.'

'He is working.' A note of defiance cuts though Hendrickje's composure.

'He has had three days' notice,' Otto says.

Someone raps on the front door.

'Wait downstairs,' Hendrickje says.

'We will wait in the side room.' For an instant, I block her path. Another rap. The notary.

'You had better let Meneer Laurens in. Or do you expect him to go to the kitchen door?'

Otto follows me into the room where the master hosts his most honoured visitors. 'Why do you provoke her?'

'She has provoked me long enough.'

How I once marvelled at the grandeur of the columns supporting the immense mantel. The painting of the shrouded figure still overhangs it. The man's wasted face is pitiful and I wonder how it ever frightened me.

No fire burns in the grate. Let Hendrickje learn for herself how quickly dampness creeps in.

Laurens speaks to Hendrickje in the hall. I picture the notary polishing his spectacles with a square of soft leather as he waits. I take a seat at the end of the table, where the mistress used to sit. Otto shifts from one foot to another, throwing glances over his shoulder as though he expects to be ordered from the room at any moment.

When the master bursts in, his chest is heaving with angry breaths. He has forgotten, or not troubled, to set aside his painting clothes. In his spattered smock and cloth cap he could be a painter of ships' hulls, of barn doors.

'You broke your promise.' His accusing finger smells of linseed; the nail is glutted with umber.

Fear jumps in my chest. I wrap my arms around my body as though calming a skittish pup. So he had me followed to the pawnshop. Perhaps he offered a reward for information.

'And what of your promise to me?'

The red vein flares in his cheek.

Behind him, Laurens coughs. 'This business is best conducted around the table.'

The master grasps the back of a chair so hard the velvet may never give up his imprint. He sits opposite me at the far end of the table, as though we are master and mistress of his fine house.

'*Godverdomme*, man, read. The sooner I am done with this, the better.'

Laurens open his folio and begins.

'*The following contract has been drawn up to cover all claims arising from alleged promises of marriage and other sundry matters as* yet unsettled between the parties, to include wages the applicant owes to Geertje Dircx.'

I interrupt. 'This is your contract, not mine. I will agree to no conditions drawn up without my consultation.'

Otto removes the awl from behind his ear, turns it over in his hands.

'Let the man finish,' the master says through his teeth.

Laurens pushes his spectacles further up his nose. 'There are but three points.'

'The applicant will pay a redemption fee for the purpose of recovering items recently pawned.

'In addition, the applicant will pay 160 guilders a year towards maintenance and lodgings for Geertje Dircx's lifetime.

'All this conditional on Geertje Dircx conducting herself in a suitable manner so that her will in favour of the applicant's son remains unchanged, and all possessions detailed therein are unburdened by debt at the time of her death.'

'What of my wages? What of the money owed to me for keeping your house and son? I have not been paid these seven years.'

I look to Otto, who has calculated the figures. He fumbles with a fold of paper, starts to speak, stops.

It was a mistake to meet here, in this room where the master celebrates his successes with glasses of chilled wine. The grand paintings with their ornate frames, the columns of red marble, only serve to discomfit Otto. I want to shout that the gold he sees is gilt; the marble, disguised wood.

'You declare yourself unsatisfied, yet this exceeds what we already agreed.' The master snatches the paper from Laurens, stamps it with his fist.

'I agreed nothing.' I am standing now. When the master rises, I do not flinch.

'I have been too generous and now you dare to cross me.'

'Your brand of generosity would not cover the cost of nursing should I fall ill. Under your dictate, the most suitable manner of my conduct would be my death.'

'Sign the paper and be gone. You will wring no better terms from me.'

'Let the magistrates decide that in the Chamber next week.'

The master laughs. 'You may wait with them all day if you wish. I would not clean my brushes with their summons.'

'Then we will summon you again,' Otto says.

The master turns to Otto. 'You have put her up to this. Lately, I heard an interesting tale about your nocturnal activities.' He laughs again. 'To think I once suspected her with you.'

Otto gets to his feet.

'We are leaving,' I say quickly. 'Close your inkwell, Meneer Laurens; you will not be needing it today.'

I open the door to the hall, surprising Hendrickje who is making much work of polishing the mistress's writing table. For a moment, her cloth stills, and the eyes meeting mine are unguarded. Her lips part. Can we at last talk freely?

Too soon, the others come into the hall. Hendrickje turns back to her pot of wax. Before any of the men can speak, I open the front door and leave the master's house for the last time.

Chapter 53

On the day of the second summons, the master does not appear.

Neither does Otto.

At the head of the table, the turret clock ticks. The commissioners close their folios and I am dismissed.

Jacob rises, his face grave, and accompanies me to the door.

'In one week's time, the painter must present himself.'

'And if he does not?'

His flat collar sits upon his shoulders like clean pages of an open book.

'I will take the notice to him myself. This time, I promise you, he will comply.'

Over the Oude Kerk, a mass of grey cloud stains the sky. Though it is not yet three o'clock, candles are lighting in casements all down the narrow streets. Women huddle in open doorways, patting their hair, clutching their shawls. On the canal bank, close to where filth drops from the privies, a woman bends to wash her linen. Passing barges slop water against her dress.

Needles of icy rain sting my face as I cross the bridge.

Otto is ill. His father is ill. Marten had an accident and could not mind the shop.

I run through the Nieuwmarkt. Tarpaulins swell over stalls like ships' sails and smack against the swaying poles. One shoe catches on a loose cobble and my stockinged foot plunges into a puddle.

I limp across the square. From the top of the street I look for the sign with the anvil and see that the windows of Otto's shop are closed. No light shines within.

When I press against the door, it gives but a thumb's width, as though some bulk obstructs it.

One window creaks open. 'Geertje!'

Marten peers out, looks up and down the street. 'Wait.' He pulls the latch closed.

There is the sound of wood dragging across the floor. The door opens and a dull metallic note sounds in place of the bell's trill.

When I step inside, Marten pushes a wooden chest back against the door.

'They smashed the bolt,' he says.

The floor is strewn with boots and shoes. Hides have been dragged from their pegs and flung about the room. The bracket of shining tools has been wrenched from the wall, and hammers, knives, chisels lie in confusion. On the table are piles of pattern pieces and tangled trimmings. The air is thick with the smell of leather and pine resin.

Marten leans on the handle of a sweeping brush. 'Have a care where you walk.'

A rough pathway has been swept through a scattering of tacks and studs. On the counter, the ledger always so neatly kept now lies face down on its crumpled pages. I lift the old book, smooth a hand across the paper, and will myself not to cry.

'Where is he?'

'Safe.' Marten turns over a grey upper, crushed flat as a glove, and stamped with the muddy print of a man's boot. 'They came in the night. The brewer heard the mischief and ran to my grandfather's house to warn him.'

'Otto is at his father's house?'

Marten shakes his head. 'Not any longer.'

A work stool lies on its side. I right it, and sit.

'Who did this?'

Marten is coaxing the stained upper back into shape. He attempts to polish the leather with his sleeve, curses, throws the half-made shoe onto the table.

'He should have left a year ago. I warned him.'

An awl lies by the foot of the table. The wooden handle is stained from years of workmen's hands but the point is sharp.

Otto always carried an awl. Even outside the shop.

'May I have this?'

Marten looks confused. 'I can lend you something better.'

'This is the one I want.'

'Take it. There must be a dozen more, I will keep only the best.' He rests his hands on his hips, surveys the ravaged shop. 'The counter will do better opposite the windows. In its place, I will have a settle where ladies may fit on shoes with ease. The back room will serve Marieke for a kitchen, and the attic, once she has cleaned it, will be our living quarters.'

'You mean to move in?'

'My apprenticeship is complete; I am to be accepted into the Guild within the month.'

I remember then that Otto's nephew is no longer a boy, but a man. A married man, soon to be a father. And now that Otto is gone, the shop is his.

Night comes early to the Rapenburgh. Wind drives rain into my face. Channels of murky water rush against my feet and my sopping shawl binds me in bitter cold. I feel as though I am submerged in the canal, struggling to escape a knotted sack. Who would miss me if I disappeared? The innkeeper would draw a line through his ledger; his wife would sell my linen. The commissioners would shrug and close the case. The master would return to the Breestraat with a lighter step, eager to tell Hendrickje the good news.

I could go to a scribe and send for Trijn. Trijn, who has not sent me a word of comfort since we last met in Edam. Pieter is at sea with no certain date of return. A shiver courses through my stiff limbs. What will my brother say when he hears how I have failed him?

The door of the Black Flounder swings open and a man stumbles out. He staggers past me, rests hands on knees, and vomits into the horse trough. From inside come strains of a sprightly fiddle competing with a drunken chorus. Perhaps the innkeeper will give me a crock of peat to warm my room.

In the tavern, smoke mingles with vapours rising from wet wool. Men sprawl on stools, pipes held between their teeth, beating their thighs in time to a red-cheeked piper. The fiddle has been seized by a girl of about seven who fights her brother for possession of the bow. A red-faced woman, her cap flattened onto her crown, quaffs a mug of ale, and aims indiscriminate slaps at her children who maintain a cautious distance from her chair.

Flames leap from the fire. At the hearth I loosen my sodden shawl, waft it in the heat.

'Did you swim all the way, Sister?' a man calls, and laughs heartily at his own wit. I keep my eyes on the fire, try to dry my stockings discreetly.

The woman in the slack cap looks up from her mug. 'Why, she is half-drowned.' She sounds amused.

'Take a dram with us, Sister. There are plenty here to keep you warm.' A brawny sailor with a stubbled chin pats the seat beside him.

'I prefer to stand.'

But already he is pouring rum into a mug, pushing it towards me.

When I drink, it is as though a second fire has been lit within me. Before I can judge the company I am keeping, the man has stripped me of my shawl and shoes, which he sets by the hearth to dry.

He talks of India, where women wear rubies large as plums and men conceal daggers in their turbans. He edges his stool closer to mine. I curl my fingers around my mug, drink deeper. His tanned forearm bears a faded pattern of blue ink. It could be the wing of a bird, or the scales of a fish.

'Have you heard of a fluyt called the *Sint Maria*?' I ask on impulse.

'Your husband is on board?'

'My brother.'

He leans back, calls over his shoulder. 'Henric, when does the *Sint Maria* dock?'

An older man sets down his tankard, wipes his mouth with the back of his hand.

'With a good wind behind her, no more than a week's time.'

Pieter may be home within the week. I jump up, but my new friend grabs my wrist, eases me back down. The innkeeper, wary of me since the doctor's visit, stands watching from the archway.

'I must go.' I break the man's hold. This time I make it to the fireside, retrieve my shawl, and look for my shoes.

The fiddle is lying on the ground and the little girl is sawing the bow over and back across the strings. Abruptly, she stops her play and gazes at me through the spindles of a chair.

My shoes are gone.

The child holds a hand to her mouth to contain her merriment. Not a theft, but some childish whim. Already I can hear her mother's protestations, the men's laughter.

The sailor smirks at me from his chair. How far can a woman run without shoes?

Rum boils in my brain. I must think. The little girl cracks almonds between her teeth, engrossed, as though watching a farce.

A hand reaches for the abandoned fiddle and a man swings it over his shoulder.

'This is no toy,' he says. 'And neither are these.'

The fiddler holds my shoes pinched between thumb and forefinger.

The company grows quiet. I wait for rebukes to rain on him for spoiling the fun, but none come.

The piper blows the opening bars of a lament, swiftly changes to a jig. Laughter breaks out. The tavern's natural order is restored.

'You are the woman who lodges upstairs, are you not? I will see you safely to your room.'

I can almost feel the prod of Trijn's finger. *And who will see you safely delivered from this stranger?*

Before I can thank him, the fiddler has plucked a lantern from a hook and is leading me through the cluttered tables, past the suspicious innkeeper, to the door.

Outside, at the bottom of the steps, he holds the lantern aloft to light the way to my room. His hair is speckled grey, his chest broad within his smock. I imagine him raising a pick above his head, driving metal into stone. He smells of chalk and sweat and ale. If I were to slide my arms around his neck, press my lips to his, would he follow me upstairs?

'My name is Geertje. I come from Edam.' I sound like a lost child.

'Goodnight, Geertje from Edam. Whenever I am in the tavern, you will be safe there.'

I climb the steps, the warmth of his gaze on my back. When I reach the door at the top, I can hardly bear to close it against his light.

Chapter 54

A week passes, and still the *Sint Maria* has not docked.

In the harbour, ships lie wreathed in morning mist, their masts dissolving into grey cloud. Along the wharves, sailors wheel carts loaded with biscuits, beer, cheese, stockfish. Vapours from open barrels of tar catch in my throat. I pass three women lamenting over a boy in an ill-fitting jerkin and slops, a knitted cap pulled over his ears. He hoists a wooden chest onto one shoulder, eager to be gone.

Titus wanted to be a ship's boy. I imagine him grown to a youth, climbing rigging by night, hands numb, arms weary, the deck and pitching waves merging into one darkness beneath him. *Which would you prefer if you fell from a topmast, Geertje, to land on deck or in the sea?*

Today, I must face the master alone.

The bells of the Oude Kerk ring ten o'clock as I walk over the bridge. Cold weather has dampened the stench of the streets, or perhaps I have grown accustomed to the foul air. The commissioners will have their volumes; the master, if he is here, will have his notary. All I have are my mementos from Edam, and Otto's awl.

Shortly before the appointed time, I go to the Chamber. Before I can knock, the studded door opens and Jacob stands before me.

'Mistress Dircx, are you ready?'

His urgency tells me the master is within. I try to smile at him, then we are walking into the room together and there is no more time to prepare.

The master sits stiffly, a velvet cap tugged low over the back of his neck. Laurens has already drawn on his oversleeves and his head is bent over a document.

The two commissioners look up as we enter.

'Good morning, Meneers.' I pass behind the master, take the seat beside Laurens. 'We shall not need the fourth chair. Today, I represent myself.'

Jacob, who is continuing around the table, halts. 'The shoemaker is not attending?'

'His shop was ransacked.' I detect a slight turn of the master's head. A flicker of something like surprise crosses his face.

Jacob places the unwanted chair against the wall. At that moment, as surely as if they had stepped into the room, Abe, Trijn, and Otto seem to fill the space beside me. I grip the carved arms of my chair, hold on to the rearing sea creatures as though they are hounds in need of restraint.

The senior commissioner reads:

Geertje Dircx, widow of the sailor Abraham Claesz, declares the defendant has made her promises of marriage and plighted his troth with gifts of a marriage medal and ring. Beyond this, she claims he shared her bed on many occasions, and now must marry or otherwise support her.

Laurens is taking rapid notes. The master stares ahead, looking out the window onto the street. His face is calm, inscrutable. There is something of Hendrickje's composure in his manner. She is a good influence on him. The thought stings.

Laurens and the master confer in low voices.

The scribe lifts his quill. 'May we have the defendant's response?'

Laurens buffs his spectacles as though polishing precious stones. He looks carefully through the lenses before replacing them on his nose.

'The defendant denies making any promise of marriage to the plaintiff. And if the plaintiff asserts that he has slept with her, we call on her to present evidence to support this claim.'

'The union produced no children?'

'None.' Laurens is triumphant, as though my fruitless womb is a damning exhibit to be passed, hand to hand, between the men.

Now it is the turn of the three magistrates to confer. Jacob writes something, shows it to the other two. Murmurings pass between them.

The senior commissioner strokes his pointed beard.

'We have considered the submissions and our opinion is unchanged. It is our view that the honourable painter cannot be compelled to marry a person of the peasant class. There is no issue from the union, therefore no dependants to be provided for. The agreement drawn between the parties at the painter's house stands, except in one particular.'

Laurens stops writing. The master's hands press against the edge of the table ready to force his chair backwards.

'Instead of 160 guilders, the defendant shall pay the plaintiff the sum of 200 guilders annually in her lifetime.'

'An exorbitant sum.' Laurens is indignant.

'A fair one,' Jacob says calmly. 'The case is now concluded. The redemption fee to be paid directly to Meneer Coppens, pawnbroker of the Oudeschans. The first instalment of 200 guilders to be paid to the plaintiff on the twenty-eighth day of June, 1650.'

The master rises, leans across the table. 'Close your books if you will, Meneers, but this matter is far from over.'

Laurens rests a cautionary hand on his arm. He shrugs it off, kicks back his chair. As he leaves, the edge of his cloak catches Laurens' stack of papers and sends the top sheets spiralling to the floor.

'There is another way out, Mistress Dircx.'

At first I do not understand, then Jacob is guiding me through a second door into a side chapel. After the confines of the Chamber, sunlight pouring through the immense windows dazzles my eyes.

'I hope you are satisfied.' His voice is gentle. 'No court in this republic could have compelled such a marriage.'

'I am grateful.' In truth, my mind is so agitated I cannot tell if I have won or lost, or remember exactly what I was fighting for.

The door closes behind him and I am left alone in the silent chapel.

What is there to do but return to the Black Flounder and live out my days in respectable loneliness? Soon, Titus will forget me. Perhaps already he calls Hendrickje *moeder*. I must think on it all, make a plan. For now, weariness besets me and I feel as though I could lie across the grave-markers paving the church and sleep for all eternity.

There is no sign of the master or Laurens in the nave. Two children chase one another around the great columns, and their laughter rises, rebounds from the vaulted ceiling.

Out in the brisk, chill air, order returns to my mind. Tomorrow I will go to the pawnshop to collect the coins, and sew them safely back into my skirt. I will stay in Amsterdam until Pieter arrives, and persuade him to let me keep house for his family in Rarep. When June of next year comes, he can accompany me to the notary's rooms to collect the master's first payment.

How I miss Otto! There is nobody with whom I can share this new resolve.

I walk down the Rapenburgh, avoiding the leering eyes of the ever-present men who fall into step with lone women, hoping to gain favour with sly compliments.

Though it is not yet noon, bright notes from a fiddle spill from the open tavern door. I pat my pocket through my skirts. My bills have been paid; what money I have left is my own. I will take a plate of stew and a dram of rum to heat my belly. If I tell the fiddler my story, perhaps he will tell me his.

Chapter 55

April, 1650

Market day in Edam. I hang back in the shade of the school-master's house. The square is filled with people who might recognise Pieter Dircx's sister, and Pieter must not find out I have been here. Already, I have told him too much of my disgrace and suffered endless recriminations.

Farmers preside over sleds stacked with yellow rounds of cheese. One takes a knife which hangs about his waist, slits the rind, and serves slivers from the blade to waiting customers. I wonder if children still gather at the end of the day to collect the shrivelled leftovers. To our tongues, those discarded wedges tasted sweetest of all.

Boys tease poultry, poking reeds through bars of cages and snatching their fingers clear of sharp beaks. The birds cluck in distress, their ribbed feet clawing at the coops. Keeping to the eaves, I pass the bakery where we used to loiter in hope of a broken twist of sugared bread, and turn onto Molensteeg.

Two little girls sit on the steps outside Trijn's house, one braiding the other's hair with deft, grubby fingers.

The windows are shuttered. I run up the steps, press my weight against the door.

'Trijn Jacobs has gone away.'

When I turn around, the two girls are looking at me curiously. The younger ducks behind her sister's shoulder, peeps at me with round eyes.

'Where has she gone?'

'You will have to buy your herbs from Lina at the market instead. And Trijn Jacobs says Lina cannot tell a thistle from a turnip.'

They giggle.

'Do you know when she will be back?' The elder girl shrugs, points her toe, hops up and down a step. Her shoes are too big and strapped to her feet with strips of leather.

Even now, the innkeeper's wife could be knocking on my door, calling for her husband, telling him I am gone away and no rent paid.

A clang from the bell tower makes me jump, as though someone had struck a pan behind my back. For a few moments, the ponderous melody fills my ears and I cannot think.

I can stay no longer.

I reach for one of the coins that was to pay for my dinner. 'Tell Trijn Jacobs her cousin, Geertje, was here.'

In the moneylender's shop, Giertgen Nanningh hands me a mug of broth without asking if I have eaten. A low fire burns in the back room. Two candles spiked on crooked prickets drip wax onto the stool serving as our table.

'I cannot stay long.'

She nods, folds her hands, and waits.

I drink the thin, gluey broth, grateful for its warmth. When I entered the shop and found her there alone, I almost cried with relief. 'Jeremias will not be home until dusk,' she had said by way of greeting as she bolted the front door behind me.

The musty air smells like clothes that have lain in chests for years. How can she bear to spend her days in a room filled with other people's desperation? I wonder if the buxom shepherdess, my mother's only treasure, ever returned to the cottage wall.

I take the awl from my pocket, turn over the hem of my skirt and pick the threads loose. The contents clink into my hand and onto the pocked stool.

This time, there are no spies to report back to the master.

'All of it is honestly got.'

Giertgen rises, takes a purse from a shelf and counts the silver and gold coins into it. The rings and marriage medal she threads onto a piece of string, knotting it, before adding them to the purse.

'I will be back at the end of June.'

'Everything will be kept safely for your return.'

A leather pouch hangs from her girdle. From it, she takes a handful of guilders, stacks them in front of me.

'Come back if you need more.'

Already, she knows too much, but I am weary of dissembling.

'Some nights I serve in the tavern, but it is not enough to pay all I owe.'

A downdraught sends smoke curling around the room. Until I get the master's first payment, I cannot be free.

My mother sits by the fire, chewing on buttered bread. I fry thin slices of salted pork, willing myself not to look at the dark patch on the wall where the shepherdess once hung.

'Too hard for my gums.' She sucks on a rind, listens to my chatter of how I have tired of the bustling city and plan to return to my friends and family.

'Pieter will help you,' she says, though I have given no hint of need.

'Even if I were a rich man's wife you would worry about me.' I force a laugh.

My mother frowns. 'Then I would worry even more. You should stay among your own people.'

Her eyes are moist and red-rimmed. How much of my face can she see? I take her hand in mine. The ridge of her knuckles presses into my palm.

'Eat well and stay strong. I will come back soon.'

'Why did you not answer Trijn's letters? She went to your master's fine house to ask for you and they turned her away.'

'Trijn came looking for me?'

Trijn, arriving on the Breestraat, borne down with bags and baskets, pushing past a confounded Hendrickje, refusing to leave until I took shape before her eyes.

'She met a bailiff there. From the town hall.' My mother's lips are cracked. Breadcrumbs cling to the corners of her mouth. I suppress the urge to take out my handkerchief, dab at her face as I would a child's. 'She waited over an hour in his company. In that time, a tailor called, complaining he had not been paid since Martinmas.'

'Did she meet the master?'

'Only a half-witted maid who swore you had left of your own accord and gone she knew not where.'

'I called to Trijn's house today but she was not there.'

'Your cousin has gone to Rarep, to ask Pieter where to find you.'

My mother plucks at my arm. 'Geertje, if you are in trouble you should seek your brother's help.'

'You must not tell him I was here. Promise me.'

'Only if you promise to come back soon.'

What would Trijn say if she came to the Rapenburgh and saw how I lived, scrubbing pots in the kitchen by day, drinking brandy wine with strangers by night? What will Pieter tell her? Pieter, who warned me not to leave Amsterdam until the master's payment was received.

I bend to kiss my mother's slack cheek. 'Tell Trijn I will be back in Edam in midsummer. Till then, she does not need to search for me; I am not lost.'

Chapter 56

At the Amsterdam docks, the *Sint Maria* lies on her side, careened in shallow water. Men on ladders scrape at her scabrous timbers. A boy no older than Titus passes buckets of pitch from the wharf to men on the slip, whose breeches are rolled above their knees. They wade to the exposed keel, fasten the fresh buckets to hoists, shout to their comrades who lean down from the tilted deck.

Up close, the tips of the boy's ears and the back of his neck are pink from wind and sun. I want to pull the ragged cap down to protect his child's skin. The men patching the hull are stripped to their waists, their backs bronzed like oiled timbers. How many seasons before this boy becomes one of them?

I hold out a stuiver.

'Where might I find Pieter Dircx?'

A smear of black grease has been pressed like a thumbprint onto the boy's cheek. He takes the coin, straightens his back, and points towards the largest of the warehouses.

The building is like a brick barn. Immense wooden doors are thrown open and a stream of men shouldering planks, pulling carts and rolling barrels flows in and out. At the entrance, groups of wizened sailors pick oakum in the sun. I am the only woman on the wharf. For what price would the boy escort me? But already, a foreman, his teeth blackened with tobacco, is shouting orders at the child. I turn and walk boldly through the sea of men, swinging my arms as I go. No one will harm the carpenter's sister.

Inside, roped crates are heaved upwards on pulleys and stacked under the lofty beams. Freshly cut timber sweetens the salty air. Men with oil-stained faces call and whistle as I pass. Their taunts are lost beneath the rasping of saws and pounding of hammers. I look for Pieter while trying not to meet any stranger's gaze.

I find my brother at the back of the warehouse, one foot resting on a stool, a paper spread out across his knee.

'I told you not to come here.'

Already, I have displeased him.

'I need to speak to you.'

'Why are you not working? For too long it has fallen to me to pay our mother's portion.'

If I tell Pieter that pouring ale and boiling pork knuckles for sailors is not enough to pay my way, he will only tell me to work harder, longer.

'There is little work to be had. Let me go back to Rarep, Pieter. I will help Marit with the children and return to collect the master's payment as soon as it is due.'

He smooths the paper flat with blackened hands and counts aloud, his finger travelling down the list. Satisfied, he folds the docket.

'I may need you here.'

How can I tell him that my nights at the tavern are passed in drinking, dancing and spending Giertgen Nanningh's money? And all the while, the innkeeper's wife keeps watch, chalking figures on slate.

My throat is dry in the dusty air.

'Pieter, why did you not tell me Trijn came to Amsterdam to look for me?'

He drops his foot to the floor. The latest voyage has aged him. His forehead looks rough as tree bark and the hair sticking out from underneath his cap is grey as a gull's wing.

'Who told you that?'

'The baker's boy saw her,' I lie.

'What a trial that woman is. Lately she came to Rarep, bleating nonsense about you being missing.'

Pieter fumbles for his pipe. Before he can fill it, a boy tugs on his arm.

My legs feel weak. I have to speak above the crack and split of wood.

'Someone has been in my room, going through my things. I am afraid to carry money through the streets but more afraid to leave it behind.'

Pieter looks around, lowers his voice. 'The jewels are safe?'

'Quite safe.'

I think of Giertgen Nanningh's leather purse, the thong she knotted around its neck.

My brother grunts, picks up another docket.

'Lately I have been so unwell I can hardly work. In the country I will grow strong again. You are a man of business; you can handle my affairs better than I.'

It is a long time since I have heard Pieter boast of business. But my brother drinks flattery like sweet wine. I see an idea sprouting in his mind.

'It is true that all would be safer in my hands.'

I wait.

'Very well, Sister. We will call to a notary and have it written down.'

'A notary?'

'You want all conducted within the letter of the law, do you not?'

'And then I can keep house for you and Marit?'

He raises a hand. 'All in good time.'

The boy is back at his elbow, saying something.

Pieter curses. 'Can they not caulk decks without me?' He turns, and I follow him back through the warehouse.

Outside in the dock, the hull of the *Sint Maria* swarms with men. A shout goes up, and all scramble to descend the ladders. Dark patches shine where pitch has been rubbed into the ship's joints. She lies pinioned to the wharf with great nooses of rope looped around mooring posts. Sailors wade back through the shallows, climb the slip and take their positions. I look for the boy who reminded me of Titus but he is lost among the men. Pieter cups his hands around his mouth, calls an instruction nobody seems to hear.

Just when I think he has forgotten me, he looks around. 'Meet me by the weigh house tomorrow at noon. We will go to the notary together.'

'Thank you, Pieter.' A surge of happiness warms my blood. At last, I am going home.

I want to embrace my brother but think better of it. He has already directed his attention back to the men. They groan in chorus, heave the ship upright on the ropes. The old vessel sends a wave lapping against the wharf and soaking my feet. Once more, her masts point skyward. I will walk away now, before the men roll their prisoner onto her other side.

'Geertje!'

I look back, shield my eyes. Pieter beckons me closer.

In sunlight, he looks younger, stronger. He grabs my arm, speaks into my ear. 'Tomorrow, make sure to bring the jewels.'

Chapter 57

July, 1650

We follow the curve of the Breestraat, past the Zuiderkerk, and down towards the canal. All morning, the sun battled a mesh of cloud overhanging the city. Now, in mid-afternoon, it surrenders. Even the master's grand house is cast in gloom.

I stop before the bridge.

'I will never enter that house again.'

Pieter frowns.

'You will go where I direct you.'

I must not anger him. Today might be my last day in the city.

In the weeks since telling him of my visit to Giertgen Nanningh's shop, Pieter has remained strangely calm. My mark on the notary's paper has worked some kind of alchemy on him. But the tighter his restraint, the further his wrath may travel when finally released.

'Do you think the master will keep his word?'

He takes the pipe from his mouth, points the stem at the house.

'The painter answers to me now, and that will keep him honest. I tell you again: go back to the tavern; you are not needed here.'

He walks away, crosses the bridge.

I cannot leave until I hear what unfolds.

My brother mounts the steps, lifts the iron ring on the door. There is movement behind the window of the side room; perhaps the master has visitors and will not entertain him. But the front door is opened quickly by someone I cannot see and Pieter steps inside.

I sit on the canal bank to wait. A moorhen's sudden flight startles me. Her yellow feet slap the water, breaking the surface into a chain of colliding ripples. Further along, two boys plunge fishing nets into the depths. They stir the murky water, raise the dripping nets and fling catches of gravel back into the canal.

I look towards the master's house and the windows of the painting room. If he were to look down the Breestraat and across the canal to the crate where I am sitting, my drab figure would blend unseen into brick and mud.

Perhaps now, Hendrickje is bending to whisper in his ear that Pieter has come.

A horse ambles along the towpath pulling a barge towards the bridge. The vessel's steady progress calms me. A seam of pondweed at the water line wavers in its wake. Now Hendrickje brings Pieter down to the kitchen to wait. I see him pacing the slate floor, calculating the cost of the meat strung from the rafters, rating the quality of the ale she pours. When the master joins them, she will sit to one side, slicing beets or grinding peppercorns, listening closely to all that passes.

The boy leading the horse dips his stick into the canal, flicks droplets at two men on board. They curse him, and he laughs. The barge slides under the bridge. A fear grips me that the boy, the horse, the men, are about to disappear; that soon the barge will drift back, untethered and unmanned.

As I strain to see the boat emerge at the other side, Pieter appears at the mouth of the alley behind the master's house, his head held low, walking as though he is being pursued.

'Pieter!' I shout.

I scramble to my feet, hurry to meet him on the bridge.

On seeing me he does not slow his pace. His face is grim.

'What happened?'

'I told you to go home.'

Home. He means the room above the tavern on the Rapenburgh. I have to run to catch up with him. His gaze is fixed straight ahead.

'Did the master pay you?'

'Why can you not behave yourself, Geertje? Did you ever pause to consider how your wanton living might affect my reputation?'

It is as though he has pitched chill canal water into my face. What has the master told him?

'I have done nothing wrong.'

'Do not lie to me; I have heard a full account of your debauchery. Drinking and dancing with sailors in the tavern. It seems you have become adept at finding ways to supplement your income.' There is cold fury in his voice, but also a hollowness to the words, as though he is not fully persuaded of my guilt.

I reach for his arm, force him to stop. 'Pieter, I swear to you it is not true. His spies have so little to report they invent stories where there are none.'

Still, he will not look at me. 'You have brought this misfortune on yourself. Your conduct foils my every attempt to help you.'

'What do you mean? Does he refuse to pay?'

'He will pay nothing until the jewels are redeemed, and my creditors will wait no longer. You have left me with no choice.' When he reaches for his pipe, there is a tremor in his hand. He abandons the attempt and his fingers close around nothing.

'Give me the money and I will go to Edam and collect them this very day.'

'You cannot be trusted. Some weakness of the mind afflicts you. A doctor's word has confirmed it.'

So this is the verdict the doctor and the innkeeper's wife reached while colluding outside my door. They think I am mad. Or want others to believe it is so.

'You know it is not true.'

'Go back to the inn, Geertje.' There is a catch in my brother's voice. He clears his throat. 'I can do no more for you.'

'You will send for me? How long must I wait?'

He walks away, leaving me standing alone on the bridge.

Not quite alone. A woman is watching me. Another of the master's spies? As she approaches, I see something familiar in her face.

'My mistress would speak with you,' Hiskia's maid says.

Am I now to endure the mistress's sister gloating over my downfall?

'Over there. We are ready to leave.' The girl points to a hired barge tethered beyond Sint Antoniesluis. She starts walking, looks back over her shoulder to make sure I am following.

Hiskia's authority pulls me like a river current. At the lock-keeper's house, the maid stops. 'I am to wait here.'

Ahead of us, the barge tugs gently on its mooring. Under the canopy, a pair of grey-gloved hands rests on a woman's dark skirts.

Hiskia can see me, though I cannot fully see her.

'What does she want?'

The girl shrugs. 'I hope she will be quick about it. We have many more calls to make.'

Already a horse is harnessed to the tow rope and a boy stands holding the reins. The boatman squats on the bank, smoking a pipe. When I approach, he hooks the barge, pulls it close enough for me to clamber on board.

The boat rocks under my feet.

'Sit,' Hiskia's voice commands.

I duck under the canopy, take a seat on the wooden bench opposite her.

She is gowned in her habitual black. A white cap, severely starched, is tied under her chin. Her hair is now more grey than black, but her eyes are sharp as ever. Even in the confines of a tow barge she holds a regal air.

'So you have been supplanted. I deem the new wench will prove a more tractable helpmeet.'

My instinct is to rise, run far from this woman, but she stops me with a wave of her glove. 'I take no pleasure in your misfortune.'

'What do you want of me if not to revel in my troubles?'

'I revel in nothing. I fear God, and strive to protect my nephew from the excesses of his father. Those are my guiding principles.' She pauses. 'Your brother came to the Breestraat on a petition.'

'He acts for me.'

'He acts for himself.'

The glove rises in admonition before I can reply.

'You were a friend to my sister in the last months of her life. You held her hand as she lay dying. I have not forgotten these things. I would not have it on my conscience that I failed to warn you.'

'Warn me?'

She glances out onto the canal bank. 'I know none of the particulars. Only that the men have struck a bargain and you are to pay the price.'

'It is the master who must pay. The law ruled in my favour.'

'Reports of your behaviour may challenge that ruling.'

'Those are lies.' My face grows hot.

'It matters not. My brother-in-law seeks to incite others against you and will pay well for such testimony.'

'If he defaults, I will summon him to the Chamber again.'

She shakes her head. 'Test his malice no further. Leave Amsterdam. Give up your sinful ways and turn your mind to God.'

Money is her true concern. She wants me away from the temptations of the city for fear I might squander her nephew's inheritance.

'I have already planned to leave, to go far from here and live among those who care for me.'

For an instant, the mistress's anxious eyes gaze upon me. The illusion passes, and Hiskia returns.

She straightens her back, clasps her gloved hands.

'My duty is done. Step out, and send my maid to me.'

All the way back to the Rapenburgh, I tremble with rage. What slanders has the master gathered, and how does he mean to use them against me? The innkeeper's wife, the doctor, the owner of the pawnshop on the Oudeschans – all are in his pay. And what deal has he struck with Pieter? I remember my brother's parting words: *I can do no more for you.*

I pass the Blue Anchor and think of Otto settled in Haarlem, perhaps by now a married man. How badly I need the counsel of a friend. Tonight I will pack my things, and in the morning I will go, not to Rarep but home, to Edam. Trijn will not fail me.

Chapter 58

The fiddler lifts the pitcher, fills my mug again.

'No more. I must be gone at dawn.' I look over my shoulder. There is no sign of the innkeeper or his vigilant wife.

The fiddler laughs. 'I have had more farewell drinks with you than with every sailor to pass under this roof.'

'This time, I am really leaving.'

The double ale served by the house is cloudy and sour. I drink in gulps to avoid the taste, and to push Pieter's harsh words, Hiskia's talk of sin, from my mind. A sailor slaps a coin onto the table, making me jump. The swaying girl he grips about the waist bumps against my stool and giggles, holding a hand to her mouth. Brightly coloured feathers in her hair remind me of those in the master's cabinet of curiosities. How afraid I once was to walk in his sacred space, to touch his precious things. The fiddler lifts his bow, strikes up a jig. The sailor and girl dance too close to the tables, jogging elbows and upsetting drinks. Soon, there will be a fight.

It is too hot for dancing. I finish my drink, move towards the open door. Cloud covered the city all day, and evening has added another stifling layer. Dock-labourers fill the wooden benches outside, their sleeves rolled up over grimy forearms as they slake their thirst. A sudden gust lifts a scattering of vegetable peelings, mussel shells and dried husks, depositing the flotsam at my feet. The forlorn hope that Pieter might come for me, see me safely out of the city, is gone. At dawn I will walk to the Nieuwmarkt and seek a cart heading northward.

What would Hiskia say if she saw me beckoning the maid, bidding her to bring me a pitcher of ale, no, a jug of rum, to take to my room? All are disposed to believe the worst; on my last night let me fulfil at least a little of their imaginings. I count coins into the maid's hand. Never will anybody accuse me of theft.

Outside, the innkeeper is occupied in supervising the unloading of a sled, and does not look around. I mount the steps, the jug hidden under my apron, as he rolls a barrel over the cobbles.

I bolt my door, set the jug down on the scratched boards. Downstairs, the music comes to an abrupt stop. I picture the innkeeper dragging the sailor across the floor, the girl in feathers shrieking, wringing her hands. I splash rum into my stained mug, drink too quickly and cough, spattering my bodice. Tomorrow, Trijn will sieve through this mess I am in, cast the waste aside, help me to salvage what is left.

I roll my belongings into the old shawl and knot the ends. When the jug is empty, I lie down and lose myself to the lurching in my head.

Someone is tapping a spigot into a barrel. When I open my eyes, I expect to find myself in the tavern. The knocking sounds again.

'Who is there?' I struggle up from the bed, hold my head in my hands.

Outside my door is a boy in a stained jerkin.

'What do you want?'

'Your brother is waiting for you at the weigh house, Mistress Dircx, and I will get another stuiver if I bring you straight away.'

It is still light out. I have slept for an hour at most.

'What time is it?'

'The clock on the Montelbaanstoren struck seven as I passed.'

Even if we leave now, it will be dark before we reach Edam. But Pieter will be with me, and he will likely bring a lantern. My clothes smell of rum. I will tell him I was serving tables.

The boy skips to the top of the stairs and back again to see if I am following.

'You will have another stuiver if you carry my things.'

On the Rapenburgh the boy runs ahead, looking back every now and then, and waiting for me to catch up. My feet are clumsy, stumbling along the streets. I will myself on, eyes burning, forehead throbbing. A few hours of my brother's censure and the rocking of a cart must be endured, then I will be home. I can think no further ahead.

By the time we reach the Nieuwmarkt, the cobbles are hitting the soles of my feet like mallets. The square bears the scars of the day's trade. Trodden cakes of manure bake in the evening sun. Piles of wooden crates lie abandoned under the trees, and a crew of children has made a game of stacking and leaping the obstacles.

The boy leads me around the weigh house to the northern side and stops, pushes my bundle into my arms.

'Where is Pieter?' I reach for a coin, scan the quiet square. For now, the taverns contain the drinkers. The only carts I see are not harnessed, their horses likely stabled for the night. A beggar leans on his stick, making slow progress towards the canal.

Two men step out of the shade. Neither of them is Pieter.

A wary look comes over the boy's face. Something is wrong. He backs away as the men approach. Fear jumps in my chest. The bundle falls from my arms. I turn and run, but the men are upon me, grabbing me from behind. I scream and struggle.

'Stop your caterwauling.' The man tightens his grip. I cry out again. He drags me back on my heels. My feet slide along the cobbles. The second man faces me, brandishing a closely written page. 'Geertje Dircx, you are arrested by order of the magistrate.'

'Arrested? I have done nothing wrong. My brother will speak for me.' But Pieter is not here. He was never here. Someone has betrayed me.

'Your brother has already spoken.' Tobacco stains streak the man's beard. He taps the paper. Swimming among the words are the first two letters I learned as a child: *P is for Pieter, G is for Geertje.* Pieter coming home from school, promising to teach me all he learned, then quickly tiring of the game. The men take one arm each, drag me towards the canal. A *trekschuit* is docked at the jetty. I am shaking now, my legs folding beneath me.

'Let me go. I am leaving anyway, I swear it.'

'We will make sure of it,' the man who pinned my arms says, and they laugh.

They hoist me onto the jetty, force me across the ramp onto the boat. A push to the small of my back sends me sprawling down steps into the cabin. My forehead hits the edge of a low table. Underneath it, a pair of coarse stockinged feet are wedged into wooden mules.

'Pick her up,' a woman's voice says.

I am lifted by the elbows, thrown onto a bench.

Cornelia Jans, the butcher's wife, sits across from me, hands folded on her lap, a thin smile on her face.

'You have a long journey ahead. It is best you spend the time in prayer.'

My forehead stings. 'Where are you taking me?'

'Be grateful to be leaving your sinful ways behind.'

Something drips down the side of my face. She curls her lip. When I touch my cheek, blood sticks to my fingertips.

The man with the stained beard stoops to enter the cabin, takes a seat beside me. His companion follows, kicking the bundle of my clothes in front of him. I grab it, hug the familiar shawl now clotted with dirt.

Cornelia Jans leans forward. 'Did you really think he would sit by and let you squander his son's fortune?'

'Enough,' the magistrate's agent says. 'See to her.'

She sits back, settles her shawl about her shoulders. 'I am no nursemaid.'

'Wipe your face on your apron,' the man tells me.

Passengers fill the cabin. Two merchants stare at me, my guards, and take seats at the furthest end of the benches. A group of labourers gets on, then a girl in a red bodice who asks the men if they would like to hear her sing. Even if I could scramble onto the deck, what could I do there but throw myself into the water, hope that the weight of my skirts would not drag me to the depths before reaching safety?

The sun is setting as the boat slides away from the dock. When darkness falls, perhaps the men will sleep. I might slip up the steps, beg the boatman to take pity on me, let me jump onto the bank. Better to be alone and lost in the dark than confined with the master's accomplices.

Grief for the life I once had swells within me.

He loved me. I want to shout it at the labourers who have taken out a deck of cards, at the merchants who are sharing a flask of brandy, at the girl who has seated herself on a man's lap and is laughing as he pretends to push her away.

No appeals will move my captors. The men sit in silence, legs spread wide. Cornelia pulls her shawl tighter, draws in her elbows, her face a study of spite. The master chose his allies well.

We travel south along the canal and onto the Amstel. Soon we are passing under the Blauwbrug and leaving the city walls behind.

Chapter 59

Cornelia Jans is sleeping, her head inclined towards the guard's shoulder, breath whistling through her nose. We pass old city walls, studded with watchtowers. Windmill sails cut the sky.

Our boat is towed into a narrow waterway and drawn to a halt. Beside me, my guard stretches his back, slaps his knees and rises. His bulk fills the doorway as he calls to the boatman. The man shouts back. A toll must be paid.

The girl is slumped on one of the labourer's laps, her cheek resting against his chest. 'Hup,' he says, swatting her thigh. She lifts her head, yawns, and he tumbles her to her feet.

Is this to where I am banished? Chill air has flooded my bones, as though my body had been fastened to the horse's rope and dragged through the waterways all night. Perhaps I am never to leave this smoke-filled cabin. My punishment is to travel the canals on an endless journey of regret.

The remaining guard twists in his seat to point out a lodging house to his neighbour. While they look out the window, the girl slides along the bench, touches my hand.

'They say it is not so bad as other places.' Her eyes are full of pity.

'Is this Rotterdam?' I am too tired to weep.

'Gouda. The town stinks, but lots of men work in the factories.'

My guard swings around to face the cabin. 'Have a care, or you will go where she is going.'

The girl shuffles back along the bench.

The boat jerks forward.

Cornelia Jans opens her eyes, scans the windows.

'Get up.' She drives a shoe into my shin.

As we dock, a powerful odour wafts through the cabin as though one of the passengers had opened a barrel of rotten meat. I stand on stiff legs, claw at the doorway to steady myself. Cornelia slaps my hand away. 'Wait.'

The labourers push past. The girl staggers and squeals. One of the merchants lifts a hand to support her on the steps and she laughs, links his arm. Her chatter continues onto the deck, along the jetty, fades into the distance. Cornelia Jans rises, then the guard's hand is on my shoulder and I am pushed after her.

Gouda blinds me. All along the bank, sun flashes against whitewashed houses.

One of the guards digs a knuckle into my back. 'Move on.'

They prod me along a street pitted with missing cobbles. Beside us, the canal is a thick soup of waste. Its stench seems to seep into my jacket, my hair, my skin. At the sluice, the bloated corpse of a dog floats, snagged against the gates.

Cornelia turns, walks into the lee of an old church. They are taking me to a convent. But then she turns again, leads us through a narrow street to a long grey building with an arched doorway. On the pediment is a carving of a robed woman, a sword tucked under her arm. She gazes at the pages of a book while at her feet a man lies, the tip of her blade entering his neck.

The men are flanking me now, each holding an arm. Cornelia hammers the iron ring against the door.

A shutter opens behind a grating. Cornelia dips her head to match its height. 'I have brought the prisoner, Geertje Dircx.'

Bolts slide back. I am pierced by fear, as though the stone sword had slipped and entered my chest. When the door opens, the men drag me forward.

'No!' I grind my heels into the cobbles.

'*Godverdomme!*' The men wrench my arms behind my back. My legs crumple. I am carried inside walls as thick as I am tall. They force me through a hallway into a room furnished only with two chairs and lit by a row of small windows set high in the wall.

'A rough one,' the maid says, looking at me.

My cap is sliding from my head. Wisps of hair torment my eyes. When the men release my aching arms, I see that my hands are streaked with grime.

The man with the stained beard swings my bundle from his shoulder to the floor.

'Tell the house mother we have had a long journey and could eat a ship's rations.'

'You may tell her yourself.' The maid turns to Cornelia. 'You and her, wait here.'

'I must see the governor immediately,' Cornelia says.

The maid smirks. 'Impossible.'

Cornelia bridles. 'I demand to see the governor.'

'You will have a long wait. There is no governor here. The governess will see you when she is ready.'

The studded door closes behind them. A key turns in the lock. Cornelia jumps forward, attempts to rap on the stout oak and succeeds only in hurting her hand.

It would take a battering ram to force that door. And even if I could scale the bare walls, my bleeding fingers would likely find the windows sealed. The only tool I have to aid me is Otto's awl, still hidden in the pocket under my skirts. How many years would it take to chip a tunnel through one of these stone walls?

Cornelia sits on one of the chairs, tilts her head forward and tightens the strings of her cap behind her neck. I slip the awl from my pocket to my garter.

When the maid returns, she leads us out to a yard and through a portico into what once must have been a chapel. Under a vaulted wooden ceiling, stained-glass windows line long grey walls. Instead of pews there are narrow benches, and a lectern stands where an altar should be. Beside it, a woman sits at a table, writing.

'I have brought the prisoner, Madam.' Cornelia's triumph echoes through the old chapel.

The woman removes her spectacles, regards her with a solemn expression. She wears a heavy gown of black damask and an old-fashioned ruff so crisp I wonder the folds do not cut her chin like blades. Her aged face is white as her linen. A widow's cap sits high on her forehead. When she looks at me, her eyes narrow. She rises from her seat. I shrink back as she approaches.

'You are hurt,' she says.

I had forgotten the cut to my forehead.

'She resisted,' Cornelia says. 'We had much trouble with her.'

'You know why you are here?'

'No, Madam.' I am weak with exhaustion, hunger, fear.

The governess frowns at Cornelia. 'Did they read the warrant?'

'It was shown to her but she thrashed about and refused to look upon it.'

'Give it to me.' She replaces her spectacles, takes the paper from Cornelia. 'You are Geertje Dircx, widow of Abraham Claesz of Hoorn?'

'Yes, Madam.'

'You are charged with dissolute living, drunkenness, disturbing the peace of your neighbours, unpaid debts and breaking terms of a lawful agreement.'

'There is more. There is writing about her erratic behaviour and disordered mind.' Cornelia jabs the page, elbows me. 'See how many have signed it.'

Pieter's name is first. For an instant I see him as a boy at the Edam *kermis*, a golden twist of bread shaped into a P and sprinkled with sugar swinging from one finger.

The rest of the names are a tangle of letters. No doubt the inn-keeper and his wife were eager to sign; the doctor, too. Is the fiddler's mark among them? It matters not; this is the master's work as surely as though he had signed his name in bone-black across the bottom.

The governess folds the warrant. 'You have the fee?'

Cornelia takes out a leather purse, hands it over.

Footsteps cross the flagstones behind us.

'Mistress Jans, the maid will bring you to the house mother's quarters where you may take some refreshment before you leave. Geertje will then be taken to the infirmary.'

'Do with her what you will.'

Cornelia Jans follows the maid to the door, calls back to me. 'At last, you are where you belong.'

The governess returns to her table, counts the money into a drawer, locks it. She opens a large book and starts to write.

'Madam.'

My whisper carries through the chamber. She looks up, removes the spectacles again.

'Yes?'

'What is this place?'

'This is the spinhouse, where you will be reformed and leave your sinful ways behind.'

The spinhouse. Where wicked women are brought to be punished before they die. My legs weaken. I sit before I fall.

'Do not be frightened. Hard work and discipline will become your truest friends. The skills you learn here will steer you to a better course.'

The maid returns, eyes the dirty shawl holding my belongings. 'You may carry that yourself. Get up.'

I follow her to the door.

I have been condemned without a trial. Anger strikes like a flint against stone. I turn back to face the governess.

'Madam.'

She looks up and frowns, but stays her quill.

'How long is my reform to take?'

'The sentence has been logged.' She turns back a leaf in her book. Her finger searches the page. When she finds the answer, she smiles to herself. Her record-keeping has been tested and not found wanting.

She lifts her chalk-white face to look at me.

'Twelve years.'

Chapter 60

'Every bedstead is full. Where am I to put her?' The matron at the infirmary props the door open with one shoulder. She wears a white apron over a heavy grey gown. A smell of lye wafts out to meet us.

The maid shrugs. 'This one is need of a basin of water, not a bed.'

'Where did they find her?'

'At a sailors' tavern.'

'Then the pox house is the best place for her.'

A groan of agony comes from within. 'Quiet,' the matron shouts into the room. She frowns at me. 'You look healthy enough.'

Lye catches in my throat as I follow her into a room lined with bedsteads where women recline, two to a bed. Those who are awake stare at me with dull eyes.

One raises a hand, calls to me.

I stop. The woman is older than my mother. Her lips move but no further sound comes.

'Ignore her,' the matron says.

The barred windows of the infirmary look onto a courtyard, and the former chapel where I met the governess. Its steeple rises like a bodkin. Swifts have nested in the belfry. Shadows of birds in flight chase across the cobbles.

Past the bedsteads, in the farthest corner of the room, a maid sets down a jug and basin on a table.

'Strip to your shift and wash yourself.'

I hesitate. Am I to undress where all may see?

'Take her linen,' the matron tells the maid.

'What about this?' The maid pokes the knotted shawl in my arms.

The matron unties the bundle, sorts through my clothes, flicks my mother's comb aside. Abe's medal, she holds up to the window.

'Tin.' She wrinkles her nose. Her mottled hands pull out Saskia's silk kerchief. 'A thief as well as a harlot.'

'I am neither. After my mistress's death, that was given to me by her sister.'

'I hope you did not murder her for it.'

They laugh.

The matron threads the silk through her rough fingers, drapes it over one shoulder to admire the folds, then rolls it up and tucks it into her pocket. 'You may count yourself lucky to have escaped the gallows.'

I could have sold the kerchief long ago, had its value in bread and meat. But every time I suffered a trader at the Nieuwmarkt to shake it out like an old towel, I finished by snatching it back, and spending another hungry night on the Rapenburgh.

A hoarse scream makes me jump.

A room adjoins the infirmary, as though a wall had been knocked into an adjacent building years ago. Down one step is a windowless annexe with a low ceiling. Inside is a box bed, and on the floor beside it, a girl lies on a pallet, her knees drawn up to meet the mound of her belly. She writhes and sobs, her hand half-forced into her mouth.

'Knot a rag for her to bite on,' the matron orders the maid.

For an instant I am back in Hoorn, the midwife at the foot of my bed, the room smelling of mutton grease and blood.

'What are you gaping at?' The matron throws a cloth into the basin. 'Be quick about it.'

In front of the women I take off my jacket, apron, bodice, untie my skirts and step out of them.

'And your stockings,' the matron says. 'The Spanish disease starts with the feet.'

Otto's awl is secure in my garter, hidden under the length of my shift. What will happen if she sees it? My hands tremble. I peel the first stocking from my leg.

A pounding comes from within the box bed. Someone is hammering at the wooden panels. They have been bolted on the outside with a crude length of timber. There is a shriek of laughter, then a choking sound.

'Now you have woken her.' The matron aims the words at the girl on the pallet. She takes a broom, beats the handle against the wood. 'Silence!'

My shaking hands tear a hole in the second stocking. I shove the awl back into my garter without her seeing. I pray she will not examine my knees.

I smear the oily scrap of soap over my skin, douse my face, neck, arms with cold water. Shiny scales of dried blood from my forehead cling to the cloth.

'Hands,' the matron says.

I turn up my palms and she begins her examination. When she has checked the soles of my feet and between my toes, she grunts. 'You are clean. For now.'

The clamour of women's voices in the dining hall is louder than the tumult of any tavern on the Rapenburgh. The uproar echoes around four tables flanked by crowded wooden benches. A dozen or so women occupy each table, marking territory with elbows planted firmly on scuffed surfaces. A grim-faced maid scrubs a splay of droplets from one of the whitewashed walls.

Supper is underway. I am led to an empty space beside a woman with lank fair hair and an ill-fitting cap.

'Alone again today, Janne?' the maid accompanying me says.

Janne turns around and smiles. I stare back at her. Bulbous growths bulge from her youthful forehead. Her gums seem to shrink from her teeth. She pats the bench beside her and I sit, take up my wooden spoon. In front of me is a dish of barley porridge, a chunk of rye bread and a half-filled mug of ale. On my other side, an old woman is rocking back and forth, muttering what might be a prayer.

Janne's swollen hand reaches over to touch mine. I try not to wince.

'Tomorrow will be better. Sometimes the mother sends to the fish market. What is your name?'

A crash resounds through the hall. I drop my spoon.

At the head of the room, a woman brandishes what looks like the leg of a chair. A plain white collar falls like a cape across her broad shoulders. The wired points of her cap pinch her slack cheeks. She surveys the subdued room, the implement resting like a bayonet against her shoulder. I want to ask Janne who she is, but all are silent. Even my elderly neighbour's supplications fade to a whisper.

The woman bows her head to recite grace. When she finishes, my companions lift their spoons, and soon a cautious hum of conversation accompanies the scraping of plates, the clattering of mugs. Janne eats quickly, forcing morsels of bread into her mouth after every spoonful of porridge. When I hesitate, she motions for me to do the same. Hunger claws at my stomach but the congealed barley clogs my throat. I push it away. Gulls at Amsterdam harbour eat better than this. I soak a piece of bread in the weak ale, take a bite.

Someone ousts the praying woman from her seat, edges in beside me. I smell stale breath and the reek of unwashed skin before I dare to look up. On my other side, Janne cowers.

'Welcome, Oma,' the newcomer says. 'What present have you brought me?'

She is a tall, brawny woman with a tanned face. I imagine her harvesting peat in the sun, a basket strapped to her back, or balancing a yoke across her shoulders, bearing more weight than most men could carry.

'I am sorry, Sister, I have nothing to give you. All I ever owned now lies in a pawnshop far from here.'

She grabs my sleeve. I am careful not to flinch from her grasp.

'No token from a sweetheart pinned to your shift?'

'The sweethearts I had took more than they gave.'

At this, she laughs, loosens her grip. 'Then you will have to make it up to me.' She reaches for the remainder of my bread, stuffs it into her mouth, smacks her lips over the last of my ale. 'That will do for now.'

The maid returns, ringing a pewter bell. The woman at the head of the room now wields a prayer book. All stand.

After prayers, we file past the house mother to ascend a narrow stairs. The chair leg catches the crook of my elbow.

'You are new.'

'Yes, Madam.'

'*Yes, Mother*,' she corrects me.

'Yes, Mother.'

The chair leg jabs my ribs. 'See that you give me no trouble. Janne will show you where to go.'

'Yes, Mother.'

I grab the rope that forms the balustrade, follow the other prisoners upstairs.

Janne is waiting for me. The dormitory is an airless attic furnished with two rows of straw pallets. Inside the door is a chair where I guess our guard will be stationed. At the other end, under the apex of the roof, a round window admits a disc of evening light. 'Over here,' Janne says.

I have to duck my head to avoid rafters cutting across the space. Already, women are fighting over bedding. At the end of the room, a rank smell rises. A young girl is squatting on one of a cluster of pots. She sees me looking at her, extends a bare leg and laughs as I trip over her foot.

This is where I am to sleep.

There are no pallets for us, only mats woven from coarse fibres. I undress in the cramped space, roll up my skirt to form a bolster. Janne lies on the mat beside mine, her small body curled like a child's. Across the room from us is the muttering woman who lies fully clothed on her mat. Another croons over an imaginary baby she has fashioned from a bundle of rags.

'Better to sleep other way round,' Janne says. 'Sometimes the pots get upset during the night.'

In my shift, I crawl into the narrowing space until my head brushes the shingles. They have baked all day in the blazing sun and now release unbearable heat into the room. Janne's breath floats across the gap that divides us. 'It gets easier, Geertje. Tomorrow will be better.'

A parade of women passes to and from the pots. The stench grows stronger. The porridge, the sour ale threaten to return to my throat. I reach for my pocket, find the mementos of my mother,

Abe, Trijn, still safe under my shift. I close my eyes. For a while I try to follow the recitations of the muttering woman but her gibberish seems closer to curses than prayers. Pain revolves inside my head.

In the dark, rafters turn to gibbets dangling phantom figures. A terror of pustules swelling all over my body seizes me and I wake myself with the frantic pressing of my fingers to my face.

Women moan and cry out in their sleep. The night is fractured with sounds and smells of bodies on pots, the passing footsteps of the warden on her rounds.

I stray in and out of sleep, dream that I am standing on a plinth above a strange city, afraid to move lest I plunge to the street below. An iron weight presses against my shoulder. I touch the blade of the sword and a drop of my blood spills down its length, falls onto the neck of the dead man at my feet.

When I awaken, I am lying on my front, Otto's awl held tightly against my chest, as though defending myself against the evils of the night.

Chapter 61

After morning prayers I follow Janne and the others out of the dining room. My head aches from lack of sleep. We enter the work-room, where four windows braced with iron bars overlook the court-yard and admit the full force of the sun. A partition wall, panelled to waist-height and topped with a row of wooden balusters, allows the sunlight to travel to the corridor beyond. Stale sweat salts the air.

Janne takes a seat at a spinning wheel. Her swollen fingers strug-gle to feed the bobbin. I want to help, but the house mother is direct-ing women to their places and I dare not move without instruction. A weaving loom clatters at the far end of the room. Elderly prisoners are already settled on three-legged stools where they braid fishing nets, the slack falling around their feet. They work with eyes half-closed, their fingers reading the strands.

The house mother leads me to a circle of women sitting with heads bent over their stitching. 'Spoil any linen and I will send you to the laundry with Beatrijs.'

Beatrijs, who took my bread and frightened Janne. I imagine her strong arms turning paddles in vats of steeping linen all day.

A seamstress wearing a pair of shears on a cord clips a length of barley-coloured thread and hands me a needle. From a basket of fabric scraps she takes a handkerchief pitted with old needle marks. 'Copy Lijsbet's work for now. Make no mistakes, or you will spend the afternoon unpicking them.'

The woman seated beside me smiles, spreads her work out on her lap to display the pattern. She is stitching a border of flowers and leaves, a design too delicate to conceal the puckers in the square of fabric I have been given. I thread my needle, try to recall the devices my mother taught me.

A howl cuts across the room. One of the spinning women has grabbed her neighbour by the cap and swung her to the floor. They tussle on the ground. In an instant one of the wardens is upon them, beating both with a slipper until they separate, gasping, skirts about their knees.

My fingers tremble. I begin the outline of the sparrow with the sprig of strawberries in its beak. I pretend that I am back in Edam, stitching peacefully by the fireside. As long as I keep my head lowered to my work, the illusion endures. With every vane on the feathers, every seed knotted onto a berry, a drop of courage returns.

'You have a talent for fine work,' Lijsbet whispers. Her blue eyes are framed with fair lashes. There is a twist in the bridge of her nose where the bone must have been broken long ago.

'My mother taught me when I was a girl.'

'It will please the house mother. The best work is sold to the visitors.'

A child seated on Lijsbet's other side touches her elbow. Lijsbet takes the girl's work, untangles the thread, hands it back.

'Your daughter?' I ask.

She shakes her head. 'Anneken has no mother.'

'Why is she here?'

'Her father's new wife said she stole a golden pin from her jewel box.'

Anneken pulls hard on her needle, snaps the thread. Lijsbet takes the work from her again.

'Have you been here long?'

'Eight years this winter,' Lijsbet says.

'When do you get out?'

'Nobody leaves before their term and I have ten more years to serve.' She turns to Anneken. 'Hold it like this.'

'Is there no other way out?'

'Those in favour are allowed out by day. Some work at the pipe factory. They sleep in proper bedsteads in the east wing, along with the white-bread prisoners.'

'How am I to gain favour?'

Lijsbet's eyes flick to the lectern where a man converses with the house mother, a large book held under one arm. His eyes rove around the room.

'At the whim of the house father.'

The man opens the Bible and commences reading, sucking in his breath after every line. His fleshy chin sits on a collar too tight for his neck and his face is blotched red, as though he had lately enjoyed an excess of food and wine. Trijn would size him up with her shrewd eyes. *I fear it may take more than a little psalm-reading to win his favour.*

I risk another question. 'Who are the white-bread prisoners?'

A blow lands on my shoulder. The house mother stands over me, wielding a distaff. 'Enough talk.' She pinches my work between her fingers, inspects it in silence, drops it back onto my lap. 'How slow you are.'

The house father drones on. Some trick of the wooden panels adds a mocking echo. In hearing him twice, we hear none of his subject.

Women rub their necks, mutter to one another. The seamstress rounds the circle, nods at my progress, moves on. Anneken shifts in her seat. Her neighbour on the other side has a habit of cosseting the child, fussing over her cap and smoothing her face. 'Stop it, Hanna,' the girl says, shrugging her off. Before long, Hanna resumes her attentions.

Lijsbet holds her square of linen to the light, frowns at some imperfection. I want to ask her how I might appeal to the governess, how I can get a message to Trijn. Trijn, who is far away in Edam and knows nothing of Pieter's betrayal. How long will it be before my cousin comes to look for me? She will find no trace of me in Amsterdam. She will seek out Pieter, but it may be months before the *Sint Maria* returns from Russian waters. And what tale will my brother tell her then?

By midday, the room is so hot I have to press my damp fingers to my apron to prevent them staining the linen. The house mother taps the distaff against her palm, remedies the slackening of spinning wheels with smacks on knuckles. When a bell rings, the wheels cease, and fat bobbins of wool are stilled for her approval. She unwinds a length of Janne's yarn, holds up the lumpy wool for all to see.

The seamstress begins her inspections. She tosses Hanna's work into the scrap-basket with little more than a glance. She nods at Anneken and Lijsbet, stops when she comes to me. The bird is yet without tail feathers; the sprig bears one strawberry but no leaves.

'Where did you learn this?'

My shoulder still throbs from the house mother's blow.

'In the village where I grew up.'

Her fingertip follows the line of my stitches. 'I have seen it before, though not so finely done as this.' She lifts the basket of scraps, turns imperfect samples over in her hands until she finds the one she seeks. 'This is the same pattern, is it not?'

A wrinkled piece of linen, frayed at the edges, bears a crude copy of my sparrow. A haphazard hatching of thread fills the wing where fishbone stitches should be, and a misshapen strawberry floats, unattached to any stem. Someone in the Gouda spinhouse has worked an imitation of my mother's design, the one which never left Edam until I brought it on a handkerchief to Amsterdam, and gave it, years ago, as a parting gift to Ilse.

Chapter 62

In the dining room I search every table, face by face. When I cannot find Ilse, I start my search again.

Janne touches my arm. 'Geertje, you must eat.'

Dinner is pottage, boiled to a thick paste. I am hungry enough to eat it. Women hunch over their food, curling protective arms around their bowls. This time I finish my bread and beer before Beatrijs approaches. Her thick fingers grab the rim of my mug. Raw patches shine where skin has been scraped from her knuckles. Finding the mug empty, she sends it sliding across the table. I catch it before it hits the floor.

'Clumsy,' she says. 'Break any ware and you will earn yourself a beating.'

Hanna giggles, presses a wrinkled hand to her mouth. On her lap is the clump of rags to which she sings at night. She snatches the bundle to her chest and strokes the folds.

'I hope the ribbon-woman comes today,' Anneken says.

'Do you have money?' Beatrijs leans across the table, her face almost touching the child's.

Anneken turns up her chin. 'None. Perhaps you would like to buy me a present?'

Lijsbet's shoulders tighten.

But Beatrijs only laughs, backs away. 'I would do better to buy Janne a veil to hide her face.'

Janne ignores her. She is busy tying and re-tying the strings of her cap. 'We must make ready for the visitors. You might meet a man, Geertje.'

'The pox has softened your brain,' Beatrijs says.

But nothing seems to dampen Janne's excitement. 'It could happen. One summer a cloth merchant from Antwerp fell in love with a girl he saw weaving and took her away to be his wife. I heard it from one of the maids.'

'Neither man nor beast would pin your rotting cunny,' Beatrijs says. A cackle of laughter breaks out around the table.

Janne continues her preening, patting the swollen contours of her nose. Today, the growths on her forehead seem more pronounced, as though her skin is straining to contain them. I remember Abe's tales of the home for old sailors, the raving men who lay tied to their beds, flesh rotting from their faces. A shiver of pity creeps up my back.

Nobody can remember who stitched the crooked bird. The seamstress presses the point of her shears to the tangled threads at the back of the sample.

'I can fix it,' I tell her.

'I see nothing worth saving.' But she stays the shears, hands me the scrap of linen.

I examine the stitches again. Ilse's impatience is in every shortcut the needle took. She must be here. Or perhaps she was here, and is now gone.

Lijsbet sews steadily beside me. *Nobody leaves before their term.*

When I open my fist, the bird is scored with wayward creases. I smooth the linen against my knee. Ilse is here, and I will find her.

Feet tramp through the hall. The whirring of spinning wheels stops. Women look up from their work and the buzz of chatter rises.

'Silence,' the house mother calls. The corridor is filling with people who stare at us through the balusters as though watching a sideshow at a *kermis*. There are ladies and gentlemen, sailors and servants. 'I want to see the bad women,' a child cries, and an obliging father holds the little boy aloft. The child sucks his thumb, regards us with round-eyed pleasure.

'Who are these visitors?' I ask Lijsbet.

'Anyone who cares to pay two stuivers to look upon us.'

A young man with a cloak swung over one shoulder provides commentary for his companion. *Thieves . . . vagabonds . . . whores.* His lady friend lifts a corner of her silk shawl to cover her nose.

A boy not much older than Titus grips the balusters, squeezes his face between the struts. Smallpox scars pit his forehead. Who deemed a visit to the spinhouse a suitable diversion for this child?

I have been looking too long at him. He pinches a coin between thumb and forefinger, stretches his thin arm through the bars towards me.

'Open your bodice.' The tip of his tongue slides over his lips.

I bend my burning face to my work. I remember the boys I saw at the Edam market, jabbing caged birds with reeds.

Peddlers enter the hall, their singsong voices offering cakes of soap and candied lemon slices. Anneken quivers with excitement. Lijsbet looks at the house mother and gains a stiff nod of permission. She slips a coin into Anneken's hand, accompanies the girl to examine lengths of twill and corded trim dangled through the bars.

A privileged few are permitted to join them while the rest of us stay seated. I try to ignore the rich smell of molasses floating into the room. One of the weavers buys a square of gingerbread. The cake is divided and divided again. The house mother raps shiny fingers with her distaff, makes the women wipe their hands before returning to their work.

A bell signals the end of the visitors' hour. After the footsteps die away, the house father appears at the door. Today, in place of the Bible, he carries a wooden coffer. Below the brim of his hat, sweat-soaked hair clings like treacle to his forehead. His eyes search the room, land on Anneken.

'I will borrow the child to count the money.' His breath is almost a wheeze.

Lijsbet's hand grips Anneken's wrist.

The house mother stiffens, sets down an armful of bobbins. 'Leave it to me,' she says. 'I would not trust any of these scoundrels with the task.'

Her husband seems about to object. He starts to say something, but already she has taken the box. Lijsbet does not withdraw her hand until the door closes behind him.

I stitch on, willing myself back to Edam and the peace of my mother's fireside. Can it be that Ilse once sat in my place, enduring the tumult of spectators, stabbing linen with her needle to pacify the house mother?

A new ribbon lies coiled on Anneken's lap, and every so often she strokes its silken weave.

Lijsbet has relaxed again. Her fingers whip neat stitches across her work.

'The prisoners in the east wing,' I whisper. 'Do they have visitors? Where do they eat?'

'We never see them. Their families pay well to keep them hidden from sight. They take exercise in the smaller courtyard beyond the kitchens and have meals in their own wing.'

'What of the women who work by day?'

'Only the youngest and fittest are afforded that privilege. Their wages are paid to the spinhouse and in return they are housed with the white-bread prisoners. At the house father's pleasure, of course.'

I trace Ilse's childish needlework, follow the meandering lines of her thread.

'Do you think your friend may be among them?' Lijsbet asks.

I nod, wipe a tear away before it can mar the linen.

'Then you must look for her at Sunday prayers. If she is in the chapel, I promise we will find her.'

Chapter 63

After breakfast on Sunday we gather in the old chapel. Women crowd the benches, breathe the stifling air. That morning we were given soap and water as well as rags to rub our skin clean. By the time my turn at the basin came, only a slick of soap remained. Under my bodice, my shift already sticks to my back.

Seated behind the table at the head of the chapel are the house mother and father. Accompanying them are two strangers: a sombre predicant, a full white beard frothing at his chin; and a woman dressed in severe black, who half-turns in her chair as though she cannot bear to fully look upon us.

Lijsbet touches her elbow to mine. She has contrived that I should sit by the aisle, and in the tomb-like confines of the chapel I am grateful for the open space beside me. She jerks her head over her shoulder. I turn as far as I dare. A procession of white-hooded women in fustian gowns approaches. I search their downturned faces. If Ilse is among them, will I recognise her? When last I saw her, she had become thin. These women are young and vigorous, broad and muscular. In silence, they file towards the front row. Only one holds her chin up.

There can be no doubt. In an instant I am transported back to the master's kitchen door, facing an inquisitive maid who looks me up and down, tells me she had hoped for someone younger. In the eight years since we first met, Ilse has grown stronger. A determined expression has replaced the old, alluring smile. Her eyes are focused on the figures at the table. She passes without seeing me.

I watch her take her seat beside the other factory women. Her shoulder blades no longer press through her clothes. She sits at the edge of the bench, her back straight, her head modestly bowed. She is but five rows away. If I were to call her name, she would surely hear me.

The house mother lifts one finger. Like a handmaid, Ilse steps forward. She takes the Bible, lays it open on the lectern. When she resumes her place, the house mother motions for all to stand.

The woman in black approaches the lectern, announces the first psalm. In a wavering tone she sings the opening bars, prolonging the words until more voices join hers. Beside me, Lijsbet sings fervently, eyes half-closed. Beyond her, Anneken holds a pamphlet, follows each line with a bitten fingernail. The woman leading the psalms turns a page, begins the next verse.

I will Ilse to look around but she seems intent on a show of devotion, her body swaying with every rising cadence. The house mother casts her an approving glance.

It is the turn of the predicant to come to the lectern, where he bends so close to the text his cloud-like beard brushes the page. His topic is temperance. Had he drunk the thin ale served in the dining room, suffered its sourness on his breath from dawn to dusk, he would not concern himself with its surfeit.

Women shuffle their feet. Hands fan faces, fingers pluck at neckbands. I long for a handkerchief to blot my forehead. The windows are sealed shut. Overhead, the vaulted ceiling seems to hang lower, its wooden ribs exuding heat. I need to sit down but the preacher keeps talking. To my left, Lijsbet discreetly flutters the pamphlet before Anneken's face. On my other side, the aisle opens like the mouth of a deep well. A film of sweat chills my skin.

Up ahead, the house mother beckons Ilse and, obediently, she approaches the table. I will her to turn around but she lowers her head to take instructions. What if the gathering finishes without her knowing I am here?

My feet move. I step into the aisle. 'Please!'

There is a gasp, as though all in the room had taken a breath together. At the lectern, the predicant stutters to a halt. The house mother rises, her face aflame.

Ilse turns. When she sees me, her mouth falls open.

I bend my knees, crumple to the ground.

Footsteps approach. Someone pats my cheeks none too gently. I open my eyes to the house mother's grimace. She is bending over me as I lie on the chapel floor, the flagstones mercifully cool against my back. Ilse stands beside her.

'Take her to the courtyard. There is water in the dog trough; splash her face and walk her up and down.'

'Yes, Mother,' Ilse says.

Ilse. I start to say her name. A warning flashes in her eyes. Then her arm is around my back, I am hauled upright, and she is leading me from the chapel into the open air.

'Geertje, is it really you?' Outside, she removes her hood, fans my face with the snowy linen. I sputter through my tears, try to tell her I will never fail her again.

'Use it for a handkerchief.' She offers me the cloth, but it is she who gently mops my eyes.

'Forgive me, Ilse,' I say, when at last I can speak.

She laughs her old laugh, screws the linen into a ball. 'Never mind about my nun's garb. They make us wear it all week to keep the dust off, and again on Sundays to demonstrate our industry.'

Her pretty face bears unfamiliar lines of care. The childish dimples that once puckered her cheeks have been lost. When she smiles, a chip shows in her front tooth, like a corner clipped from a page.

'We have little time.' She takes my arm, looks into my eyes. 'He did this, did he not?'

The story of the master's betrayal pours out as we round the cobbled yard. Ilse interrupts with instructions. 'Slow down. Lean more heavily against me. You must not recover too quickly or we will be called back inside.'

We sit on a stone bench outside the infirmary, and I tell her about the warrant that brought me here.

'They had not your mother's mark on the paper? Nor those of your relatives in Edam?'

'Pieter's name was enough.'

Ilse shakes her head. 'They cannot keep you here without your family's consent. You must have your mother fight for you.'

'She is too old.' I cannot bear to think of my frail mother hearing of my plight, knowing she is powerless to help.

'Your relatives then. What of your cousin?'

'Trijn does not even know I am here.'

Ilse frowns. 'What is her name and where does she live?'

'Trijn Jacobs. She lives in Edam on the Molensteeg, a stone's throw from the bell tower.'

Ilse falls silent.

I take her hand. 'Tell me what has befallen you since we last met? Did you ever find your cousin?'

She laughs. 'I found her in a Rotterdam alley, in more need of help than I. For a while I stayed with her, but that shelter came at a cost, and soon I moved on.'

'Where did you go?'

'I headed for Utrecht but never made it that far. It was not all bad; for a time I lived with a tobacco trader, then with an ostler. One mistake, and now I knead clay and sweep dust all day.'

She keeps a wary eye on the chapel door across the courtyard. A desultory burst of song penetrates the stained-glass windows. The psalms have started again.

Swifts circle the belfry, their quietude disturbed.

'I have a daughter, Geertje. Not yet four and already she can pick out her letters.'

'A daughter? Oh how you must miss her!'

She nods, bites her lip. 'A widow keeps her for me in the country.'

'Ilse—' I begin.

She stops me. 'You must not call me that here. It is best you pretend not to know me at all. They want to keep me five more years but I mean to get away.'

'To get away? How?'

She looks around. The psalms from the chapel rise in intensity.

'The foreman at the pipe factory will help me. But I have to wait until the evenings grow dark.'

'What if they catch you?'

She laughs, pats my hand. 'Do you remember when I brought you to the master's cabinet of curiosities? How afraid you were, and how I teased you, making you touch his monstrous things. The foreman will make certain I am not caught, or else his wife will hear a pretty tale of his conduct.'

So I am to lose Ilse as soon as I have found her.

'What can I do to help?'

'Do you have any money? Or a knife?'

'There is this.' I slide the awl from my garter and in an instant it is gone, her hand moving faster than my eyes.

'Better than nothing,' she says. 'And I have a little money of my own.'

The door to the chapel swings open. The house mother stands, watching us.

'She is much improved, Mother,' Ilse calls.

The woman nods and waits.

Ilse helps me to my feet, slips her arm through mine.

'First I must see my daughter,' she whispers as we cross the courtyard. 'Then I will find Trijn Jacobs who lives by the bell tower in Edam.'

'Is there something I can do?'

'Have patience.' She squeezes my hand. 'And stay alive.'

She answers the house mother's curt queries at the door and leaves me without another look.

Back in the chapel, I slide onto the bench next to Lijsbet and mouth the words to the latest psalm, the melody of the Edam bells ringing in my heart.

Chapter 64

Winter gales bluster through the courtyard, whipping grit into our eyes when we are forced to take the air. By day, a stove is lit in the workroom. The meagre heat is soon lost through the wooden bars of our cage. In the dormitory, rain trickles through broken roof tiles, drips onto our faces as we sleep. The spinhouse swells with damp.

Every Sunday I see Ilse in the chapel but cannot find a way to speak with her. I dare not contrive to faint again. The old grey walls that seemed impenetrable in summer freely admit the bitter cold. On numb feet, I endure ponderous sermons, watch Ilse perform the house mother's bidding with perfect diligence. Nobody gazing at her bowed head could guess the stratagems planned beneath the linen hood.

By night, I lie on my mat listening to coughs and moans, the endless tread of feet to and from the pots. Janne teaches me to safeguard my blanket. 'Pin it with your weight lest it be taken while you sleep.' I wrap the thin weave around my body like a mantle.

The creeping damp stiffens my limbs, sharpens the monthly pains in my womb. I awaken with my knees drawn to my chest, my body in spasm. I roll from the mat, seek relief in pacing past the sleeping women wound in their threadbare coverings. But the warden says my wandering unsettles her and I must lie down again.

In the workroom, we draw our stools around the stove. Lijsbet rubs warmth into Anneken's hands. My fingers struggle to force the needle through the linen.

'That vine is ill-wrought,' the seamstress tells Lijsbet. 'Fix it before the mother sees.'

Lijsbet turns over her work, slides the eye of the needle under her painstaking stitches to unpick them.

'How can you bear it?' I whisper.

'I have hours enough to work it a hundred times over if I must.'

'But how can you bear this place? You never complain.'

A winding stem is reduced to coils of thread. She prises a stitch from the corner of a leaf, undoes the work of hours in moments.

'I must take the punishment I deserve.'

'You cannot deserve this misery.'

She stays her needle, looks at me with her mild blue eyes. How lovely she would be were it not for the bone broken in her face.

'I do deserve it, Geertje. I tried to kill my husband. And were I sent back to him, I would likely try again. So you see, I cannot be free.'

'Look!' Anneken has spread her work out over her knees. Lijsbet turns to inspect it. The child wriggles with pleasure at her praise.

Shame scalds my cheeks. What torment have I rekindled? Never will I question her again. Gentle Lijsbet, who accepts every privation with unfaltering grace, seeks only to protect those around her. Even the house mother affords her some respect.

Hanna reaches over to pet Anneken's head, tries to caress her face, but the girl twists in her seat, takes up her needle again.

A shower of hail clatters against the windows. The stove smokes, wind whistling down the flue.

Lijsbet's head is dipped low over her work so that when she speaks I strain to hear. 'Hanna abandoned her newborn in a barn in the dead of winter. In the morning, the farmer found it frozen to death, its fingers clutching the cord.' Her voice is calm, as though describing the pricking of a thumb, or the breaking of an egg.

Beside Anneken, Hanna is caressing her bundle of rags, humming a cradle song under her breath. 'They caught her rinsing her bloodied skirts in a stream,' Lijsbet says. 'She still denies the baby was hers.'

I close my eyes, hold my hand to my mouth. Trijn once told me of a girl found drowned in a well. Nobody understood, until a tiny corpse was drawn out after hers.

The seamstress taps my shoulder.

'What ails you?'

'I need the privy.'

One of the wardens keeps watch from under the eaves as I cross the yard through sheets of icy rain to the outhouse.

Inside, I cling to the wooden seat, vomit a churned mess of porridge into the hole. My retches turn to sobs. How am I to bear another day in this place? I will not live to see out my twelve-year sentence. Perhaps that is the master's plan. I see him in the salon of his great house, reading letters by the fire, a glass of wine glowing in his hand. Close by, Hendrickje is trimming his quills, sloughing off the old tips, sharpening the new.

Have patience. Stay alive.

Ilse will find a way.

When I return, my skirts are heavy with rain. The warden looks at me apprehensively as though she expects me to spew across her apron.

Back in the workroom, the piece of lawn swims before my eyes. I squint at the fabric, hold it closer to the candle. My bodice cleaves to my back. Lijsbet whispers something I cannot hear. The seamstress trims the candlewick, releasing a waft of rancid tallow. My forehead sears as though my face were pressed to a hot iron. The needle slips from my shaking fingers.

The house mother lifts my chin with the point of her distaff. She beckons the warden. 'Take her to the infirmary before she spoils the linen.'

Not the infirmary, with its reek of lye and moans of dying women.

'I am much improved.' I try to stand, sink back onto the stool.

'Mother, it may be catching.' The warden hesitates, presses the hem of her apron to her mouth.

'Take her.'

I am hauled from my seat, half-dragged out of the room.

'Bring her to the annexe,' the matron says. 'Best to keep her apart.'

The maid leads me along the narrow ward, past the bedsteads where bodies lie trussed in blankets. I stumble down the step into the adjoining room. The matron's candle flickers as though there is not air enough to sustain it. The panels of the box bed are open, ready to draw another prisoner into its depths. I shake in terror.

'Leave her here.' The matron toes the corner of the chaff bed where the writhing girl once lay. What became of her, her baby?

Without the maid's support I crumple onto the pallet. 'You may count yourself lucky to have a fever,' the matron says. 'Else you would be sharing with one who nightly pisses the bed.'

They leave me in darkness.

I sweat through the night. Ghost babies crawl into my dreams, wrap their cold fingers around mine. A stone-faced woman steps down from a plinth and I fear she will tread on their bare heads. She holds her sword aloft. I scream.

A rustle of skirts. A wet towel is pressed to my forehead.

'Close your eyes,' a voice commands.

'And your mouth,' another adds with a laugh.

I roll over on the damp straw. It hurts to move, hurts to lie still. My body is caught in a vice and some wanton hand is turning the screw. I sail on waves of heat, plunge into chattering cold. I search for my mother, for Trijn, but the spinhouse visitors mock me and will not let me pass. I smell linseed oil, hear a woman sing. The strangers press closer.

Somewhere, bells are ringing, dogs are barking. Out in the yard, a man shouts an instruction. A gate opens, closes.

How long have I lain here? I lift myself onto elbows, then knees. It is dawn, or it may be dusk. The annexe is in near darkness but dim light enters the infirmary through the windows overlooking the courtyard. I slide my feet to the floor, walk towards the light.

The matron and maid stand at one window, gazing across the courtyard. The bells toll too close to be those of Sint Jan's kerk. There is no music in their clangour.

'Is it Sunday already?'

The maid glances over her shoulder. 'She is awake,' she says, looking at me, but not leaving her post.

The matron crosses the room, presses the back of her hand to my forehead. 'Bring a basin of water,' she calls to the girl.

The maid gathers herself. 'How much longer must they ring that bell?'

'She will soon be found,' the matron says.

'What has happened?' I am dizzy. I feel my way to the table, lower myself onto a stool.

'One of the factory women has run off.' The maid joins me, soaks a rag in the water and wipes my face. 'The bells have been ringing since first light.'

'Enough of your talk,' the matron says. 'Bring her a bowl of porridge and a draught of buttermilk. Once fed, she may go back to work.'

When they leave me, I go to the window and look across to the chapel. A halo of blush light surrounds the steeple. The swinging bells must have scattered fragments of the swifts' nests across the courtyard. Perhaps Ilse is now lying beneath a sheet of tarpaulin on the back of a barge, or crouching in a cart among placid sheep, gazing up at the dawn. Perhaps she hears the bells, knows that I must hear them too.

The swifts will return in spring, gather moss and straw, build their homes anew.

I eat the steaming porridge. Before the maid comes for me, I am ready to leave.

Chapter 65

February, 1655

One morning when my braid falls over my shoulder, I do not recognise it as my own. My hair has turned grey as hammered pewter. I shrug it off, as though it were the tail of one of the mice that nightly run around our feet. I have not looked in a mirror since I left Amsterdam nearly five years ago. And Ilse has been gone for four of those years. If she came back now, would she even know me? The worn face reflected in the workroom windows is more like my mother's than my own. My true self was left behind at the spinhouse door, under the stone woman's sword.

Every day I walk through endless pathways in my mind. Hope torments me. Ilse is in the countryside, hiding from bailiffs seeking a runaway with a chipped front tooth. Or Ilse is sleeping in barns by day, walking barefoot through fields and fens by night. More often, I am in despair. Ilse is dead. Ilse is lost. Ilse is in the Amsterdam spinhouse, never to be released.

At night, I lie on my mat, its coarse weave pressing into my skin, repeating Ilse's words in my mind. *Have patience. Stay alive.*

After Candlemas, Janne begins to suffer nightmares. On the mat beside mine, her body twists in agitation. In the mornings she lies shaking, eyes wide with fear, unable to tell me what she has seen.

On a cold spring dawn, her screams wake me. I crawl to her side. 'Janne, hush, you are safe.'

She grabs my throat. I swat her hands away but it is too late; the warden has seen, and women are jumping bare-legged from their pallets shrieking for help. Janne cowers on her mat, covering her ears.

I kneel beside her. 'Janne, it is me, Geertje.'

She looks at me and shudders. There is no recognition in her eyes.

When the house mother arrives, the warden rolls up her sleeves. 'No,' Janne says. 'No.' But they pull her to her feet, twist her arms behind her back. Her whimpers are worse than her screams.

'Let me go with her.' I follow them to the door where a maid bars my passage. Already, they are forcing her down the stairs.

'Janne!' I call.

She does not look around.

In the workroom, my stitches shift and blur. The sparrow I have worked so many times before defeats me. Its raised wing no longer suggests flight. It seems to flounder, as though one ankle has been tethered to a perch.

The house mother frowns. 'Perhaps you would do better at the spinning wheel.'

Janne's wheel has sat idle since she was taken away. Nobody will use it, for fear her disease lies dormant in the wood, ready to leach into the next hand to touch it. I wind the crank, feed the bobbin. The wheel pulses like a living thing. How Janne's weakened fingers must have struggled to keep the rhythm. I try not to think of her in the infirmary, locked inside the box bed, pounding on the panels for mercy. *Tomorrow will be better.* I crank the wheel faster, try to muffle her voice in my head.

Anneken's sobs grow louder as the morning progresses. The house mother abandons attempts to chastise her. Lijsbet rocks the girl in her arms, murmuring words of comfort. Anneken has turned sixteen and her sentence is served. Her father will not have her back, and so she is leaving for Amsterdam, where a ship will take her to the New World. Anneken, who marks the passing of each year by measuring her height against the brickwork. *See Geertje how I have grown since you first came.* I catch a tear on my knuckle, wipe it on my apron.

When it is time for her to go, Anneken embraces us one by one. 'I will write to you all. Marking letters on paper must surely be easier than stitching them on a sampler.'

'Forget this place. Forget us.' Lijsbet stands dry-eyed at the workroom door, still waving when Anneken is taken out of sight.

In the afternoon, visitors stream into the spinhouse. I bend my head, work the wheel until the flyer is a blur. Today, nobody has heart for the hawkers' offerings. The ribbon-woman calls through the bars that she has brought a parting gift for Anneken, and Lijsbet tells her she has come too late.

Out in the hall, the house father is embroiled in an argument. I imagine him clutching his coin box to his chest, his fingers rubbed with dirt.

A visitor is protesting. 'Two stuivers? To see my own cousin? Young man, you should be ashamed to use an old woman so meanly.'

I stop the wheel, lift my head.

'Madam, it is the rule.' Uncertainty has crept in. He cannot decide whether the compliment or the insult bears more weight.

'Make way!' The woman barrels through the throng, wielding a basket in triumph. Visitors skip aside.

A twist of wool slips through my fingers. I rise from the stool.

The woman sets her basket down and I cannot see her face. Someone stumbles, jostles her arm. 'Tread not on my apples, I beseech you.' She peers between the balusters, frowns, searches the room.

I am afraid to move lest the slightest action proves this wonder a dream.

'Geertje, what have they done to you?' Trijn cries.

She is the same Trijn, her forehead a little more wind-chafed, the mesh of veins across her cheeks a little redder. Her best cap has been freshly starched and she wears a worsted jacket I have not seen before. She takes my hands through the wooden bars.

'You have put me to sore trouble though I do not mean to scold you. How thin you have become, tell me are you well, do you eat at all? What a wearisome journey I have had, I ache all over, but no matter, I am an old woman, it must be expected and I do not complain. Is that your watchdog? How free she makes with her hands.'

The house mother is slapping one of the weavers.

'She will not let us talk for long.' I squeeze Trijn's hands. Her eyes are still bright, though the skin around them is creased like worn linen. 'How are you? How is my mother?'

'Well, we are both alive. Pieter told your mother you had found a position in Eindhoven and that your new mistress could not spare you for visits home. But I have never trusted that brother of yours. So I went to Rarep, and his scarecrow of a wife came flapping out to the yard to tell me he was not at home. She would have had me leave without stepping inside their door but I was not put off so easily. Do you know she permits her children to caper about the kitchen like chickens in a coop?'

The house mother hovers, the distaff resting on her shoulder.

Trijn switches to a dramatic whisper. 'But enough of that. I have been to the painter's house.'

I have a vision of Trijn crossing the bridge to the Breestraat, shoulders up, chin held high, her wooden shoes clattering over the cobbles. Hendrickje opening the door, climbing the stairs in her slippers. The master bolting from his canvas, the red vein blazing in his cheek as he comes pounding into the hall.

'You saw him?'

'At first he sent his proxy, that artful maid who looks up at the world through her lashes. "Madam," said I, "I will engage with no go-between. Summon your master or I will have the magistrate here within the hour, for I have heard that good gentleman is well-acquainted with this house."'

Trijn stops for breath and the house mother cuts in. 'Your visitor keeps you too long from your work, Geertje.'

Trijn draws herself up, performs a low bow. 'Madam, I have brought you a humble gift.' She passes a berry-red apple through the bars. The house mother turns it over in her hand as though expecting a worm to break out through the spotless skin. Perplexed, she nods at Trijn, turns her attention to one of the spinners who is laughing too loudly at a sailor's wit.

'Where was I in my tale?' Trijn has pulled a second apple from her basket.

'The master,' I prompt her.

'Ah yes. Well down he came, like a rampaging Jove, in a moth-eaten tabard spotted with paint.

'"I have found you out, Sir," said I. "You are the author of my cousin's misfortune and I mean to remedy it."

'"Speak to her brother," said he. "Dircx signed the papers, not I."

'"I am going to Gouda to release Geertje from unlawful detention. And you are going to write to the magistrates to support it."'

Trijn produces a knife from some concealed place on her person, halves the apple and hands me my share.

'You cannot use a knife in here!' I look towards the house mother. She is lecturing on the dangers of consorting with sailors, a topic she relishes.

'How else are we to manage, Geertje; would you have me bite off pieces for you as though you were an old horse?' Trijn crunches through her half.

I take a breath. 'Tell me what he said.'

She spits a pip delicately into her handkerchief.

'He turned a most peculiar colour, like rhubarb overstewed. For a moment I thought he would have a fit and I would be obliged to call on the skulking maid to revive him. But alas, he recovered himself well enough to speak.

'"Do not go there," said he. "You will be sorry if you go there."

'"Wag your finger all you please, Sir," said I. "Geertje's family supports her cause. And when her brother returns from sea next month he will not dare oppose his kin."'

'Oh Trijn, can you really have me released?'

'It will not be easy.' Trijn wipes her sticky fingers on the handkerchief. 'My poor hip troubles me daily. I may be dead within a matter of days.'

It is too much. Better to have no hope than have it dashed away.

'Geertje, do not cry! Of course I will get you out. It will take a little time, that is all. I must have the notary draw up a letter.'

I am sobbing like a child.

Trijn pats my hand. 'Hush, Geertje. Eat your apple before the watchdog sniffs it out.'

The bell rings to mark the end of visiting hour.

'I must make haste. I take the *trekschuit* to Amsterdam and travel on by cart to Edam. I promised Marje I would be home before the cat has kittens, though what novelty anyone can find in a litter of mouse-catchers I cannot tell you.'

'Who is Marje?'

Trijn looks at me as though I have lost my wits. 'Why, she is Geertje's daughter.'

I stare at her. My head hurts.

'Your friend! But of course you know her by a different name. When you come home she will have to choose another, for my house is too small for two Geertjes.'

In all our conversation I had not thought to ask about Ilse.

'She found you,' is all I can say.

'Indeed she did, or rather Marje did. A stubborn little miss; she would not release a handful of my skirts till I came to where her exhausted mother had set herself down.'

'They are well?'

'Quite well. And determined to bring you home.'

The house mother looms. 'The bell has already rung.'

Trijn reaches for something. For a moment I think she is about to proffer another apple. Instead she lifts the basket to her shoulder.

'A pleasure, Madam,' she says to the house mother. 'Geertje, I will come again soon.'

With a bow of her stiff cap and a swing of her basket, she is gone. I wait for the very last sight of her before going back to my work.

'What did you get?' The woman at the wheel next to mine angles her head to see.

My hands are cupped in front of me as though they hold a precious liquid. I show her the cut apple, fuzzed with brown.

'Is that all?' She looks at me with frank disappointment.

I can no longer contain myself. Laughter gladdens my heart like a burst of long-forgotten song.

Chapter 66

The old chapel looks bigger without its usual gathering of women. Sunlight assails the stained-glass windows, throws their colours onto the slabs before my feet. I walk through the mosaic and am draped in its hues. Trijn is sitting on the front bench where Ilse used to sit. She rises to embrace me, upsetting the basket at her feet. 'At least the watchdog is not here,' she says in too loud a whisper. 'That one would gnaw our bones for sport.' The vaulted ceiling catches her words, sends them bouncing back around our ears.

The governess is seated at the table beside the lectern with two men I have never seen before. The older of the two is dressed in black bombazine. One tassel of his collar has escaped the button-hole of his coat and I imagine it dipping into the inkwell and spattering the ledger in front of him. His companion sits back in his chair, an idle arm draped across the table, and seems absorbed in admiration of his lace cuff. I could be back in the Oude Kerk, with the commissioners of marital affairs.

The governess clears her throat. 'You are Trijn Jacobs of Edam, widow of Albert Jansz, and the cousin and sole representative of Geertje Dircx?'

Trijn stands. 'At your humble service, Madam.' Her bow threatens to throw her off-balance.

'You may sit. Mistress Jacobs, I have received a letter from a notary of Edam concerning your wish to remove your cousin from this house of reform before the appointed time.'

Trijn bustles to her feet again. 'Through your excellent efforts, my cousin is fully reformed and I am willing to take on the burden of her care and spare you the trouble of extending further hospitality.'

The man with the ledger taps the curling corner of a page. 'The expense is considerable. Why, pray, was this woman received into our jurisdiction? The city of Amsterdam should have been tasked with her subsistence.'

The governess puts on her spectacles, lifts a letter from the bundle before her. 'I have also had letters from a citizen of Amsterdam, an instigator of the original complaint.'

The master. I lean forward, strain to see some inflection of regret in his hand upon the paper.

'He forbids the release of the prisoner until such time as her brother returns from overseas.'

Five years and still his anger is not spent. I turn to Trijn who has righted her basket and is rummaging through the contents. A ball of cheese wrapped in muslin rolls out. She picks it up, dusts it with her elbow.

'A moment, I pray you.' She hands me the cheese, continues rummaging, and pulls a fold of paper from among her parcels.

The governess extends a hand. Trijn delivers the letter with a flourish, looking expectantly at her audience as though they might divine the contents before opening it. For a moment, I think she will draw up a chair and join them at the table.

'You may sit.' A testy note has crept into the governess's voice.

Do not anger her, Trijn, I pray. Not now, when we have won her attention.

The governess reads in silence. Trijn repacks her cheese. My eyes travel the walls of the chapel, the plaster pitted with nail holes, the patches of shade where paintings once hung. Still, the governess studies the paper, her face pale as stone. She could be a statue, stepped down from one of the empty niches.

Finally, she sets the letter aside.

I sit, rigid, awaiting her verdict.

She removes her spectacles, rubs her eyes. A word from her could break me in two.

'Fennel,' Trijn says.

The governess raises an eyebrow. 'I beg your pardon?'

'A handful of seeds infused in boiled water. Strain the liquid well, and when cooled it will soothe your eyes.'

'This woman is rambling and I am wanted at town hall.' The magistrate half-rises.

'A moment.' The governess hands him Trijn's letter.

He grunts, stops in his seat.

The governess blinks at Trijn. 'Every summer, my mother used to bathe her eyes with fennel tea. I had forgotten the remedy.'

'All kitchen gardens grow it,' Trijn says. 'I could teach your cook my method.'

The governess inclines her head. 'Tell me, what do you advise for irritations of the skin?'

Trijn describes a poultice of mashed dock leaves. The governess nods, makes notes. I look from one to another. Finally, the magistrate interrupts to read from the letter.

'Pieter Dircx, ship's carpenter, residing at Ransdorp, withdraws his support for his sister's detention. Without malice, and witnessed by a notary.'

The second man stirs, takes the letter.

'The woman is ill?' The magistrate directs his question to the governess.

'A condition of the womb. The house mother reports a decline in her work due to the failing of her health.'

'Then my recommendation is to let her be a burden on this person instead of on the city of Gouda.' He gestures in Trijn's direction.

Trijn takes my hand.

The second man leans forward. 'You cannot mean to release her? The woman has not yet served half her sentence. Are we to entertain the whim of a too-fond brother and suffer a miscreant to roam our streets?'

'A valid consideration.' The magistrate examines the letter again.

In the silence that follows, Trijn's grip on my hand does not falter.

The magistrate folds the letter, hands it to the governess and closes the ledger. 'I sanction the release of the prisoner on condition of her immediate removal from the city of Gouda.'

A tinge of colour warms the governess's pale cheeks. 'Mistress Dircx, in your five years of detention I have heard no complaint of your conduct and deem you suitably reformed at this time. Mistress Jacobs, I am satisfied of your capacity to maintain the welfare of the widow, Geertje Dircx. I therefore release her into your care on this, the thirty-first day of May, in the year of our Lord, 1655, at one o'clock.'

When I stand, I sway on my feet. The governess is still speaking but it is as though a gate has been opened, a great body of water released, and I struggle to hear her above the din. There are to be no goodbyes. I am to leave the spinhouse in my prisoner's homespun. We will be escorted through the studded doors and delivered onto the street.

Trijn leads the way. We reach the chapel door without a hand falling on my shoulder or a voice calling me back.

In the courtyard, the warden thumbs through her ring of keys.

'What of your belongings?' Trijn asks.

'All I own is here.' From my pocket I pull my mother's comb, Abe's medal, Trijn's tattered prayer. Things nobody wanted to steal. 'Your prayer I kept with me all this time.'

Trijn pokes the fragment. 'I do not remember a prayer. Are you certain it is not a recipe of some sort?'

The warden fits her key to the lock.

From across the courtyard comes the hum of voices. The women have finished their midday meal and are returning to the workroom.

The warden opens the door to the gatehouse. There is but one more door between us and the street.

I turn, run back across the courtyard to the workroom, push my hand through the bars and rap on the window.

Lijsbet is the first to see me. 'Geertje!' She hurries to the glass. The tears she withheld before Anneken well in her eyes. The house mother crosses the room to accost her, but when she sees me she hesitates, raises a hand in sober farewell.

Trijn joins me at the iron bars. 'Look, Geertje!'

I take a step back. Women fill all four workroom windows: the stitchers, the weavers, the spinners; Hanne with her cloth doll; the seamstress with the shears hanging from her girdle. For a moment, I think I see Beatrijs. Some wave, some clap their hands. All are smiling.

Trijn takes my arm.

With my cousin by my side, I step into the gatehouse, and walk out the door through which I was dragged five years ago.

The sun is too bright, the sky, too wide. I stretch out my arms, as though I could embrace it all. We take a few paces, then I turn back to face the stone woman on the pediment. The impaled man lies at her feet. A broken wheel rests, half-hidden by her robes. Serenely, the woman reads on, the sword under her arm a seeming afterthought.

'Sint Catharina,' Trijn says. 'I was named for her.'

In the distance, swifts flit in and out of the chapel belfry, their nests remade around the silenced bells.

Behind me, hooves ring on cobbles. A horseman passes close by and Trijn seizes my arm. 'Lean on me, Geertje.'

She walks me down a busy street. Today, the pungent vapours of the canal are strangely comforting, like an unwashed garment to which an infant clings. At first I expect the citizens of Gouda to pass through me, prove me a ghost. At any moment I might slip into a crack between the cobbles or dissolve into the torpid water of the canal.

A washerwoman shouldering a basket smiles as we step aside to allow her to pass. The scent of clean, damp linen lingers a moment behind her. A tottering child follows his mother across our path, holding out a griddle cake for us to admire. Trijn shoos away a hawker before I can take a curling head of cabbage into my hands, marvel at its forking white veins.

At the bridge, a fisherman unloads his catch. Gulls shriek and swoop over the nets. Somewhere, hammers are pounding metal. I want to press my hands to my ears but Trijn is telling me about Ilse's escape. How she slept in barns and stables. How a blacksmith helped her to file her tooth smooth. How she spent her days gathering peat and gutting fish until she could reach her daughter safely.

'She works all day in the dairy and scrubs my house when she comes home. So far she has refused all the young men I have found, but I will not be dissuaded. The little girl practises her letters by making labels for my remedies and I have promised her we will dig for bulbs and make bluebell glue to fix them onto the jars. She is teaching me to recognise the names, though it is no easy task for my poor eyes. Are those fresh baked this morning?'

We have reached the square, where Trijn pauses at a stall to prod a loaf. She wrinkles her nose, moves on.

'I almost forgot. A letter arrived some weeks ago, much tattered and torn, and no wonder, for it must have been misdirected many times. Tell me, does your shoemaker friend think there is but one Trijn in the whole of Edam?'

'Otto! What did he say?'

'Marje will read it for you. I am glad he followed my advice and has married, though he forgot to thank me amid his inquiries about you.'

Trijn buys hot *wafels*, and we sit on a bench near the dock to await the next *trekschuit*. Cinnamon-scented butter shines on my fingers as I eat.

The bells of Sint Jan's kerk chime the hour. If I close my eyes, I could be back in Amsterdam where the bells of the Zuiderkerk measured every day I spent in the master's house. I see Titus, now a young man of fourteen, unrolling the canvas I left him, puzzling over the woman's familiar face. I see his father, adding his signature to the dry paint, attempting to pay creditors with encumbered goods. I remember how I searched for any trace of his hand in my painted face, as though his touch could be extracted and preserved before it spoiled.

'Are you ready, Geertje? It is time.'

Trijn is peering at me, her bright eyes filled with concern. A *trekschuit* has passed through the toll gate and is travelling up the canal towards the dock.

I get to my feet, shake the last crumbs from my apron.

Acknowledgements

Heartfelt thanks to my agent Ger Nichol who believed in this book when it was still a work in progress and whose unwavering encouragement and expert guidance propelled it to becoming a finished manuscript.

I am infinitely grateful to Deirdre Nolan at Eriu who immediately engaged with Geertje's story and brought so much enthusiasm to this project. Her sensitive editing and care throughout the process have made this a better book. Thank you to Lisa Gilmour for her support and all at Eriu and Bonnier Books UK. Thank you to Djinn von Noorden for her thoughtful copyediting.

This book was first pitched to agents and publishers at the Novel Fair run by the Irish Writers Centre in 2023. Thank you to Betty Stenson and all at the IWC. This book would not exist without you.

Back in 2011, I had the good fortune to meet three incredibly talented writers: Marie Gethins, Danielle McLaughlin and Marie Murphy, who became stalwarts of my writing group and steadfast friends. This is your book, too. Thank you.

The generosity and goodwill of the writing community in Cork is legendary. People to whom I am indebted for their encouragement along the way include Madeleine D'Arcy, Laura McKenna, Billy O'Callaghan and many others. Thank you to Cork ETB, the Munster Literature Centre, the West Cork Literary Festival and the Crawford Art Gallery.

Thank you to David Brennan and John Mee. Thanks also to Jennifer McMahon and all participants at the 2023 Novel Fair. Special thanks to Elizabeth O'Connor for her expertise on the craft of spinning!

The Rembrandt House Museum in Amsterdam offers unique insight into the years that Geertje shared with Rembrandt. Walking through the rooms where she cared for Titus, where she fell in love, and where she finally packed her things and left to face a precarious future was incredibly moving and immensely helpful when researching and writing this novel. Special thanks to Marie Murphy and Catherine Twomey who accompanied me on visits and humoured me as I paced out the kitchen, counted steps and tiles and took more photographs than I could possibly need.

The Rembrandt Documents Project, a digital collection of primary documents relating to the life and work of Rembrandt van Rijn, was hugely helpful when researching this book.

Geertje Dircx, a woman of remarkable courage and dignity, inspired me from the moment I first learned of her existence. I would like to acknowledge those who spoke up for Geertje long before I discovered her. These include Hanneke Leroux, Julika Marijn, Simone van der Vlugt, and art historians Simon Schama, Gary Schwartz and the late H.F. Wijnman. This list is far from exhaustive. To those I have unwittingly omitted, I salute you.

Thank you to all my friends, relatives and colleagues, I've been truly overwhelmed by your support. To my dear friends Emma MacCarthy and Catherine Twomey, thank you for being the Trijns in my life!

In loving memory of another Geertje, my late grandmother Gertie Gavin, who inspired me in so many ways.

To my brothers, Paul, John and Conor for their unfailing love and support. To my nephew Matthew, and nieces Evie and Iris who all love reading as much as I do.

Unending love and gratitude to my late father Bill whom I never stop missing.

Finally, to my mother Rosemary, my best friend and loyal supporter in everything I do. This book is dedicated to you with all my love.